SAFE FROM HARM

"So, that is the story of your mother and me," said Don Miguel. "Now you know why we must leave. If Tecolote finds us here, he would slaughter us all and never even blink an eye."

Estrellita touched the locket on her neck and thought of Jeremiah. By now, he would be up in the mountains. He would not even know that she was gone. "When will we return?"

"When it is safe. When Tecolote is killed or captured."

Corazon noticed her daughter's trembling. "Do you have fear?" she asked.

Estrellita nodded.

"Do not worry. Your father will keep us safe."

Estrellita felt Jeremiah's strength within her, felt his love swell her heart, brace her from harm as though his arms were around her.

She touched the silver eagle on her locket and drew comfort from Jeremiah's words. She and Jeremiah were like two eagles. Eagles of destiny. Together they could scale the heights, soar freely above the earth and its turmoil, safe from harm.

Taylor—made Romance From Zebra Books

Whispered Kisses (2912, $4.95/5.95)
Beautiful Texas heiress Laura Leigh Webster never imagined that her biggest worry on her African safari would be the handsome Jace Elliot, her tour guide. Laura's guardian, Lord Chadwick Hamilton, warns her of Jace's dangerous past; she simply cannot resist the lure of his strong arms and the passion of his *Whispered Kisses*.

Kiss of the Night Wind (2699, $4.50/$5.50)
Carrie Sue Strover thought she was leaving trouble behind her when she deserted her brother's outlaw gang to live her life as schoolmarm Carolyn Starns. On her journey, her stagecoach was attacked and she was rescued by handsome T.J. Rogue. T.J. plots to have Carrie lead him to her brother's cohorts who murdered his family. T.J., however, soon succumbs to the beautiful runaway's charms and loving caresses.

Fortune's Flames (2944, $4.50/$5.50)
Impatient to begin her journey back home to New Orleans, beautiful Maren James was furious when Captain Hawk delayed the voyage by searching for stowaways. Impatience gave way to uncontrollable desire once the handsome captain searched *her* cabin. He was looking for illegal passengers; what he found was wild passion with a woman he knew was unlike all those he had known before!

Passions Wild and Free (3017, $4.50/$5.50)
After seeing her family and home destroyed by the cruel and hateful Epson gang, Randee Hollis swore revenge. She knew she found the perfect man to help her—gunslinger Marsh Logan. Not only strong and brave, Marsh had the ebony hair and light blue eyes to make Randee forget her hate and seek the love and passion that only he could give her.

Available wherever paperbacks are sold, or order direct from the Publisher. Send cover price plus 50¢ per copy for mailing and handling to Zebra Books, Dept. 2965, 475 Park Avenue South, New York, N.Y. 10016. Residents of New York, New Jersey and Pennsylvania must include sales tax. DO NOT SEND CASH.

SANTA FE TRAIL

EAGLES of DESTINY

JORY SHERMAN

ZEBRA BOOKS
KENSINGTON PUBLISHING CORP.

ZEBRA BOOKS

are published by

Kensington Publishing Corp.
475 Park Avenue South
New York, NY 10016

First printing: April, 1990

Printed in the United States of America

DEDICATION

For Loren D. Estleman

Prologue

Don Miguel Santos de Rojas y Montez always thought of that day as being dark, stormy, the clouds hanging low in the skies like gray cotton batting. Yet there was sunshine, golden like the honey in the *ollas,* and birds were chirruping in the pine tree thicket above the hacienda. From the balcony, he could see his sheep flowing over the hillsides like a woolly river, streaming from the bedding grounds to the rich, irrigated pastures along the Pecos. The shepherds emerged moments later, from tree-shadow, white-clothed young men, their faces brown smudges under straw sombreros, following the migration, hooting to one another, the sounds of their voices rising above the faint blatting of the sheep.

The youthful-looking hidalgo stood there for a long moment, wondering what was different about this day, wondering what was wrong. He watched the growing flock as he always watched it, with pride, a sense of accomplishment. This morning, however, he was filled with dread, a foreboding that all was not well on the vast rancho with its more than a quarter million sheep, its cattle, goats, chickens, guinea hens, geese, ducks, deer, doves, rabbits, and game birds.

Don Miguel was not a tall man, but he stood straight, and with his square shoulders and narrow hips, his wiry musculature, he appeared taller than he was. The high heels of his polished riding boots made him still taller, of course. Today he was dressed in black clothing, with no piping of colorful thread on his tailored shirt and trousers. He had not yet put on the flat-crowned hat and his thick dark hair flowed backward from his high forehead, glistened in the rising sun. He had the blue eyes of the Castilian Spaniard, the hawk-beaked nose of his father, the olive cast to his skin from Moorish ancestors.

He knew what this day was, of course, but the fluttering in his stomach came from the uncertainty of his plan. There were so many people involved that he did not know if they could pull it off.

"Miguel, I am here."

The hidalgo jumped as if someone had cracked a whip.

He turned to the woman who had climbed the stairs silently, padded soundlessly onto the balcony. She carried a hammered silver tray laden with fired clay cups, sugar bowl, cream pitcher, pot of strong, steaming coffee. She, too, was garbed in black. Her long black hair, brushed to a high sheen, was tied under her ear with a dark-wine bow of velvet held with a turquoise-and-silver clasp.

"Corazon," he said to his wife, "I did not hear you. You made me jump inside my skin." He looked at the tray in her hands, frowned. "Why do you carry that tray up here? Where is that wretched girl, that shameless servant?"

She forced herself to laugh as she set the tray down on the table, a light ripple of throat-tones that never failed to delight him.

He forgot, for a moment, the odd heaviness in his heart, as he gazed at Corazon's face, beautiful, her ruddy skin radiant as if glowing with an inner light, her white teeth even and sparkling as pearl beads, her dark eyes flashing a radiance of their own. She was a proud woman, loyal, strong. He, and possibly a few others, knew of the source of some of her strength, but this was not something that was mentioned between them. Not until this day, when she would be reminded of her past, and her shame.

"Miguel, it gives me pleasure to wait on my man, my dear, sweet lover," she said, her voice liquid and soft with the Spanish accents, although she had never been to Spain. Miguel took some comfort in her accent and diction, because he had tutored her hard after what had happened, after he had fallen so much in love with her he could not bear to give her up, even though there was much *amargor y orgullo*, bitterness and pride, to swallow. "Now, would you have liked it better if we had that chattering magpie of a serving girl, whose name you can never remember, fussing about us? I came up here to be alone with you, before he comes. Besides, it is so unusually quiet this morning. It cannot be such a bad day, even so."

"Quiet? Yes, it is quiet. But it will not be a good day. I do not know if I can lie well enough. I am afraid that I have left out something. That my plan will fail. And if it does . . ." The distant bleat of the sheep just scarcely intruded on the stillness of the hacienda. "*Where is Estrellita?*" he asked suddenly, his voice sharp as the *cuchillo flacco*, the thin-bladed knife he used to castrate the sheep.

"Miguel! What is wrong? You know she is safe in Santa Fe."

"What if he goes there first? What if he starts trouble? Someone will talk. Someone will say something wrong. He will be suspicious." He could not bring himself to say the name of the one they all dreaded.

Corazon rose from the table and went to her husband. She put her arms around his shoulders and drew him to the comfort of her breasts.

"You must not be so upset. He will not know. He will come straight here and you will lie because . . ."

"Yes, yes," he said, and the thing that had been between them all these years rose up again so they could almost touch it. But they could not say the true words that were behind this ugly cloud-thing that made his day turn so suddenly dark.

He stiffened and he knew that she could feel him stiffen. He was immediately repentant, but it was too late. A shadow passed over Corazon's eyes, a fleeting look of inner pain. She

9

jerked her arms away from him in a reflexive movement, as if burned on a hot stove. His stomach twisted with a wrenching pang that seemed born of fear and remorse. The fear came from knowing he had hurt her, she who had known so much pain in her life. The remorse was his own quick conscience suddenly rising up unbidden, shaking a scolding finger in his heart for what he had so unthinkingly done.

"Corazon . . ."

She turned away from him quickly, not out of disrespect, he knew, but because she did not want him to see the hurt in her face, the tears welling up in her eyes. He strode to her, grasped her shoulders with hands that trembled slightly. He drew close to her, until his loins cupped her rounded buttocks, until he could smell the faint perfume of flowers in her hair, the lingering aroma of love-musk on her skin.

They had made love in the soft shadows of their bedroom before dawn, caressing like blind people, coupling naturally and with tenderness. He could still hear her cries in his ear, her low moans of pleasure, like a cat's throaty purr when it is in season.

"I'm sorry, Corazon," he whispered. She turned, inside his arms, looked up at him. Her eyes were wet with tears. "It is not you I shun, but myself."

"You do not have to say that, my husband," she said. "I understand your feelings. You have been very good to me."

"Not good enough." He kissed her impulsively on the cheek, the salt of her tears like the taste of bitter wine.

For a moment, he was transported in time, back to that day when he had first met Corazon and learned the story of her mother and the bold Comanche chief, Matadiez, Tenkiller.

Corazon's mother was Spanish, born of royal blood in Cádiz, taken for bride by an adventurous nobleman, Don Fernando Aguilar de Peña y Iglesias, who was from Madrid. Don Fernando journeyed to the New World, became one of the great hidalgos who settled along the Rio Grande, where he raised more than a million sheep, earned the respect of the townspeople of Caballo. In those days, as now, the Comanches often raided such villages and occasionally entered into treaties with the Spaniards. Don Fernando made such a treaty with Tenkiller, but the warrior looked with lust on the rancher's wife, Magdalena. One day, he swooped her up, carried her off to his tribe.

Don Fernando hunted Tenkiller for five years, six years, seven. In the eighth year, he found the Comanche, raided his camp, rescued Magdalena. He killed the haughty chief and took back his wife. But Magdalena had given light to a girl-child, Corazon. When the victorious Spaniards returned to Caballo, bringing Don Fernando's wife and bastard daughter with them, the village wanted to celebrate. Don Fernando, bitter at what had been stolen from him, furious that his wife had been violated and had given birth to a bastard daughter, wanted to kill the half-Comanche girl. He was ready to defy the priest and order the girl beheaded.

Corazon was already a legend among the Comanche. She brought much honor to the tribe because of her beauty and because her father had insulted the hated Spaniards by taking his wife and siring a daughter.

Young Miguel Santos saw Corazon, who was two years his junior, saw that her beauty was beyond compare, and begged his father to save her from such a violent death. There was much talk, many negotiations. Don Fernando gave his decision.

"As long as I never see her again, you may take her. I will spare her life but, I will not have this shadow in my house."

Miguel's father, himself a wealthy hidalgo, moved north to the Pecos east of Santa Fe. He was a deeply religious man and felt that it was wrong to kill an innocent child who had no control over the accident of birth. Still he did not want Miguel to marry a half-breed, to disturb the bloodlines. And, too, there was the fear of reprisal from one of Tenkiller's sons or brothers. The Spaniards knew that there was honor among Comanches, as well.

11

Miguel fell in love with Corazon, even more so when he learned that her mother, unable to cope with Don Fernando's jealousy, his constant references to her time with the Comanches, took her own life with poison. Following this news, Miguel stepped up his efforts to get his father to give him permission to marry Corazon.

"There has been enough tragedy, my father," he pleaded. "Let me take this girl as my bride or I will kill myself as her mother did."

So it was that, at the age of sixteen, he married Corazon, who was fourteen. Two years later, Corazon gave light to Estrellita, who had the dark beauty of her mother, the clean visage of her father, and the proud mien of her grandfather, Tenkiller.

"We must never tell her of Matadiez," said Corazon.

"She will hear the story, eventually," argued Don Miguel.

"We will deny it!"

"But blood is blood."

"She had our blood and that is enough, my husband. Please, I beg you, grant me this one thing."

And so, the secret was born between them and whispered of at the church in Santa Fe, in the little villages along the Rio Grande and the Pecos, spoken of among the shepherds. Sometimes, like now, it rose up between Corazon and Don Miguel, like a shadow, bringing with it a nameless fear, because the Comanches also knew the story and knew that Corazon was the daughter of a famous chief, and therefore one of their own people.

Don Miguel lived in dread that the Comanches would one day come back to claim Corazon. His wife knew this and when he brooded, she would comfort him, caress him tenderly so that he would become calm again.

"Come," she said now, "let us take our coffee before it turns cold."

They sat at the balcony table, sipping the lukewarm coffee, looking into each other's eyes. Corazon reached across the table, touched her husband's hand.

12

"*Te quiero mucho, mi esposo,*" she said softly.

"I love you, too, Corazon. It is just that I have the dread in me."

"Is it the Comanches?"

There had been reports of raids along the Rio Grande, many sheep stolen, some ranchos burned, pillaged.

"Just one."

"Can you not say his name? The priest says that one need not fear anything with a name. Besides, perhaps he will not come back this day. Perhaps those are other Comanches who are raiding to the south."

"No. It is . . . Tecolote. I know."

There. He had said the name. The Comanches called him Owl Face in their Shoshoni tongue. The Spanish called him Cara de Tecolote, shortening it to "Owl."

Don Miguel knew something of the Comanche, their origins. He had learned much since that day almost twenty years before when Don Fernando returned to the hacienda with his rescued wife. He knew that his own people had lived in fear of the Comanche for almost two hundred years. Their name was not Spanish, but came from the Ute tongue. The Utes were also of Shoshonean stock and, like the other tribes of the southern great plains, greatly feared their warlike cousins. They called them *Komantcia,* which meant "anyone who wants to fight me all the time." The Comanches did not use the word. They called themselves "the human beings." The people.

The coffee turned tepid as Don Miguel reflected on the day when Tecolote had first come to the hacienda. Estrellita was only seven, but she was already more beautiful than her mother. His own father had died and his mother was soon to join him in eternal sleep. The Comanches appeared, two dozen of them, rode into the yard of the hacienda looking fearsome, frightening the maids and the shepherds who began crossing themselves, moaning and weeping as they prepared to meet their maker.

Don Miguel had met them, unarmed. He was looked to as the

leader of the little community along the Pecos and he saw at once that the Comanches were not painted for war.

Tecolote made the hand-sign of peace. Miguel returned it, offered him tobacco.

"We come from the range you call Sangre de Cristo," said the Comanche chief. "We have heard of you. They say your heart is not turned against the human beings."

"No. My heart is good for the people of your tribe."

"We would make a treaty, trade you furs for food and blankets."

Don Miguel knew that this was sometimes done, despite the animosity between Spaniard and Indian. Usually, the Comanche would call a truce with one village but go on pillaging others. At such times, there was more to trade than furs trapped in the mountains.

"*Tenga usted cuidado,*" whispered Corazon who had come to stand a few paces behind him.

Tecolote's eyes had narrowed when he saw Corazon, but he said nothing.

"We will make a treaty with you," said Don Miguel. "I will butcher some sheep and we will eat."

"No sheep. Cow."

Thus had begun a treaty that had lasted almost eight years to this day. Tecolote came and went. Sometimes he and his sons worked in the gardens and learned about raising vegetables. Not a word was said about Corazon and who she was. However, Tecolote had a son who was about Estrellita's age. One day, a year ago, when Estrellita had turned fourteen, he had asked Don Miguel to smoke a pipe with him so that they could talk.

When the Comanches came to trade, they set up their lodges below the hacienda, along the river, in a spot where the sheep did not graze. Over the years, Don Miguel had seen the band grow, become prosperous. When they had been raiding to the south, they would return with wounded, and some of the young men who had gone along did not come back. Sometimes the Spaniards would see fresh scalps and cringe, wonder if the

14

hair belonged to Apache or Spaniard, but no one said anything. A treaty had been made.

"I will smoke with you," said Don Miguel, starting to walk toward the Comanche camp.

"No," said Tecolote. "We will smoke where you have the flat stones."

Miguel led the chief to the patio. One of the maids brought strong coffee, cigars. Tecolote opened his blanket and brought out his pipe. He offered tobacco to the four directions, to the earth and to the sky, so Miguel knew it was a serious talk. The two men smoked and drank coffee. Finally, Owl said what was on his mind.

"You have a daughter who has already passed the time when she can give light. I have a son who is strong and brave. His name is Yellow Wind, Viento Amarillo in your tongue. He has worked beside your daughter in the place-that-grows-corn and his heart sings like the lark for her. He wants her for his wife before she grows too old and cannot bear children."

Don Miguel felt a stabbing in his chest, but he did not show Tecolote any sign that he was uncomfortable. He looked up at the sky and felt it darken as he always did when he was in anguish.

"Why do you ask this, Tecolote? Estrellita is Spanish. Your son is . . . Indian . . . a human being."

"Estrellita is the granddaughter of a great chief. This marriage would make our treaty strong. It would last for as long as the sun burns hot and the grasses grow."

"She is but fourteen. Too young to marry." He did not tell Tecolote that Estrellita had been promised, shortly after she was born, to Augustino Armijo. It was Miguel's intent to clean up the bloodlines, erase the past, if he could. Over the years, he was even more pleased that the promises had been made so long ago, for now Augustino was an important young man, a soldier, and his uncle, Manuel Armijo, was once the governor of Mexico. Surely such an alliance would do much to quash the stories of Corazon and her mother. Miguel himself was one of the biggest ranchers of Santa Fe and he would grow even more powerful once it was known that his daughter had married the governor's nephew.

Tecolote had laughed.

"Good. We will wait twelve moons. When she has one more summer, my son will take her to his lodge. We will have peace as long as rivers run."

Don Miguel knew that to refuse was tantamount to an act of war. He had no doubt that Owl would swoop down on them and murder them. Worse, he would take Estrellita away by force. He shuddered to think of what they might do to his virgin daughter.

He needed time to think. Tecolote had given him a year.

Don Miguel had talked to the priest in Santa Fe, made a novena, prayed for guidance.

Finally, a week ago, he had come to a decision.

He would never give his daughter to Yellow Wind. He would kill her first.

"Aquí vienen los Indios!"

Corazon's face drained of color, froze in a pale, translucent wax. She and Miguel looked over the low roof and saw the dust in the sky.

Miguel's face turned rigid. His lips tightened down on his teeth.

"You heard the cry?" she asked. "The Indians are coming here."

"Yes, I see them now. It is Tecolote."

She reached across the table, squeezed his arm in a desperate grasp.

"I must be strong," he said. "He must believe me."

"I will go with you. He will believe both of us."

He looked into her eyes and knew that, as usual, she was the wiser. He could not do it alone. He would need her support. Tecolote was no fool. He could tell when a man was lying. He

16

could smell the clammy sweat of fear. Miguel was afraid.

"Yes. We will do it together. I will carry a pistol."

"No, Miguel. You must believe what you will tell him. In your heart, you must believe that what you say is so. Only then will he believe you."

Again, he mentally bowed his head in respect for her wisdom.

"I will try," he rasped.

"No," she hissed, "you must believe that Estrellita is dead. Dead, do you hear? Stone-cold dead. *Claro?*"

He stood up.

"Yes, my dove, I will do this thing. Pray for me."

He was ready. He held out his arm. Corazon slipped her arm under his. They walked down the stairs together. He could feel her trembling. It masked his own nervousness. He knew what he had to do, yet it was so difficult to imagine. But everything had been prepared for this day, this one terrible moment. The fate of his daughter hung in the balance. The fate of all of them, in fact, was at stake. Yet, he knew that even if Tecolote believed him, it would not be over. Someday he would learn the truth and he would seek vengeance. By that time, perhaps, Estrellita might be safe, married to Augustino, living far away in a big city. After that he would not care what happened to himself.

Tecolote was waiting for them.

His son, Yellow Wind, sat atop his horse, next to his father. The Indians were not painted, but their horses were dusty, blowing from distended nostrils as if they had ridden far and fast. The band of Comanches stood their horses some distance off, but they held their war spears proudly as if ready to use them at their chief's urging.

Corazon had already begun weeping. She and her husband walked out along the flagstone path, holding on to each other.

The chief and his son murmured greetings in a Spanish turned guttural, the liquid consonants strangely twisted in their Indian mouths.

"My son, Yellow Wind, wants your daughter," said Tecolote in Spanish. "He has waited a year."

Miguel steeled himself.

"Where is Estrellita?" demanded Yellow Wind.

"Do you not see my wife weeping?" asked Don Miguel. "She is in mourning. That is why we wear the black clothes."

"Who has died?" asked Tecolote.

"Come," said Don Miguel somberly. "Dismount and follow us to the graveyard. You and your son."

Yellow Wind's face darkened. He started to say something, but his father quieted him. The two Comanches dismounted. Tecolote called for one of his braves to take their horses. Father and son followed Miguel and Corazon to the little hill above the side of the hacienda. There were four or five mounds there, servants who had died. One of the graves was fresh. There was a wooden headboard, flowers strewn below it.

"There lies my daughter," said Don Miguel.

"I do not read the marks in the wood," said Tecolote. He was a burly, bronzed man with a blunt nose, small, dark eyes, deep-set behind chunky cheekbones. His son, Yellow Wind, was slightly taller, his chest scarred from the hooks of the sundance. His nose was straight, his eyes wide-set.

Don Miguel knelt by the grave.

He traced the words carved into the wooden marker.

Here lies our beloved daughter
ESTRELLITA
born May 30, 1818
died June 5, 1833
May God keep her safe in heaven

Don Miguel read the words. Corazon sobbed loudly, pulled her hair, tore at her bodice.

"What killed her?" asked the chief.

"The pox. It came on suddenly. She died but yesterday. My wife and I cannot bear our grief. We are going away for a while to try and forget this sadness."

"Where will you go?" asked Yellow Wind, suspicious.

"To the east, to a big city called St. Louis. When we return, we will bring you presents."

Slightly mollified, the young brave turned away. He sang a song of grief and pulled his own hair.

Tecolote turned and stalked back down the slope to his horse.

Soon, Yellow Wind followed.

Don Miguel and Corazon stood there by the fresh grave. She put her arm around his waist. They watched the Indians ride down to their camping place on the Pecos.

She looked up at him and smiled thinly.

"They believed you," she said. "It's going to be all right."

"We must leave for Santa Fe tonight," he said softly. "And be gone from there tomorrow."

"When will we come back from St. Louis?" she asked.

"Someday."

She sighed. "Miguel, what were you thinking of when they were here? When you touched the grave marker, I shuddered all over."

"I was thinking that if that savage married my daughter, she would be as good as dead. She must marry Augustino Armijo."

"What if she does not?"

"She will. He will be in St. Louis and I will tell him he is free to court her. She is nearly of age."

Corazon squeezed her husband's waist, drew strength from him. He was wise and strong.

He loved Estrellita.

But he did not know his daughter. She was very much like him, and she had already told her mother she would not marry a man she had never set eyes on, no matter the custom. Corazon had not told Miguel this, nor would she tell him unless it became necessary. For she agreed with Estrellita, and now she realized that her husband still had that blind spot. He thought that breeding could erase the Comanche bloodlines.

19

He was wrong. He called them savages because he was ignorant. Estrellita was part Comanche, although she did not know it. Even if she married Augustino, her blood would not change.

Nothing could change who she was, where she had come from, who her parents and grandparents were. That was the finality none of them could escape.

Estrellita was part Comanche; now and forever.

Chapter One

Estrellita stretched languidly on the soft bed, her coal-black hair rustling on the plush down pillow. A golden shaft of sunlight slanted through the thin opening in the curtained window, splashed on the rug. Her sky-blue eyes opened slowly, filling with the light from the room. Her gaze fixed on the pale pink canopy above the four-poster bed. She smiled, remembering where she was, delighting in the luxury of the silk sheets, the softness of the light comforter that snugged against her breasts. She pulled the down-light spread up to her mouth, rubbed the satin border across her lips. She made a low sound in her throat, a secret little groan of pleasure that expressed her joy at being in such a nice house, where it was quiet and she could not hear the monotonous rumble of wagon wheels on rough roads or the creaking springs, the constant whine of coach wood and leather under strain. Gone, too, was the smell of horse sweat and the choking dust, the stifling heat that no amount of furious fanning could relieve.

She lifted several strands of her long dark hair, smelled them as if to prove that she really was clean, no longer masking her bathless scents with flower water, no longer shaking inside her father's coach as the bleak countryside streaked by while her chaperone spoke endlessly of bad storms, natural disasters, savage Indians, the likelihood of road agents and robbers. Poor

21

Lucia; she was prone to self-conjured fears that seldom materialized. It was almost as if she wished for such bizarre excitements because her spinster life was so uncommonly dull. Estrellita's father once told her mother that they would always be safe from Indian attack and thieves because "Lucia Delgado is not only ugly outside and sour inside, but she has the evil eye." Estrellita had once thought that her father had hired the woman because she was somewhat unattractive, if not downright *fea*, only to discourage young men from ogling her, but she had since learned that Lucia had worked faithfully for Corazon's parents and would have been forced into poverty had not the Rojas family taken her in as nanny for little Estrellita. In many ways, Estrellita felt closer to her *dueña* than to her own mother, but that was because Lucia had been her tutor, her mentor, her friend during her growing-up years, while her mother had been involved with ranch matters and social obligations. She was reminded now that her father, Miguel, had not left Pecos entirely because of the incident with Tecolote and his son, Viento Amarillo. Rather, he hoped to make amends for the treatment of French traders in Santa Fe and had set up a trading post of his own to take advantage of the opportunities that now existed as more and more expeditions invaded the wilderness. Her mother was a needed ally when his own persuasiveness failed. She believed in her husband's ideas and was not hesitant to speak out on his behalf.

In fact, the Rojas family were guests in St. Louis of none other than Julio Garcia, one of those adventurers associated with Pedro Vial, who had been sent by the governor of New Mexico to trace out a road from Santa Fe to St. Louis, back in 1796. Even though there had been problems, Garcia had elected to stay on in St. Louis and do business with the French and the American merchants. Now, Julio was anxious for Miguel Rojas to establish a trading post in Santa Fe. Today, in fact, her father was to meet with several American merchants at the Missouri Hotel to try to assure them that there would not be a repeat of the incident that had happened over a dozen years before. She had heard her father talking about the two ill-fated expeditions that had effectively blocked trade between the people of New Mexico and those in Missouri Territory.

When the Hidalgo revolution broke out in 1812, everyone along the Mississippi thought that this would finally break Spain's dominion over Mexico. So, three Americans, Jim Baird, Sam Chambers, and Bob McKnight, organized a trading expedition to Santa Fe, hoping to open the trail again and reap the first profits. Instead, when they reached the city, they learned that the revolution had failed and Hidalgo had been executed. The three men were arrested and shipped to prisons in northern Mexico. They were not released until Iturbide succeeded with his own revolution, returning to Santa Fe in 1821. While they were still in prison, in 1815, A.P. Chouteau and Julius De Mun, trying to read the winds of change, organized a Santa Fe expedition, fully believing that they would receive favorable treatment by the New Mexican authorities. Upon their arrival, they were promptly arrested, put in irons, and imprisoned. Their trade goods were confiscated and they were imprisoned for almost three years before they were released and allowed to return to St. Louis. They figured their losses at around thirty thousand dollars. Their story served, for a time, to deter any other major expeditions to Santa Fe.

However, a few bold traders managed to slip into Santa Fe and return with profits large enough to curry the interest of other businessmen. In 1821, Bill Becknell, who lived in Howard County, published an advertisement in the *Franklin Intelligencer.* He hoped to recruit "a company of men destined to the westward for the purpose of trading for horses and mules and catching wild animals of every description for advantage to the company." Becknell hoped to enlist seventy men, but only seventeen showed up at Ezekial Williams's, the "Lost Trapper," on the Missouri River, five miles north of Franklin. Becknell was elected captain, and he shaved his requirements to thirty men. The expedition left in September, crossing the

23

Missouri at Arrow Rock, returning in January, 1822.

Becknell had done what no one else had managed, and now Estrellita's father was anxious to become part of the trading community in Santa Fe. It was exciting to Estrellita because she knew that her father would handle expensive clothes and jewelry, which she and her mother could wear.

"Feliz cumpleaños," said a voice. "Happy birthday."

Estrellita jerked the coverlet up to her breasts in startled surprise. She turned, saw a face peering through the door.

"Oh, Lucia, you scared me!"

The *dueña* entered the room carrying a breakfast tray. Coffee steamed from a silver pitcher. There was cream, sugar, hot pastries. There was also an envelope, unsealed, stuck between the napkin ring and the sugar bowl.

"Are you not going to thank me for remembering this day?"

"Thank you. A million of thanks. Oh, Lucia, why did you bring this tray to my room? Where is my mother? Is she not here? I thought she would bring a little present for me. Is she still asleep? Did she go riding without me?"

"Te-te-te-te-te, Estrellita, you ask a dozen questions and you do not listen for an answer. You chatter like a magpie. The good lady has gone to town with your father, but she will have us to meet her at the fine hotel. There we will eat the good meal and then we will shop in the fine stores. Tonight you are to meet your future husband, have you forgotten? Augustino Armijo is here in St. Louis. Oh, I'm so excited. My heart flutters like the wings of a bird."

Estrellita's face turned cloudy as she bounced out of bed with a flicker of her lean legs beneath her nightgown. She stretched and stalked to the table where Lucia had set the tray. She picked up a pastry, tasted it with her tongue. She talked while licking off the thin layer of sugar that coated the French brioche.

She fixed Lucia with a pouty look.

"So, I am to meet the governor's nephew, am I? He is probably a dull-witted soldier in a fancy uniform who struts

24

like a peacock. They all do. Smug, vain, stiff-backed, straight-legged, *ay de mi*, I can see him now—a boring dandy who smells of horse sweat and stable droppings . . ."

"Estrellita! Take care with your tongue! And, yes, he is a soldier. A captain."

"I don't want to meet him—ever!" Estrellita began to mimic what she thought Augustino looked like, pooching out her buttocks, strutting about the room with her head tilted, her nose stuck up high, her arms and legs straight and stiff.

The *dueña* did not laugh. Lucia, a dark-skinned woman with a big Roman nose, wide forehead, high cheekbones, stood there in her severe black dress with its high, frilled collar, her black hair brushed straight back and coiled atop her head. She frowned at the antics of her charge, clucked to herself in wordless disapproval.

"You must not make fun of the man you are to marry," said Lucia. "It is not a good thing to make such slanders, even in jest."

"More of your superstition, Lucia?" Estrellita stopped strutting and glided back to the table, a mischievous twinkle in her clear blue eyes. "If I joke about my future husband, he will laugh over my grave."

"Hush, girl! Don't say things like that! They might come true."

Estrellita laughed, the sound a melodic ribbon of notes that echoed off the walls of the room. She crunched into the brioche, poured herself a coffee. She could not bring herself to look at Lucia, for she dreaded seeing the stern look on her face. Lucia took everything seriously. Her life was one of regimen, of order, of custom. There was no room for frivolity. Even when she dressed Estrellita, she was meticulous, painstaking. Sometimes her rigid, careful ways made the young woman want to scream. Still, she should not have teased Lucia so. She could not help the way she was. But now, Estrellita knew her one cocked eye would be flaring, while the other would be squinting almost shut, giving her the look of one with the "evil eye," the *malojo* her father referred to so often.

"I'm sorry, Lucia. It's just that I hate having to meet a stranger whom everyone has talked about all my life. My own mother and father do not know Augustino."

"They know his father and mother. That is enough. The custom—"

"Oh, spit on custom. I don't like soldiers. They are so arrogant, so boastful. They strut and brag, act so superior. I want to marry a good, strong man who is light-skinned and handsome. He must have fiery eyes like my father, and powerful arms to hold me. He must be tender and loving and he must not know other women like the soldiers do. He must have soft hair and a wide chest. He might even be an American, or an Indian . . ."

Lucia gasped. "This is not good talk," she stammered. "A lady doesn't say such things. A lady doesn't think such things. You must tell this to the priest in confession. These are sinful thoughts, young lady. You must say penance and not think these bad thoughts anymore."

Estrellita sat on a chair. She stretched out her legs, crossed them at the ankles. She sipped, stared up at the ceiling.

"Did you not ever think of the perfect man, Lucia? Even when you were a little girl? Did you never pretend you had a secret lover, a man who was perfect in every way? Did you not burn with a fever at night thinking of such a one after you began to have blood?"

The girl's voice dropped to a husky whisper. Lucia's face darkened with a sudden flush of embarrassment. The *dueña* sat down quickly, held on to the table for support. Her wild eye flared in its socket. It seemed to expand and contract like some bulging fish eye, and Estrellita shrank away from her, afraid that she had gone too far in revealing herself while trying to probe Lucia's wisdom for answers.

"Come close, girl," said the chaperone in low, conspiratorial tones. "You have sixteen years today and yet you are like a

26

little child."

Estrellita moved her chair close to Lucia, eager to hear what she had to say. The old woman took the girl's hand in hers, squeezed it gently.

"Listen to me," she said. "I had these thoughts once. When I was younger than you. I loved a man above me in station. He did not even see me, did not even know I was alive and full of love for him. I ached in my heart for him. When I saw him riding his fine horse, my heart beat fast and my stomach filled up with little caterpillars. I thought I was going to die, for I could not breathe when he came near. I pretended he loved me, and when I dreamed at night, I dreamed of being in his arms. I dreamed of his kisses on my mouth and his arms holding me tight."

"Yes, yes," said Estrellita, "go on, Lucia."

Lucia looked at the girl, her eyes clouded with the pain of a bittersweet remembrance. So sad her eyes, thought Estrellita, like the wind that blows through the olive trees stirring the dark fruit before harvest, wafting a smell of old Spain to the nose, the Spain that Lucia had told her about many times, and the story of the olive-tree cuttings coming over on the schooner, then overland by mule and into the ground of the New World. Lucia knew the path of every object that came across the seas to this terrible Mexican colony with its heathens and sinners, derelicts and savages.

"It was a sickness in me. I could not eat, could not sleep. My mother was worried about me. Finally, I told her what was wrong."

A deep note of melancholy crept into Lucia's voice. In the stillness of the room, Estrellita shivered involuntarily.

"Was she sympathetic, your mother?"

"*Ay, de mi.* I thought so. But she told my father, and he flew into a rage. He called me into his room and shouted at me in anger. I was struck dumb with fear of him. He began to beat me until I fell senseless and bleeding at his feet. Truly, he broke my eye, and at first I thought it was an accident. It swelled up with blood, and for a long time I could not see. Nothing more was said to me, but I was kept inside, away from the young master. When I complained about my eye, my mother told me that this was the lesson my father had given me, never to look on forbidden things, never to want those things which I was forbidden to have."

"Forbidden . . ."

"Yes," hissed Lucia bitterly, "forbidden!"

Estrellita drew back in her chair, surprised at the passion she had unleashed. She looked now at Lucia with new eyes, wondering at the depths she had discovered in the old crone. Perhaps she had been beautiful once, and most certainly she had loved, even deeply. It was a side of Lucia she had never witnessed.

Lucia clucked to herself, shriveling back up in her clothes as if certain she had gone too far, been too loose with her tongue.

"There is a surprise for you," she said. "When I have finished dressing you."

"A surprise? For me? What is it?"

"Tss, tss, child. It would truly not be a surprise if I told you. Aren't you going to look in the envelope?"

Estrellita noticed the envelope on the tray. It was made of fine paper, dyed pink. She stuffed the remainder of the pastry in her mouth, plucked the envelope from the tray. She opened it carefully.

"Dearest one," read the note on the fancy stationery, "we wish you a happy birthday. We have gifts for you in town. But a very special one will be there soon. With love." She recognized the handwriting as her mother's, but the note was signed Mama *and* Papa. She clutched it to her breast, looking dreamily at Lucia.

"It must be something very nice," she said. "Won't you tell me what it is, Lucia?"

"It's time for your bath. I'll lay out your clothes. Quick! Quick! There is much to do this day."

"Will I see it after I bathe?"

"Soon, soon. Hurry, child."

Estrellita did not mean to languish in the big wooden tub, but the water was so warm and the soap made bubbles so soft and perfumy on her skin that Lucia had to chide her several times before she climbed out to rinse. She thought of dozens of things her parents might have gotten for her, savoring each wish until Lucia's coaxing drew her back to the bedroom.

"You will be late for your own surprise if you don't hurry," said the *dueña*.

Estrellita, wrapped in a large fluffy towel, looked around the room in disappointment. Her gaze stopped on the bed where her clothes were set out. There were no frilly pantaloons, no satin dress, no silk accessories.

"Lucia, what have you done? I'm not wearing those old things."

"Yes, you are."

"Those are my riding clothes. I thought we were going to town."

"Not until later. First, you wear these. Do not argue."

Estrellita pouted, tossed her towel at Lucia. It fluttered harmlessly to the floor several feet from its target.

"My, what a temper you show on your birthday," clucked Lucia. "Maybe your gifts should be given to someone more appreciative."

"What gifts?"

"You'll see. Patience."

Estrellita went to the dressing table, began to dab her bare flesh with scented powder. Lucia helped her dress, handing her each item, fussing over her like a mother hen with her chick. She combed out the girl's hair, tied it back with a ribbon.

"I hate this skirt," said Estrellita, "and you laced my boots too tight. I don't want to go riding."

"Yes, yes," said Lucia agreeably. "Just come with me to the window."

"To the . . ."

Estrellita gasped as a determined Lucia jerked her across the room. The *dueña* opened the curtains wide, dragged the girl up to a position beside her.

"Look," she said.

Estrellita looked down into the courtyard. She saw a young man leaning against a tree. She could not see his face, which was shielded by a cap, but his clothes were homespun, plain. Peasant's garb, she thought.

"I see only a boy," she said loudly.

The lad, hearing her voice, looked up, gaped at her. His mouth fell open.

Lucia suppressed a titter.

"What are you staring at, boy?" taunted Estrellita in English.

"You talkin' to me?" The youth pointed to his chest, hairless under the muslin shirt that was open at the collar.

"You're the only boy I see down there."

He stepped away from the tree, drew himself up.

"Well, I ain't no boy, ma'am, but full growed and on my own."

Estrellita laughed.

"Are you my surprise?"

A puzzled look crept over the young man's features. Then Lucia stepped up to the window, nodded to him.

"Uh, yes'm, I mean, no, ma'am. I brung you . . . Uh, well, you come on down here and I'll fetch what it is you're hankerin' for."

Estrellita turned to Lucia.

"Are you playing a joke on me? Who is that down there? He's one of those unmannered Americans."

"Yes, yes, but you must see what he has brought you. Come, we will go downstairs now."

Estrellita looked out the window one more time.

The young man still stood there, wide-legged, glaring up at her with deep-set eyes. The morning sun seemed to shine on him, on his wide square shoulders, his swelling chest, tapering torso. He wore boot moccasins, she noticed, and a knife on his belt. As she watched him, he folded his arms across his chest, flashed her a scornful smile.

She drew back from the window, tossing her hair.

"I'll give him a piece of my mind," she told Lucia. "How dare he look at me that way?"

"And how were you looking at him, child?"

Jeremiah York thought that the old crone must have poisoned him.

Something was surely wrong with his heart, and his head swam with dizziness.

He looked away from the window. The girl had gone. He had never seen one so beautiful as she, but she was obviously mean. She was a "furriner" like the woman who had served him breakfast in the kitchen shortly after dawn when he brought the horse in from the stables in St. Louis. The people who had bought the horse from him were Spaniards, too. He knew that much, although he had never seen the likes of Miguel Rojas in Bowdoinham, Maine, on the Kennebec River, where he was born. He guessed the Spaniard was some kind of gentleman, since his clothes were so fancy and he had not balked at the price of the mare.

Nor had he ever seen so many Frenchies in one place before, or Negroes. They seemed to be all over St. Louis, talking in so many different languages, he sometimes felt as if he was in a foreign country. He had not yet found the man he had come to see, but he would, as soon as he was through with this business. This was the last of the horses he had brought in from Kaskaskia, Illinois—good, strong Tennessee horses that Mister Morrison had told him would bring good prices on the frontier.

William Morrison was a merchant, a right smart one, and Jeremiah had listened to him talk so much about the money to be made in fur trapping, that one day York had upped and told him he wanted to make his mark in the world and would he help him get started. Not only had Morrison been eager to stake the boy, but he told him the man to see in St. Louis. He arranged for the purchase of the horses, and gave Jeremiah a message to deliver to Baptiste Lalande, a fur trader, a man who lived most of his life in the wilderness, where savage Indians roamed, and bears and other wild critters stalked the land.

Yet, he had not found Lalande, although he had inquired about him in the taverns and grog shops, at the Green Tree Inn and Rocky Mountain House, all the places where trappers and mountain men told their rich, tall tales, while he stared at them in wide-eyed envy, wishing to be one of them, knowing he would be someday soon.

He had been in St. Louis for a week, had not seen the man who had come with him, Benjamin Snopes, since two days before. Snopes, who had taught him much about horses, but had little patience, had told him, "You keep the sorrel gelding for your trouble, York, and if you sell the Arabian colt, you got your stake."

"What about you, Ben?"

"I be goin' back to Kaskaskia for more horses, and to give Bill his share. You be sure you tell Lalande about Morrison's offer."

So for two days he had walked with a lump in his throat, hoping someone would buy the pretty colt before his meager funds ran out. Then the Spaniards had come down to the stockyards, a whole passel of them, looking for a young horse. Rojas had looked a long time at the Arabian, asked a lot of questions. He had felt the legs, the chest, looked into the mouth. He had put a saddle on the young mare and crawled underneath it to see if it was gentle. Finally, the Spaniard had brought a comely, dark woman with him and paid half the money, with the rest due on delivery this day.

Jeremiah had arisen from his bed of straw in the loft at the stockyards and begun currying the mare before dawn.

Armed with directions to the Vial hacienda, Jeremiah had ridden his own mount, leading the mare on a rope halter. The old vulture of a woman had met him earlier, ordered him to put the horses in the stables. She showed him a brand-new saddle, carved of leather and inlaid with silver, told him to put it on the mare, bridle her, and wait in the courtyard until he saw her at the window.

"This is a birthday gift for the daughter of Don Miguel," Lucia said in her halting English. "It is a surprise, so you will not show the horse until I tell you. Do you understand?"

"Uh, yes'm, I ain't to fetch the horse till you tell me to. But I got to get on my way and . . ."

"Do not spoil the birthday."

Then the foreign woman had left him and he had seen her no more until a few moments ago. He knew that the two-year-old Arabian was a birthday gift for the girl who had appeared at the window, looking down at him with scornful eyes, teasing him. He had wanted to spoil her surprise right then, but also saw the stern look from the old woman. He wasn't afraid of her exactly, but she could cause him trouble. She was to give him a note for the Spaniard that would let the man know the horse had been delivered.

It would soon be over, and he would ride back into town, meet Rojas, and get the rest of his money.

Impatiently, Jeremiah began to scuff his bootheel at the base of the acacia tree where he had been waiting. His belly was full because of the generosity of the old Spanish woman, but he was anxious to be on his way. He would not feel right until he had the rest of the money in his hand. He did not want to be cheated. Morrison, the merchant, had warned him about such things.

York heard a sound, turned, and saw the girl and the old

woman coming toward him across the courtyard.

From the way she walked, Jeremiah could tell that the girl was angry. Her leather skirt flapped against her boots, making a sound like a bullwhip cracking across a mule's rump. She took long strides, her shoulders square, her head, covered by a small flat-brimmed hat that was tied under her chin, held proudly high.

"Who are you? What are you doing here?" snapped the young lady.

Jeremiah had never seen eyes so blue. They sparkled with spirit, contrasted sharply with the girl's flawless olive skin. They were like prairie sky and summer lakes under the sun. They pierced him with brightness and beauty, and drew him close to her, made him want to look deeper into their dazzling depths.

He opened his mouth to speak, but the old woman began waving her hands at him.

"Do not say anything," she ordered. "Bring the surprise."

"Lucia," said Estrellita in Spanish, "let me finish. I do not like the way this boy looks at me. He has no manners."

Jeremiah stared at the girl, wondering what she had said in her staccato tongue. None of it made any sense to him, but his ears stung and he knew they must be red with shame.

"Please, Estrellita, do not pick at the boy. He means no harm."

Jeremiah stood there, baffled at the talk he could not understand. Up close, the girl was even more beautiful than he had imagined, and he had seen beautiful girls in St. Louis, even back in Bowdoinham.

"All right," pouted Estrellita.

Then she spoke to Jeremiah in English. "Where is this surprise you have brought me?"

"It's in the stable."

"Well, don't just stand there like an idiot," she snapped. "Bring it to me."

But Jeremiah could not move. He tried, but his boots seemed

to be planted firmly in the earth, like hardwood roots in the Maine woods. A dizziness assailed him, and he felt his heart pounding so loudly, she surely must hear it throb against his rib cage. Certainly it hammered in his ears with a ragged drumbeat, trilling at high speed like a woodpecker's beak against a hollowed-out hickory trunk in high summer.

An eternity went by, time crawling like a lazy yellow caterpillar, and still Jeremiah stood there, totally smitten by a girl who was no older than he, and who looked at him with dancing, sparkling, spearing, scornful blue eyes.

Chapter Two

Lucia saw the dumbstruck expression on the boy's face and frowned. It was the worst possible thing that could happen. If Don Miguel had seen it, he would have known. Corazon would have been horrified. This was a mere stableboy, a peon, yet he stared at Estrellita as though she were stark naked.

"Well," she said sharply, "you must not just stand there." Lucia began to wring her hands in anguish. She stole a sidelong glance at her ward, saw a bemused expression flit across Estrellita's face. She jabbed the girl sharply in the side as if to communicate her displeasure with a single poke of her finger. Estrellita seemed to snap out of her fascinated gaze, but there was no doubt in the *dueña*'s mind that some damage had been done. She had seen such looks before, had been the subject of several many years ago when she herself was a young woman. Now her heart fluttered wildly in her chest, and she longed to sit down before she had a stroke.

She turned again to the boy, who stood there, transfixed. Jeremiah saw the movement, blinked his eyes.

Then, without a word, he turned on his heel and disappeared from sight.

"What's wrong with him?" Estrellita asked in Spanish.

"He is a stupid," said Lucia quickly. "Do not concern yourself with the likes of him. Did you see his threadbare clothes? The poor boy doesn't have a *centavo* and feels intimidated in your presence."

"Was that it? He does seem . . ."

"Rude. Very rude. Without shame, too."

Estrellita spoke in a faraway voice, still staring after the young man as though his image had been burned into her mind, lingered there still, blazing.

"I did not think . . ."

"Child, you do not know what you think. It's the excitement of your birthday. Put him out of your mind."

"Eh? Oh, yes. I wonder what he is bringing me."

Lucia's heart sank. She wanted to shake the girl, jiggle out the nonsense in her mind. Estrellita did not know what had happened, but she, too, had seen the look of a young man gone suddenly mad, stung by Cupid's arrow, pierced to his heart by a beauty he could never possess.

Instead, she began to tap her foot impatiently, hoping it would all be over soon. The boy would bring the horse and Estrellita's interest would shift to the surprise her father had arranged.

It seemed forever before the youth returned, leading the Arabian. The horse stepped out, prancing under the new saddle, fighting the alien bit in its teeth. Its flowing mane draped over its handsome neck, flaxen as its graceful tail. The mare's coat, the color of dark champagne, glowed in the sunlight. Its small hooves danced as York led the animal in a circle to show her off to the young lady.

"This be the horse your father bought you, miss," he said. "Ain't she beauteous?"

Estrellita brought her hands to her face and let out a scream of delight.

"He's mine? Oh, he's beautiful!"

"It's a her," said Jeremiah. "A right fine horse, you ask me. I druv her clear form Kaskaskie, and she warn't no trouble a-tall. Rode her a time er two, and she's plumb soft-gaited. Like ridin' a cloud, she is."

Estrellita went to the horse, began stroking its mane, caressing its withers with delicate hands.

"How beautiful!" she said in Spanish. Then, in English, "What's her name?"

"Name? Why, I don't rightly know. Mine's Jeremiah York."

"I am Estrellita Montez y Rojas."

Lucia's face blanched, but she was powerless to undo the damage. She stood there, scowling, her face dark as a stormcloud.

The two young ones stood close together now, Jeremiah holding the reins, gazing raptly at the girl, Estrellita stroking the horse's neck, but staring, mesmerized, into York's deep brown eyes.

"You, there, stableboy!" called Lucia. "That will be all. Come, I will give you the note for Don Miguel."

"Huh?" asked Jeremiah, his gaze still locked on Estrellita's.

"She's talking to you," said Estrellita.

"Yes, you, the stableboy," reiterated Lucia.

York turned to the chaperone then, his jawline hardening in sudden anger. The flesh at the corners of his eyes pinched up ever so slightly.

"Ma'am," he said politely, his voice pitched low, resonant in his swelling chest, "beggin' your pardon, but I ain't no stableboy. I'm a freeborn from Bowdoinham, Maine, on my own, beholden' to no man, ner no woman, neither."

Lucia did not understand all that York had said. She turned to Estrellita, her eyebrows lifted in puzzlement.

"He says," Estrellita told her in Spanish, "that he is not a lackey. He serves no master but himself." Her almost arrogant tone did not escape the chaperone's notice. It was as if the girl used his words to defy Lucia's authority.

"Take caution with your own tongue, daughter," said Lucia in rapid Spanish. "While the boy is here, he is under Don Miguel's orders, and he will obey me as if the master was here himself."

"This American looks pretty strong to me, Lucia. If you

push him, he might strike back."

Lucia recoiled at this near-sacrilege. Her eyes seemed to turn incandescent with rage. Yet Estrellita was right about the American. He was young and probably poor as a churchrat, but his muscles were well developed, his hands strong. Yet, certainly the daughter of Don Miguel was making too much of this little thing. The boy had done his job. He must be on his way. Estrellita would forget him soon enough.

"Are you talking about me?" York asked Estrellita.

"It is nothing," she replied. "My chaperone did not understand your funny English."

"Funny English?"

"The way you speak is foreign to her."

Jeremiah laughed.

"I reckon she don't talk it much better."

Estrellita laughed, too, and Lucia's tight collar drew even tighter. She felt faint, wished for her fan, something cool to drink, a shady place to stand. She was beginning to perspire. These young ones were beginning to get under her skin like itching mites.

"You, sir," said Lucia, changing her tone, "come with me. You no needed here no more."

Jeremiah looked crestfallen. He looked down at his boots, then at the girl. He flashed a weak smile.

"Reckon I done wore out my welcome," he said. "You know how to ride?"

"Yes. I grew up riding horses. But I never had one so fine as this."

"Are you going to ride her now?"

"For a while. Then I am going into town."

"Well, maybe I'll see you again. I got to go back there too. Your father owes me some money."

Estrellita said nothing. She, too, looked as though she did not want the conversation to end. Lucia, however, walked up, took the young man's arm, and began leading him toward the house.

"Good-bye," said Jeremiah. "Hope you like that little filly."

"Good-bye," said Estrellita wistfully.

"You wait until I return," Lucia said, in her native tongue. "I will go riding with you."

"No! I want to go alone!"

Lucia did not break her stride, but looked back over her shoulder.

"Wait!" she said, fixing Estrellita with her single bad eye. Jeremiah turned, began walking backward. He watched the girl climb into the saddle, sit straight, work the reins expertly. Lucia glared at him, applied pressure to his arm.

"Ma'am," he said, "you'd better slack off. A man don't like to be shoved about like a danged mule."

Lucia suddenly lost her ability to converse in the English language.

"*No comprendo,*" she said tightly, twisting York around.

As the two left the courtyard, the air echoed with the clatter of the Arabian's iron hooves on the cobbled walk.

"That's some girl," breathed Jeremiah. "She's got spunk."

"*Hijo de mala sangre,*" hissed Lucia under her breath. "Son of bad blood."

Lightheaded, Jeremiah led his horse out of the stable, climbed into the saddle. The old crone was nowhere in sight, but she had written out the note and it was tucked safely in his trouser pocket. He clucked to the horse, a little bay gelding he called Fleetfoot because the animal had good bottom and speed. It was chunky, compact, stood nearly fourteen hands high, short-tailed, dark mane long and untrimmed. He knew the importance of owning a horse, especially out here on the edge of the frontier. He knew about horses because his father had given him his first one when he was only eight years old. That had been Jeremiah's first taste of freedom, mobility. That had been the beginning of his wandering days, the first stirring of restlessness in his heart, a restlessness that had brought him to Kaskaskie first, and now to St. Louis. A restless urge that would take him beyond the big river and into the mountains, to the far, shining mountains.

But even before that, Jeremiah had heard the tales of the mountain men. At first he had thought they were just stories, told at the mercantile store by men sitting around the potbellied stove in winter, at the summer picnics when the men were lighting their pipes after the lacrosse games and the feasting.

"Are there really mountain men?" he had asked his father one day, when he had heard the talk once again down at Vestal's store.

"Seems like," said his pa, Stanley York, a blacksmith.

"You ever see one?"

"Nope."

"What do they do?"

"Fur trappers. Bear hunters. Odd ones, the lot."

And Jeremiah had liked what his father said about them being odd because that was the talk at Vestal's and at the picnics by the river and sometimes at Cap's Barber Shop or when the old men were whittling in the town square, chewing on their tobacco twists, or from the travelers who came to his father's blacksmith shop and from those friends who hunted partridge and grouse on land his father owned beyond the river in the deep woods. He listened to them and the mountain men grew big in his head and he began to memorize their names, the deeds they had done.

There was talk of Jim Bridger, the Sublette brothers, Thomas Fitzpatrick, Kit Carson, Joe Meek, and Jedediah Smith, true names of real men, heroes in his eyes. He learned the story of Fitzpatrick and Smith, who had spoken with wild Crow Indians in their tongue, learned of the great and secret South Pass through the Rockies, gone into the Green River Valley which was thick with beaver, easy-trapped, coats shiny silk, tails good for eating.

Mr. Morrison had talked of little else once he found out that

42

Jeremiah wanted to join an expedition. But when he spoke of Lalande, there was a bitterness to his voice. Jeremiah had no idea what was in the message he was to deliver to the trapper, but Morrison had hinted that it was a kind of letter of introduction.

"You find the man, see if he will take you on, Son."

"And if he does?"

"Then I will buy your pelts and make you a rich man."

So, in York's mind, he was in Morrison's employ. All he needed to do was to find Lalande and ask to be taken along on the next fur-trapping expedition.

He thought of those things now, as he rode slowly away from the Vial hacienda, out through the thick prairie grass, belly high on his horse, looking for the Indian mounds in the distance, the landmarks he had left behind in the predawn dark.

But, first he must deliver to Don Miguel Rojas the note the old Spanish woman had given him and get the rest of his money. Then he would be free to look harder for Lalande. He had not been able to spend time in the places where the trappers drank and smoked, because he had little money. Now he would go inside one of the taverns where the mountain men congregated, sit and listen to the talk, try to find someone who knew Lalande.

He rode out, wishing the country would open to him now that he was almost his own man, but he knew he was still with civilization and he had been there all his life. He was ten years old when he heard the tales of the mountain men, and he knew that he had been only six or seven years old when Ashley and Henry had gone west from the mouth of the Yellowstone, founded an empire that they proclaimed in 1825 at Henry's Fork of the Green River when the first rendezvous brought all the brave men, the fearless trappers and the Indians, together. The names of the men and the rivers, the places where they traded, rang in his ears and made his blood run hot. Kit Carson, he remembered, was only a boy like himself when he had come

43

to the wilderness and made his name famous among all the famous names of men who were his elders.

So he had pestered his father for stories, and later, Morrison. And each time he heard the names mentioned, the places spoken of, his blood ran fast and made his skin tingle, his stomach flutter with winged insects. He made legends of the men who *were* legends and they grew into giants and he dreamed about them when he lay on his cot, his muscles sore from hard work in his father's fields, his shop, at Morrison's store and the sweat smell strong in his nostrils, the night sounds of crickets and owls purring throaty in the deep woods, calling to him from another place, another time.

He longed hard to be on his own, in the far wilderness, trapping beaver and other fur-bearing creatures, shooting his own game, cooking blooded meat over an open fire under the bright stars. He took to the woods, and he did those things, but they were not the same. He wore only simple, homespun clothes and could hear cattle lowing, and he knew the bears were gone and the deer scattered, the elk pretty much gone, too. And there were no men telling tall tales in the firelight, their rifles laid across their laps, their handmade knives jutting from leather sheaths they had cured themselves far from the dangling lamps of towns and chinked log houses in a settlement.

The pull was strong in him, and it had grown stronger when he saw St. Louis and knew that this was the place where the mountain men came to buy knives and hatchets and rifles, drink from the burning cup, and swagger among lesser men like gods descended to the earth for a time from high mountain camps where the air was thin and the grizzlies taller than a cabintop.

He saw the pall of smoke threaded over the river, could almost hear the calls of the *voyageurs*, the slap of water against hulls, the crackle of burning wood, the hiss of steam, and he imagined the flow of boats up and down the Mississippi, the grunts of the stevedores wrestling goods on to the docks, the "twee" of water birds as they flapped above the decks, dove, thieving, for scraps of waste food clinging to the scuppers. The sky above, so blue it made him ache inside, made the call in him stronger than ever.

Behind him, he heard the ragged thrum of hoofbeats. Turning in the saddle, he saw the dark-haired girl, riding the Arabian, riding like the wind. Her dark tresses streamed from under her hat. She sat straight in the fine saddle, her shoulders square. Jeremiah looked at her with envy. She rode better than most men.

She came up on him, working the horse, bringing it up to a singlefoot gait, making it prance alongside. She smiled at him wide, and something inside him melted, turned soft. He had never seen such a flawless complexion, her skin smooth over the fine bones of her face, her nose delicate, her lips full and ripe, the veins in her neck like sculpture, her shoulders still square. He avoided looking at the part of her leg that showed between the skirt and her boottop, but he knew it was slim and sleek, graceful as anything he'd ever seen.

"I love her," she said, her voice breathless. "She's such a fine, good horse."

"Uh huh, she shore is," he replied in that flat, crisp Maine accent, slightly nasal.

She patted the Arabian's neck with affection, her gloved hand sliding over the hide like some winged creature, like a dark bird gliding.

York slowed his horse, looked at the Arabian dancing alongside, part of the girl now, regal under the new Mexican saddle, proud head bridled in new leather. The two had made friends fast, and he knew that this was because she was in command of the horse, that she knew how to ride, how to make such an animal respond to her. She wore no spurs and he thought that was a good thing because he had seen the big Mexican rowels and the raked flanks of Mexican horses, scarred and trembling from the cruelty of their riders. The rich Spaniards treated their horses much better.

"Thank you," she said, getting her breath back now, her breasts rising under the cloth of her blouse straining at the material until he felt a heat rise up his neck and burn the lobes of his ears.

"Warn't none of my doing," he said sheepishly. "Your pa . . ."

"I know. For my birthday. But you brought her to me."

"Yeah, I reckon so." He did not know what to say. He wanted to bask in her praise, listen to the sound of her voice, the way the words came out in English, faintly accented but somehow prettier than pure American talk.

"What does your name mean?" she asked. She stopped petting the horse, looked at him with an intensity that made him squirm.

"Huh?"

"Your name. I have never heard such a name before."

"Jeremiah?"

She laughed. "Yes. Cheremiah."

He chuckled at the way she said it.

"What's *your* name mean?" he asked.

A smile played on her lips. He felt dumb, but he had never heard such a name before. He had no idea what it meant. Nor any person's name for that matter. Names were just names.

"Little star."

"That's what it means?"

"Yes. You don't speak Spanish."

"I don't hardly speak good English, I reckon."

"You could, if you wanted to. My father hired a tutor for me, but there are books you could . . . Do you know how to read?"

His face flushed a pale rose.

"Some," he said. "I ain't never thought about it much. Readin'."

"Oh, I didn't mean to hurt your feelings. It's just that you talk very strange sometimes and I have trouble understanding you. I read a lot of books written in English and I listen to people speak. I had a hard time learning English."

"You did?" he asked hopefully.

She nodded, smiled warmly at him. She patted her horse's neck again and Jeremiah felt envious. He didn't want her to leave. He wanted to sit there for hours and listen to her. Her horse snorted and he wanted to kick it. The Arabian shook its head impatiently, rattled the bit in its teeth. It stretched its neck, began nibbling on the sparse grass.

"I have sixteen years today," she said suddenly.

"Huh?"

"It's my birthday."

"I know. You told me. You're sixteen years old?"

"Yes, that is how you say it? See what I mean? I still have trouble with the English."

"No," he said quickly, "no, you don't."

"How many years have you?"

He started to lie because he did not want her to be older than he was, but something inside him told him it would be wrong. More than that, he had the feeling that she would find out if he lied.

"Fifteen. Going on sixteen."

"Oh." She sounded disappointed.

"Come October," he said, "I'll be as old as you." He drew himself up, sat straight in the saddle.

"I'll come to your birthday if you come to mine," she said.

He felt a thrill that was like going into a cold stream on a hot day without any clothes on, going deep under the water like a diving otter, the shock of the cold water sudden, exciting.

"Uh, I don't have no good clothes and no present," he said, self-consciously.

"That doesn't make any difference, silly. Come tonight."

"Where?" Maybe he could buy a shirt and trousers. Maybe he could buy her a little gift. He wanted to see her again—at any cost.

"At the Hacienda Vial. Where you came this morning."

"Yes."

"And where will your birthday be?"

"Huh? Oh, well, I reckon I don't know. You see, I'm bound for the mountains, goin' after beaver and such."

Her face fell, darkened.

"That's so far away. And so dangerous."

"Um, I reckon. I'm going to be a businessman, make a lot of money." The moment he said it, he believed it. He wanted her to believe it. Somehow, it had become important that Estrellita understand that he wasn't always going to be poor. He did not think beyond that, but his heart thumped like a caught rabbit in his chest and his head seemed as if a wind was drawing everything out of it, filling it with a dizzying emptiness.

"Maybe you will also come to Santa Fe. That is where my father says the fur traders will come in the spring."

"Oh, I don't reckon we'll be gettin' down Mexico way."

"Not Mexico. *New* Mexico."

"I reckon I don't know where that is," he said, again conscious of his ignorance.

"My father says there will be a lot of business between St. Louis and Santa Fe someday. He talks of many people becoming rich. You must come to Santa Fe. From there, the big mountains are not far away."

He didn't know what to say. She had voiced this strange invitation to him and her words filled him up inside, all over, filled up his heart and his mind until he thought he would burst with it, because her words were so full of wonder and so powerful, he felt smothered by them. It was as if she was burning the words into his brain, branding "Santa Fe" into his mind so that it would never go away. She was telling him where she lived, where her home was, but she was telling him so much more, as well. She was telling him so much that his ears burned and his heart kicked up like a colt's until it hurt inside his chest. He wanted to reply, but he was struck dumb with the enormity of what she had said, because he knew that he should have just ridden back to St. Louis and gone about his business. He should not be here at all like this, talking to this beautiful foreign girl. He should have ridden away from the Vial hacienda and, by rights, never seen this girl again, never learned her name nor spoken it over and over in his mind as he was bound to do forever after.

She looked at him for a long time and he was sure that she thought him stupid and that hours had gone by since she had spoken. But her gaze shifted from him, and her sky-blue, lake-blue eyes widened until he looked over his shoulder and saw what she was staring at on the horizon. A dark shape, growing larger, moved toward them, a horse and rider, and even without seeing the figure exactly, close up, for certain, he knew who it was.

"Quick," she exclaimed. "I know where there's a little stream, where the horses can drink. Follow me."

Before he could say anything, she touched her heels to the Arabian's flanks and the horse's muscles bunched up underneath her. The animal bounded off, turned under the deftness of her reining, galloped away like the wind. Jeremiah looked over his shoulder once at the advancing *dueña* and kicked his own horse into action. He raced after the Spanish girl, his stomach knotting up in mock terror, as if he was fleeing a fire-snorting dragon. He chased after her, watched her disappear over a hill, and when he reached the spot, turned in the saddle and looked back. The dark dot was very small now, hidden behind a scrim of dust, and he could picture the old woman's face, dark as a raincloud, hideous in its wrath. Jeremiah began to laugh, and he let out a whoop of joy as he rode over the crest of the hill, leaving the chaperone way behind, so far behind that she would never catch up, even if they rode a thousand miles.

He was still laughing, and his side was aching from the laughter and the hard ride, when he caught up to Estrellita. She sat her horse by the shady banks of a creek. The Arabian's neck stretched out until its muzzle buried itself in the water. Its rubbery lips moved under the rippling water, giving the animal a comical expression.

"What are you laughing at?" she asked.

He jerked a thumb back over his shoulder.

"Is that a relative of your'n?" he asked.

"No. She is my chaperone."

"It just seemed funny, us runnin' off like that and her comin' up on us."

"You mustn't laugh. She'll be very angry with me."

"Why, shucks . . ."

"Listen . . ." she said urgently, "I should not be here with you like this, but I . . . I wanted to talk to you."

His horse moved up the creek. He let the reins go slack so that it could drink.

"I reckon I'm plumb glad," he said, grinning, trying to fight down the panic that rose in him. Panic and a certain terror that had to do with the old woman, the forbiddenness of this moment alone with Estrellita.

"I want you to come to my birthday party. Tonight."

He was dumbfounded.

"Me?"

"Yes," she said softly, and he felt the word whisper in his ear, and the whisper made the little hairs tickle on the back of his neck.

"Well, I don't know. I mean, will it be all right?"

"Yes. Just come. Have you some nice clothes to wear?"

"Why, sure," he lied. "Heck, I don't have no present for you, though." Doubt assailed him, clouded his mind. What kind of a present could he possibly get this girl? And, he had so little money for himself . . .

"I don't want you to bring a present. Just come. There'll be music and singing and dancing . . ."

"Well, what time of the day and what if that old woman don't let me see you no more and . . ."

She shot him a look of exasperation. Once again, he was struck with the blueness of her eyes, the blue against the dark of her skin, her hair.

"After dark. Come."

Suddenly, she pulled her horse's head from the stream with

a decisive tug of the reins. Before he could say anything, she rode away, leaving him there. He turned in the saddle, saw the reason why she had left so quickly. She rode toward the dark figure on horseback, the old woman who watched over her like a guard.

Jeremiah swallowed hard. He saw Estrellita stop, saw the old woman wave her arms, point in his direction. Then, after a few moments, they rode away, over the sloping crest, getting smaller and smaller until only their shoulders showed.

Then Estrellita turned, and he saw her arm rise in the air, her hand flap.

Stunned, it took him a moment to realize that she was waving to him.

He raised his own arm, waved back.

But she was gone.

Chapter Three

Jeremiah rode back to St. Louis in a numb state of shock. He tried to sort out his feelings and they only became more tangled. He had met a girl, a foreigner, and he had never seen anyone so beautiful, so fascinating. Her eyes were emblazoned on his mind, yet when he tried to envision her face, he could not set it right. Her skin, the smell of her, her hair, these things he could picture clearly, but not her face. He could see the essence of it, the high cheekbones, the finely chiseled nose, but he could not get all of her features to stay still in his mind's eye.

Yet, when he rode into the city, he saw Estrellita everywhere. Each time he passed a dark-haired girl on the street, he saw Estrellita. He knew this was not possible, yet more than once, he felt his heart leap in his chest, and one time he opened his mouth to call out, only to see the object of his interest turn and present to him an entirely different face—that of a total stranger.

Impatient to get to the hotel and obtain the rest of his money from the sale of the horse, Jeremiah stopped at the little tavern and eatery on Market Street owned by a French couple. Their prices were fair, the food good. He gulped his food, listened to the talk among the buckskinners as he always did, hoping to hear word of Baptiste Lalande. But these were the same old people: trappers bragging about the furs they had brought down to rendezvous, the number of buffalo and antelope they had killed, the women they had bedded. He could only understand a small part of their talk, but he was getting better at it. The slang fascinated him. Their language was sprinkled with idioms, with the words of French and Indian origins, words they had made up themselves. And all of it was said peculiar, as if they had created their own language.

He would have left Etienne's Corner earlier if Madame Dupris, Etienne's wife, hadn't engaged him in conversation.

"You are zee boy who keeps asking for Baptiste Lalande, no?"

"I am."

"*Bien.* He is arrive. Someone say they see him in Saint Louis thees morning."

Jeremiah became excited.

"Where?"

Madame Dupris shrugged, smiled. She was middle-aged, had owned the small tavern even before the names of some of the streets had been changed from French to English.

"Ah, I do not know. But, M'sieu Lalande, he sometimes come here, drink. He come here and to the Red Boar."

"Yes, yes. Well, I'll be back, Madame Dupris. You tell him Jeremiah York's a-lookin' fer 'im."

He paid her, his hands shaking so badly he was embarrassed. He stumbled over a chair and bumped into a table as he left. The buckskinners paid him little attention, but Etienne and Marie Dupris laughed, waved him on his way.

York made his way to the corner of Main and Oak, looked at the massive stone building that housed the Missouri Hotel. It was here he was to meet Don Miguel Rojas. Men and women of several nationalities passed him along the street. Horses pulling fancy carriages clipclopped by him on hard-packed earth. Vendors called out their wares as they pushed carts on rickety wheels down Oak. The streets flowed with the commerce of city life, reminding Jeremiah that he, too, was a part of it. He had business with a wealthy man in a fancy hotel.

He hitched his horse to a rail, walked up the stone steps to the side door. Suddenly he was filled with fear, wondering how he could face the man who was the father of a girl he had just met, of a girl he could not get out of his mind. Would the Spaniard see the look on his face, read what was in his heart?

Jeremiah entered the hotel with a heart-gripping sense of dread.

The men seated at the long oak table seemed to be almost a cross section in miniature of St. Louis's cultural blend. Pedro Vial, his hand shaking with a tremor, his gray hair falling straight down from his bald pate, sat next to the younger Don Miguel Rojas, who leaned over the table as if in a pugilist's crouch. His cloak hung from the back of his baronial chair, his hat from a clothes tree near the entrance to the private dining room. Baptiste Lalande, a burly, bearded Frenchman, sat farther down the table, isolated by the greasy buckskins he wore, his foul smell. His knitted cap lay on the table in front of him, next to a *cenicero* of fired clay which held the stubs of three cigars. On the opposite side sat a huge American, also clad in leather, named Mike Finnegan. There were others, too, but they all faced a man in his mid-seventies who sat at the head of the table: Pierre Chouteau, one of the great builders of St. Louis, certainly its wealthiest citizen. He was a broad-shouldered man, with gray hair parted down the middle, a long, straight nose, slightly flared at the tip, high cheekbones, thin lips, a jutting chin. His sideburns bristled down the sides of his face on age-thickened jowls. He was flanked at the table by his two sons, Auguste Pierre and Pierre "Cadet" Jr., both of whom had vital interest in the proceedings that day.

Pierre Sr.'s brother, Auguste, had died in '29, leaving his younger brother to manage their considerable holdings, the recognized head of a large family, his and Auguste's. Both were strong family men, concerned with the welfare of their children. Pierre had used his influence to win appointments to the U.S. Military Academy for his eldest son, Auguste Pierre, and for his nephew, Charles Gratiot. Both men had graduated from West Point in '06, but, to Pierre's disappointment, his son had resigned his commission to enter the fur trade. Most of his ventures had failed, and the financial successes that came so easily to his father and other members of his family had eluded him. He had, however, inherited his father's congenial personality, which stood him in good stead when dealing with the Indians on the frontier. Indeed, his affinity for the red man's culture made him one of the best known and best liked of the Indian traders. He was, however, not as shrewd as his father, so did not make the money his brother, Pierre Jr., did. Cadet, too, entered the fur trade, acting as agent for John Jacob Astor's powerful American Fur Company, seemed destined to become wealthy as a successful merchant-capitalist.

The Chouteaus wielded considerable influence not only in Missouri, but in the East, as well.

"Gentlemen," said Chouteau, his accent thick, oily, his voice still strong, resonant, "in eighteen hundred and twenty-four we sent twenty-five wagons to Santa Fe. They carried thirty-five thousand dollars worth of merchandise that was sold for one hundred and ninety thousand dollars in gold, silver, or the equivalent in barter. Since then, hundreds of wagons have made the eight-hundred-mile journey from Independence to Santa Fe, bringing our annual volume of business to a figure totaling almost one million dollars."

Some of those at the table let out sighs, reminded once again of the staggering wealth generated by enterprising men, reminded of wealth yet to be made. Chouteau paused to let his words sink in. When he quoted figures, his dark eyes took on a light of their own. He licked his lips, smiled, and there were some who said, their words laden with respect and envy, that old Pierre spoke of money as some men spoke of food, with much the same effect on a starving man.

"Soon after those first wagons left Franklin, bulging with American calicoes, tables, chairs, chests, foods, spices, medicines, wines, tobacco, tableware, inks, oil lamps, paints, jewelry, they returned with rugs, furs, blankets, gold and silver coins. Such wealth! And it did not take long before the New Mexicans began to come here, bringing Spanish-backed pack trains and merchants to compete with ours in Independence and here in St. Louis. One of the most profitable items the New Mexican brought here has been the mule, and this has helped us all. Yet we are in danger of foundering, even though we have not yet reached a peak. Why?"

Chouteau's dark glance swept the table. His eyes fixed on Pedro Vial, then on Don Miguel.

Don Miguel did not flinch.

"Armijo," he said evenly.

"Exactly!" spat Chouteau. "Manuel Armijo, who used to be governor of your province, now director of customs. Manuel Armijo, who brags 'God rules the heavens and Armijo rules the earth.' Well, by all the most holy saints in heaven, Armijo must be made to see that he is killing the goose that lays the golden egg. Don Miguel, I charge you with this responsibility. You must entreat your most esteemed director of customs to forgo charging one hundred percent duty on imported goods or there will not be one New Mexican pack train allowed inside our borders."

Don Miguel nodded soberly. It had been his sad duty to convey this information to Chouteau, and now he was being charged to ask Armijo to rescind this oppressive duty. But he, too, had a stake in this matter of commerce.

"I will see what can be done, Pierre."

"No," said Chouteau evenly, "you know what must be done. Do it."

Chairs scraped as Pierre Chouteau stood up from the table, signifying that the meeting was at an end. His son, Cadet, signaled to a waiter by the door, snapping his fingers. He turned to the assemblage, smiled warmly.

"Gentlemen," he said, "please step up to the bar. Even though I must take my father home, he wishes you to

57

enjoy yourselves."

Big Mike Finnegan roared his approval, patted his elephantine sides with plate-size hands. His palms made a hollow sound on his ribs. Baptiste Lalande, who had ridden in from Independence just that morning, slid a damp tongue across dry lips as servants began to set up drinks at the bar, set out foodstuffs.

Auguste Chouteau embraced his father before Cadet led the elderly man away. Then he joined Don Miguel and Pedro Vial, demonstrating his father's wishes that he act as emissary in the elder Chouteau's absence. He was a handsome, rugged man, resembling his father when Pierre was a young man, dressed in simple but expensive clothes. Yet he carried himself like a man more familiar with buckskins and moccasins than fine cloth and calfskin boots. Indeed, he knew both worlds well, but his heart was with the red man more than with the white. His interests lay in the mountains rather than on the plains of progress, in the empire carved out by his father and his uncle.

"Do you think you will be able to do anything about the levy?" asked Auguste as he walked with Don Miguel and Don Pedro to the bar.

"Of course," said Don Miguel confidently. "Armijo is a reasonable man. Besides, my daughter Estrellita is going to marry his nephew."

"That is so?" exclaimed Auguste with delight. "Then you will become a man of considerable influence."

"He is a man of influence already," said Vial dryly.

Lalande and Finnegan, whiskies in hand, moved along the bar to confront Auguste.

Baptiste spoke in rapid French to Auguste, much to the latter's annoyance.

"I think we had best speak English," said Auguste politely, "since that appears to be the common language here. To answer your question, Baptiste, my brother Cadet has formed a partnership with our brother-in-law, Bartholomew Berthold, and is negotiating with John Jacob Astor."

"Ah, then they will have American Fur by the balls, *non?*"

"That is my understanding, yes."

"*Sacrebleu,*" exclaimed Lalande, exchanging a glance with the gigantic Finnegan. "Mebbe so, he will give someone some big trouble, no?"

Auguste shrugged, lifted a glass to the Spaniards, as if to show them that he did not mean to leave them out of the discussion. For that matter, Don Miguel was most attentive, while Vial, used to the labyrinthine schemes of the fur traders, paid more attention to the brandy in his glass than to the gabbling Frenchman.

"Are you talking about Sublette?" asked Don Miguel.

Lalande's eyebrows arched.

"Ah, then you know that Sublette, he beat out American Fur last year, *non?* He plenty smart, eh?"

Don Miguel nodded. It was true that Sublette's Rocky Mountain Fur had beat the competition to rendezvous on New Fork by three days. It was a buyer's market, and, after ten years of mountain trapping, the fur companies had managed to keep out most other competition. Even though Bonneville and others tried to encroach on the established trusts, the fur companies had a virtual monopoly on the trapping industry. Last year, veterans could draw up to fifteen hundred dollars in advances for the next year's work, and plews had sold for as high as nine dollars a pound, which was much less than they were worth back in the settlements.

American Fur was trying to break Sublette and Rocky Mountain Fur. Astor had money, RMF was deep in debt. And Bill Sublette and Bob Campbell were building forts on the Missouri, putting them up right next to the Company forts.

"Maybe not," said Don Miguel. "If his forts hold up and his other schemes work, he might survive. But he is wrong not to use the Santa Fe trail."

Lalande's eyes narrowed. Financially, everyone was in trouble this year. RMF was signing notes payable to Bill

Sublette, that was all they could do. He had them by the short hairs. It was his goodwill and his credit that they relied on to break American Fur, the Company.

"So," he said to Auguste, in French, "this Spaniard is not so dumb, eh?" To Don Miguel, he said, in English, "You plenty smart, my fren'. Bill Sublette, he made the big gamble this time, I think."

"Isn't there more to it than that?" asked Don Miguel. "I have heard that Jim Bridger is fuming."

"Ah, he is one mad bear, that one," laughed Baptiste. "Eh, Mike?"

Finnegan's body shook as he roared with laughter.

"Ay, he's fit to be tied, he is, old Jim, swearin' blue smoke over the damnable marks them fellers put on papers, claimin' he don' unnerstan' 'em, sayin' ever' damn one's robbin' his pockets of money. True, he froze his balls in the high cricks and trapped with the Blackfeet a-breathin' down his hindside, but that don't make him king of the trappers, no matter what he says."

"Bridger may smell something," said Don Miguel, not content to let Lalande slide away from the issue. "Sublette and Campbell have something up their sleeves."

Lalande sobered.

"I think you plenty smart, Rojas, eh? I look at dem forts up on the Missouri and I wonder to myself what is Bill Sublette up to. He big man with Rocky Mountain Fur, but he not little man with American Fur, eh? So, why he building all these big forts, eh? Bridger, he say it competition, but I think Bill and Bob Campbell, they hoping the Company she buy him out, and they make plenty money. *N'est-ce pas?*"

Don Miguel frowned. He did not discount what Lalande had to say about the situation. He was a Frenchman, with close ties to both RMF and American Fur, but he was essentially a loner, an opportunist. He kept his ear close to the ground, and he made the best deals he could, often in disregard of firm contracts. The man had a bad reputation in some circles, but he

60

knew where the beaver were and he brought back the plews. He was shrewd, probably knew more about the fur trade than any man alive, because he was both an outsider and an insider.

"I wonder," said Don Miguel, "if you knew that Nat Wyeth had made a deal with Milton."

Although Lalande opened his mouth to reply, he did not get a word out. Instead, there was a loud commotion beyond the doors of the room, with men shouting and cursing. There was no mistaking the sounds of a scuffle, building like an orchestral drumroll just outside the room.

Big Mike Finnegan grinned wide.

"Hey, I think we got us a fight!" he exclaimed.

The men at the bar moved, as one body, toward the entrance. A loud crash rattled the doors.

Mike Finnegan led the way, was the first to reach the closed doors. He grasped both handles, wrenched them downward.

A moment later, as the doors burst open, he went down, bowled over by an inward tide of kicking, scratching, cursing men, all chasing what appeared to be a young boy.

Jeremiah entered the lobby of the Windsor Hotel feeling dwarfed by the immensity of the room. Potted plants stood next to chairs and divans where people sat and talked, read newspapers or books. Others bustled to and fro, speaking in subdued tones. He heard a woman's tinkling laugh, the graveled voice of a man speaking under his breath. He stood on the red carpet, looked at the polished hardwood floors gleaming under woven throw rugs. Fluted stone columns rose to the high ceiling, past the balcony with its wrought-iron railing, more potted plants, desks, chairs, people chatting, at ease, as though they lived there, were used to such magnificent surroundings. York looked around him, bewildered, wondering how he would ever find Don Miguel in such a busy, teeming place. A man in a beaver hat jostled past him, stared at him with a look of utter disdain. A pair of pretty young women, bearing fancy parasols, strolled past, ignoring his presence with noses jutted high in the air as if to avoid smelling him as well.

York looked toward the long desk across the lobby where couples waited with their luggage, and a clerk on the other side wrote in a ledger with a quilled pen. A uniformed pageboy walked stiffly through the lobby, calling out a name.

"Mr. Estleman, paging Mr. Estleman."

The page, wearing a pillbox hat cocked to one side, looked up the stairs, began to climb them to the balcony where people sat next to the railing, seemingly oblivious to the activity below. Jeremiah wondered at the luxury of such a place, and now had misgivings about even being inside the elegant hotel. But Don Miguel had told him to bring the proof of delivery here, to this place, and ask for him by name. Jeremiah had not thought to ask any questions, and now he stood with his mouth half open gazing at a world completely alien to him. Another boy, dressed in livery, a gray uniform with black stripes, crossed to the counter-desk, lifted a pair of bags made of fine leather, beckoned to the waiting couple, who followed him up the wide, curving flight of stairs.

Sensing that the registration desk was the place to seek information about Don Miguel, York strode toward it, his boots scuffing the crimson carpet that marked the path. He stood at the desk for a moment, oblivious to the stares of people around him, looking at all the small boxes back of the clerk, little cubbyholes, some with keys dangling from their shelves, others vacant, still others stuffed with letters, postal cards, and messages.

He cleared his throat.

The clerk, scribbling earnestly in a ledger, did not look up.

"I'm looking for Mr. Don Miguel Rojas," said the youth, his voice quavering with nervousness.

"He's with M'sieu Chouteau in the Salon Royale."

"Where's that?"

"Just off the lobby to your right. Just what is it you wished to see him about, sir?"

The clerk looked up then, saw the boy standing there in shabby clothes, seedy cap. He sniffed twice through his nostrils.

"Thank you," said York, turning to leave, his eyes fixed on the doors at the other side of the lobby.

"Wait a minute," spluttered the clerk. "You can't . . ."

But Jeremiah was already striding toward the huge oaken doors that bore the legend above them, in wooden letters gilded with gold paint: SALON ROYALE.

The clerk, snorting with a sudden flash of temper, reached quickly for a brass bell on the desk, jangled it furiously. A pair of men at opposite sides of the lobby, seated in overstuffed chairs, looked up from their *Enquirer* newspapers, their puffed bulldog faces scowling. They rose, almost in unison, made their way to the desk. They were burly men, wearing ill-fitting suits, rumpled ties. They looked more like stevedores than house detectives, more accustomed to working as bouncers in waterfront dives rather than in genteel hotels.

"Stop that boy," said the clerk. "He's not to disturb the men in Royale."

The two men looked in the direction the clerk was pointing, saw the young man reach the double doors of the salon.

"Won't take a minute," grinned one of the men, starting off at a lope.

The other followed, grunting with the unexpected exertion.

Jeremiah reached the door, heard footsteps pounding behind him.

"Hold on there," called one of the men.

"Huh?" said Jeremiah.

"Don't go in there," said the other man.

As they loomed closer, Jeremiah braced himself.

"I have business here," he said, "with the Spaniard, Mr. Don Miguel Rojas."

"You don't have no business here, boy." The bigger of the two men, the one in the lead, halted a few feet from York.

"Just come quietly," said the other. "We're gonna take you outside where you belong."

Jeremiah's face flushed with a combination of rage, embarrassment, and anger. The two men glared at him, bracketing his position with solid stances as if expecting him to try to make a run for it. He felt their menacing stares scorching his face as his blood ran hot.

"I ain't goin' nowheres till I see Mr. Don Miguel Rojas." He said the name again, hoping they would understand.

"You ain't goin' nowheres is right," said the big man closest to Jeremiah. Then he reached for the youth, lunging forward, stretching out hands the size of baby hams.

Jeremiah ducked, slid away.

The second man reacted, doubling up his fists. He waded on bowed legs toward the boy, determined to stop him by force if necessary.

People in the balcony leaned over the railing to see what was causing the commotion down below. Many of those in the lobby turned to stare at the boy and the two house detectives. Newspapers and magazines rattled as necks craned. A woman gasped in mock fright, began to flap a paper fan in front of her face.

"Get him, Horace," said the first detective. "He's slippery, this one."

Jeremiah backed into the door, tried to reach behind him to open it.

The second man shot out a fist, straight at the young man's face.

York moved his head. The fist crashed into carved oak with a resounding thud. The detective screamed, cradled his hand, hopped away in pain.

The first man made a circle of his arms, rushed at Jeremiah.

York kicked out, landed a boot on the man's knee. The second man turned, grabbed York's sleeve. Jeremiah scooted away, felt the cloth of his shirt tauten. Panic lit his eyes with a fierce flame until they glittered like dark pulsing coals sunk in white ash.

It was a fight now, he knew. The men were angry, wanted to hurt him. They were bigger than he was, and they were mean.

They both came at him, and he swung a fist at the nearest one. He felt the shock go up his arm as the blow landed on the man's jaw.

"You little bastard," muttered the man Jeremiah had struck.

"I'll give him what for," said the other, raising his arm for a hammering strike.

Jeremiah slithered away.

A man in the lobby cheered the boy.

People rose from their chairs, the divans, struggling for a better view of the fracas.

"Leave that boy alone, you bullies!" shouted an elderly woman descending the stairs.

"Maybe he's a thief," someone offered, as sides were taken by the spectators.

The bigger man grabbed York by the waist with a single swoop of his girdling arm.

"I got him, Horace."

"Hold him, Ned," said the second man.

Jeremiah felt the grip around his waist tighten. He brought up a knee, hard into Ned's groin. Ned gasped, doubled over in agony. His arm slid away. Jeremiah tried to run, but Horace shot out a leg, tripped him. York crashed into the double doors. They rattled with sound.

His head spun with dizziness.

Ned and Horace came for him then.

"Now, you little bastard . . ." growled Ned Ames.

York got to his feet as a cheer of encouragement sang out from the spectators who now had made a half-circle around that end of the lobby.

"Make fools of us, will ye?" snarled Horace Beeker.

Jeremiah knew they had him braced. These were big men and he could not go around them. Or through them.

He panted, sweat oiling his face. But the blood-heat of battle was strong in him, and he would not give up easily. He doubled up his fists and charged between the two detectives, flailing his arms wildly. A roar of approval arose from the small crowd.

65

The two hotelmen lowered their shoulders, caught York by his arms. They drove him back, into the double doors. His body slammed into the hardwood with a resounding crash. The doors shuddered under the impact. Jeremiah cried out in pain as his shoulder blades rammed into solid oak. A collective "ooooh" emerged from the clutch of spectators.

Jeremiah felt himself being lifted up in the air.

He began to kick wildly in protest at this indignity.

At that moment, Corazon, her daughter Estrellita, and the *dueña*, Lucia, entered the lobby from the tea room at the opposite end. They heard the commotion, saw the clerk running in front of them. They joined the throng in front of the Salon Royale.

"Why, that's Jeremiah," exclaimed Estrellita.

Lucia's face twisted into a dark scowl.

"Yes, he's the *joven* who sold your *papá* the horse," said Corazon.

The women stood there, transfixed, wide-eyed as a pair of owls. Then the clerk leaped into the fray.

"Stop this, stop this," he shouted, pounding on Ned's back. "Look what you're doing."

Ned only grunted as Jeremiah kicked him in the stomach.

The doors swung open and the four men burst into the salon, toppling over big Mike Finnegan, Baptiste Lalande, Don Miguel, a waiter, and Don Pedro Vial.

Horace's head slammed into Mike's chin. Ned had the misfortune to knock Lalande down.

Jeremiah, at the bottom of the pile, looked up into the clerk's surprised face.

Finnegan glared at Beeker.

"What's the big idea?" asked Mike, grabbing the detective by the shirtfront and shaking him like a rag doll.

"Turn me loose, you big ox," said Ned foolishly.

And the fight was on.

Chapter Four

Mike Finnegan planted ham-thick hands on the chest of the house detective and gave a mighty heave. Horace tumbled backward off the heap of tangled men. Jeremiah shoved the clerk aside, scrambled to his feet. Don Miguel rolled over to avoid being crushed under the pile of men. Finnegan stood up, swayed for a moment like a clapboard building in a windstorm, pumped his legs into a running start. He powered forward and waded into Beeker, swinging his meaty fists like a pair of wrecking mauls.

Beeker, no shy stranger to impromptu brawling, braced for the giant buckskinner. He leaned into an imaginary wind, tipping forward on the balls of his feet. He rammed his arms upward like a pair of crossed fenceposts to ward off Finnegan's blow. Mike, however, more accustomed to roughousing with grizzly bears, war-painted savages, and fellow mountain men, did not fight according to Beeker's rules. Rather, he slammed into Beeker like a rolling boulder, shoulders massed like the bunched frame of a two-thousand-pound bull buffalo. He knocked Beeker flat without ever throwing a punch, though his fists were still compacted into lethal weapons.

Beeker did not rise again under his own power.

Baptiste Lalande took on Ames, dancing with him for a

67

moment as he twirled him in a tight circle before he planted a pair of solid bootkicks into the man's rump. Ned, for his part, struck out like a blind man in a dark room. Still, he landed a knuckle-cracking fist square into Don Miguel's temple and another that grazed the hapless clerk's Adam's apple, then glanced off young Chouteau's shoulder with all the force of a thrown dandelion blossom.

When Ames stopped doing the minuet, he found himself facing off Jeremiah York. Growling low in his throat, Ames charged. He drew his right fist back, cocked it like a leather-strapped catapult to deliver a serious, if not fatal, blow to the bridge of Jeremiah's nose.

York saw it coming, ducked under the swishing fist. Agile as a cat walking on boiling tar, the youth brought up a steaming right uppercut from floor level. His fist struck the detective's jaw plumb square on its most prominent point. The resounding crack rose above the grunts and groans of the men massed in the doorway of the salon like the losing team in a tug-of-war.

Mike Finnegan stared in stupefied admiration as Ned's legs turned willowy underneath his bulk. Don Miguel gazed at the erstwhile bouncer in abject fascination as Ames's eyes rolled back in their sockets, revealing the whites as if they were a couple of boiled prairie hen's eggs. And Lalande, his mouth gaping open in an ox-yoke of wonder, leered as Ames toppled over as though clubbed senseless with four feet of six-inch oak lumber.

Ned Ames let out a long sigh and crumpled into a senseless heap as York stood over him with ready fists, his legs widespread, a look of dark intent sharpening his features into a fierce scowl.

The clerk, groggy from being caught in the middle of the scramble, gasped as he stared blank-eyed at the two detectives sprawled lifeless as Saturday-night sots on the expensive carpeting. He screamed and dashed back to the desk as if the seat of his trousers was ablaze.

Lalande and Finnegan threw back shaggy heads and roared

with spontaneous laughter. The laughter was as contagious as the three-day measles. It spread to the men in the salon, to the spectators, and, finally, to York, whose face had started to regain some of its color after being drained chalk from exertion.

Estrellita waved at Jeremiah, but he didn't see her. She and her mother, and the *dueña*, Lucia, stood at the far edge of the crowd. The young woman's face flared crimson, the excitement having triggered a deep blush that crept up her neck in a raspberry glow and spread out over her cheeks like foxfire. Her pulse hammered in her temples, her bosom swelled against the bracing stiffness of the wire in her bodice. Butterfly wings flapped inside her stomach.

For a moment it seemed as if the laughter would continue until it spilled outside onto the street.

Mike Finnegan broke the spell of the moment.

He walked over to Ames, grabbed him by the back of his suit collar. He lugged him to where Beeker lay, grabbed the latter by the back of his coat. He dragged both men out into the lobby, dropped them like a pair of steamer trunks, from a distance of six or eight inches, to the floor. Then he made a swiping motion with his palms as if dusting off his hands, turned, and walked back into the salon. He closed the doors with mock formality to a smattering applause from the onlookers in the lobby.

Finnegan clapped York on the back, almost knocking the youth to his knees.

"I don't rightly know what them Micks were a-chasin' ye for, boy, but you brung 'em to the right place. You pack a fair punch with that puny frame of yours, bejasus. I'd like to shake your fightin' hand, me bucko."

The big man's hand swallowed up Jeremiah's and his enthusiastic pumping of the youth's arm rattled York's teeth, threatened to dislocate his shoulder.

"I . . . I come to see Mr. Don Miguel and get my money," stammered Jeremiah, looking around at the men in wide-eyed wonder. He knew now why those hotel men had come after him. He didn't belong here in this private gathering, in such plush surroundings. His eyes scanned the baronial tables and chairs, the heraldic shields set in velvet on the walls, the heavy Doric footings on the doorframes, heads of wild game: antelope, buffalo, bear, elk, and deer. There, too, were the dusty-feathered carcasses of ring-necked and golden pheasant, blue- and green-winged teal, mallards, canvasback, pintail, quail, sage hen, and gray and fox squirrel, placed at strategic places so that the roving eye in such a room was never bored. The room seemed big enough to swallow him up. He wished, at that moment, that it would. He should have waited outside for them to finish whatever they were doing. He was blamed all-fired eager to get his dadgummed money, buy himself some needed things, that he had just rushed in like a yokel without sense enough to come in out of the rain.

"Is that so?" asked Chouteau.

Don Miguel nodded. He looked at Pedro Vial with a faint smile flickering on his lips.

"Did you deliver the horse for my daughter?" asked the don.

"Yes sir, mister, I sure did. I got this here note." Jeremiah searched through his pockets, brought forth a folded piece of paper.

Don Miguel's hand reached out for the paper.

"Nope, that ain't it. That's the one I brung from back home to give to Baptiste Lalande when I catch up to him."

Finnegan and Lalande exchanged amused looks. Jeremiah continued his search for the note the old Spanish woman had given him. It was in another pocket.

"Here," said York. "This is it."

Don Miguel read the familiar scrawl, Lucia's gratuitous warning below her signature: *Cuidado con ese joven. No vale nada.* The rancher from Santa Fe suppressed a smile.

"Well, young man," he said heartily, "it seems I owe you some money. Was my daughter pleased at her *regalo*, her gift?"

"Oh, yes, sir. Very much. She likes that filly a lot. A whole lot. She rode it real good, too."

"You saw her ride?"

"Uh huh." Jeremiah failed to see the shadows rise up in Don Miguel's eyes. A warning. Fleeting, but there.

Don Miguel reached inside his coat as the others looked on, extracted a long, thick wallet. He opened it and pulled out several specie, bills of various denominations.

"Here," he said, "that should be sufficient."

Jeremiah counted the money.

"You give me too much," he spluttered, trying to hand back a five-dollar note.

"No, that's extra, for your persistence in finding me."

"You ought to give him another fiver, Don Miguel," said Finnegan, "for providing us a little fun to boot."

Everyone laughed.

Jeremiah's face flushed a pale salmon color.

"You give him five dollars," retorted Don Miguel. "You had more fun than anyone."

"By God, kid, what's your name?" boomed Finnegan.

York told him.

"Come on, I'll buy you a drink." Finnegan blanketed York's shoulder with a bear-size arm, started herding the youth toward the bar. "You say you been lookin' fer that Frenchie, Baptis' What's-his-name?" The big Irisher looked over his shoulder, winked a merry eye at Lalande.

"Lalande," said Jeremiah. "He's a fur trapper. I got a message for him, and I'm aimin' to hire on with him next time he makes up his brigade."

"What is this message you have for Baptiste Lalande?" asked the Frenchman.

"Oh, I don't know what's in it. But it's from William Morrison, back in Kaskaskia, Illinois."

"I am Baptiste Lalande. Give me the message." The Frenchman's face darkened with a scowl.

York handed him the note with a trembling hand. It was in an envelope, sealed with a glob of wax bearing Morrison's personal imprint.

71

Lalande ripped open the envelope. He handed the message to Finnegan.

"Read the words," he said, his voice soft.

The big Irishman squinted, moved his lips without speaking for several seconds, then began to speak in his lilting brogue. "To Baptis' Lalande," he read, "Saint Louie. You, sor, contracted to sell me trade goods and to date I have not received any of the monies. Nor have I heard from you regarding the disposition of said trade goods. This will introduce Master Jeremiah York who will act as my agent in this matter. I pray you will pay him the full amount owing me with all promptness. Your faithful servant, William Morrison."

"Pah!" spat Lalande. "That pig! He don't understan' nothing about business, eh? By Gar, he lucky he not come here and lose his scalp. Baptiste, he damn near lose his hair to the Pawnee over that deal." Lalande's chest swelled until Jeremiah thought he would burst with indignation. The Frenchman's eyes seemed to shoot sparks as he glared at the boy who had brought him the unwelcome note.

"So," he continued, "what does he do? He sends me a mere boy to demand money from me, eh? What he think? I cheat the Yankee trader? Eh, he make the big mistake, I think. I show him what I do to this stupid messenger boy."

Before anyone could stop him, Lalande strode to York, picked him up by the collar, and shook him like an empty grain sack. Jeremiah hung there, above the floor, stricken speechless by the savagery of Lalande's sudden rage. His teeth clacked together as Baptiste shook him from side to side, and up and down.

The trapper's anger against the merchant seemed to surge up in him, focus on the hapless messenger. Lalande shifted his grip with one hand, clamped the other around York's neck. The youth gagged, made a croaking sound in his throat. Lalande drew back his other hand, doubled it into a fist, and drove it straight at Jeremiah's jaw. His fist slammed into the boy's chin with a thwack. The sound was like that made by a sixteen-pound maul striking a steer's skull inside an abbatoir.

York's eyes rolled backward in their sockets. His head jerked back with a snap. His spinal cord cracked like morning knuckles.

Big Mike Finnegan stepped in between the youth and the Frenchman as Lalande drew his fist back for another strike. He intercepted Lalande's arm, grasped it gently but firmly.

"You knocked the lad cold as a Columbia salmon," he said, his brogue thick as potato broth. His tone was soft, laden with quiet menace. "Leave him be."

Lalande shook his head, seemed to come to his senses. He loosened his hold on York's neck, let him fall from his grasp.

Jeremiah dropped like a discarded scarecrow, sagged onto the polished hardwood flooring in a pathetic heap. His face was pale and waxen, his lips blue as Arkansas wellspring clay. He did not move.

At that moment, a pageboy slid through the doors, peered about. He saw Don Miguel, hurried to his side. He whispered something in the Spaniard's ear. Rojas nodded, and the boy took one quick look at the figure on the floor, swallowed, dashed back to the foyer.

"Is he dead?" asked Vial.

"Eh? Maybeso," said Lalande, drawing out the last vowel until it rasped in his throat. "I go a little crazy, eh? This man Morrison, he make me so mad with his stupid letter and he send this *garçon pauvre* to tell me I owe him the money. I just want to break the bastard's neck."

The men stood in a circle, staring down at the floor. They did not immediately notice the doors open to admit three women: Corazon, the *dueña* Lucia, and Estrellita. A bellboy preceded them, but it was plain to see that he had admitted them to the sanctum reluctantly. His face was flushed and his pillbox hat hung askew from his grease-slick hair. He tried to outdistance the women, but Estrellita, as if sensing something was wrong, overtook the hapless youth. Her mother lashed out a hand to stop her, but to no avail. Lucia opened her mouth in silent protest, nearly tripped over her long dark skirt as she hurried to catch up with Corazon.

The huddle of men parted as the three women drew near. Estrellita knifed through the opening and scurried toward the fallen Jeremiah without a thought of impropriety. Don Miguel, seeing his daughter suddenly appear amidst the mass of men, stepped toward her, hoping to intercept her before she saw the unconscious youth.

"What have you done to Jeremiah?" she accused, upon seeing York sprawled out on the floor. She knelt, bent over the young man. "Oh, he's dead!" she exclaimed. "You've killed him."

"Estrellita," said her father sharply, "leave this to us. The boy's not dead."

Corazon, peering over her daughter's shoulder, could not help seeing the pale face of the young man, the blood on his lips. She gasped. Lucia pushed her way into the pack of men, took one look at York, and knelt beside Estrellita. Despite herself, the old crone felt sympathetic to any poor creature that was hurt, man or beast. She chattered in Spanish about the brutality of grown men picking on a boy and how the saints in heaven would shudder to see such animal behavior among civilized men who ought to know better.

"Sin verguenza! Animales! Salvajes!"

"He's hurt terribly," said Estrellita, her voice shrill with anguish. She lifted York's head in her arms, crushed him to her breasts.

Lucia looked at her ward in dismay, a shocked expression contorting her face.

Corazon blinked hopelessly, wondering at her daughter's open display of affection toward a complete stranger. Yet she was touched by Estrellita's obvious compassion.

"Oh, *pobrecito*," wailed Estrellita, "he's dying." She rocked him in her arms, looked up at the sea of faces, the wide eyes staring down at her. She looked down at York's face, his pale lips. Something welled up inside her, a

74

warm feeling of tenderness, a floodtide of compassion. Her stomach fluttered, her skin tingled all over as if she had rolled in a bed of thistles. Her breasts, a cushion under York's head, swelled with her breathing, the nipples grew tumescent, much to her embarrassment. She looked on his face and flushed with a private, wicked shame. He was so close, she wanted to kiss his sallow lips, breathe life back into him. She knew he was not dead, but he was badly hurt and so frail and helpless-looking that her maternal instinct was aroused. Yet this instinct mingled with another, a more primal one, and for that she felt ashamed and confused.

"Leave him be," muttered Lucia. "You will, *por cierto*, smother him to death."

Corazon tugged at her daughter's sleeve in a futile effort to pry her arms from the unconscious youth. "Yes, Estrellita," she said, "leave the poor boy be. He's no concern of ours."

Estrellita, afraid to look up and reveal the embarrassment and shame on her face, stared blankly at the young man in her arms.

"No, no," she pleaded, "we must help him. I must take care of him." Before she realized what she had said, she heard the twin gasps from Lucia and her mother. Her father cleared his throat audibly in the ensuing silence.

No one spoke for several seconds.

Corazon stood up straight, squared her shoulders. She met her husband's gaze, a querulous look in her soft brown eyes.

Lucia drew in a long breath, held it.

"Maybe," said Pedro Vial diplomatically, "we should summon a doctor."

The bellboy, scarcely noticeable at the fringe of the group, piped up just then.

"Mr. Don Miguel Rojas, I have a message for you, sir."

"Eh? What is it?"

"Sir, there is a gentleman to see you. He's waiting in the lobby."

"Who is he?" asked Don Miguel, his features drawn taut in

75

an impatient grimace.

The boy looked at the card in his hand, read the name on it. His lips moved as his eyes scanned the unfamiliar syllables.

"Cap-tain Agus-tino Army-joe," he said, mispronouncing the man's title and both Spanish names.

"Augustino Armijo," said Corazon breathlessly. "The governor's nephew."

"Your betrothed," whispered Lucia to Estrellita. The accusation in her tone was not lost on the young woman.

"Very good," said Don Miguel. "Tell the gentleman that I and my family will join him presently." Don Miguel gave the boy a coin. The lad saluted smartly and turned on his heel. "And send for a doctor at once," the Spaniard ordered, almost as an afterthought.

"With smelling salts," amended Pedro Vial.

Estrellita shot him a look of gratitude.

"It seems Augustino has not forgotten your birthday, Daughter," said her father. "Leave this boy to us. You and your mother may wish to go ahead and speak with the captain. I will be along in a little while."

"No," snapped Estrellita, hugging York tightly. "Not until I know Jeremiah is all right. Please, Father."

"What is this young man to you? He is merely a delivery boy."

"He . . . he was nice to me, and if he had not brought me the horse, the present would not have been so fine."

"Estrellita," her mother exclaimed, "mind your tongue! How dare you speak to your father this way?"

Don Miguel, taken aback by this exchange in front of his friends, rocked on his bootheels, clutched the lapels of his coat for support. He looked at the appeal in his daughter's expression, the faint shadows in his wife's eyes, as if she was begging his forgiveness for the impetuousness of their daughter. Lucia wore her usual dark scowl, made even darker by the lace frame of her towering black mantilla. The men around the don all seemed to be waiting for him to make a decision in this delicate matter. Baptiste Lalande, especially, the trace of a mocking smile playing on his lips, his thick arms folded across his buckskinned chest, hovered on the edge of the silence like a vulture waiting to pounce on carrion.

"I . . . I'm just concerned about Jeremiah," mumbled Estrellita, dipping her head to avoid her father's stern gaze. "He . . . he looks so hurt and helpless."

Lalande snorted.

Don Miguel's eyes flashed a warning to the Frenchman. This was his knot to untangle or cut through with the blade of his sword.

He quickly made his decision.

"Very well," he said, "let us see what the doctor says. I don't think the boy was hurt very badly, but he was caught by, ah . . . surprise." He very nearly said that the blow had been cowardly struck, but he had business with these men and did not want to spoil the progress that had been made this day.

The doctor, an officious, portly man in a gray morning coat, bustled into the room, his nervousness evident in the flickering of his eyes as he encountered the group of men and women encircling the stricken boy. He reeked of cigar smoke, stale wine, and crushed mint. He licked dry, liverish lips, tugged a worn leather satchel in a pudgy, hair- and freckle-stippled hand, immaculate except for the smoke-yellowed index finger and thumb.

"What happened here?" he asked as he knelt, thumping his physician's bag on the carpet. A faint, rectangular puff of dust arose around the border of the satchel. He grasped Estrellita's elbow, moved her aside with a practiced firmness. He began folding back York's eyelids even before he received an answer.

"There was an altercation," volunteered Chouteau with surprising vocabulary, attesting to his formal schooling. "The boy was struck, fell unconscious."

"Hell," swore Mike Finnegan, "he was hit by a fist."

"Umm, I see," said the doctor, glancing into the vacant pupils of his unwitting patient. His fingers kneaded York's face

77

as though it was a lump of sculptor's clay, feeling for fractures, clots. He opened his bag, withdrew a stethoscope which he attached to his ears. He slid the amplifying button underneath the youth's shirt, listened as he looked up at the men leaning over him like viewers in an operating theater.

He removed the stethoscope, stuffed it back in his bag. He fished thorugh the satchel, found a small, corked vial. He waved it under York's nostrils. Jeremiah coughed. His eyes fluttered open and then closed. He let out a low sigh.

The doctor held the young man's head between his hands, then ran a finger down the knuckles of his spine, probing for separated vertebrae. He slapped York's face gently, patting both cheeks with light, jarring smacks. York did not awaken.

The doctor then felt the back of the youth's head for bruises, soft spots that were mushy as the flesh of overripe fruit, contusions, any telltale knot. Finally, he stood up, panting from just that slight amount of exertion.

"The boy likely has a concussion," he said. "He should be watched for a day or two. I can't find any broken bones. No contusions. Vertebrae intact. If he wakes up, see if his pupils are dilated. They seem contracted at the moment. He should be kept awake as much as possible. If he falls asleep again, goes too deep, his brain might forget to tell him to breathe. I'd say he was hit pretty hard, probably on the point of his chin. A glancing blow, or one that jars the brain sufficiently, would cause such a condition. Yes, concussion, I'd say. Could be dangerous if he's not watched pretty close."

"Yes, that's right," said Don Miguel. "He was hit on the chin."

The doctor sized the Spaniard up with a raking glance.

"If you're going to take care of him, I'll be on my way. Ah, that'll be two dollars, please."

Don Miguel did not move.

"I will pay," said Lalande, swaggering forward. "I hit the young whelp. But, I won't nursemaid him, by Gar."

Estrellita glowered at the Frenchman, gripped by a sudden

78

hatred toward him. Lalande pressed a pair of crushed notes into the doctor's fleshy palm.

"Papa," said the young woman, "we must take Jeremiah with us, care for him."

"No," said her father sternly. "He is not our responsibility."

"But . . . but he might die." Her voice rose to a pitch close to hysteria. "We can't just leave him here—leave him to these ruffians . . ."

Lucia, her scowl wrenching her face into a wrinkled mask, reached out and grasped Estrellita's wrist, yanked the girl toward her.

"Child," she said in rapid Spanish, "listen to your father. He's right. This boy is just trouble. Look at him, fighting with grown men, and now he has to pay the price for his foolishness. Come along now, quickly. Your betrothed is waiting for you."

Estrellita's eyes rolled as she caught her mother's attention, and she pleaded silently for Corazon to come to her rescue.

Don Miguel saw the look in his wife's eyes, started to shake his head. Corazon turned away from him quickly, unwilling to contradict his wishes to his face.

"Perhaps she is right," she said. "After all, the boy is hurt and someone must care for him. It's obvious that no one here is going to. If he dies, Don Miguel, I would be forever heartbroken, feeling that we might have saved him with a little charity."

Lucia retreated, unwilling to speak against her mistress's heartfelt plea. But she was not happy over this intrusion. She had convinced Don Miguel, she was certain, but she would not come between a man and wife.

"Oh, yes, Mother," said Estrellita quickly, "that is the thing to do. He will be no trouble. I can care for him, see that he doesn't die in his sleep."

Corazon let out an exasperated sigh. She snatched her daughter's hand from Lucia's.

"Someone will look after him, Daughter," she said firmly, "but it will not be you. Now, come along. We'll see to it that your young friend is taken to the Vial ranch."

Corazon looked at her husband. A look of understanding passed between them like a cloud shadow over the land. He nodded somberly.

"I'll see that a wagon is brought for him," said the Spaniard.

But Estrellita balked at leaving with her mother just then, even though Lucia was prodding her from behind, jabbing a closed fan into the small of the girl's back.

"Come along now, Estrellita," said her mother. "Your father will take care of the young man."

Estrellita opened her mouth, started to say something, but Lucia shushed her with a warning gesture and a flash of narrowed dark eyes.

The young woman looked longingly at Jeremiah one last time before she was whisked away by her mother and chaperone, an unwilling prisoner between them as they marched through the hotel lobby like royalty.

Estrellita let out a sigh as she stepped into sunlight, her heart beating like the wings of a frightened bird against the wooden bars of its cage.

Chapter Five

Augustino Armijo sat ramrod stiff in one of the anterooms of the hotel, one arm resting on a small table, his dark uniform spotless, the golden epaulets gleaming. The nephew of the Mexican tax-collector, Manuel Armijo, Augustino was a swarthy young man with slick black hair, dark Moorish eyes, a thin, severely trimmed mustache. His military bearing and the braided epaulets declared him to be a captain in the Mexican Army. On the other side of the small table sat his aide, Lieutenant Merito Salcedo, another whose rank depended totally on family ties. Merito's father was none other than General Nemesio Salcedo, the commandant general of all Spanish forces in New Mexico.

Merito, too, was young, cocky, completely loyal to his captain, Armijo. Fair-skinned, he was a true Spaniard, with pale-blue eyes, sharp features. He sat and stood straight-backed, and there seemed to be a perpetual sneer on his thin lips. He, like Armijo, held his plumed hat on his lap. A sword in its sheath jutted from his waist, touched his polished boot, and a flintlock pistol, ornately engraved, the butt gracefully curved, protruded from his crimson sash. Merito was spit-and-polish and looked down his sharply hooked nose as if from a great height, despite the fact that he was shorter than many men of lesser rank.

The two men sat in graceful, spindly legged chairs, waiting for Don Miguel. Augustino tweaked his mustache impatiently, while Merito slapped his immaculate white gloves repeatedly against the top of his calf.

The curtains parted and Don Miguel stepped into the room. The military men rose in unison, stood smartly at attention.

"My friends," said Rojas in rapid Castilian Spanish, "how much I lament having made you wait. Certain matters detained me, but I bid you welcome to St. Louis and beg your forgiveness."

"There is nothing to that," said Armijo, beaming, his smile wide and white in contrast to his dark skin.

"It imports nothing," agreed Salcedo.

"You came up from Independence by boat?" asked Don Miguel.

"Yes," said Salcedo. "We left our small troop there a week ago. It was a good trip."

"No Indians on the road east?"

"None," said Armijo. "And no bandits."

The three men laughed. Don Miguel put his arm around Augustino's shoulder. "It is a pleasure to meet the nephew of my good friend, the governor, at last. Come," he said, "let us meet the ladies and take a meal together."

"My uncle sends his good wishes to you, Don Miguel," said Armijo. "May I present my friend, Merito Salcedo, who accompanied me on the journey. And, I look forward to meeting your beautiful daughter at last."

"She looks eagerly toward meeting you, as well, Augustino." Don Miguel shook Merito's hand. Both young men were nervous, and the lieutenant's palm was slick with sweat. "I take much pleasure in knowing you," said Rojas. "You are welcome, too. My daughter, Estrellita, will be pleased to have two such handsome young men greet her on her birthday."

A look passed between Armijo and Salcedo. There was little else they spoke of on the long ride from Santa Fe. Augustino had heard how beautiful Estrellita was and took great satisfaction in knowing that she would one day be his bride. Merito had teased him about the woman, saying that she was probably horse-faced and plump, but Augustino knew that this was not so. Although he had never seen her, he had sent spies to the church in Santa Fe who told him of her beauty.

"There will be a party at the home of Don Pedro Vial this evening," said Don Miguel as the three men crossed the lobby of the hotel. "Music, dancing, a fine fiesta."

"I have brought presents for the family, and a very special one for the señorita," said Augustino.

Don Miguel summoned a carriage, and the three men climbed in. The soldiers rattled their sabres and found it difficult to sit properly until they had adjusted themselves in the seats.

Don Miguel spoke to the driver of the open carriage as curious onlookers stared at the three New Mexicans.

"To Planters' House, if you please," he said.

"Look at them greasers," said a passerby to his companion. "Think they're better'n white folk."

Augustino's face flushed dark; the veins stood out on his neck like blue earthworms in rust soil. Merito, too, pulled himself up on the seat to a rigid pose, and his fingers tightened around his sabre's silver scabbard.

The carriage lurched away from the hotel entrance as the driver flicked his whip over the big bay's back. On the backsnap, the whip made a sound like the crack of a flintlock rifle. The wheels of the carriage creaked and groaned under the strain.

"You must not listen to such talk," Don Miguel said in Spanish. "We Mexicans have much stronger words than 'greaser' for their kind."

He smiled, and his words broke the tension between the two soldiers. Armijo sat back against the leather cushion, flicked a gloved hand as if to brush away the remark. Merito glowered for a moment, then grinned.

"It is of no import," he said. "I have been called worse names by my own men."

The three laughed heartily as the carriage rocked over the cobblestone street. The carriage stopped at a corner to allow a procession of Chippewas to pass on the cross street.

The Indians rode slowly, pulling springy travois laden with birchbark sacks of maple sugar, skins of wild honey, salted buffalo tongues, bear grease, moccasins, horsehair lariats, wild herbs, along with antelope and deer hides. These they would trade for blankets, saddles, bridles, coffee, tin cups, knives, and tobacco.

"The Indians are going to Chouteau's big stone warehouse," said Don Miguel.

"I have seen it," said Augustino. "Stacks of fur in rows that stink to the skies."

Merito made a face, crinkling up his nose. The other two men laughed, recalling the aroma down near the levee.

The carriage lumbered onward once again, passing the strolling men and women in silk and satin as well as the mountain men and Indians who crowded the boardwalks, the shoppers and gawkers who streamed in and out of the shops on Olive Street. Soon they passed the large stone houses where the ladies and gentlemen lived, and overtook the Planters' House wagon bearing the guests who arrived by boat. Two black drivers in resplendent red-and-white livery and black boots, drove the four horses that pulled the large wagon. Ladies sitting on upholstered seats clung to their large shade hats and floppy gingham bonnets. Men in eastern garb, chewing on pipes or cigars, sat stiffly next to the womenfolk as if unruffled by the jouncing over the rutted and potholed road.

The buildings gave way to trees and pastures, stock ponds where cattle grazed, and swards where horses and mules stood hip-shot in the shade of oaks and hickory trees. The imposing facade of Planters' House loomed up behind the sworl of dust left hanging in the air by the wagon ahead. The driver turned into the lane, and the three men swayed into a clump until the vehicle straightened, headed toward the old mansion with its stately Grecian columns, wide veranda, and lattices where the wisteria and the honeysuckle climbed and intertwined.

As the Planters' wagon jostled to a halt, with the don's carriage right behind it, slaves rushed from their stations in front of the porch to unload the baggage, assist the new arrivals. The blacks spoke but little, replying to the guests' questions with "yassams" and "no sahs," as the caravan from the levee was led up to the massive porch by a dark-coated butler.

Don Miguel paid the driver with Mexican silver and the three men strolled toward the inn. The Gothic columns were already showing signs of age, the paint had peeled, and fissures made dark jagged cracks in the wood. The building had been standing since 1817, and, while still elegant, the inn had stiff competition since Judge J.B.C. Lucas and his associates had built his hotel on Fourth, between Chestnut and Pine. Lucas charged a dollar twenty-five a day and management was strict about the dining hours. Breakfast was served from seven to eleven, dinner at one-thirty, tea at five-thirty and supper from nine to twelve. Planters' House was much more relaxed about such things, and the guests came and went at their leisure. But Lucas had made his point. St. Louis was a growing center of commerce and business thrived on punctuality.

Don Miguel spoke to one of the servants beyond the massive double doors and the three men were ushered to one of the parlors that served as waiting rooms. Corazon's fan stopped in midwave and she rose from her chair, received her husband's chaste and formal embrace, then curtsied to the soldiers.

"I have the honor to present Captain Augustino Armijo and Lieutenant Merito Salcedo," said Don Miguel. "This is my wife, Corazon, my daughter, Estrellita, and her companion, Lucia Delgado."

Estrellita looked over the edge of her fan at the man who was her betrothed. Her eyes focused on his sharp, aquiline nose, his sensual mouth, the confident, almost cruel, jut of his chin. She looked especially at his hands, saw that they were clean and well manicured, delicate like a violinist's hands, slender, with the veins rippling a faint blue under the skin's surface.

Augustino bowed politely, took her proffered hand. He brushed his lips over the soft flesh and Estrellita felt a faint thrill, a brief tingle as his lips lingered on her hand.

"I have much pleasure in meeting you," said Armijo. "Your beauty is already legend in the city of Santa Fe and now St. Louis shines in the radiance of your presence."

Estrellita's face warmed with a ruddy blush and she smiled self-consciously. Her mother beamed. Even Lucia's countenance lost its stern cast for a brief moment.

A butler appeared at the entrance to the parlor, bowed with a majestic sweep of one arm.

"Your table is ready," he said in a soft drawl. "Will you all be so kind as to follow me."

"May I escort the señorita?" asked Augustino, offering Estrellita a stiffly crooked arm.

"Why, thank you, sir," she said quickly, linking her arm in his. Corazon smiled, took her husband's arm, and Lucia fluttered like a disheveled hen turkey as Merito offered his services as escort.

The servant ushered the party into the large dining room. Seated at tables were many of the winter guests, the new arrivals, and some of St. Louis's upper-class patrons. Potted plants broke up the expanse of the large room and gave each table a modicum of privacy. As they made their way to the large table by a window that looked out over the greensward, Estrellita felt the intensity of the curious stares and was grateful for Augustino's arm.

They sat down to a crystal setting, as a young black man poured clear spring water into their glasses. A stately steward presented Don Miguel with a wine list printed on deckle-edged parchment in fancy script. Slates chalked with the bill of fare were presented to the men as the hum of conversations rebuilt around them in soft, flowing murmurs that blended with the tink of glass and utensils striking china plates. The other seated patrons had accepted the newcomers, though many of the men glanced longingly more than once at Estrellita. They had watched her as she walked through slanting columns of sunlight that seemed vibrant with the dazzling dance of dust motes stirred by her passing. Birdsongs, the lyrical trill of the meadowlark and the piping peal of the mockingbird, floated through the windows from the green fields and there was the faint aroma of clover and sunflowers on the breezes that rustled the leaves of the potted plants. Estrellita seemed unaware of the glances that tugged at her, but she sat in a place where the sunlight played through the open window and her chair, to those who watched her settle gracefully into it, looked like the throne of a princess born to be a queen.

"You must come to our daughter's party tonight," said Corazon, after inquiring politely about Augustino's family back in Santa Fe. "There will be music and dancing and good food."

"We will be honored," said Augustino, as Merito suppressed a smirk.

Don Miguel ordered the famous planter's punch drink for himself and the soldiers, after which he asked that a delicate rosé wine be served to the ladies, a strong burgundy for the men. He chose lamb, catfish, and crayfish from the menu, rice, turnips and peaches as accompaniment to the entrées.

The three women began to notice the other ladies at nearby tables, and the sound of a half dozen tongues, including French, English, Portuguese, German, and Italian, assaulted their ears. As the women began to chat, discussing the hats and gowns in the room, the men drew away from them, cleared their throats.

"And how did things go at your meeting with Chouteau this morning?" Augustino asked Don Miguel.

"Ah, very well, I thought," replied the Santa Fe landowner. "With the others there, as well. Pierre is very optimistic about the fur trade, thinks it will grow even bigger in the years ahead. He has big plans."

"Is he as rich as they say?" asked Merito, smacking his lips as the bright tang of the punch bit into his tongue.

"I believe he is even richer," said Don Miguel. "Maybe not as rich as that Greek Croesus, but richer than the first pope."

The men laughed. Corazon and Lucia shot looks in his direction that barbed him for his flirtation with sacrilege.

"He and his partner, a relative by marriage who is called Bernard Pratte, Senior, went into business two years ago," Don Miguel continued. "The American millionaire, John Jacob Astor, is retiring. So Chouteau and Company are buying his company."

"American Fur?" asked Armijo, frankly astounded. Astor's reputation as a millionaire businessman was well known, even in Mexico and its territories.

"Yes," said Don Miguel with solemnity. "Astor did not want to give up control, so Pratte and Chouteau purchased the western department. Pierre now owns the Upper Missouri Outfit, the trading region."

"Ah," chorused the two soldiers.

"He is gloating over it," Don Miguel said.

Augustino and Merito grinned.

"This is good news, for sure," said Armijo. "Some of his riches will surely flow into Santa Fe."

"Clearly," said Don Miguel, basking in the warm feelings his announcement brought to the table. Corazon held herself proudly straight in her wicker chair; Estrellita looked at him with adoring eyes, and even the old crone, Lucia, seemed almost radiant. "It is said that Chouteau's annual trade in furs and buffalo robes will be worth three hundred thousand American dollars."

The soldiers looked at each other. Augustino let out a long breath.

"But, enough of business," said Don Miguel with an extravagant sweep of his hand. "Today is Estrellita's sixteenth birthday, and I offer a toast to her."

Rojas stood up, lifted his dewy glass of punch. "To you, my daughter," he said, "I wish good health, long life, and much wealth."

"And many fine children," blurted out Merito. The women laughed, and their laughter was infectious. Don Miguel and Augustino joined in the merriment. They all saluted Estrellita with their drinks and drank with gusto.

Waiters served the steaming platters of food, and the people from Santa Fe dined and spoke of inconsequential things during the meal. The men ate with a rabid Dionysian relish and the women picked at their viands with delicate, birdlike probes, their forks glittering like crochet needles in their hands, chattering among themselves, their voices smothered by the louder, more robust talk of the men.

"Surely you will receive many fine gifts," said Augustino when he was finished eating and had caught Estrellita's eye. "This must be a happy day for you."

"I already have a fine gift," said Estrellita, "brought to me by a prince very handsome and fair."

"Oh, my daughter," said Corazon, slightly giddy from the rosé, "you think a stableboy to be like a prince? You must truly be happy with your gift."

"Oh, I am," said Estrellita. "And I'm worried about Jeremiah. I hope that he is well by now."

Augustino began to stiffen in his chair. Merito looked dumbly across the table at the women, feeling the first fidgety bristle of tension.

"The sooner you forget about that young lout, the better," said Don Miguel.

"*Basura,*" muttered Lucia.

"Who is this American?" asked Augustino.

"He is just a boy," replied Don Miguel. "I bought a horse from him as a present for Estrellita. A good horse, but the boy is a peasant off the farm. He is nothing to us."

"Where is he?"

Don Miguel told him of the incident at the hotel. Estrellita squirmed in her chair, closed her eyes when he told of the boy being knocked unconscious.

"So, he is at Pedro Vial's?" asked Augustino, with a tone of barely disguised hostility in his voice.

"You'll meet him, I think," said Estrellita, a trace of teasing devilment in her voice. She felt her mother's shoe tap against her shin under the table, and did not miss the dark look that Lucia shot her from her watchful vulture's perch.

"I do not want to meet him," said Augustino stiffly.

"He's very nice, truly. No manners, perhaps, but he can be taught some."

"And who would be his teacher?" asked Augustino, fixing Estrellita with a bold, challenging stare.

She picked up her fan, flicked it open.

"Oh, I don't know. Most anyone, I imagine," she said coyly, unfurling the fan across the lower part of her face so that only her eyes showed above the pleats. "Maybe I will, if he wants me to."

Sensing a growing hostility between her daughter and her betrothed, Corazon cleared her throat.

"That is enough talk about that American boy," she said. "He really doesn't matter. We are just being kind to him because he was hurt."

"I see," said Augustino, his tone icy with resentment. His features hardened to cast iron.

A waiter appeared at Don Miguel's side. The don ordered pastries and cordials as the servants cleared their table of emptied plates.

Smacking his lips in satisfaction, Don Miguel slipped cigars from the inside pocket of his coat, offered them to Augustino and Merito. He rose and bowed to his wife and daughter.

"We will smoke on the veranda," he said, "and you may join us if you wish when you have eaten your pastries. If not, we shall return in a little while."

"Thank you, my husband," said Corazon.

After the men had left, she looked at her daughter as though she pitied her.

"Your manners," she whispered. "There goes your betrothed and you irritate him by speaking of another man. A boy, in truth, and for what good reason? Estrellita, you are without shame, I tell you, and I hope you will not offend Augustino again with your rudeness."

"But, Mother, I was merely answering his question. If Augustino is a man, as you say, he should not be bothered by a boy."

"An American boy," replied Lucia. "And I hope he has recovered and gone on his way."

Estrellita went silent as the pastries were served. She and the other two women did not speak as they ate daintily, sipped their peach cordials. It was not until she saw the men returning that she spoke again.

"Well, I hope Jeremiah stays," she said quickly, dabbing at a gout of creamy filling at the corner of her mouth. "After all, I invited him to my *fiesta de cumpleaños.*"

"You did what?" stormed her mother as the men reached the table.

"*Ay de mi,*" said Lucia, throwing up her hands in a gesture of despair, as if she was one of the women standing beneath the cruel cross of Jesus as he suffered in Golgotha.

The men sat down uneasily, unacknowledged by the women.

"I hope he stays in St. Louis as long as we do," pouted Estrellita, pushing her half-empty plate of cream-filled pastry away from her. "And I hope he comes to Santa Fe someday soon."

"But the young man is an American heathen," said her mother. "He can mean nothing to you, Estrellita. Maybe he will not be at the house when we return."

Estrellita drew a long angry breath. "I am sick of hearing everyone talk badly about Jeremiah. I don't care if he is an American or not. He is nice and I like him. I like him very much. I want to go home this minute and see if he is all right."

Augustino smoldered with suppressed rage. He did not know who this American boy was, but he did not like the idea that he was staying in the same house as his betrothed. He glared at

Estrellita, determined to show his displeasure by frosting her with the withering look in his eyes.

Estrellita caught the dark, lancing look and tossed her head defiantly, fixing him with a haughty gaze. The afternoon sunlight streamed through the nearby window, washed her olive complexion with a golden spray, bathed her face until it shone with a startling, beauteous glow.

Augustino stifled a gasp as he looked at her face, saw the lovely contours illuminated, carved by light to perfection. The sun seemed trapped in the sleek, dark depths of her tresses, boiling molten gold and hammered foil into each silken strand. Her cheekbones stood out in finely chiseled relief and her eyes flashed with sparks like the flickering lights in diamonds or sapphires. Her lips pouted with a moist invitation. He wanted to touch her, crush her lips against his. For a long moment he stared at her and did not realize his fingers were trembling as if expressing the desire that flared in his veins like ignited phosphor, gnawed, like soft fur afire, at his loins.

Merito, as well, was struck with this sudden illumination of her rare beauty. He glanced sideways at Augustino and then at her father, Don Miguel. Both men seemed frozen in the awesome radiance of her beauty, just as he, too, was held transfixed for a moment as though turned to stone.

Don Miguel looked at his daughter and memories flooded to his brain in a flutter of images. He saw the chubbiness of her baby face swept away by the light, remembered her sweet child's smile, and realized that Estrellita was a woman grown and had become more beautiful than he ever could have imagined. He saw the child in her, too, and he saw the woman, saw the grace and bearing of her mother, and her mother's forebears, the strong bloodlines in the sunstruck profile of her face, the savage heritage of an Indian ancestor visible as a raw smear of vermilion across her cheek.

And the men at the table fell in love with Estrellita in that special moment when the sun poured over her like honey and highlighted her loveliness. They each fell in love with her in different ways and for all time because they knew she was no ordinary woman, but a Thoroughbred, a champion sleek and fleet and strong-minded, who would demand a very strong man to tame her wild heart, to temper the savage blood that flowed in her veins as the lava flows from a restless volcano.

Her mother saw the looks in the men's eyes and so, too, did Lucia, whose face darkened like a stormcloud and whose pulse raced with long-forgotten tremors.

"Yes," choked her mother, "we must be leaving. Let us return to the hacienda to complete our preparations for the fiesta."

But no one moved, for the sun still glistened on Estrellita's face and rippled in her hair, gently brushed faint shadows across her lips like an invisible kiss, like a kiss from a forbidden and secret lover.

Chapter Six

Jeremiah felt a tingling rush of blood course through his veins when he heard her voice.

"Jeremiah! Jeremiah! Where are you?"

He lay stiff and still, flat-backed on the bed in the upstairs room at the back of the house. He had not heard the carriage arrive, but now his muscles quivered in his abdomen as they always did when he sensed danger. He closed his eyes, felt the quivering inside his stomach, felt the flutters turn to a cloud of flying insects.

He heard a door slam, footsteps on the hardwood floor down the hall. Another door opened, whining on its hinges like the lost cry of a peacock. It slammed shut a moment later.

"Jeremiah?" she called again, and the sound of footsteps echoed down the corridor, closer. The door to the guest room was still closed. This was where the servants had brought him, had stripped off his shoes and left him to lie under a flounced canopy that hung over the four-poster bed. He had never been in such a room and he felt dirty lying on the fresh coverlet, an eiderdown pillow under his head. The room smelled of lilac and the mint that grew in the flowerbeds two stories below.

It seemed he had been there for an eternity, listening for the sounds of voices, of hoofbeats, of approaching footsteps, long into the afternoon, his stomach squeezing and gyrating with hunger. He had memorized the room with its framed prints, its dark paintings of European boar and fox hunts, oddly hung among various prints of religious figures painted by medieval masters. Brass lamps with painted glass chimneys adorned the end tables and a pewter one stood tall on the low dressing bureau with its large mirror, its wood painted white and covered with flowers that had delicate yellow and blue petals. Throw rugs lay like islands on the floor and there was a highboy dresser, a porcelain pitcher, and bowl atop a lace doily.

He had seen the wisteria vines clinging to the trellises and climbing up the walls of the great house, and he had looked out at the green fields beyond the sill, a haven for blackbirds and meadowlarks and quail whose piping broke the droning stillness of the interminable afternoon. When he looked out the window, he was flooded with such a wave of homesickness that he had to turn away, ashamed at this sudden weakness that struck him without warning. He bit back the tears, refused to let them flow as his lips clamped together, hardened like a snapping turtle's mouth. He threw himself on the bed and thought only of Estrellita, wishing they were riding together again, racing in the wind to a place of trees and silence, to a place where he could look at her face in soft sunlight and drink in her rare beauty.

Now she was here and he wanted her to feel sorry for him, to touch him and hold him as she had before. He wanted to feel her bosom pressing against his ribs and smell the scent of wildflowers in her hair, hear her voice like a song in his ears.

"Jeremiah? Where are you? Where is everybody?"

Jeremiah ran his fingers quickly through his hair, lay back down on the pillow just before the door opened, and closed his eyes.

"Jere . . . *ay de mi*, there you are. Oh, you're still hurt."

He suppressed a smile as he heard her footsteps pattering on the floor. The bed gave under her weight and he rolled into her, his eyes still closed. She took him in her arms, cradled his head to her bosom. His heartbeat picked up speed as his blood pumped fast like water through a millrace.

"Oh, *pobrecito*, you are still bad hurt. Are you awake, Jeremiah? Can you hear me?"

He felt her fingers stroke across his forehead delicately, trace small furrows through his hair. He wanted the moment to last forever. He wanted to reach out and draw her lips to his and hold tightly to her while he kissed her. His pulse throbbed in his temples, roared in his ears like a sea tide, rumbled like distant summer thunder.

"Wake up, Jeremiah," she pleaded.

He could no longer hold back his mirth at deceiving her this way. Jeremiah opened his eyes, smiled at her.

"Uh, hello," he said sheepishly.

"What? You are fooling with me?"

"No, not rightly," he said lamely.

She dropped him from her lap, scooted away. He lunged for her, caught her shoulders.

"Please. Don't run away. I . . . I wanted to see you. I wanted to come here to your house."

She did not struggle, but pushed his hands from her shoulders.

"So, this is what you do," she said. "You make a fool out of me. I was worried about you. I thought you were hurt."

"Ah, Estrellita, please. I know your folks didn't want me to come out here, so I just did some pretendin' a little. Don't be so dadblamed mad at me."

"Ah, you pretended," she scathed. "Pretended so that my heart jumped and I almost fainted from worry. And now what do I tell my mother and father? They will never believe me again, nor you, either. Maybe they are right. Maybe you are not worth anything. Maybe you are just trouble. Maybe you are just a common liar. So. Are you a liar, Jeremiah?"

Her words stung him and he winced visibly.

He could almost hear his mother's voice saying the same things. Calling him a liar. He could almost see his father standing behind her, his arms folded across his chest, silent as stone, his eyes dark and accusing. More than anything else, his parents hated lying. "You can be anything you want," his father used to say, "as long as you aren't a liar." The word was like a whiplash across his face now. Coming from Estrellita's mouth it hurt worse than the switches his mother used to cut from the base of the black locust trees, long, slender, supple branches that she laid across his bare back until the welts rose up in angry red streaks and burned like fire. And he heard his father Andrew's voice again in his mind, clear and stern and deep: "That's enough, Edna. You don't want to ruin the boy." Heard his mother's panting, saw her still quivering in rage, her mouth drawn up tight and bitter, the switch vibrating in her hand like a cane fishing pole with a five-pound bass on the line. In the shadows, Andrew, unable to strike him, but angry, too, a tall, lean figure whose shoulders slumped from years of pushing a plow behind a team of shaggy mules.

"Look, Estrellita," he stammered. "I . . . I sure am sorry I pulled your hair. I didn't mean nothin'. I didn't mean it like lyin'. I . . . I just wanted to have you like me some."

"You didn't pull my hair," she said, a look of puzzlement on her face.

"I, uh, I mean, well, I guess I made myself into a fool same as I did you. Without meanin' to."

He looked down at his lap, shamefaced, contrite.

Estrellita felt a tug at her heart. She looked at Jeremiah's tousled hair, the flicker of a muscle along his jawline. Something inside her melted, was drawn to him. He looked so forlorn at that moment she wanted to hold him in her arms again, clutch him to her breast as she had earlier. Yet she held back, conscious that the circumstances had changed. This was not a hotel meeting room. There were no people about. This was a bedroom, and they were alone.

Jeremiah raised his head then, saw the look in her eyes. It was a look he had never seen before, but he knew what it was. He recognized something he felt inside himself, something he had felt the first time he had seen Estrellita. A tremor of excitement raced through him, a rippling tingle such as he had felt on winter evenings when he ran his hands over the quilt and then through his hair, the kind of thrilling excitement he got during a thunderstorm when the lightning was very close and scary.

The look that passed between them crackled like that same lightning, danced and shimmered in their eyes like the glow of will-o'-the-wisp on summer marshes at eventide. It generated heat and light like a miniature sun. They could feel the heat on their skins, like the glow from a bright fire, and they could feel the warmth inside them like bread baking and rising in an iron oven. He lunged for her then, impulsively, without thinking, and grasped her slender shoulders. His palms burned as if he had placed them on the belly of a warm stove and he drew her to him across the bed and kissed her lips as if drawn to them by the force of a powerful magnet. It happened so fast, Estrellita did not have time to ward him off or spurn his dramatic impulse. Caught by surprise, she grew limp, pliant in the sturdiness of his grasp. The blood drained from her face as his lips touched hers and she closed her eyes, on the verge of a deep swoon. She felt as if the bed and the floor had fallen from under her and she was plunging earthward from a great height. Breathless, she felt faint until the fire of his kiss caught hold, drove into her, drove deep like flamenco music, like the sad, sweet songs the Mexicans sang, their voices rising over the plaintive notes of a guitar, blending with the music, striking sad chords in the heart, bringing unwitting tears to the eyes and hurting with their words of love and betrayal and jail and death. The *son huastecos*, the sad songs they sang in the cantinas and over their campfires, the songs that tore at the heart and squeezed it with haunting melodies that lingered long after the last note was sounded.

Jeremiah could not believe what he was doing. He was like a man who had gone over the edge of sanity. He knew, somehow, that he was taking liberties not granted to him. He had violated every instinct, every inbred grain of decency, in kissing this girl who had befriended him. Yet he was not able to release her, to draw his lips from hers. The fire in him was too hot, the insane desire to possess her too strong. Her lips seemed to open a magical realm to him, take him to some dizzying parapet far above the earth, where eagles soared, traced wide circles on some invisible carousel of wind currents, oblivious to gravity, mindless to the laws and customs of man. Her lips were soft and yielding, and his own lips felt numb and fiery at the same time, bristled with heat that went beyond the numbness and coursed through him in knee-weakening rivulets of molten lava.

Summoning her senses, Estrellita drew up tiny fists and flung them weakly against Jeremiah's chest. Her fists opened and she drummed on his shirtfront with trembling fingers, tapping at him with a silent plea to release her. Yet she clung to him despite herself, held on to his lips with hers as if magnetized and felt the current go through her, hold her fast in a giddy swirl that was beyond her power to control. Her heart beat with the flutter of rosewood castanets chattering in the hands of a flamenco dancer until she felt herself whirling and whirling and sinking down and down into a spiral whorl that was like the tidepools of the sea, like the wet-warm pudding of quicksand on the Rio Grande.

He broke the kiss and she fell away from him, pushed off. He stared at her, wide-eyed with wonder, his face ruddy with the rose-flare of passion, his lips swollen, still warm and tingling. Estrellita's dark eyes widened, too, and she brought a hand to her crushed lips, touched a finger to them in bewilderment.

"Estrellita, g-g-gosh all, I . . . I'm sorry," he stammered.

"Wh—what have you done?" she said, her voice small and husky and far away as if shrouded in mist.

She scooted back, away from him, slid from the bed. She stepped backward, stood there trembling for a long moment.

"I'm sorry," he said, dropping his head until it drooped over his chest. "I didn't mean no harm. Honest."

"We . . . we can't stay here like this," she said softly. "And you must never do anything like this again. Do you promise?"

He lifted his head and looked at her. He wanted to kiss her again and, from the look on her face, he was pretty sure she wanted him to. But there was that lingering shadow of doubt and he felt lost, as though he had journeyed too far into a land he did not know. Lost in the aura of Estrellita who was now so far away from him, who, a moment ago, had been close to him, almost inside him. Now he wondered if he had imagined it. Maybe the kiss had never happened. But, no, the sting of it was still on his lips, the hurt of it in his heart. Still, he did not understand why he had done such a thing, why the kiss had happened, so easily it seemed, and now she stood away from him and he knew he could not run fast enough to catch her and kiss her again.

That was part of the mystery, too. The sudden change. The changes in him, in her. She looked now like a young girl, a stranger, but for a moment she had been a woman, and he a man. That was the mystery, the strangeness of it all. He had felt things inside him that he had never felt before, odd stirrings that left his thoughts tangled and jumpy. Did she feel these things, too? He did not know and that was another edge to the mystery. He knew he could never go inside her thoughts, might never know how she had felt when he kissed her, how she felt now. There was no sign on her face. Her hair was not mussed. She appeared as before, as if nothing had ever happened.

Well, he wondered, what *had* happened? He had stolen a kiss, taken it without permission, and she was angry at him. Maybe. Maybe the kiss was good for her, too. But there was no sign. No visible mark of him on her. And that hurt, hurt deep. How could she just stand there and not want to kiss him again? Did she have no feelings? It kept hurting that he could not touch her again, could not draw her close and be intimate with her. There was a barrier there now. There was a wall between them, and he had built that wall by grabbing her like that and taking a forbidden liberty.

"Oh, Estrellita," he blurted, "I am so sorry. Please don't be mad at me."

"Just stay here," she said, and her voice sounded cold to him, "and don't go away. I . . . I'll be back in a *momentito*."

"Wh-where are you going?"

"Just wait for me," she said emphatically.

She turned around then, and ran out the door before he could say another word. He was scared now. Was she going to tell her mother, her father? His stomach knotted up and the muscles tightened down and the fear began to build in him.

The house seemed alien to him and he almost felt like a prisoner. But if he was, it was his own doing. He had wanted to come here, to see Estrellita again. But where was she? She did not seem part of this world, either, although he knew she was. The people here were foreigners. Rich foreigners. He did not understand their language or their ways. Somehow Estrellita did not seem like them. She was different, just as he was different. He believed that, he told himself. He had to believe it.

Jeremiah had never seen clothes so fine.

"These . . . these are for me? To wear?" His voice cracked, shifted from the lower register to the high and back down again so that he sounded like a man who had swallowed a bagpipe or a concertina.

Estrellita laughed.

"Yes, but you must not say anything. They are for you to wear to my party and to keep. I hope they fit. I had to guess at your size."

Jeremiah looked at the clothes, dumbfounded. She had bought him, secretly, he suspected, a pair of velvet trousers, dark with a purple sheen, a pair of fine men's hose, a frilly white linen shirt with puffed sleeves and a high collar, a silk cummerbund, and a pair of boots that were as fine as any he had seen, coal-black and shiny.

"I . . . I don't understand," he said.

"Wear these to my fiesta," she said. "Now, go down to the

102

bathhouse, quickly, and I'll have a tub drawn for you. Wash clean and wear these clothes. I will see you when the fiesta begins."

"I . . . I can't take these . . ."

"Be quiet. Do it and just don't say anything. I want you to look handsome."

"Where is the bathhouse?" he asked, an odd, queasy feeling of anticipation, not unlike fear, roiling his stomach.

"Just outside, in the back. It is where the men who work here go. No one will see you if you hurry."

"But . . ."

Before he could ask another question, she was gone. He looked at the clothes again, at the wrappings on the floor. His stomach twisted and he knew he had best be getting on or he would never summon the courage to go downstairs. He wrapped up the new clothes and walked through the door. If he didn't lose his bearings in the big house, he would surely find the bathhouse.

Estrellita sat before the mirror at the dressing table in her room, marveling at the clarity of her image. She brushed her hair gently, turning her head to catch the light's sheen, made faces, smiled, made little moues with her lips, arched her eyebrows, crinkled her nose, winked, posed to display every expression she could think of, tilting her shoulders, shrugging them, taking deep breaths to raise her breasts against the tight-wired bodice of her birthday dress.

She imagined herself in various kinds of situations with her suitors. She tucked a dainty fist under her chin, extended a limp hand to an imaginary man, withdrew slightly, as if he was gallantly kissing it. She bowed from the waist in a mock curtsy, looked at her eyes in the wavy mirror, checking the angle to see if she still appeared comely. She bared her teeth, concealed them behind a worldly smile. And the brush kept moving, sliding expertly over silken, dark hair until each strand shone like the back of a crow's wing in sunlight.

The door opened suddenly and Estrellita jerked upright while her heart pumped fast and seemed to sink in her chest.

"Mother!" she exclaimed as Corazon glided across the room. "Do you not tap first before coming in?"

"My dear one," her mother said, "if you had not wanted me to enter, you should have turned the key in the lock. Is there some reason you want me to warn you before I come into your room?"

Corazon looked quickly around as if searching for something out of place. She was already dressed for the party, her hair drawn up on one side in a bun, her lace bodice framing her chest in a V, her dark silk gown dotted with red cactus flowers made of satin. She looked, Estrellita thought, young and beautiful—almost like a sister instead of a mother. A graceful mantilla rose above her, tilted backward slightly, its veil draped becomingly over her sleek dark hair.

Estrellita drew herself up straight on the dressing bench, offended.

"There is no one hiding here."

"No? Well, at least you show some sense, Estrellita. I have not seen the young American who was brought here and no one seems to know where he is now. I suppose he went back to the town to be with his own kind. But I didn't come here for that. You'd better give me the purse your uncle Pedro gave you for your birthday this morning. That is a lot of silver to leave lying around. Many people will be here, and the guests will be roaming about this grand house of Garcia, curious to see all of us from Santa Fe."

Estrellita's face blanched as the blood drained from the tiny veins, then turned crimson as the blood rushed back.

Pedro Vial, bless his soul, had sent a servant to her in town that morning bearing a purse with one hundred silver dollars inside. A birthday gift from a sweet and dear old man.

"Oh, I have it safely hidden away, Mother," said Estrellita quickly, her voice quavery. "The purse, ah, yes, no need for

104

you to worry about it."

"May I see it?"

"Why, Mother? It is mine, after all. Tío Pedro wanted me to have it."

"That is why it must be kept in a safe place. I will lock it in your father's big trunk."

Estrellita's gaze wandered. The air in the room seemed close, almost suffocating.

"Not now," she said. "I must finish dressing."

"You are dressed, except for your shoes and your mantilla."

"Please, Mother. Later."

"Now," said her mother.

"Motherrrr," she purred. "Please."

Corazon strode to the large cedar-lined closet. The doors were open. She saw the purse Pedro Vial had given her daughter, lying toward the back amid a jumble of shoes and boots. Corazon snatched it up, opened it before Estrellita could cry out in protest.

The woman stepped into the light, dipped a graceful hand inside the velvet purse with its fittings of Mexican silver. The coins jingled and Corazon looked up, fixed her gaze on her daughter once again.

"Why, there are only a few pesos left. What have you done with the rest? When you left me in the town to go off by yourself, did you buy something for your birthday? I saw the extra packages and did not think to ask."

"Y-yes," stammered Estrellita, her face still flushed with embarrassment and shame.

"May I see what you bought?"

"No—no—I—not now, Mother."

"You're hiding something from me, young lady. I want you to tell the truth."

For a moment, Estrellita considered that she might want to cry. But she thought of how her eyes would look if she did that. She fought back the tears, clenched her fists in frustration. She rose from the bench, stood there, trembling in every limb.

Why couldn't her mother leave her alone? Why did she have to pester her so? Why did she dig and dig and ask so many questions? What she did with her birthday money was her own business, not her mother's. It wasn't fair. She was sixteen now and should not be treated like a child.

The minutes stretched to an interminable length and the silence in the room became unbearable. Corazon's eyes were like banked fires and Estrellita squirmed like an animal caught in a snare. There was no escape for her.

"Oh, you'll know soon enough anyway," Estrellita blurted. "I bought clothes with some of the money. Not for me, but for Jeremiah. I wanted him to look nice for my birthday and I felt sorry for him. It's my money. Can't I do with it what I want?"

Her mother said nothing. She glared at her daughter, restraining her rage.

"Mother?"

"I shall not tell your father of this foolishness, young lady," said Corazon. "It would break his heart to see you throw your shameless self on this American boy. If I were you I would go to confession and tell the priest how you have sinned in your thoughts over this boy."

Estrellita blushed. She wondered if her mother knew how close to the truth she was.

She could not speak. Her throat was constricted. Her mother flashed one last look at her and flung the purse to the floor before she stalked out, slamming the door behind her.

Estrellita stood there, on the verge of tears, fighting to keep her composure. Then she took long strides to the door and angrily twisted the key in the lock.

The men gathered at the miniature bullring in the back of the stables and the stock corrals, took seats in the bleachers. A stableboy handed out goatskins of wine and straw hats to those guests who came bareheaded.

"What are we to see here?" asked Don Miguel, "a *tienta?*"

106

"More than that," said Don Garcia, his host. He was a lean man of grace and bearing, originally from Andaluz. He knew horseflesh and knew the bulls. "Not quite a *corrida,* but more than a *capea.* We have no *novilleros* here, only some of the young men who have made their own *muletas* and think they are brave."

The men around them laughed, swarmed over the seats as the sun raged in the sky at four of the clock, the traditional time that bullfights started in Spain. The bleachers were *en sombra,* in the shade of tall oaks and leafy box elders, leaving the tiny ring, which actually served as a large corral most of the time, bathed in afternoon sunlight.

The doors to the large barn and stables that led into the circular corral opened and a trio of musicians stepped out smartly into the ring. They began to play "La Virgen de la Macarena" on trumpet, bass, and lead guitars. They were followed by two men on horseback serving as picador and banderillero. Their horses were draped with drab, padded quilts. After these a sword handler bearing a cushion with a gleaming sword atop it walked hesitantly into the arena.

A young man strode into the ring wearing, not a *traje de luces,* a suit of lights, but tight-fitting trousers and blouse, a small cape draped over his shoulder. He bowed formally to the congregation and blushed as the men laughed.

"A young rooster," said one spectator, a neighboring rancher who was interested in talking to Don Miguel about raising mules.

"We will give him a young bull, Lorenzo," said Garcia.

"Hornless, I hope," replied Lorenzo Arrubia.

The men swigged from their *botas,* began to chant for the bull.

"*Anda de prisa,*" said Don Garcia, "*traigale el toro.*"

"*Traigale el cabron,*" exclaimed a wag. "Bring the billy goat."

The men laughed, but their attention was diverted when a servant led Jeremiah York to the small bullring. Don Miguel

107

frowned and the others just stared at the American youth. Muttered questions passed among them and Don Miguel felt compelled to explain the boy's presence. He was surprised to see that the young man was wearing new clothes.

"Come, boy," he called, "you might want to fight a bull yourself."

Jeremiah took one of the straw hats from the stableboy and a goatskin of wine, although he did not know what it was at first. He could guess, though, because it sloshed and smelled musty. He saw a man in the bleachers lean back and hold the *bota* up high overhead and squeeze the bottom until a stream of red juice arced into his mouth.

He scrambled up into the seats just as the door to the pens opened and a young, rangy bull with four-inch horns jogged stiff-legged into the ring.

"Take yourself a seat," said Don Miguel, waving toward an empty spot below him. Pedro Vial smiled when he saw the young man, gave Don Miguel a knowing wink. Augustine Armijo and Merito Salcedo jostled each other with their elbows and scrutinized the American closely.

Jeremiah took a seat near the bottom of the bleachers. He did not look over his shoulder, but he felt several pairs of eyes on him, sharp glances burning into the back of his neck. When he had finished bathing and dressing, he had started for the house, but a young servant who spoke English had told him that he was to join the men.

"I thought there was going to be some kind of birthday party," he said to the boy.

"Yes. It will go on for many days. A week, I think."

The boy whose name was Mario led him to the bullring without further comment and then disappeared.

Jeremiah felt out of place and very alone.

This was not his idea of a birthday party.

The boy in the ring stamped his bare foot on the hardpacked earth and twirled the cape. The Spaniards and the New Mexicans laughed. Some of them had seen fullblown *corridas* in

Spain or in Mexico and they knew that this was not sport, but fun. There would be more events during the week of celebration, of course. This was but the preliminary offering from their host, Garcia. There would be horse races and other feats of horsemanship. There would be lavish feasts and good wine and strong liquor, the late nights of talk and revelry. Now they smacked their lips and imagined that they were in Seville or Madrid and remembered the stories they had heard of Francisco Romero, who was legendary and immortal because he was the brilliant *torero* who had invented and perfected the use of the *muleta,* the red cloth draped over the sword used in the closing moments of a bullfight. He was the one who had introduced professional bullfighting to Spain, forming the teams they called *quadrillas,* and he was the one who had taught Pedro, who became Spain's most famous killer of bulls, credited with more than five thousand during his active career. Pedro, a legend, as well, who said "the coward is not a man, and to fight bulls, men are necessary."

But this was not Spain and the bull was not from one of the great ranches, but only a gangly gringo bull with less than formidable horns and the boy did not know how to use the cape well. They drank the wine and laughed at all the mistakes the boy made.

The boy's name was Umberto Calderon and he weighed a hundred pounds. The bull weighed more than twice that, and though he was not much of a bull yet, he had been teased and taunted to a fine rage for this afternoon's festivities. Umberto's stomach quivered with fear and his knees felt as if they would buckle at any moment.

Olé!" shouted Garcia, and the others joined in, urging the boy to begin. Unlike a regular bullfight, there was no barrier behind which a *torero* could hide and no ragamuffins to harry the bull so the matador could watch his movements. Umberto stepped away from the rails and twirled his cape. The young bull snorted steam and moisture, blew it through rubbery nostrils. The bull lowered its head, charged the boy.

109

Umberto made an awkward pass, flicking the red satin cape at the bull, backing away. The men in the bleacher seats grumbled their disapproval.

Jeremiah watched as Umberto made more awkward passes but each time, he noticed, the bull came in closer. Now, the bull's horns caught the cape as the animal jerked its head sideways in a vicious swipe. The cape fluttered to the ground and Umberto dashed over to it. He snatched it up quickly as the bull turned and came after him. Umberto jumped out of its path to the jeers of the crowd. The picador moved in between the bull and the boy until Umberto could recover his composure.

The boy made two or three more passes but his heart wasn't in it. His suit was limp with sweat. He wiped his hands. He tried a Veronica, and the bull took the cape away, bumped Umberto's leg. Umberto went down, and the two horsemen moved in, backed the bull off until the boy could regain his footing.

Umberto, shaking, called for the picador to spear the bull's shoulders. This would weaken its muscles so that its head would lower for the kill. But there would be no kill this day.

As Umberto stepped toward the rails, the bull avoided the horseman, charged the boy.

Jeremiah rose from his seat, shouted a warning.

Umberto turned, stood transfixed, his eyes wide in horror as the bull rumbled toward him. He put up his hands, but the bull went under them and caught the boy in the groin with his horns. Umberto went up in the air, screamed, and did a somersault.

Jeremiah leaped from his seat, crawled through the rails, and scrambled into the bullring.

The men in the bleachers rose up as one, hissing and booing.

Umberto cried out in pain, tried to rise, as the bull charged again.

Jeremiah raced toward him. The bull, seeing the movement, altered its charge. Blood streaked one of its horns and its eye

110

glared with anger as the animal barreled toward Jeremiah at top speed. The horsemen were caught off guard on the opposite side of the ring.

There was no one between the charging bull and Jeremiah. He stood alone in the center of the ring, without anything to defend himself against the rage of an animal gone berserk.

The men in the stands froze in horror.

Jeremiah crouched and braced himself for the terrible, bone-crushing savagery of the bull's impact.

Chapter Seven

Jeremiah heard the men shouting as the bull charged straight toward him. The sound of voices seemed to come from far away, then moved inside him until it was in his brain and filled his ears like a resounding thunderclap. The bull loomed large as it fixed him with murderous eyes and lowered its head with the dangerous horns aimed at his groin. It seemed to Jeremiah that his own feet were mired in thick mud or clutching quicksand, that his knees were locked and frozen. But this illusion lasted for only a split second. He moved, jumping to his left and dancing just out of reach of the horns.

The bull swerved to follow him and Jeremiah stumbled, pitched headlong into the dirt.

The bull lowered its head still more, snorted, and seemed to come down on him like a falling mountain. Jeremiah doubled up, drew his legs up tight against his belly, knowing he could not roll away, that the bull was going to gore him. There was no time to think, and he could not see anything but the bull's head and its ugly horns. He kicked out then, with both feet and felt a horn ram into his calf. He rolled as his feet struck the bull's chest and leg and the horn slid along his leg like a hard bone. He heard the sound of ripping cloth, felt a hoof dig into his back. He lurched, sprawled facedown in the dust as the bull stormed past him.

He looked up to see the Mexican boy stagger into the bull's path, blood pouring from a wound in his groin. Umberto snatched up the fallen *muleta* and shook it until the bull charged into it, snatched it from his grasp. Jeremiah struggled to his feet, groggy, the pain throbbing in his leg like an enormous pulsebeat. The horn had not punctured his skin, but the bruising went deep.

The bull, its vision blocked by the cloth over its eyes, charged blindly past the Mexican boy and shook its head as it turned to find the enemy once again. Jeremiah saw the cloth sail away as the bull wrenched its neck and tossed its head to free the horns from the alien material. The bull saw him, snorted, and raced toward him at high speed.

"Get the American out of the ring," someone shouted from the tiered seats.

Jeremiah dodged away from the charging bull, ran to the fence rail. The bull stiffened its legs and skidded to a halt. Umberto, weak from the loss of blood, toppled over, gushing blood into the dirt of the arena. The bull saw this movement and altered its path of charge. Umberto looked up in horror, gasped a cry filled with fear.

"Hoouh!" yelled Jeremiah and ran at an angle to head off the bull. He did not think of his own danger, but only of the Mexican boy's predicament. The American lowered his shoulder and bowled headlong into the bull. The bull, rocked off its course, swung sideways and Jeremiah reached out blindly, grabbed its hind legs. He tightened his grasp and the bull went down.

The bull struggled, dragging the youth across the arena as the men in the bleachers swarmed down the tiers and boiled over into the ring. The picadors backed their horses away to keep from trampling the American. The bull bawled forlornly, but Jeremiah hung on, determined to wear the surly beast down to manageable size.

At that moment, the women came down from the house, drawn there by the odd tone of the shouting. Estrellita, in the vanguard, led the procession, followed by her mother, Lucia, and the wives of the male guests. They saw the clot of men in the bullring and little else, but they heard the men's curses and the awful bawling of the bull.

As the women stood there, twirling their parasols and fanning their faces, the men jostled for position and their combined weight knocked down one row of corral posts. The bull, seeing an opening, charged on two front feet, freed a third and kicked Jeremiah's shoulder. Jeremiah twisted until he heard the fourth leg snap. The bull turned on him then, horns raking a three-foot arc that caught two men at the shins and dumped them like sacks of meal.

Augustino dashed between two men and dove at the bull's head. He lashed out with both hands and grabbed the animal's horns. The veins on his hands bulged under the strain and the muscles in his wrists tautened as he pulled backward, bending the animal's neck. Cords stood out on the soldier's neck as the bull struggled to free itself and gore the nearest human.

The Spaniard dug in his heels and hauled the bull over on its side. Jeremiah released his grip and jumped to his feet. He grabbed one of the horns, helped Augustino pull the head down until the bull collapsed, sprawled awkwardly on the ground under the weight of the two men. Its tongue lolled and its chest rose and fell as it fought to draw breath into tortured lungs.

"Good work," said Jeremiah.

"*Sí, está bien,*" grunted Armijo. The picador dismounted and other workers came and sat on the bull. Jeremiah and Augustino faced each other. The American's face was streaked with dirt and sweat; Armijo looked barely ruffled from the brief exertion.

"Come," said Don Miguel, stepping in close to the two men, "let's all go inside the hacienda and have a drink. We must forget this little broken *corrida*, and join the women. Augustino Armijo, may I present the brave American, Jeremiah, ah . . . York, I believe."

"York, it is," said Jeremiah, grinning, holding out his hand

115

to the New Mexican soldier.

"Ah, you are the young man who sold the horse to Don Miguel," said Augustino, frowning. "I thought you had a broken head."

Jeremiah laughed.

"No, there's just a lump on it, kinda sore is all."

Augustino's eyes narrowed as he looked the youth up and down. He did not see much competition there. In fact, he suppressed a laugh as he drew himself up straight and brushed off his uniform. This was a mere boy, dressed in sullied finery, *por seguro,* but obviously poor with his uncut and unkempt hair and loutish bearing. No competition at all, he mused.

"Good. Let us take a drink together then, when you have washed your face and brushed your clothes," said the New Mexican in a thick Spanish accent.

Jeremiah was not so sure he liked Augustino Armijo, but the man had come along at a bad time and taken the proverbial bull by the horns. That would make a good story to tell the mountain men when he saw them again in St. Louis. And he fully intended to pursue his mission with Lalande and secure the funds owed his sponsor back in Illinois.

The women scurried back to the house, out of the heat, but Estrellita lingered, looking over her shoulder at her father, Augustino, and Jeremiah, all walking together, with Merito a few paces behind them. She averted her gaze as her mother tugged at her arm and looked back no more. She was dismayed at Jeremiah's disheveled appearance. The clothes she had bought him appeared ruined and there was nothing she could do about it. But her curiosity was piqued that the two rivals were walking side by side as though they intended to become friends.

Later, after Jeremiah had brushed most of the dirt from his new clothing, he walked down the stairs, looked in rapt wonder at the throng of people streaming in and out of the rooms, many of them carrying drinks in fancy glasses. The sounds of Mexican or Spanish music—he did not know exactly what to make of the tinny horns, the screeching violins and thrumming guitars—wafted through from the courtyard patio, and he heard the buzzing sound of Spanish conversation and the lilt of unrestrained laughter on the afternoon air.

He walked, favoring his sore calf, toward the sound of the music, threading his way through the crowd, but not feeling a part of them, conscious of their questioning stares, the odd looks on their faces. Sweat gathered under his collar, dampened his armpits, soaked through the back of his shirt. He looked for Estrellita, Don Miguel, but he did not see them. He had gotten most of the dirt off his clothing, and luckily he had not bled, but he was aware that the garments were no longer immaculate and were wrinkled, tinged with dust from the bullring.

He reached the patio, saw a bewildering throng of people, some dressed formally, others in less costly clothing, but all of them laughing and smiling, obviously at home with one another. They spoke in Spanish or in heavily accented English, and he heard also the flat twang of the East and the warped and exaggerated vowels of French-speaking residents wrestling with his own native tongue. He saw fair faces in the crowd, too, and took hope that he was not the only stranger there, but the men looked like merchants or bankers and the women like society folk in their fine gowns, their elaborate dresses.

A young American boy came up to Jeremiah, seemingly from nowhere.

"Hullo," he said. "You lookin' for Estrellita and the others?"

"I reckon."

The boy was no more than fourteen, with thick curly hair the color of dark coffee. He wore a white muslin shirt and gray trousers, polished black shoes.

"Come on with me. My name is Benny White. I'm almost fifteen. What's your name?"

117

"Jeremiah York. Do you know Estrellita?"

"Nope. My folks just brought me here for her birthday party. I talked to her, though. She's pretty. I heard you fought with a bull. You must be brave."

"Where are we going?" Jeremiah asked as they walked away from the patio, went under a vine-covered arch and followed a flagstone path around the house.

"They got a big table set up under the trees out back. A swing and everything. You hungry? They got lots of good food and some peach punch in a big old bowl."

Jeremiah was hungry, but his stomach was quivering so he didn't think he could eat anything. The sound of the music faded but he could still hear the buzz of conversation, snatches of foreign words. The White boy walked fast and Jeremiah had to lengthen his stride to keep up with him. Sore muscles tugged like hard fingers digging into his calf.

He saw the trees then, a grove of oaks and elders, a long table set beneath them, and ropes hanging from one of the elders. The ropes were quivering and whatever they were holding was hidden by a group of young people standing around it in a tight circle.

Jeremiah and Benny reached the edge of the circle, crowded into the pack. Estrellita sat in a swing, surrounded by young men and women. She sat there alone, regally, smiling and laughing, her feet dangling just above the ground. Jeremiah thought she looked beautiful. There were other girls there, but none of them had her beauty. He forgot all about the pain in his leg.

"Hello," she said to him, and his heart turned to melting wax. "This is Jeremiah York, everyone, who brought me my best birthday gift . . ."

Everyone turned to look at him and his face reddened. He saw the dark eyes of Augustino boring into his, and then his gaze shifted to the soldier standing next to the New Mexican, Merito, and he saw a flash of hostility in the man's piercing glance.

118

Estrellita laughed and leaped from the swing. "Of course I did not tell you what Jeremiah brought me. Can anyone guess?"

"A pretty parasol," said one girl.

"A doll," said another, much younger than the others.

"A necklace," said a young man.

Estrellita laughed and shook her head.

"No, no, no," she said. "He brought me a beautiful horse and I'm going to ride it everywhere."

"A horse! That's fine, fine," chorused some of the boys. The girls oohed and aahed, but they sounded disappointed.

Boys slapped Jeremiah on the back and the girls looked at him shyly and smiled as they fluttered their eyelashes. The group moved to the table and began dipping into the punch bowl, grabbing chunks of food and putting them onto baked clay plates.

Estrellita led the pack, but she only poured herself some punch and nibbled at a black olive. She poured a cup for Jeremiah, handed it to him, then took his other hand. She pulled him away from the table, walked to a nearby oak, stood under its shade.

She sipped at the punch, looked over the rim at Jeremiah through long eyelashes. Beyond, at the table, Augustino looked longingly in their direction, but he and Merito were surrounded by young ladies anxious to hear stories of Santa Fe and Indians. They seemed enthralled with the handsome young uniformed soldiers and encircled them so that they could not leave without appearing rude.

"I'm glad you're here," said Estrellita softly.

"Me, too. It's a nice party."

"Oh, it's fun, but I don't know anyone here really well. Just you."

"Me?"

"Yes, you. And I heard my father talk about how foolish you were today. You could have been killed."

"Well, that Mexican boy got into a little trouble. I just tried

119

to help him out."

"I know," she crooned, "you were very brave."

Jeremiah cleared his throat, drank a swallow of punch from his cup. The punch tasted sweet and he could smell the peaches in it.

"Who is that Mexican soldier?" he blurted. "He keeps looking at you like you was chattel. His chattel."

"You know who he is."

"I reckon I know his name, is all."

"My parents want me to marry him," she said solemnly.

"Want you to?"

She looked away from him, a wistful look in her eyes.

"I am to marry him," she said so quiet he could scarce hear her.

"What? You want to marry him?"

"I . . . I didn't say that, Jeremiah."

"What did you say, then?"

There was the beginning of an anger in him, but there was something else, too. A big pit was opening in his gut, a hollow place where disappointment gnawed like some savage predatory animal. The emotions he felt fought down there on the edge of the pit, where the sand was loose, beasts without shape or form.

"Jeremiah, let us not talk of this now. This is my . . . my birthday and I want us to be happy. You and me. Both of us."

"Well, I don't like the idear of you a-marryin' some soldier. That one ain't for you, Estrellita. What you wanta marry him for?"

"Because. Because this is something that is the custom among our people. I know you do not understand. I have heard that your customs are different."

"I reckon. So, are you sayin' that this feller and you got to marry up with one another?"

"My father and Augustino's father made an agreement a long time ago, when I was a little girl and Augustino a boy."

"I never heard tell of such a thing, 'cept maybe with

120

matchmakers and such and that only with spinsters that nobody wanted to marry."

She had trouble following his speech because it was nothing like the refined English she had learned from her private tutor in Santa Fe. He spoke in a vernacular strange to her, exasperating. She had heard enough English to know that Jeremiah was no silver-tongued orator, but she believed he could learn, as she had learned.

"Well," she said, "it's nothing like that. When two families wish to strengthen their ties to one another, they arrange for their children to marry. This is a good thing."

"Haw!" he exclaimed. "Good for who? You know this feller Augustino pretty good?"

"No, not very well. He comes from a good family."

"Heck, I come from a good family, too."

"I know you do, Jeremiah. Please, let us not talk of this anymore. It is upsetting to both of us."

"What if I was to get rich and come to Santa Fe and, uh . . . well, what if I was to do that and then ask you to marry up with me?"

"What are you talking about? You must not say such things."

"Why not? I just might come riding up one day, with my pockets full of gold and take you off to the preacher."

"No, no, no, Jeremiah. This could not be done. We are of the Roman Catholic faith and we live like civilized people. Besides, my father would probably shoot you. Augustino might shoot both of us."

"I am not afraid of either of them," he said.

"Shush, now. You do not understand these things. But there is something I wanted to talk to you about. To give you."

"Me? You've already given me these clothes. Sorry I messed 'em up some." He paused, drew a breath. "And I don't even have a gift for you."

"You look very nice and you are nice, but you must guard your tongue lest someone overhear you. I am promised to

121

Augustino Armijo and that is that."

He opened his mouth to protest, but she put a finger over his lips and shook her head. He wanted to take her into his arms at that moment, but he saw Augustino and Merito Salcedo out of the corner of his eye. They were walking toward them.

Estrellita saw them, too.

"Hush now," she said, "and listen. I want you to meet me out back in a little while. When I give you a sign. I will open and close my fan very quickly, and when you see me do this, you must leave and go out back and stand under the balcony."

"Will you be there?" he asked as she drew her finger away from his lips.

"Yes," she whispered.

The two soldiers swaggered up to Estrellita and Jeremiah. Augustino looked at her accusingly and Merito glared at the American.

"Estrellita," said Augustino smoothly, "you have been away from us too long. Your guests are impatient."

"It is you who is impatient," said Estrellita saucily.

"You should not be talking with this clumsy oaf so much," said Augustino in rapid Spanish. "He is a fool."

"Please do not be rude," she told him in Spanish. "Speak in English and do not order me around like a servant."

Stung, Augustino backed away, his face drawn. He quelled his anger, faced Jeremiah.

"I was saying," he said in English, "that we should go into the big house and do some dancing."

Quickly, before Estrellita could protest, Augustino took her arm in his and marched away toward the patio. Jeremiah started to lunge after him, but Salcedo blocked his way.

"Do not interfere," Merito said softly. "Come with me and we'll both find pretty girls to dance with."

"I don't want to dance with anyone but Estrellita," said Jeremiah defiantly, but his heart was heavy as he saw her and Augustino reach the patio and join the other dancers. The young people flocked after them, running across the greensward like a gaggle of geese.

"Isn't the music pretty?" asked Merito, leering at Jeremiah with a grin.

"Just go on," said Jeremiah. "Just go on and leave me alone."

Merito shrugged and strutted away, squaring his shoulders and pooching out his buttocks.

"Pompous ass," Jeremiah muttered. The truth was that he did not know how to dance and the music's tempo had picked up so that the dancers swirled around the patio, bobbing and swaying like riders on a carousel.

He stood at the edge of the crowd, alone, until the dancers blurred and the music turned dull and tinny in his ears. His thoughts drifted back to his homeland, to his parents and the simple life they led. All of this was alien to him: the music, the people, the dancing, the talk. His father did not play a musical instrument, nor did his mother. Once he had seen a fiddler in the town square and he had heard an old sailor play ditties on an instrument he squeezed between his hands.

Jeremiah walked away, suddenly homesick. This was not what he had come west for, and he wondered why he had made such a fool of himself over a girl who lived so differently. Estrellita did not care about him. She was curious about him and probably laughed behind his back. He stopped and turned, thought he heard her laughter above the sound of the music and the noise of the dancers.

He walked around the corner of the big house and looked across the big lumpy field. Far off he heard the hooting of the boats on the big river, and the sun made green light in the trees and the trees made shadows across the sward that stretched long and thin. He stood in the shadow of the house, facing west, and saw the sky change subtly as the sun fell farther down toward the horizon. He imagined that the days would be longer in the high mountains. That was where he wanted to go, into the wilderness. He wished that he was riding toward the sunset, traveling with the mountain men he had met in town, carrying a good rifle and riding a good horse.

The sadness gripped him then, and he wanted to run away, to just keep running away from this place and forget all about her and her soldier, her husband-to-be.

But he stood rooted there, pulled by something stronger than his will.

And the homesickness rolled over him again and gripped him tight.

He would not be beaten, he vowed. He would not give up. He wanted Estrellita. He wanted to hold her in his arms again and kiss her and have her kiss him back until neither of them could stand it any longer.

He wanted this woman, wanted her more than anything else in the world.

"Someday," he said softly, "I will have her for my own."

Don Miguel followed Pedro Vial to the study where the others were waiting. Both men carried wineglasses filled with Spanish sherry.

"Gentlemen," said Don Miguel as he entered the room. "Please have some sherry."

The three men rose from leather chairs, held their full glasses high.

"We have already been served," said Auguste Pierre Chouteau, Pierre's son. "We thank you for your hospitality."

"Please be seated," said Vial, taking a chair for himself. The room was well lit with finely crafted oil lamps, and dark wood gleamed under the glow. Books filled the bookcases and the walls were studded with the heads of game animals mounted on wooden shields. Spanish rifles and swords hung on wood and brass mounts. This was a man's room and it was large and comfortable.

"Did your father send you?" asked Don Miguel, taking the chair behind the large oaken desk with its globe of the world on one edge. He toyed with a small brass telescope that lay atop the leather mat that protected the polished wood.

"No," said Auguste, "but he knows I am here. You know my brother, Cadet," he said, pointing to his left. "This man is his partner, Bartholomew Berthold."

Berthold did not rise, but nodded soberly. He was a swarthy-complexioned young man, with an ascetic, scholarly mien accentuated by the delicate pince-nez that straddled his aquiline nose. His eyes were so close-set they almost appeared to cross, but this was only an illusion made more emphatic by the intensity of his gaze. He looked to be, and was, a serious man, with big plans.

"It is a pleasure," said Don Miguel. "We have heard you have been talking with Astor."

"That is so," said Berthold. "But . . ."

"I know," said Don Miguel, holding up his hands in an expansive gesture of admission to something unpleasant. "You, too, wish that the tariff for the furs and goods was not so high."

"More than that," said Bartholomew, "we feel that the Santa Fe Trail is most vital to our trade. Auguste has agreed to work with you on Armijo. We can't fight Sublette and Wyeth and Campbell and buy out Astor if we don't have that trade route opened, free of excessive tax."

"What will you do, Auguste?" asked Don Miguel.

"I will tell Armijo that if he does not cooperate he will find Santa Fe cut off by all American trade. He is killing the goose that lays the golden egg, has been ever since he was governor. He is corrupt and his minions are tyrants."

"True," said Vial.

"He is worried about the forts," said Don Miguel. "I think he is afraid the Americans will take everything away from him. So am I."

"We are prepared to offer him bonuses," said Cadet.

"Bribes, you mean," said Don Miguel.

Everyone laughed.

"I will show him how easily money can slip through his

fingers," said Auguste. "My brother is prepared to finance Lalande's brigade, have them pass through Santa Fe with their plews, and not sell them there for nine dollars a pound."

"Ahh," breathed Don Miguel. "You will make more money that way."

"Yes, but it will be more costly in the long view," said the practical Berthold. "For us and for the New Mexicans."

Don Miguel saw the clarity of this ploy. Political conditions were still unsettled in Santa Fe. Manuel Armijo understood that he held the upper hand for now. The General Government left him alone, gave no aid, and he could plunder freely from the caravans coming and going through his territory. Yet he had reservations, not about the Chouteaus, but about Baptiste Lalande.

"Do you trust this Lalande?" he asked bluntly.

"He knows his trade," said Auguste. "He is smart. But, no, I do not trust him much. But, that young man who got into the fight . . . What is his name?"

"York," said Don Miguel tightly. "Jeremiah York." He pronounced it "Yeremiah Jork."

"Yes, that one. He will prove useful, I think, if he joins the brigade. He seems determined to see that Baptiste pays off his father's debt to an eastern businessman."

"He is but a boy," said Don Miguel.

"But he has eyes and ears."

"You will use him as a spy?"

"Maybe. It is important that Lalande make a good showing in Santa Fe, that he bring many plews to show Armijo. And, he must be prepared to fight and to carry his furs to St. Louis unless Armijo removes the high tariffs on all goods."

"You will talk to York, then?"

"I will talk to him. But, there is something else we must discuss."

"*Por seguro*," said Don Miguel. "Of course."

"It is you we are most worried about."

"Me?"

126

"Yes. It is my understanding that your daughter is to marry an Armijo."

"Yes, but I bear no strong love for Manuel Armijo, even so. He is a tyrant. He is, as you say, a thorn in my side, and if we do not open the Santa Fe Trail, keep it free of savages and brigands and high tariffs, then Santa Fe will wither and die."

"Good, that is all we wanted to hear," said Auguste. "Let us work together then, to bring profit back to trading between our two countries."

The men all stood up and shook hands, then finished their sherries.

"Now," said Auguste, "I would meet this York and have a talk with him. It is my understanding that he is here, no?"

"He is here," Don Miguel frowned. "But I have not seen him since this afternoon. Come, enjoy some food and drink. I will try and find the boy."

Auguste looked at his brother, Cadet, and at Berthold, made a Gallic moue in satisfaction.

The night made him feel better. The long shadows had finally lumped together and the sunlight faded from the sky, leaving the land soft in darkness. It was cool when he went to the table and ate some of the delicacies. He drank more punch, and when he saw a pair of young people come toward him, he stole away, circled the house again, looked at it from a distance. A lamp was lighted in an upstairs room and he saw a shadow move behind the amber pane. Then the lamp was extinguished and the darkness thickened behind the house once again.

Strains of music and bursts of laughter floated on the night air, strangely disembodied. Jeremiah began to pace by the back porch, looked around in the darkness, listened for a footfall.

Estrellita had said she would come. Where was she?

Chapter Eight

"Pssst. Jeremiah."

Jeremiah turned, startled.

"Estrellita?"

"Yes," she whispered. "Over here."

He saw her then, a few yards away, standing in the shadows. He had not heard her come up and wondered how she had managed to do that. She was like an Indian, he thought. He walked toward her, puzzled that she had sneaked up on him so easily.

"Where have you been?" she asked, as he drew near. "I have been looking for you. And now my father is looking for you."

"Your father? Why?"

"I don't know. But I must hurry. I think Augustino saw me go upstairs. He may have seen me go out the side door. And Lucia, she is like a hawk. Her eyes are everywhere."

He started to laugh, but she put a finger to his lips. He saw, then, that she carried something tucked under her arms.

"Why does it matter what this Augustino does? He don't own you."

"No. Nobody owns me. It's just that—well, he takes certain things for granted."

"Like what?"

"Oh, Jeremiah . . . don't make so much of it."

"Well, I hate to sneak around in the dark. I don't like playing hidey-seek with that—that toy soldier."

"But you stayed away from the fiesta. I kept looking for you."

"You did?"

She touched his arm, then handed him the packet she carried.

"What is it?" he asked.

"Open it."

The package was wrapped in oilcloth, shiny, smooth to his touch. He unfolded it carefully. A pair of books fell into his hands.

"Huh? Books?" A tone of suspicion crept into his voice. "What's in 'em?"

Estrellita laughed.

"Words," she said. "Language. I thought you might enjoy reading them."

"I, uh, don't read too good."

"But you do read, do you not?"

"Some, I reckon. But books. These are . . . are heavy and probably got a lot of words in 'em I likely wouldn't know.'

"That's why you read books," she said. "Partly. It will help you with your speech."

"I don't give no speeches."

"The way you talk, silly." Estrellita sounded apprehensive.

"What's wrong with the way I talk?" He bristled as he said it.

"Nothing, really," she said quickly, "but . . . but you could learn much from reading. And listening to good English."

"I listened to good English all my life."

Estrellita suppressed the urge to laugh. Her gift, she realized, was doing more harm than good.

"Jeremiah, please don't take this wrong. I thought you might like to improve yourself while you're out there in the wilderness with those rough, crude men. It would give us something to talk about when you return—when you come to Santa Fe."

"I don't know where my feet will take me. Packin' books, well, I might not have time to read 'em."

"You must come to Santa-Fe, Jeremiah. There will be much to see and do there. You must come."

"Well," he said, mollified, "I reckon I could come there, all right."

"Good. I hope you like the books."

"What are they about?"

"They're written by a very good American writer. Washington Irving. They're very exciting. One is *The Conquest of Granada*, the other, *The Alhambra*."

"Where's Granada?" he asked. "And what's this Alhambra?"

"Granada is in Spain. And the Alhambra, too. That one is all about the Moors and the Spaniards."

"Your people?"

She laughed then. "Maybe."

He hefted the books in his hands.

"Lordy, it would take me the rest of my life to read these," he said.

"Perhaps I can help you—someday. But, let's go back before Lucia comes looking for me. I want you to dance with me." She took his hand and dragged him around the side of the house and back to the patio. She took the books from his arms and set them by a table. The small band of musicians started playing a lively tune and dancers flooded the patio. Estrellita grasped Jeremiah's hands and began the steps to the fandango.

"Just watch me," she whispered, "and follow me. Lift your feet, that's it."

She swirled to the music and he followed her, caught up in her beauty and the graceful way she moved in time to the music. He stumbled, but she twisted his arms, brought him back upright. He faltered, but she whirled him with her so that he felt lightfooted and lightheaded. Soon, he found it less awkward to follow her lead.

131

They bumped into other dancers and he saw Estrellita smile warmly and glide away, taking him with her. He drew her close and she slid backward, away from him, pulling him after, but keeping him at his distance. He looked at her tiny waist and saw her shoes tapping out the rhythm, felt the rhythm come into him and sweep him up, carry him away from his self-consciousness.

It was like riding a wild horse, racing in the wind. The music came into him and moved his feet, his body. Estrellita was light as goosedown, an enchanting, lovely creature who seemed to be so attuned to the music that she was part of it. She smiled at him and he danced after her, chased her across the patio as if she was some wild creature taunting him, staying just out of reach, but ever so close.

"See?" she said. "You're a natural-born dancer."

"I don't know," he said. "It seems easy, but I don't know what I'm doing."

"Just follow the music," she said. "Let your feet be light, as if you were walking on pillows."

He laughed then, and swirled her around without losing his balance.

People applauded them as the music came to an end. Estrellita bowed in mock solemnity, while Jeremiah just stood there, dumbfounded, the rapture gone, lost in the dying notes of the trumpet and the guitar. He looked at Estrellita, then at the people ringing the patio. Don Miguel stood there, his face expressionless, and Corazon, rapt and smiling wanly. The dark-faced Lucia stood behind them, scowling. Nearby, the two soldiers stood stiff as sentries, watching him with cloudy eyes, tight-lipped and stern as schoolmasters. Jeremiah flashed a smile of triumph at Augustino.

"Come," said Estrellita gaily, "let's drink some punch. Are you hungry? Did you eat?"

Jeremiah shook his head, stumbled after her as the music started up again, the band playing a light American air slightly off-key.

Before he reached the punch table, Don Miguel stepped toward him, blocking his way.

"Mr. York," he said, "there is someone who would talk with you."

Estrellita stopped, turned around to look at her father and Jeremiah.

"Me? Who?"

"Come with me," he said. "Estrellita, your mother wishes to speak to you."

"Yes, Father," she said, biting her underlip. "Hurry, Jeremiah. I'll be waiting for you."

Jeremiah felt himself being pushed along by Don Miguel, gently but firmly, and they soon passed through the foyer and into the living room. A man rose from the divan, stalked across the floor, his hand outstretched.

"This is Jeremiah York," said Don Miguel. "I will leave you two alone."

"Thank you, Don Miguel."

The older man closed the doors to the room. Jeremiah felt his hand bob up and down in the grip of the Frenchman.

"I am Auguste Chouteau. I saw you put up a pretty good fight at the hotel today. I hear you did not do so well against the bull, eh?"

"I didn't do too good at neither," said Jeremiah. He had heard the name Chouteau. That was about all one heard in St. Louis. But he would have expected a much older man, a man who appeared to be wealthy, wearing fine clothes and perhaps a silk or beaver top hat. Instead, this was a very ordinary young man who wore a suit that did not look particularly costly. His boots were dusty, and his coat slightly wrinkled.

"Would you like some sherry?" asked Chouteau, waving Jeremiah to a high-backed chair.

"No, I better stay away from that stuff."

Auguste laughed, sat back on the divan. He looked at Jeremiah closely, fished a cigar from his inside coat pocket. He offered one to York, but Jeremiah shook his head.

133

Chouteau bit off one end of the cigar, raised the chimney on the lamp next to the divan, and leaned close to the flame. He drew on the cigar until it caught, and sat back, lowered the glass chimney, blew thick plumes of bluish smoke into the air.

"You do not like all these people here, *non?*"

"I don't know 'em," said Jeremiah.

"But you like the girl, eh?"

"I like Estrellita. A whole lot." Jeremiah squirmed in his chair. He did not like talking about Estrellita with a man he did not know, but he sensed that this man was important, that he was only beating a stick around the bush hoping to flush something out before he got to the point.

"Don Miguel, he says you are one who is like the mule. One who goes his own way. Stubborn."

"He don't really know me."

"Well, Jeremiah, you and I, maybe," said Chouteau, his accent thick with Gallic overtones, "we are much alike. I do not like being in a room with a lot of people. I feel like the chicken in the coop. No, I feel like the eagle in the chicken coop. I listen to them squawking and I want to fly away, high in the sky."

Jeremiah laughed. He looked at the older man more closely now. Auguste was saying things that he himself felt inside, but could not express.

"I reckon I feel that way sometimes," said York. "I wish I could just take Estrellita and ride away and marry up with her."

Auguste laughed heartily, drew on his cigar, let the smoke out until it obscured his face. He let the smoke waft away, then began speaking again, gesticulating with the cigar.

"Ah, but maybe you jump too quick, my hot-blooded friend. If you marry now, you miss the adventure."

"The adventure?"

"*Mais, oui*, the adventure of youth, the good years when one can sow the wild seed, enjoy the grand company of men, explore the wilderness. Ah, but you have not been to the

134

frontier, to the great land with the shining rivers and the big mountains."

"Have you been there?" Jeremiah's eyes widened and his mouth opened in wonder.

"Ah, many times. I go back there again, soon. Very soon, I think. Maybe you will go, too, to catch the beaver, the mink, the marten, the lynx. You would like that, no?"

"I'm a-goin', I reckon. I got business."

"With Baptiste Lalande?"

"Him, yes."

"Good. That is good. But this Baptiste, he does not want to take you, I think. He makes up the brigade, but he likes only the experienced trapper, the good hunter."

"I can hunt, and I can learn to trap," Jeremiah said stubbornly. "I trapped muskrat, back home."

"That is good, very good, my friend. But I tell you this, and maybe you want to work for me, too. This Lalande, he work for me. If I say you go with him, you go with him, is it not?"

"Really?"

"Yes. If I say he take you, he take you."

"What do I have to do?" Jeremiah's questioning words softened with the faint quaver of suspicion.

"You will be my eyes, and my ears, Monsieur York. I cannot go with the brigade, but I go to Santa Fe for the business. You understand?"

"I reckon I do."

"This Lalande, he is the son of the man who cheated the merchant who sent you here."

"He is?"

"Yes, Baptiste's father worked for me after the war, and he cheated me, too. He was named Baptiste, too. His son has paid me back and he will pay your merchant back, too."

"He will?"

"If you want to work for me and make sure that Baptiste does not cheat me."

"I do," said Jeremiah, beaming. "Oh, I surely do."

"You will work hard. You will carry the traps and make the lead ball, keep the powder from getting wet, and you will clean the rifle and sharpen the knife."

"I don't care. I want to go." Jeremiah's heart soared to think about it. He had thought of little else for months. He would be going to the wilderness with real trappers, with the mountain men. He would see all the things he had dreamed about. He would have an adventure.

"Then, you will go," said Auguste Pierre. "You come to see my brother Cadet in the morning. He will give you a rifle, pistol, knife, powder, ball, flint, things you will need."

"But . . . I don't have much money."

Auguste waved his cigar.

"I will charge you for these things out of your pay. You will need them when you go with Baptiste."

Jeremiah's heart seemed to stop beating. He looked at the Frenchman, dazed by his offer. He sat there, stunned, his mind full of tangled visions of wide rivers and cursing mountain men and fat beavers in spring-swollen streams, swimming sleek in the curl of backwashed waters, diving to open traps. He had listened to the stories back in Illinois and he had dreamed of going to the mountains with men such as Baptiste Lalande.

"You come to Front Street, to the river, walk up Laurel, and you will find my office. I will be busy elsewhere, but you ask for my brother, Cadet. Be there soon after the sun is up, eh?"

"Y-yes," stammered Jeremiah. "I can find it. I'll be there."

Auguste stood up.

"Good. You had better leave here tonight. I will talk to Baptiste before I go to sleep. Do we shake the hand?"

Jeremiah lurched to his feet. He stuck out his hand. The older man took it, gripped it strong, and moved their hands up and down in affirmation of their agreement.

"Ah, Jeremiah, you must not tell Baptiste or any of the men that we have this contract between us, no? It will be our secret. I will tell Baptiste that I met you and that he should take you on as a helper. But you must act as the dumb one, and when you take count of the plews, you must not write things down, but keep them in the head."

Jeremiah nodded. He did not want to tell Auguste that he could do little more than write his name and make crude letters with a pen.

"I won't," said Jeremiah. "I mean I will. And won't."

Auguste laughed then, and Jeremiah laughed with him. The two walked to the doors and Auguste opened them, let Jeremiah pass through first.

"*Bon soir*, Jeremiah. Good night."

"Goo' night."

He watched the Frenchman stride across the foyer toward the stairs. He climbed them and did not look back.

Why, thought Jeremiah, he must be nigh fifty and walks straight as an Indian.

He was so excited, he just stood there, bewildered, wondering what to do next. He wanted to find Estrellita and tell her the good news, but he thought about that for a moment and realized that he could not say too much for fear of it getting back to Lalande. But he would have to tell her that he was leaving, that he would not see her for a long time.

He turned from the rising column of stairs, headed toward the patio once again. Above, he heard a hearty laugh that sounded familiar, then a door slammed and the sound shut off abruptly.

"I wish to speak to the señorita," said Augustino. "Away from all these people."

Lucia's expression did not change. She gripped the handle of her fan tightly to hold down the fluttering of her heart. A few feet away, Estrellita stood alone, staring at the dancers, seemingly unaware of Augustino's request, but Lucia could read the signs better than most *dueñas*. At last she had the opportunity to manage an important part of the life of her charge, to set the rules and maintain protocol in matters of the

137

heart and libido.

The *dueña* looked sharply at the young man in the thrilling army uniform, at the golden piping, the gleaming brass buttons, the polished boots. Then she looked sternly into Augustino's eyes as if seeking honesty and decency in them, as if reading a history of his life and soul. Augustino did not cringe under the scathing rake of her scrutiny, and she liked that. Surely, here was a fine young man with a bright political future. Surely, here was breeding stock of high quality. And here, too, was a man of destiny, a man that Don Miguel himself, and Corazon, as well, approved of, and, for that matter, had chosen as the one they most wished to be the husband of their only daughter.

"What are your intentions?" she asked, not unkindly.

"I wish to give her compliments away from prying ears," Augustino said boldly. "I wish to look into her eyes without seeing the reflections of others who are about. My intentions are most honorable."

Lucia's heart skipped a beat, and she quelled the impulse to show the slightest trace of emotion. She must, she knew, establish her authority at the outset and figuratively grasp the young man's ear between thumb and forefinger as if he was a schoolboy under the headmistress's disciplinary control.

"There is a parlor where you may speak to the young lady, under my strict supervision, of course."

"Of course," said Augustino.

"Go there now," she said. "The young lady and I will come there soon."

"Thank you, most gracious woman," said Augustino. His eyes narrowed as he arched his eyebrows in conspiratorial agreement. A faint smile flickered on his lips.

Augustino clicked his heels together and strode across the patio toward the wide doorway, passed through it with straight backbone, head held high. Merito, who was coming down the hall toward him, stopped in his tracks.

"I have just spoken to a man in Lalande's brigade," he said.

"You will not have to worry about that young American anymore."

"Oh?"

"I gave this man money, promised him more if the boy does not return. As you asked me to, 'Tino."

"Good. We will talk later. I am meeting Estrellita in a few moments."

Merito winked at him and suppressed a knowing smile. It had been so easily arranged. The boy thought he was working for the Chouteaus and he would feel important. But he would not last the season. There was one going with Lalande who would welcome his gold and silver to assure that York did not ever come out of the mountains alive.

Lucia waited until she saw that Estrellita was about to explode with curiosity, then crossed the few paces between her and Estrellita with remarkable rapidity, a large, swooping bird in a black dress, her mantilla perched on her head like a crown.

"Quickly, Estrellita," Lucia whispered. "Your betrothed wishes to speak to you. Come."

"Who?"

"Why, Augustino Armijo, of course. Come, child, already he awaits us in the parlor."

Estrellita looked around the patio, searching for a glimpse of Jeremiah, but he was not there. Lucia grabbed her wrist firmly, pulled her toward the doorway. Estrellita shook off the grip, rubbed her wrist.

"That hurt," she pouted.

"Don't dawdle then," said Lucia.

The two women crossed the patio. Merito, entering at that moment, looked at Estrellita, smiled thinly. She avoided his gaze, perturbed that she was being forced to meet Augustino. Still pouting, she followed Lucia through the doorway to the study.

Augustino stood near a love seat, smiling. Lucia fell behind, nudged Estrellita toward the soldier. The girl walked slowly in his direction.

"You wanted to see me?" she asked.

"Yes, very much. Will you take a seat by me?"

"It is all right."

She sat down primly. Augustino sat beside her. Lucia took a chair some distance away where she could pretend not to see and hear, but she sat rigidly, her ears and eyes attuned keenly to the couple under her guardianship.

"You are beautiful tonight," said Augustino softly. "You will make a fine wife."

"For you?" she taunted.

"Well, of course for me. I will make you a good husband, too. I will make you proud."

"And give me babies, too, I suppose."

"Of course. That is the reason for marriage."

"Is it?" she snapped. "What about love, and affection?"

Taken aback, Augustino twisted in the chair, looked at her in slight bewilderment.

"Already you have the sharp tongue," he said. "Maybe you will need some spanking."

"No man will ever do that to me."

He laughed quietly, slid closer to her. "I like a woman with fire," he whispered. "I like a little resistance, as well."

"You will find fire, and more resistance than you bargain for. I do not know you and already you speak of marriage and babies."

"Is that not why we are here?" he said, slightly disconcerted. Augustino had known women before, the young girls of Santa Fe who admired him from a distance and who brought him his cup in the taverns. To some he had given coin and to others he had given only sweet words, *piropos*, the smooth, empty compliments a young man gives a young maiden when he wishes to take more than kisses from her. He had filled their ears with what they wanted to hear and toyed with their tresses, touched their hands, and brushed wicked fingers down their thighs. He had learned the little tricks that made the young ladies of the pueblo melt like candlewax until they

140

submitted to his masculine demands. But he had not approached the fine ladies of the city, the daughters of landowners and merchants. Until now.

Estrellita, while beautiful, seemed insensitive to his charms. He was not accustomed to being rebuffed by women. Perhaps, he reasoned, she would be different in Santa Fe. Perhaps it was this place, this foreign land that made her behave so coolly toward him. And that American peasant, York, he was only a passing infatuation. She would soon forget about him. Once the boy was out of sight, he would be out of mind, as well. Merito had done well. The name of Manuel Armijo worked magic with these Americans who wanted to reap the riches of the Santa Fe Trail. It did no harm to be the favorite nephew of the ex-governor. It was well to have influence, and perhaps his position would be better known to Estrellita once she was back on her native soil.

"We can talk about these things at another time," he said. "Do you not like me even a little?"

"I do not dislike you," she said. "I am told by all of the other girls that you are considered quite dear, as precious as jade. It's just that you take too much for granted where I am concerned."

"Well," he said, forcing a laugh, "I will try not to do that too much."

Estrellita was flattered by Augustino's attention. Inwardly, she chided herself for being so critical. One part of her wanted to return his affections, but another warned her to be wary, to be on guard. She wondered about this, since she had long looked forward to becoming a lady, marrying a handsome, prosperous man such as this one, and raising a family she could be proud of, grandchildren she could take to her father's hacienda and show off. Yet, since she had met the young American, she had felt other stirrings. She did not feel these with Augustino, although she had seen the way the other girls looked at him, and even the older women who glanced at him with hooded eyes, like falcons waiting for the pigeon to fly.

"My father and my esteemed uncle very much want to meet you formally," said Augustino, taking another approach. "They have not seen you since you have grown so beautiful. I have already arranged with your father to call on you when we return to Santa Fe."

"To begin the formal courtship," Estrellita said, trying her best to quell the sarcasm.

"Yes," he said, and his hand stole toward hers, touched her little finger. She started to pull away, but his index finger twined around her little finger and clasped it sensually. She felt the strength in his hand, and when she looked up, she saw that he was smiling, that his eyes were those not of a beggar, but of a conqueror. She looked toward Lucia and saw that the old woman was gazing at the wall, trying her best to stay awake.

"Augustino," she said softly, "you must not be so bold."

"And why not?" he whispered. "A woman of fire must certainly demand a man of boldness."

He switched his grip, slid his fingers between hers, and lifted her hand until it rested on his leg, against the tightly stretched cloth of his trousers. Estrellita could feel his warm flesh underneath, the suggestion of muscular strength, the hardness. Lucia dozed, her eyes fastened shut.

"The waiting," he purred into her ear. "It is agony for me."

Jeremiah passed the study at that moment, carrying the novels Estrellita had given him, and looked inside. At first he saw only Lucia, asleep in the chair, and then he saw movement, saw Estrellita's hair, the profile of her face. He saw Augustino leaned toward her, his lips close to her ear, and he saw their hands intertwined as if they were clutching each other prior to embracing.

Something sank in his stomach. He opened his mouth wide in surprise, just as Estrellita glanced his way.

He felt as if a knife had been driven into his heart. Estrellita rose from the chair, shaking her hand loose from Augustino's, started toward him.

"Jeremiah," she breathed, but he could not hear her. He saw Augustino rise, too, and grab Estrellita by the shoulders, turn her around and kiss her.

Jeremiah had seen enough. He turned on his heel and stalked away, his face dark as a raincloud. He began to run for the front door, suddenly ashamed of himself. All this time, he thought, she has been playing me for the fool. All this time, I believed her words. I hate her, I hate her, he said in his mind and the words took on shape and weight and made him blind and angry.

He reached the door and opened it wide. He bounded outside, then stopped. Turning, he tossed the books she had given him back inside, saw them skid across the floor and slam into the banister of the staircase. He left the door open and raced to the stables, tears streaming down his face. It was over. She wasn't worth it. She had betrayed him, let him believe she liked him, when all the time it was untrue. She wanted the Mexican soldier. That was plain as a fly stuck in the dough.

Well, by God, he didn't need her. He was going to the mountains to make his fortune. He would find another girl someday, one better than this one. What was she anyway? Just a high-class Mexican girl who thought she could play with his feelings and get away with it. He hated her. He hated all of them and he couldn't wait to get out of St. Louis and go with the brigade to the Rocky Mountains.

He came to the dark stables and felt a calmness overtake him. He found his horse and saddled it in the darkness, pulled the cinch tight, and led it outside. He put his foot in the stirrup, grabbed a hank of mane and the reins with his left hand, steadied himself on the cantle with his right, and climbed into the saddle. He clucked to the animal and felt it step out. He heard the music and the laughter drift away as he rode toward St. Louis, down the long lane from the hacienda. He wiped the streaks from his face and took a deep breath.

He did not look back, but he thought he heard her voice calling to him one last time.

"The devil take her," he muttered bitterly. "The devil take all of them."

Chapter Nine

Estrellita caught only a glimpse of Jeremiah's face before Augustino whirled her around and took her into his arms. Before she could protest, she felt his lips touch hers and crush them in a fiery kiss. His arms held her in a tight embrace, mashing her breasts against his chest. Her senses swirled in confusion and she scarcely heard Lucia's sharp cry of protest.

Augustino moaned with pleasure as he tasted the sweetness of Estrellita's lips. He closed his eyes, locked her in his embrace, oblivious to the gathering whirlwind across the room.

Lucia saw only that Augustino had taken Estrellita in his arms, was kissing her. She had not seen anything else, had heard only footsteps in the foyer. Quickly, she rushed to the doors, closed them, lest anyone see what she had unwittingly allowed to happen. Then she sighed deeply and snatched up her skirts, began trotting toward the two lovers, looking like a wild-eyed turkey hen on the attack.

"Mmm," mumbled Estrellita, trying to speak through Augustino's kiss. She squirmed in his arms, drew her arms away from his waist. She pushed on his midsection, began backing away. Her hands groped at his chest in protest as, with a quick jerk of her head, she broke the kiss.

She looked up into Augustino's face, saw the arrogance

there, the slight curl to his swollen lips. *The man is insolent,* she thought, but her own lips still tingled from the intensity of his kiss, and the heat of his embrace still lingered on her breasts.

"How dare you!" she exclaimed breathlessly.

Augustino smiled, as Lucia braked a few feet behind Estrellita.

"I did not want you to rush away," he said quietly. "And maybe I wanted to discourage further attentions from that American lout."

"He's not a lout," she hissed. "You had no right . . ."

Lucia approached them, uncertain of her ground.

"Now, now," she soothed, "what's this all about? A lovers' quarrel, so soon? That is a good sign. But you two should not be embracing, giving kisses . . ."

"Oh, Lucia, be quiet!" wailed Estrellita. She glared once more at Augustino, then turned on her heel and swept past the startled Lucia toward the doors.

Estrellita flung the doors open and rushed into the foyer, looking desperately for Jeremiah. The front door yawned wide and black. She saw, out of the corner of her eye, the two books on the floor. One lay against the base of the banister, the other a foot away, its pages open in the middle, the gilt edges shining in the glow of the overhead candelabra.

She raced to the open door, ran outside onto the porch. She peered into the darkness, saw only the faint stripes of lamplight painted across the trunks of trees, the waving blades of grasses stirred by a faint, empty breeze. She stepped off the porch and called softly, fearful of the darkness, embarrassed that someone might hear her. The sound of the dance music drifted to her ears, the gabble of laughter and speech underneath, and the sound of the rushing air only sounding more empty and forlorn as it riffled through the leaves of the trees.

She walked to the lane, heard the soft, faraway thunder of hoofbeats. She saw nothing, but a pang of fear clutched at her heart. *Jeremiah, don't leave me,* she sobbed soundlessly in her mind. *Jeremiah, please don't go now.*

146

Behind her, she heard the creak of a board, the scrape of a bootsole. She turned, saw Augustino stepping onto the porch.

"Did you call me?" he asked.

"No," she said, shaking her head. She saw the dark silhouette of Lucia standing just inside the door. "Please, Augustino, I want to be alone."

"It's that *americano,* isn't it? He has made you cry and gone away."

She walked back to the house, lifting her skirts above her ankles now, even though the hem was already dusty. She climbed the steps, swept past Armijo. An arm shot out, grabbed her by the elbow.

"We were not finished yet."

"Let go of my arm," she demanded. His grip tightened. "Or, I'll scream," she added, her voice dropping lower, the tone venomous.

"Estrellita . . ."

She broke away from him, wrenching her elbow out of his grasp. She stalked past Lucia who stood there in surprise, her mouth open, and, for once, silent. Estrellita stooped, picked up the fallen books, then climbed the stairs without looking back.

Augustino strode back inside, stood next to Lucia, watching Estrellita flow up the stairs, her hand gliding along the polished banister.

"Where is she going?" he asked numbly.

"She is angry, Señor Armijo, but I think not at you. Perhaps at herself."

"Why?"

"Ah, it is a passing thing. Please, go back to the fiesta, enjoy yourself. I will talk to her."

Augustino started to say something, then thought better of it. Lucia saw that he was angry at being rebuffed and was glad when he departed, striding toward the patio like a man who wanted to strike something with his fists. She sighed, shut the door. She had not failed to see the books thrown on the floor. Well, she would not have to worry about the American youth any longer. He had refused Estrellita's gift, and that was the last they would hear of him. She took a breath, went to find Corazon, tell her what happened. Perhaps she could do something with her daughter. Lucia had no desire to talk to Estrellita in the girl's present mood. Let her sulk a while. She would soon realize that her infatuation with Jeremiah York was a big mistake. Ah, if only the young ones would listen to their elders.

Corazon tiptoed to her daughter's door. The candle lamp in her hands threw light and shadow across the wall, shook from her trembling. She listened for a moment, then tapped on the door. There was no reply, so she turned the brass knob. The door was unlocked.

Inside, the room was dark. She heard sobbing, saw the dark form of her daughter lying facedown across the bed.

"Estrellita, what is the matter?" she said softly.

"Oh, Mother, I want to die."

Corazon went to her, placed the candle carefully on the night table. The flame flickered inside the glass chimney. A thin, dark plume of smoke streamed upward for a moment, then disappeared, leaving the faint scent of burnt cloth and oil lingering in the air. The curtains at the window rustled with a light breeze. The silence was like the quiet before a storm.

Corazon sat on the edge of the bed, stroked her daughter's hair, touched her shoulder.

"I do not like to see my daughter unhappy. This is your birthday, my dearest. You should not be weeping so."

Estrellita's body shook as fresh sobs wracked her body. Her mother's hand wiped at the tears flowing down her cheeks. Corazon sat there, saying nothing, until the sobbing spasm passed. She turned her daughter over on her back, looked into the hollows of her eyes. She withdrew a handkerchief from her sleeve, dabbed at the tears on Estrellita's face.

"Please. Do not cry anymore."

Estrellita tried to hide her face. Her eyes were puffed from weeping, and the tears had streaked her cheeks.

"I must look awful," she whimpered. "I feel awful."

"Why are you so sad? It would be good to talk, I think. Just mother and daughter. You and me."

Her mother's voice was soothing. Estrellita raised a hand, touched her mother's arm. Corazon leaned over, hugged her daughter tightly to her breast. Estrellita began to weep again, softly this time, the tears flowing without restraint. She tasted the salt on her lips, felt the tightness in her chest, the squeezing pain in her heart.

Corazon patted her daughter's back, rocked her as she had when Estrellita was a baby suffering from the colic.

"I do not like to see my baby hurt," soothed her mother. "What happened? Did you quarrel with the American? Did he treat you badly?"

There was no reply.

"It is that boy, isn't it? Is he the one who makes you weep so much?"

"N-no, y-yes," Estrellita stammered.

"There, now, my daughter, do not fret so. Why does this one mean so much to you? Do you not care that your father has made a good match for you with the nephew of the ex-governor?"

Estrellita scooted away from her mother's embrace, brushed her hair back from her face. In the soft light of the candle, she looked wan and weary from weeping. Her hands trembled as she wrung them, and her lower lip quivered as she struggled to put her feelings into words.

"Mother, I . . . I can't tell you what you ask. I just know that when I see Jeremiah—when I'm near him—I feel funny inside. I feel warm and scared at the same time. I want him to hold me and kiss me and make me feel safe. With Augustino, I don't feel any of this."

"You will, in time," said her mother, but there was no conviction in her tone.

"No, my mother. I know this in my heart. Don't you know

149

what I'm feeling? Don't you know how it feels to want someone so much you ache deep down inside?"

"Yes," said her mother softly. "I know. But you are young and your feelings are confused. This American boy, he is no educated, he has no breeding. It is your father's opinion, and mine, that he will never be anything more than he is, a man o no substance, no money, no value as a human being worthy o being your husband . . ."

Corazon's words were like arrows piercing Estrellita's heart They were like fistblows to her soul, pounding away at the beauty in her heart, twisting it, mashing it, crushing it like a rosebud underfoot.

"Mother, stop . . ." Estrellita pleaded. "You don't know how he is. You just don't know. He is sweet and kind and strong. Not like Augustino, who is arrogant and proud and pompous. Jeremiah is not what you and Father say he is. I don't want to marry the nephew of the tax-collector. I wan Jeremiah."

Corazon drew back in shock. Her face drained of color, and her eyes flashed with a sudden anger. She drew back her hand to slap her daughter's mouth, but she held it, frozen there in midair as Estrellita sat up straight and held her head up high and proud.

A look of defiance crept into Estrellita's eyes, burned in their depths like coals fanned by a blacksmith's bellow. Her lips flattened together and her chin jutted out as if daring her mother to strike her.

Corazon relaxed her hand, stood up, glaring at her daughter

"I can see that you are blind, my daughter," she said sadly "This boy has turned you against your own people, agains your father, and against me, your mother. This only prove what I say, that he is no good for you. You have an infatuation that is all. Very well. That will pass. Once he is out of sight, h will be out of your mind. I do not want you to mention tha boy's name again in front of your father. Do you understand me, Estrellita?"

"Yes," muttered Estrellita numbly. She dropped her head

unable to bear the coldness in her mother's warning. The hurt rose up in her but she could cry no more. She could only sit there, her heart crushed, and bear the pain of disappointment that burned in her breast like thorns driven into her heart.

"Now, straighten yourself up and come downstairs. I will tolerate no more rudeness from you toward our guests."

Corazon turned on her heel and stalked across the room. She slammed the door behind her and the silence rushed in like the backwash of a tidepool until it screamed in Estrellita's ears.

She scooted from the bed, touched her feet to the floor, stood up. She couldn't face her guests just yet. She knew she could not hide the anger she felt toward Augustino at that moment. She walked to the window, pulled the curtain aside. Light from the lanterns slashed the shadows that stretched across the sward. She looked down on the place where she and Jeremiah had stood that evening, all alone, away from prying eyes, the admonishment of her parents.

Estrellita sighed. A wave of intense loneliness swept over her as she gazed out the window into the darkness, heard the strains of the music wafting on the night air, the babble of voices from the patio, and the bright ribbons of laughter that floated up to her window. Something tugged at her heart as she thought of Jeremiah running away from her, perhaps forever. If only he had stayed so she could explain that Augustino had taken advantage of her. If only he had given her a chance.

Bitterly, she turned away from the window, her eyes once again filled with tears. The anguish of Jeremiah's departure wrenched at her, twisted her senses. Everything seemed so hopeless now. She had nowhere to turn. Her parents were against her. Augustino was so sure of himself, and why shouldn't he be? Her marriage to him had been arranged. It didn't matter that she didn't love him. It didn't matter that she knew she could never love him. She wanted Jeremiah, and she couldn't have him. The thought crushed her, and she felt the squeezing of her heart again. She felt the pain in her breast and she wanted to scream at all of them and run after Jeremiah, follow him to the mountains, to wherever he might go.

But the scream died in her throat, and a resolve rose up in her to replace the bitterness and anger she felt at this moment.

"I will never marry Augustino," she whispered, and the words gave her courage and strength. "Never!" she exclaimed loudly. "Never, never, never!"

Jeremiah leaned over, opened the gate to the corral in the stockyards. The stable was dark and he knew the night watchman had probably gone to bed. The man slept on a cot in one of the stalls near the tackroom. York knew him only as "Mr. Leeds."

He dismounted, brushed himself off. The air smelled of urine and horse droppings. He stripped the saddle off Fleetfoot and slipped off the bridle. He gave the horse a quick rubdown with his hands, reached outside the fence for the bag of feed he had bought, left in a nail barrel. He put grain in the feedbin and heard the horse whicker in the darkness. A restlessness grew in him, born of the loneliness he felt after leaving the fiesta. He did not want to think of Estrellita. He did not want to think of her kissing that Spaniard at the Hacienda Vial. Yet he longed for human companionship, longed for some defense against the emptiness inside him.

He entered the stable, felt his way along the stalls in the dark. He tripped over a bucket, heard it clang as he lurched forward.

"Who's that?" called a voice.

"It's me. York."

"Damn, Son, you woke me up."

"I can't see."

"Hold on, I'll light a lantern." The watchman at the other end of the barn made noises as he fumbled in the darkness. Jeremiah waited, saw the spark of flint and steel, the glow of tinder. Finally, the shadowed face of the night watchman took form as he touched a taper to the oil-soaked wick.

"Lotta trouble," said the watchman. The glass chimney

clanged against brass. The man turned up the wick, headed toward York. "Got yourself all fancied up, eh?"

Jeremiah looked down at his trousers sheepishly. "I'm gonna change," he said.

"Kin you see up there?"

York looked at the ladder, up toward the loft. "I reckon. You hang that lantern on that center post, I can see enough."

"Goin' to bed?"

"Maybe not."

"I don't want to be waked up a third time, Son."

"Somebody been here?"

"The post rider come in a while ago. Brung you a letter."

"A letter for me, Mr. Leeds?"

"It's what I said, didn't I? I got it in my kip."

"Who's it from?"

"How in hell would I know, Son? Looks like it come over the Natchez Trace and was dragged ever' inch o' the way."

"Must be from my ma. She said she would write me."

"I reckon. Kin you read?"

"I can. Some."

Mr. Leeds hung the lantern on a wooden peg jutting from a post near the center of the stable. The lantern swayed for several seconds, moving the light around, nudging the shadows. The watchman stood under it, scratching his beard and blinking his owlish eyes, eyes that nestled behind several striations of wrinkles. He was rotund, virtually bald on top.

"You get changed, I'll fetch it," said Leeds.

York scrambled up the ladder, waded through straw to the place where he made his bed, kept his few things. In a corner of the loft, he stripped out of the clothes that Estrellita had bought him, rummaged through his knapsack for trousers and a shirt. He changed quickly and went back down the ladder. Leeds emerged from the tackroom carrying a small, wrinkled letter.

"Here you go, Son," he said.

Jeremiah took the letter, walked back to the post where the

153

lantern hung. He looked at the letter, held it up to the light. He recognized the fancy scrawl. It was from E. York, Kaskaskia, Illinois. It was addressed to Jeremiah York, St. Louis, Missouri Territory. He broke the wax seal and opened the envelope.

Dear Jeremiah, it read. *I hope this letter finds you well and happy. I been meaning to tell you something. It's been hard to tell you. Your pa and me wasn't married right off. You are a year older than we told you. It don't make no sense to keep this secret no longer. You are sixteen and a man now. Be good. Pa and I sure hope you come back soon.*

Jeremiah's hands were trembling when he looked up. The paper rattled as he folded it back up. He drew a deep breath, swelled out his chest. He felt the down on his chin, rubbed it with tremulous fingers. Leeds cleared his throat.

"Bad news, son?"

"No. I'm sixteen. Almost seventeen."

"Huh? You didn't know that?"

"I . . . I, yeah, I did, I reckon. My legs hurt most ever' night, painin' me like they was a-growin'."

"I figgered you was done growed."

Jeremiah smiled. He walked over to Leeds, tucking the letter inside his pocket.

"I feel growed up," he said. "Can you direct me to where I might find Baptiste Lalande? Them mountain men?"

"You goin' to wet your swallerer?"

"I got money."

"Best keep some of it back. Saint Louie, she's rough at night on a boy."

"I ain't no boy," said Jeremiah.

"That's right, I reckon. You bein' sixteen a'ready. Well, they's some as drinks at Rocky Mountain House and others at the Green Tree, but most likely you'll find Lalande and his bunch at the Red Boar this time o' evenin'."

"The Red Boar?"

"On Vine Street, up where it runs into Broadway."

"Point me that way, Mr. Leeds."

154

"Son, they eat youngsters in there. Man or boy, you ain't hardly dry behind the ears."

"I got to see Lalande. I'm joining his brigade."

"Goin' to be a mountain man, are ye? Well now, I wouldna figgered."

"I'm real anxious to be goin', Mr. Leeds."

"Sure, son. Come on. I'll show you where to go, and you be real quiet comin' back, hear?"

"Oh, I may not be back tonight. I got money. I can stay in a room if I want."

Leeds snorted. He walked outside the stables with York and told him how to get to the tavern. Jeremiah set off in the dark, heading for the first streetlamp, its light gauzy in the river fog. He whistled a tuneless song that popped into his head.

"Sixteen," he said aloud. "Almost seventeen. I'm a man. Dadgummit, I'm a man!"

Chapter Ten

Jeremiah looked at the weathered sign that hung above the street. He could barely make out the lettering: The Red Boar, but he saw the reddish hog and he could hear the raucous laughter within, the faint clink of glasses and tunk of brass tankards. He felt a renewed swelling in his chest, a fluttering in his belly.

A moment later, he felt a dampening of his spirit, a brief sputter of doubt in the flame of his yearning. He felt as if he was a boy about to step into the company of men, men he had long admired and envied. He hesitated, then swallowed his fear as if it was a tangible lump in his throat. He pushed on the door, felt it give and swing open. He stepped inside the tavern, feeling that he was all eyes and trembling legs, useless hands.

Men sat at tables in the lowered center of the room, and others stood at the long bar at the side, or sat on tall, three-legged stools with padded seats of cowhide. The smoke hung in a blue pall over the drinkers and there was the tang of ale and whiskey mingled with the aromatic fumes of the pipes and cigars permeating the air. He saw sailors and stevedores, farmers and drovers, and, taking up an entire corner of the room, with three tables jammed together, the mountain men he had come to see sat drinking and talking loudly.

At the far end of the tables, Baptiste Lalande sat, holding

court, a large tankard of ale in his fist.

Jeremiah stepped down into the cellarlike room. The sailors raked him with worldly glances and a stevedore winked at him lewdly, leering with a mouthful of tobacco-stained teeth. His mouth bulged with a chaw of Climax and he spat into a brass gobboon at his feet, the leer never leaving his face.

Big Mike Finnegan spotted Jeremiah as he wove his way through the tables toward the rear corner.

"Wal, me byes, looky who's here. The messenger boy hisself!" exclaimed Finnegan.

Jeremiah's face flushed hot, and he felt a sudden clutch of claustrophobia at his chest. Someone patted him on one cheek of his ass and he turned quickly, but saw no sign of who had done it. Laughter broke out all around him and his embarrassment deepened.

"Ah, it is York," said Lalande, "come to clean out my pockets."

The others at the table watched the lad dance out of the way of a sailor's brawny, tattooed arm and their eyes glittered like the eyes of spiders. Jeremiah sidled out of the way and made it to the back tables, his face burning as if it had been scorched by a blast furnace.

"No, sir," said Jeremiah, "just come to tell you I'm going to the Rocky Mountains with you."

"Oh you are, are you?" boomed Lalande. "Well, by Gar, not until you get drunk with us. And, if there's fighting tonight, you'll bloody your fists with the rest of us or I won't have you in my brigade."

"Yes, sir."

The men at the table laughed, and York felt better. A man he did not know grabbed his hand, jerked him into an empty chair. Someone shoved a stein with the pewter top broken off into his hands and another man slapped him on the back. He felt his spine crack.

"Drink up, York," said the man next to him. Their faces blurred as Jeremiah struggled to get air back in his lungs. He looked at the man, who had a snowy beard, crackling hazel eyes, a clay pipe jammed in his teeth. "The ale tastes like pepper and panther piss, but it'll boil the city pizen out'n yore innards. You'll know yo're full up when yore teeth float out yonder door."

Jeremiah lifted the stein, poured the ale into his mouth. It tasted like rainbarrel water and lead at first, and then he smelled the fumes that wafted to his nostrils and swallowed. The ale was warm and turned his stomach when it first hit, but he kept it down, wiped foam from his mouth.

The men cheered him and lifted their tankards, drank heartily.

"You work, boy, by Gar," said Lalande, "and you get wet and cold and stink plenty, eh, like the he-bear in the rut, but we make a man of you if you live, eh, Bloody Hand?"

Lalande looked at the snow-bearded man seated next to York, a puzzled glint in his eyes.

"That one, he is Bloody Hand Andersen, York," explained Lalande, "and Big Un there you know, Mike Finnegan, and that man on the other side of you is Drew Ballentine. We call him White Buffalo, and over next to Big Un is Jim Karns, Possum Killer, and the thin man with the red hair is J.R. Asterwold. Good men, eh? Strong. Good fighters. Good hunters. Good lovers."

"We call Asterwold 'Al,'" said Andersen. "Sometimes. We call him Squire at others. Squire Al."

J.R. sat there, his thin face almost cadaverous, a slow smile on his lips. Next to him sat another man, leaned back in his chair, his face in shadow, and no one mentioned his name or offered to introduce him. Jeremiah could only see the outline of his face and it was strong and hard, even in the dimness of the shadow and the smoke. He looked away because he could feel the man's eyes burning through the shadow, through the smoke, and he felt the heat, like a firebrand held close to his own face.

York looked at their faces and at their hands. Their hands

were scabbed and broken, healed over, but rough, raw appendages that made him wonder if they were not diseased. The man called Bloody Hand had the worst hands of all. They looked like ginger root lumps, laced with deep cracks and mottled with liver spots.

"What happened? You get your hands caught in the traps?" asked Jeremiah. "That why they call you Bloody Hand?"

Laughter. Andersen plucked his pipe from his mouth and swigged from a tankard of ale.

"He won't tell you how he got his name," said Karns. "Has to do with being clumsy. He's alluz cuttin' hisself on an iron sight or a lock or a blade or somethin'. Hands alluz bloody by Jesus."

"An' if ain't any o' that," said Finnegan, "we all got blood on our hands and the skin wore out from dunkin' in the cold o' the mountain waters and dryin' an' freezin' and the wind eatin' at 'em." Big Un held out his hands as if to show York the damage done by water and weather. They were cracked and peeled, same as the others, only twice as big, big as small hams, all boiled and cracked like lumpy, overripe vegetables.

The men were not dressed in buckskins this night, York noticed, but wore regular clothes, such as they were—made of cloth, but decorated with beads and strips of bright fabric, and all had hats on, Andersen the wide-brimmed beaver felt hat with a beaded band, Ballentine a crumpled felt hat that looked dirty and worn and chewed on, Lalande with a *voyageur's* knit wool cap, and Big Un with the same kind of hat that Bloody Hand wore. J.R. wore a Hudson's Bay hat, with a turkey feather at the back, and the man in the shadows had a tall hat made of fur, beaver maybe, or fox, and Karns wore a flat-crowned hat with a beaded band and an eagle feather jutting up from the band.

And Jeremiah sat there, drinking the ale and drinking in all that he saw and felt inside him. He was with the men now and they seemed to accept him. He listened to them joke and poke fun at one another and knew it was in good fun and not mean or anything, but it seemed they were making him welcome with their talk, with their jokes, and that made him feel good, better than he had felt since leaving Kaskaskie. He saw the girl then, a young woman in a bright dress, and she carried a tray laden with pitchers and glasses and she moved like a dancer around the tables and smiled at the rough men, flirted with them, Jeremiah thought, and then she looked at him and he felt a tug of sadness because it was not Estrellita. Then he began to think of her, of Estrellita, and he drank more of the ale and Bloody Hand filled his tankard again as the girl came up to the table and asked if they wanted more ale. She looked right at him when she asked that, and he was sure that he smiled at her and that the smile was idiotic.

"Sally, we got us a young'un here," said Andersen, "green as buffalo bile and soppin' wet behind the ears, but you can have him for a hour if you don't wear him out none."

"Swen, you devil," she said, "I told you. I'm a nice girl."

"An' this here's a nice boy," said Karns. "He's got hay in his ha'r and no ha'r 'tween his legs, but I'll bet he's sweet as candy cane."

Sally blushed and Jeremiah wanted to crawl under the table and disappear. Lalande nodded to her and she whirled away before it got any worse, and Jeremiah was relieved. He drank more of his ale and wished the men would stop looking at him the way they did, all owl-eyed and mischievous, as if they were going to josh him some more.

The man in the shadows leaned forward then, and rose from his chair. He was big, tall, maybe six foot or a little more, with wide shoulders and dark hair, piercing brown eyes. He was the only man among them who wore no beard, but there was a ruggedness to his features that made the others look soft. He nodded to the men at the table, looked long and hard at York, a wry smile on his lips. He stood there, it seemed an eternity to York, and looked the youth square in the eyes and Jeremiah could not read what was in his glance, whether it was friendliness or pity that the man felt. Finally, he shrugged

161

slightly and stalked through the room. When he walked through the doorframe, he filled it. He ducked and swung his shoulders sideways as he stepped outside. He wore moccasins and leggings, a knife on his ornate, beaded belt and a sash with a flintlock pistol sticking out of it at the small of his back.

"Who was that?" asked Jeremiah. "You never did say his name."

"Hear the boy-o now," said Finnegan, "wanting to know it all in a single night. Sure, and he's bound to find out the man's name sooner or later, eh, Baptiste?"

"What do you call him? Does he have a nickname?" asked York.

The men at the table all turned solemn. Sally brought more ale and they were still silent, all looking at York as if they held some big secret. York felt like a fool once again and wondered if he would ever understand these men who lived so much in the mountains.

"That one, he has no nickname," said Baptiste. "We all have the mountain-man names, but no, not that one. He is one good man, eh? He hunt, he trap, he find the beaver. But he don' say much, I think, because he like the waters of the big river, he go deep. He plenty smart, that one."

"Why did he leave? Was he mad?"

"Naw, he warn't riled, Son," said Karns. "He don't drink much and he don't smoke none at all. Says the smoke makes it hard to smell. He can smell a Injun in the middle of next week."

"Oh, yes, sure and the tales are all true," said Finnegan, expanding his girth as he sucked air into his lungs. Mike seemed to inflate and deflate like a bellows. Jeremiah had never seen a man as big or more likable. "Come to the mountains when he was a pup and grew up with the griz and the wolf, they say, and jerked his first scalp when he was no more'n twelve or thirteen. Raised by the heathen Sioux, he was, or maybe the Cheyenne, no matter. I seed him fight off a half dozen Pawnee once't, run circles around 'em on a little dappled Nez Perce pony. I fair crapped my britches an' he was just as cool as a high green lake in wintertime. He comes back, he does, and skins out a buff cow we'd shot and never said a bloody blue word."

"What do you call him?" Jeremiah asked, exasperated. "Doesn't he have no danged name?"

The men at the table laughed as one.

"Why, shore he's got a name," said Andersen, smiling. "Eyestone."

"Eyestone?"

"His given name's Cooper. Some calls him Coop, most just call him Eyestone. He don't answer to none other than them two."

"Cooper Eyestone," said York, "I never heard no name like it."

"You hain't seen no man like Eyestone, neither," said Ballentine. "Man don't mix much. He goes where the wind blows, the rivers run. Goes off for days or weeks, always comes back with prime plews in his pack. He knows the mountains, he purely does."

York drank the ale and listened to the talk. He hardly noticed when Sally started bringing whiskey to the table instead of the ale. But when he took a drink from his stein, he felt the fire in his throat. He coughed and spluttered, gagging on the whiskey. His stomach churned and he thought he was going to be sick. He hardly heard the laughter that blared around him like hooting horns.

"Man goes to the mountains, he better be able to hold his whiskey," said Drew. "This is the best yo're gonna get 'twixt Saint Louie and rondeevoo. Likely the onliest, too."

"Ain't no decent likker on the Missouri no more," said Karns, "since Congress stomped on Bill Clark year or so ago."

"'At's right," said Andersen, "damned Congress. I 'member when them gov'ment agents ruint a thousand gallons of whiskey last year on the Yellowstone boat and then Leclerc slipped by Fort Leavenworth in his boat with the only whiskey in the territory."

"Yair, but I heard Cabanné sent his own men after Leclerc and stole his likker," said Karns. "Then Leclerc come back to Saint Louie with his hackles up a-bristlin' and climbed on Chouteau's back like ugly on a bear."

"Chouteau paid Leclerc more'n nine thousand to settle," said Andersen, "kicked Cabanné outen Injun country for a year."

"Them whiskey traders'd sell their own mothers' pussy if they was any market on the Missouri," said J.R., his tongue thick with the whiskey.

"Hell, so would American Fur," said Karns, and the other men laughed.

Such talk was all over Jeremiah's head, but he laughed with them. He was beginning to feel a part of them, part of their lives and their talk, and it was a good feeling, even with the whiskey in him, making his brain fuzzy, his tongue an outlaw slab of meat over which he had little control.

"I heard tell we could get whiskey up at Fort Union," said Drew when the laughter died away in whiskey throats.

"Bool sheet," said Lalande, his accent more pronounced under the brain-choking influence of alcohol, "that *fils de chien*, McKenzie, he set up the distillery, *non*, but the traders, they scream their balls off in St. Louis. I don' see no whiskey at Fort Union."

"There will be, time we get back up that way," said Andersen. "I saw 'em loading kegs on the wagon for Independence today. Drovers said they was bound for McKenzie at Fort Union."

Everyone knew about Kenneth McKenzie and his scheme to bypass the law. Nobody blamed him. Whiskey was still king among the traders. McKenzie had set up a distillery at Fort Union right after Congress had banned it. Before that, American Fur sold liquor to the Indians in monitored quantities on the Missouri below the Mandans and more extravagantly above, mainly because that was the only way they could compete with Hudson's Bay Company. William

Clark, the superintendent of Indian Affairs at St. Louis, was sympathetic to the realities of commerce and competition and graciously issued American Fur permits for ample supplies of liquor "for use of the boatmen." Everyone knew what the whiskey was for, and Congress got wind of it and passed a bill in July, 1832, "excluding spiritous liquors from the Indian country," whether intended for boatmen or Indians.

McKenzie might have gotten away with his distillery, but rival traders passing through Fort Union on their way to St. Louis hollered loud and long until Congress heard about it and called Pierre Chouteau, Jr., on the carpet in Washington. He did his best to explain to Indian Commissioner Elbert Herring that McKenzie had been making wine from the few wild pears and berries that grew in the region, claiming it to be "an innocent botanical experiment, nothing more." Nobody believed him, but Chouteau still had power and influence and the matter was dropped after Pierre agreed to conform to the law. However, he had no intention of doing any such thing. As he explained later, "It could not be expected that the traders should be very observant of the law, when the officers appointed to enforce it neglected to do so."

There was more talk, most of it over Jeremiah's head, because it involved the changes at American Fur, with Astor selling out and Cabanné useless after the Leclerc business, and the trappers wondering if Cadet Chouteau was man enough to run it. Hearing the name Chouteau so much reminded Jeremiah that he had to meet with Pierre Chouteau, Jr., whom they called Cadet, and get his outfit from him in the morning.

"I . . . I got to go," said York, as the hour grew late. "Mr. Chouteau, he's giving me a rifle and such." He pronounced the name Show-Tow.

"Wal, Son, you get yoreself a good Hawken rifle and larn how to use it, you'll do 'er," said Andersen, suddenly turning paternal.

"That's what I aim to get is a Hawken," said Jeremiah.

"Ain't no better piece, I'm thinkin'," said Karns. "First 'un

I had was a thirty-two caliber and it'd pop the eye out of a jay at a hunnert paces or more."

"You get yoreself a good skinnin' knife," said Drew, "one like this'n here," and he drew the largest blade York had ever seen. It gleamed silver in the lanternlight and Jeremiah pushed back from the table as if afraid Ballentine would use it.

"That ain't no knife," said Karns, "that's a plowblade."

"Looks more like a tin shingle with a handle on it," joshed Asterwold. "What you need, York, is somethin' small and sharp, like this." Asterwold slipped a knife from his sheath that was half the size of Drew's but still a formidable weapon. Jeremiah's eyes grew like grapes as he looked at the two blades. Then the trappers began to brag about their knives as Karns and Andersen drew theirs. When Jeremiah arose from the table, Drew and Karns were engaged in a mock sword-fight at the table. It looked dangerous to York and he scooted around the table before one of the swishing blades could decapitate him.

Only Baptiste Lalande acknowledged Jeremiah's departure. He flashed the youth a sardonic smile and touched a pair of Gallic fingers to the brim of his hat.

"Eh, you get your pack ready, York," said the Frenchman, "we ride out tomorrow."

"Tomorrow? So soon?"

Lalande nodded and his eyes glittered from the whiskey. He wagged a drunken finger at York.

"You go to the church and say your prayers, little boy, eh? Mebbe you no see St. Louis for long time, eh? Mebbe you never come back."

There was an ominous tone to the Frenchman's words and York wondered how much the man knew.

"I am to see that debt paid," said York defiantly.

"Go on, before I stick you," said Lalande. "Go on quick, eh?"

"Pay him no mind, Son," said Swen Andersen, "it's just the grog in his gullet."

Jeremiah staggered through the maze of tables, and lurched out the door into the fogbound night. He stood there under the swinging sign for a moment, getting his bearings. The street swam in the darkness, the buildings wavered and flickered in and out of focus. York sucked in air, tried to clear his head.

His stomach turned queasy, rolled and tilted until he thought he was going to be sick. He leaned against the building and drew in more air. He started to walk and almost fell. His legs didn't work right. One seemed to be shorter than the other. He teetered from side to side, as he headed for the stockyards, the fog wet against his face, and chill. He could smell the big river in the mist, smell its fishy tides, its marine mud, the garbage floating in its swirling waters, the wood and metal of boats and piers, the rank fumes of wet hawsers and oily wood-burning steam engines belching smoke from grimy stacks. The smells were different at night; sharper, thicker.

The city seemed to grow in him and to grow around him, a city of shadows and mist, impenetrable, enigmatic, exciting. He saw men in the street, strange forms that moved in and out of cloudy clumps of fog. Here and there, the lamps and lanterns of taverns illuminated the motes, made them dance golden and silver, made the mist sparkle and shimmer like fairy light, like will-o'-the-wisp and the dankness had a texture to it, like wet cotton. Jeremiah's head cleared and he exulted in being alive, in having been with men who had roamed the mountains and come back to earth, bigger and stronger than before. He would be like that someday, he vowed, be rough and muscular, self-assured, have money in his pockets, a pair of good pistols, a blade on his belt.

He heard the disembodied voices from a tavern on some side street, a fluttering rag of laughter floating through the fog, the clip-clop of a mule somewhere up ahead. He passed a pair of Indians, arms locked, leaning into each other as if to keep from falling down. He smelled their breaths, the rank, cloying aroma of stale whiskey wafting around him like tainted smoke. It was good to be alive, in this time, at this place, a city that hid its secrets in the dark, but pulsed just the same, pulsed with life that he could feel deep in his bones.

He watched the Indians disappear and marveled at their soundlessness, wondered if they had ever taken an enemy's hair. He shuddered, shutting out the image of a man's skinned head, the blood smeared on a skull like raspberry jam. He laughed at himself, laughed because he saw such thoughts flash across his mind, unbidden, and the laughter drove them away and he walked lightly now through the fog, free of that tic of fear that had touched him like a phantom finger for just a fleeting moment.

He passed a brick building, then another, and he looked behind him, not because he heard anything, but because it was so quiet and he had the feeling, the feeling that someone was following him. He wondered if he could run if he had to, if his legs would respond to the command he would give them. He slowed his pace and looked back over his shoulder. He crossed the street and looked at the vacant buildings shrouded in fog, wondered how they looked in the light of day, their doors open, their goods displayed. He passed a vacant lot and stopped for a moment. It seemed, then, that whatever, whoever was behind him, stopped, too, and he peered into the dark sworl of mists and wondered if his imagination would overpower his common sense, make him do something foolish.

"Who's there?" he called, and was immediately sorry he had asked such a question. As if he really expected someone to answer.

He didn't see or hear the man cross the street until he was right on top of him. Then Jeremiah jumped inside his skin. His feet would not move and a cold shower of sudden fear drenched him, made his skin erupt in goosepimples.

"Kid," said the voice, and it was deep, resonant with a strange, rich timbre. "I'll walk along with you a ways."

"Huh? Who are you?"

"Eyestone," he said, and Jeremiah looked closely at the shadowed face.

"What do you want?"

"Let's walk on to where you're goin'."

"Sure. I reckon."

Jeremiah started walking again and Eyestone picked up his step, came along with him. The man walked soundlessly and York felt his skin crawl with goosebumps. They passed one of the many carriage houses in the city, another church, turned down a lane with more buildings, the last a raucous grog shop blaring with noise and voices, and then they were crossing the wide street to the stables, heard the horses whicker in the moist night, smelled the piquant aroma of manure, the acrid ammonia tang of urine.

"This be where you're stayin'," said Eyestone.

"Yeah. In the barn."

Eyestone stopped then and listened, looked back in the direction from which they'd come.

"Kid, you better sleep with one eye open."

"How come?"

"Just be better you do that, Son. You had yourself a couple of shadows when you left that tavern. I cut atween 'em and they drifted off. Wouldn't surprise me none if they come back, though."

"Who were they?"

"Can't say. City's full of thieves."

"I didn't see 'em."

"Likely they didn't want you to."

"Bad men?"

"I don't know. Curious, maybe. Kid like you doesn't show up every night at the Red Boar."

"What did they want then?"

"It don't make no difference now. You go on, watch yore topknot."

"Yes."

"Kid, you goin' with Lalande tomorry?"

"Uh huh."

"You watch him."

169

"I don't know what you mean, sir."

"Don't turn yore back on Lalande. Frenchie's got his eye on you."

"You go with him. Don't you?"

"I work out of his brigade. I don't trust Frenchie much myself."

"Why, then?"

"He's a fair trapper, knows the country. He don't work it all out with too many in the brigade."

"But you don't trust him?"

"I don't trust nobody, kid. And neither should you."

Eyestone brought the fist out of the darkness, sailed it out of the night. Like a hammer, he struck York square in the jaw, like a crushing, smashing hammer, made of pigiron and raw steel. The blow rocked Jeremiah off his feet, struck sparks in his brain, sparks that danced like dizzy lights. Pain jolted him as he felt his feet go out from under him. He struck the ground with a thud and Eyestone's face swirled above him.

Before Jeremiah could regain his senses, Eyestone turned on his heel, disappeared in the brume. York listened for a long time, but he never heard his footsteps. It was as if the man had never been there. Finally, he shook off his grogginess, went to the stables, climbed up into the loft. It was dark and he had to feel his way. He lay in the straw for a long time listening, but heard nothing out of the ordinary. He wondered why Eyestone had taken the trouble to follow him, warn him about Lalande, then knock him down. Did Lalande know that he was to be spying on him? Or did he just dislike York because he came to collect that old debt of Baptiste's father?

The whiskey and ale made him sleepy, but Jeremiah could not keep his eyes closed. His jaw throbbed where Eyestone had struck him. He kept hearing things: noises, footfalls, breathing. He kept seeing Eyestone's dark face, hearing his words of warning. He kept seeing that brain-jolting fist coming out of nowhere. When a barred owl hooted, Jeremiah sat up, his heart pounding.

In the silence, he thought again of Estrellita. His anger floated to the surface again. He saw her again in Armijo's arms, winced when he envisioned the Mexican kissing her. He hated Armijo, hated him more than he had ever hated anything or anyone in his life.

Now, there were two people he hated. Armijo and Eyestone.

He thought that he hated Eyestone most of all. There was just no reason for him to do something like that. No reason at all. He could understand Armijo. He wanted Estrellita. What had Eyestone wanted? Nothing. He was just cruel, maybe like all the rest of them.

"If Eyestone ever hits me again," he said aloud, "I'll kill him."

Finally he slept, his anger like a fever in his brain, like a heavy drug that took him down and deep, deep and down into dream.

Chapter Eleven

Estrellita smiled at Cadet Chouteau, curtsied.

"Thank you so much," she said.

Chouteau bowed from the waist. "Do not mention it. I will see that the books are delivered. Is there anything . . . ?"

"No, that is quite enough. I am most grateful to you, Monsieur Chouteau."

The door closed softly behind her and Estrellita glided to the top of the stairs, grasped the banister. Lucia stood at the bottom of the staircase like a dark sentinel, her eyes glittering. Estrellita reached for the fan dangling from her wrist, grasped it and spread its struts. She took her time descending the stairs, delighting in the *dueña's* exasperation. She could almost hear Lucia's fiery breathing, feel the tapping of her foot on the floor as the woman waited for her.

"Estrellita!" Lucia hissed. "Whatever were you doing up there?"

"Talking," said the young woman lightly. "Just talking to a kind and understanding man."

"Come, we will speak of this later. You must bid your guests farewell. Many wish to return to their homes this night. The hour grows late and your mother has been looking for you."

"Yes, yes, Lucia. Must you be after me like my own shadow?

173

The party has been spoiled anyway. I wish it had never happened."

"You must not say such things! Don Miguel . . ."

"Be quiet, old woman!" Estrellita snapped and she was immediately sorry. She swept past the startled Lucia and forced a smile on her face. Her anger at Augustino, and yes, Jeremiah, still smoldered, even though she felt better after having visited with Cadet Chouteau. She wanted to be by herself, she wanted to think.

Her mother beamed when Estrellita appeared in the salon where the dancers were all standing around, buzzing like so many mindless bees. Augustino and Merito stood together, stiff as sandhill cranes, and she ignored them as she went to each guest in turn and thanked them, said good night. The people began to stream from the room. When she came to Augustino, she whispered to him under her breath.

"I want you to go, Augustino."

"May I call on you in the afternoon?" he asked.

"No. You took liberties. Now go."

"Good night," he said curtly, and she merely nodded to Merito Salcedo, ignored his proffered hand as she had ignored Augustino's. Finally, only her mother and father remained in the room. The musicians had retired to drink the rest of the night in one of the guest houses, leaving their instruments on the bandstand like useless ornaments tossed on a rubbage heap. The scent of flowers and perfume lingered on the air like stale wine, like the sadness of deserted rooms in an empty house.

"You did not break the *piñata*," said her mother.

"It is no matter, *mamá,* I was not in the mood."

"But everyone is disappointed." Her mother pointed to the large papier-mâché bird hanging above the streamers of colored crepe at the center of the room.

"I am tired," said Estrellita. "I want only to go to bed and rest."

"For certain, my cherished one. Happy birthday."

"Thank you, *mamá*."

Her father took her in his arms and held her tightly for a moment. She fought to hold back the tears.

Estrellita wore a mask on her face as she stood on the front porch waving good-bye to her guests. She forced herself to smile once again, to give the appearance of gaiety, but her heart was sore, the hurt in her deep. She watched the fog roll in and the carriages disappear in the swirl of mist. She was glad to see them go, for she wanted to be alone with her sorrow, the sadness that swathed her heart, muffled its beating.

Behind her, Lucia waited, ever vigilant, until the last carriage rumbled away in the darkness.

"Come, child," said the *dueña*, "I will walk with you to your room."

"Thank you, Lucia," said Estrellita, turning toward her. "I am deeply sorry I was so sharp with you."

"It is of no importance. We will talk. Would you like some tea?"

"No. I am so tired."

"There, there," soothed the old woman, patting Estrellita on the shoulder, "I know, I know."

Estrellita knew her father and many of the other men would stay up all night talking and that many of the guests would return in the morning to continue eating and drinking. She wanted no part of the celebration any longer. She never wanted to see Augustino again.

She sighed and ascended the stairs, piqued at herself for behaving so badly on her birthday. Lucia would be full of questions and she would not know how to answer them. Best to tell her what she wanted to hear and be rid of her quick. She did not mean to be cruel, but Lucia would want to pick her over like a chicken carcass, examining each bone for a shred of meat, each joint for a scrap of tasty gristle.

She opened the door to her room and Lucia scurried inside

to light the lamp. When it was glowing brightly, Estrellita entered the room, grateful for the calming shadows, the peaceful sight of her bed so smooth and soft and inviting. She slipped the fan off her wrist, tossed it on her dressing table.

"I'll lay out your bedclothes," said Lucia, rattling a drawer in the bureau. Estrellita shook out her hair, sat down at the dressing table. She slipped off her shoes as Lucia set the nightgown at the foot of the bed. She wriggled her toes, rubbed the soles of her feet before peeling down the silk stockings that sheathed her slender legs.

"Let me help you undress, child," said Lucia.

"I don't want to talk about what happened tonight," said Estrellita, as Lucia's fingers slid deftly under her straps, tugged them over her shoulders.

"Of course not. It's such a shame to see a beautiful young lady lose her senses over a worthless swain like the American. But this will all pass and you will have a beautiful wedding, a most magnificent ceremony in the grand church of Santa Fe. You will look so lovely in your white gown, with the most graceful train and the regal mantilla of snowiest white atop your head. Everyone important will be there, the governor and his lady, all the dignitaries, and the priest will say the wedding mass and there will be a fantastic fiesta, a celebration such as Santa Fe has never seen."

Estrellita let her prattle on as she slipped out of her birthday gown. She stepped naked over to the bed, Lucia still chattering like a treeful of magpies, and stood there while the old woman shook out her nightgown and slipped it over her head. Estrellita squirmed into it, fluffed the bodice, and aligned her breasts beneath the pink pleats.

"It was a fine birthday party for all the small unpleasantness," said Lucia, stepping back to admire her ward one last time. "But that will all be forgotten, you'll see. With the light of day, all will appear regular again and that boy will go off to the mountains and never be seen again."

Estrellita bit her lip to keep from lashing out at Lucia. Did the woman not know how she felt in her heart? Was she so stiff-minded she could not see that her tongue was hateful and mean?

"Lucia, I am very tired. Good night."

"Oh, yes, for certain. But wasn't Augustino handsome tonight and he bears himself so well. I thought he . . ."

"Good night, Lucia."

Lucia hugged Estrellita, sighed deeply.

"Dream the sweet good dreams," said the *dueña*. "I will see you in the morning. Shall I bring you something to break your fast, the little sweet rolls, perhaps some *café*, or *jamón*, or . . ."

"No, nothing. I wish to sleep late."

"Yes, yes. Well, good night then, and happy birthday, my most esteemed young lady. Don't forget to say your prayers. Be sure and ask our Lord for his forgiveness. You will feel much better until you finally get to confession—"

"Yes, yes, Lucia," Estrellita interrupted. "I promise. I will see you in the morning."

It seemed to take Lucia forever to cross the room, but finally the door closed and Estrellita heard her heels clicking on the hardwood as she brisked down the hall to her room. She heard a door squeak open, then slam shut. She suppressed a titter as she heard the latchkey rattle and the slam of the heavy oaken bar.

"Who is she afraid of?" Estrellita said aloud. "Does she think a man will break down the door to get at her?"

Estrellita flounced onto the bed, crawled under the covers. *Poor Lucia,* she thought. *She was so disconcerted she forgot to turn my bed down.*

She leaned over, turned down the lamp. Darkness flooded the room and she listened to the ticking of the house as it settled in the nightcool. The sound was very soothing and she lay back against the pillow and closed her eyes. Despite herself, she grew sleepy. She drew in a deep breath and nurtured

177

herself with one last thought.

I must see Jeremiah before he leaves. I must tell him that I love him and no other.

Lucia struck the sulphur match and began lighting all of the lamps. She filled the room with blazing light, light that shimmered on the walls and the ceiling and floor as she turned the wicks up high.

She went to each window and vigorously pulled the drapes tight. Satisfied, she began to undress. She carefully hung up her dress and mantilla in the wardrobe closet, placed her shoes with the other pairs, folded her undergarments neatly and placed them atop the chest of drawers, then retrieved a shining white nightgown from the bottom of a valise, donned it like a ceremonial robe, and smoothed it over her body. She looked at the religious pictures she had hung on the walls when she moved in, the sacred heart of Jesus, the Madonna with child, the print of the Christ in the Garden of Gethsemane, and finally her gaze locked on the large crucifix made of rosewood and Mexican silver. Moving a lamp closer to the icon, the silver shot beams of fractured light in all directions. It seemed to her that the crown of thorns was ringed by a halo of light and she took this as a sign of personal holiness in her life.

She knelt by the bed, crossed herself, and began to mumble her prayers. She begged forgiveness for her sinful thoughts, prayed for the souls of those she held dear. Finally, she crossed herself again and rose from her genuflection, gazed again at the crucifix on the wall, the tortured body of Jesus illuminated by the lamps until it stood out in almost blinding relief.

She opened the top bureau drawer and removed a coin purse hidden beneath blouses and panties. She fished out a key, walked to the foot of the bed. She bent down, inserted the key into the lock of a small wooden trunk. She opened the lid, found the rouge and a pair of silk panties with ruffles. She slipped the panties on, sat at her dressing table. She applied the rouge to her cheeks and lips, smeared the color in deep. She licked her lips, touched up her eyelashes with mascara, posed for the mirror. Satisfied, she set down the key, stood up, smoothed her gown once again until it crackled with electricity, clung to her body.

Lucia crawled atop the bed and sat against the headboard, her eyes fixed on the crucifix, the naked body of Jesus floating in the light, his legs bent at the knees, chastely crossed to conceal his manhood, the blood dripping from the wound in his side, from the embedded thorns in his head. The look of infinite sadness on the face of the Christ never failed to touch her deeply.

She gazed transfixed at the crucifix, her eyes glittering like the hypnotic eyes of a snake. Her lips began to move slowly in a silent prayer. She looked at the naked figure long and hard and her hips began to undulate. Her wrinkled face began to lose its cinquefoils and riven lines of age, seemed to smooth as the rapture seized her in its beatific grip. Her legs slid apart and she raised her knees. Her gown began to snake toward her beckoning hips like a gliding sheet of still water. Her tongue slid out of her mouth and caressed her lips, leaving them with a crimson sheen as if she had been sucking ripe berries.

Her eyes took on a glassy sheen and she moaned deep in her throat, a low, animal sound that was like the soft keening of a creature in torment. Her hips moved up and down now and her gown flowed around her hips in a silken puddle. She touched delicate, bony fingers to her breasts, teased the nipples in slow twirls until they stood hard, like rubbery acorns, dark nubbins that pressed excitingly against the bodice of her gown. She pulled the straps from her shoulders, exposing her breasts to the lampglow and caressed them, made them young again, made them tingle with shoots of electricity that coursed through her body like faint lightning. She moaned and writhed there, her eyes never leaving the icon on the wall, the crucifix growing large in her mind, the suffering man on the cross moving, gliding toward her, his body sheened slick with sweat and the blood throbbing in his veins, flowing down his face and his side. She could feel him now, feel his gentle, healing touch, the joyous tingle of his hands on her breasts.

She could feel Jesus come down off the cross and descend to her bed, top her. She spread her legs and the rapture consumed her, consumed her like an evangelical fire. Her hand fled to her loins, wormed its way inside her panties. She touched the softness of her sex, probed the steamy, supple, bubbling-pudding depths and saw Chrsit's face before her, looked deep into his sad brown eyes. She cried out in fervent pain and joy, felt the Savior penetrate her, bore deep inside her, his manhood a hard, throbbing shaft goring her like a ram's ancient and savage horn.

She became young and vibrant, her skin smooth and tingling, and the years of deprivation and anguish fell away, swept by a religious fervor that had replaced the shriveled woman's passion of her wasted, weed-choked youth. Now she was the ultimate woman, the virgin giving herself up to the Master, the Christ whose naked, suffering body she had gazed on in cathedrals and humble adobe rooms, gazed on raptly until his image was emblazoned on her fertile, yearning mind like a burning bush on a barren, rock-strewn, Old Testament field. Her passion was the blood-sweat of Gethsemane, the excruciating hours on the cross at Golgotha, the supreme ecstasy of that glowing moment of divine transfiguration and resurrection when the peach-tinted stone of morning was rolled away from the crypt by mysterious, halo-crowned angels.

Lucia gasped in the convulsions of orgasm and felt the hard muscles of the imagined Christ-man pressing against her loins, against the pulsating cushions of her breasts. She felt bathed in the light and blood of the Lamb, reborn in that one startling moment of light and silent, rippling thunder deep in her womb.

"*Animale! Salvaje! Sin verguenza!*" she cried, gripped in the throes of a sanctified climax that ripped through her flesh and scourged her, surged up in her muscles and shook her into a mindless dance, a series of volcanic convulsions that left her breathless and sweat-soaked.

"*O, Jesus!*" she screamed, and fainted with the sudden rush of blood to her brain, fell away in a swoon, her senses washed to a brilliant whiteness by a raging celestial fire that swept away all sin, all rational guilt, in one awesome, blinding explosion.

The lamps burned on, through the night, until they sputtered out, one by one, leaving the room in peaceful darkness, except for the faint glimmer of white clinging to the limp figure on the bed like the tattered remnant of a wedding gown.

Chapter Twelve

Auguste Pierre Choteau ran the Company out of modest offices on Laurel Street, but he already had dreams of building larger offices in the same block. Now that Astor was out, he envisioned an even larger empire built on the fur trade, with American Fur as the unchallenged leader. With the Santa Fe Trail opening up, he saw the possibility of even greater riches as trade between Mexico and the United States increased. Still, he had his problems in that summer of 1834, problems that nagged at him like gnats at a sore.

Free trappers sat outside, lounged in the chiaroscuro of the building as the sun scrolled down the weatherbeaten boards. Jeremiah walked up to the battered door, pushed it open, read the faded lettering: Chouteau and Co., and underneath it, in fresher paint, American Fur Co. There were more men waiting inside, a low banister separating the office from the waiting room. A pair of clerks sat behind desks, shuffling papers, writing in ledgers. Jeremiah felt awkward, out of place. Neither of the clerks looked up, and he scanned the walls, covered with maps, framed prints, old traps, a calendar, certificates, a few stuffed heads, a dusty pheasant mounted atop a file cabinet looking glassy-eyed at a ruffed grouse on another. The office smelled musty and the boards creaked underfoot. Jeremiah stepped up to the railing and cleared his throat. One of the clerks looked up. He looked not much older than Jeremiah himself.

"You want something?"

"I'm sposed to see Mr. Chouteau."

"Which one?" asked the clerk, dryly.

"Pierre Chouteau. Junior, I reckon."

"You mean Cadet. Who are you?"

"Jeremiah York."

"I'll ask him if he wants to see you." The clerk got up after a moment, knocked on the closed door that bore the legend: *Office du Directeur.*

The clerk stuck his head inside, muttered a few words. He waited, then closed the door.

"Monsieur Cadet Chouteau says to tell you to come on in," said the clerk. "Do not speak. Just wait until he talks to you. There are some men with him. Take the empty seat just to the right of the door when you go in."

"All right," said York. He took off his hat, pushed through the gate. The clerk opened the door again, ushered York inside. Jeremiah saw the empty chair, walked over to it, and sat down. Pierre did not look up, but continued to stare at the two burly, mustachioed men across from his desk. He sat behind piles of documents, fiddled with a turkey quill pen that he kept dabbing in and out of an inkwell sunk into his desk. He rubbed the point against the sides of the well each time, doing it without looking.

"Much as Pilcher irritates me at times, he's a good man," said Chouteau, his Creole accent contrasting sharply with his diction. He was an educated man who dearly loved the French language, but when he spoke English, he did not sprinkle it with French words. When he spoke French, he spoke it pure, as well. "His Otoe Outfit up at Cabanné's Post is doing well, even though he can't rely on his traders in the field yet."

"Joshua Pilcher won't give none of the tribes credit," complained one of the men talking to Chouteau. His name was Robert William Letterman. "Seems to me, he's missing a bet."

"Yair," said the other man, Letterman's brother Leo, "them

184

Otoes ain't the onliest Injuns. Them Omahas and Pawnees do some fair trappin' and we'd like to get some Sioux down to Cabanné's Post. They'd come in more if'n Pilcher loosened up his credit some."

Chouteau sighed and jabbed the quill pen in the well, riffled through a stack of letters on his desk. Before he found what he was looking for, he spoke about the bourgeois, the chief trader, Joshua Pilcher, almost affectionately.

"Pilcher," said Chouteau, "has a damned good reason for not giving credit to the Indians. He wrote me about it and said that anything the Indians bought on credit they considered a gift. In the past, he was liberal, and when he pressed for payment of the debt, the Indians just took their furs and skins to another trader."

"What about them Omahas last fall?" asked Robert William. "He give them credit."

"Powder and ball," said Chouteau. "However, that was a bribe."

"A bribe?"

"Those Omahas were exhausting his hospitality at Cabanné's Post and he wanted them out of there before they ate up the corn crop."

"Eh?" asked Leo, the elder of the two brothers.

"Corn for McKenzie's still," explained Chouteau. "Joshua has planted a bigger cornfield this spring so that he can provide McKenzie enough for his whiskey supplies at Fort Union."

"You are a shrewd man, Chouteau," said Leo. "I reckon we was wrong about Pilcher. Thought you and him didn't get along."

"Quite the contrary. I admire and respect Mr. Pilcher very much. He was the very man to take over Cabanné's Post, following that trouble with Leclerc. It is true that he admonishes me for writing letters to my agents in French and has so told me his displeasure in his letters. But Joshua does not read French and he distrusts my using a foreign language to communicate to my posts." His fingers extracted a letter from the pile and he rattled it as he held it up to read.

"Here's a typical missive from Joshua," said Chouteau. "This in reply to a letter of mine telling him of Cabanné's dislike of certain statements made to me last summer. In this one, Pilcher warned us all not to step on his toes: '. . . while my letters are open to the *criticism* of every gentleman—the man has yet to be born . . . who is to dictate the particular stile or phraseology of any communication I may think fit to make; or to restrain me in offering any suggestion which I may deem proper.' Now there's a man who knows what he's doing."

"He pays too low," said Leo Letterman bluntly.

"Ah, not so," said Cadet. "There is not much competition at present, but I have another letter from Pilcher here which tells me that he has instructed his traders in the field to hold to the exchange rate set at the post for all pelts. However, if another trader offers more, he has informed his men that they may outbid the competition."

"Last year Sublette and Campbell were plenty of competition," grumbled the younger Letterman.

"Well, they have gone from the Missouri now," said Cadet. "You will have to outrun them in the mountains, where they have gone."

"It does not look like a good year," said Robert William.

"It will be a wonderful year," said Cadet evenly, "but you will have to work hard for the pelts. You will find trading at Council Bluffs better than ever, I'm sure."

With that, Cadet stood up as if to dismiss the two traders. They rose, too, and the men shook hands all around. Chouteau graciously escorted the two brothers to the door, closed it behind them.

"Ah, young York, and how are you this fine summer morning?"

"Just fine, Mr. Chouteau. I come to get my outfit from you. Lalande plans to ride to Independence today."

"Good, good. I have your outfit, and a letter of introduction drawn up by one of my clerks. All that remains is to sign it and you can be on your way. Come."

Chouteau opened another door in the back of his office. It led to a storeroom laden with traps, rifles, powder, ball, knives, axes, pistols. Jeremiah's eyes widened as Chouteau pulled the curtains to let in the light of day. There were bales and boxes piled clear to the ceiling and, atop each one, a sample of the items they contained.

"Pick out for yourself a knife, a tomahawk, and then we will look at the rifles," said Chouteau.

"I don't know what kind of knife to get, but maybe it ought to be big," said Jeremiah.

"Ho, you've been talking to the men in Lalande's brigade. They like the big knives. Drew Ballentine carries one more suitable for skinning men than beaver. But, come, I will show you my choice. You want an all-purpose knife, one that can be used to butcher buffalo, elk, antelope, or the small animals you will trap."

Chouteau led Jeremiah over to a place where several barrels sat lodged snugly to one another. He tapped a lid and it swung open. He lifted it off and York saw the knives all laid out neatly inside the barrel. Their blades gleamed in the streaming sunlight and he could plainly read the legend on each smooth surface of those on the top, *Hiram Cutler, Sheffield.*

"Take one," said Chouteau. "I'll find you a scabbard, but you will one day want to make your own."

Jeremiah picked up one of the knives, hefted it in his hand. He grinned, and Chouteau slapped him on the back. Those knives had cost him nine cents apiece and sold for more than two dollars each at rendezvous or at one of the posts.

At another barrel, Jeremiah selected a Kentucky tomahawk with a fourteen-inch handle, a five-inch blade and a cutting edge of one and seven eighths inch. It weighed between three and four pounds, felt good in the hand.

"You'll have to make your own sheath, but it'll tuck in your belt or sash until then," said Cadet.

Jeremiah wandered through the stacks of blankets, the barrels of traps, to the wall where the rifles stood. Chouteau smiled, looked Jeremiah over closely. He felt the muscle of one arm, squeezed it as if it was a piece of fruit.

"You can handle a twelve-pound Hawken, perhaps," said the Frenchman. "Here's a .52-caliber rifle with a thirty-six-inch barrel. It throws a two hundred fourteen-grain ball with seventy-five grains of powder in the breech." He took the rifle from its storage rack, handed it to York. Jeremiah put it to his shoulder. He looked at the barrel, the muzzle, felt the steel lovingly. "Anything lighter might not stand up for you. You want to grow into it. That one will put some iron in your muscles. The lock on that one was made by Charles Siever in Hawken's shop. I saw him put it in. No markings on that barrel, but it's a genuine Hawken."

Chouteau explained the finer points of the rifle to York, told him it was officially listed as Hawken Plains Rifle on the company's books. It had a heavy, octagonal barrel, low sights, set trigger, percussion lock with a steel basket called a "snail" cradling the nipple, half stock, ramrod carried under a metal rib, sturdy butt stock with a crescent-shaped butt plate. "Throws a half-ounce ball of lead anywhere you point it," said Cadet.

"I like it."

"Good. I'll fix you up with powder and ball, percussion caps, throw in a possibles pouch. We've got some around here that will do you fine, I think. I'll ship your traps over with Lalande. You'll have enough to carry without that extra burden."

Chouteau gave him a knife sheath, and York selected a good wide belt with a massive buckle. He was proudest of the rifle and couldn't wait to shoot it. It grew more beautiful each moment he held it in his hand, looked at it. He liked the idea of using percussion caps instead of flint and steel. It made him feel he was almost a full-grown man.

Back in Cadet's office, he called in one of the clerks. The clerk, answering to the name of Terence, seemed familiar to

York. He wrote down the goods on a piece of foolscap, listing the items, but not the prices.

"Young Mr. Asterwold will give you a receipt," said Chouteau.

"You any kin to J.R.?" asked York.

"My brother," said Terence.

"J.R. is the wanderer," said Chouteau. "Terence has the eye for the money. He is my best clerk."

After Terence had left, Chouteau reached behind his desk, scuffled with something on the floor. He set the books on his desk.

"There is no charge for these," said the trader.

York looked at them, spluttered before he could speak a plain word.

"Wh-where did you get them?" he asked.

"A very beautiful young lady asked me to give them to you. She thinks you will enjoy reading them when you are holed up this winter."

"I don't want them," said York stubbornly, holding on to the rifle like a life preserver.

"Oh, I think it would be very rude to refuse such fine books. Reading them might make you many friends. Not many trappers can read such books."

"What did she tell you? Estrellita, I mean."

"She's a very headstrong young lady. I think she cares for you, York. Now, her family is another matter, but if I were a young man and I wanted her, I would try my best to see that I measured up to her father's standards, no?"

"I reckon. It's just that—that she made me mad."

Chouteau smiled. "The course of true love never runs smooth," he said. "It is a platitude, but true. I think this young woman likes you very much. She may give compliments to the young soldier, but she gives you the gift of knowledge. Is that not something?"

"I reckon," York said sullenly. He looked at the rifle again. It seemed the only real thing in the world at that moment.

"Take the books," said Chouteau quietly. "You will thank her, and me, someday."

"Aw, sure, Mr. Chouteau."

"Well, I think that concludes our business. There are many outside waiting to see me. Remember what I asked you to do. I will expect a report from you by the time of rendezvous in the spring."

Chouteau rose from the table, shook hands with York. He ushered the young man into the outer office. Terence Asterwold gave Jeremiah a receipt, complete with totals. The amount was staggering to him. York opened his mouth to protest, but he saw that the two clerks were already back to business and the door to Chouteau's office was closed. One of the men waiting was clearing his throat. Jeremiah folded up the receipt and walked outside carrying his gear. The knife hung awkwardly from a sheath attached to his belt. The leather was new and stiff. He carried the new belt over his shoulder, slung the possibles pouch, with powder, ball, and percussion caps over his left shoulder so that the bag hung on his right hip. He carried the books tucked under his arm. They were the most unwieldy of his possessions.

He looked up into the bright sunlight, squinted. His horse stood on the shady side of the street, reins tied to a hitchring in a cemented stone cairn. His bedroll was neatly tied behind the cantle, the saddlebags draped over the horse's flanks. Before, the horse had stood alone. Now, there was another hitched next to it, and his heart sank a foot when he saw it. No amount of squinting could erase the mare. She stood there, hipshot, next to Fleetfoot, dark leather saddle with silver inlays, freshly curried, sleek.

Then, out of the shadows, behind the horse, Estrellita appeared and Jeremiah's heart shot back up a foot and a half, lodged in his throat as if he was stricken. His eyes lost their squint and took on the contours of bright marbles. He gurgled something in his seized throat, stood there in the middle of the street as if rooted in stone.

"Jeremiah," she called, "come here. I want to talk to you. Hurry. I don't have much time."

He walked toward her as if plowing through a mud field. He felt like a goose heading toward the farmer's axe, all neck and bowlegged, waddling feet attached to stubby legs.

"Whatcha want?" he rasped, feeling more stupid by the second.

"I want to see you," she said insistently. "What's the matter with you? Did you get stung?"

"Huh?"

"You've got a lump on your chin. It's all swollen."

Jeremiah reached to touch his sore chin. The books dropped from under his arm. He grabbed for them and got tangled up in the Hawken. Estrellita laughed, ran to him. She bent down to retrieve the books at the same time that Jeremiah squatted to do the same. They looked into each other's eyes.

"Godamighty, Estrellita," he said.

"Don't swear," she said sweetly as she picked up the books and dusted them off.

They stood up, and she took his hand, led him across the street to his horse. She packed the books in one of his saddlebags as he stood by dumbly, staring at her shining black hair, the smooth olive texture of her face, her slender, graceful neck. He breathed in her perfume, a delicate aroma of honeysuckle and gardenia, summer flowers kissed by sun and rain, aromatic as a leaf-laced trellis in a garden grotto.

"Anything else you want to put in your saddlebags, Jeremiah?"

He shook his head dumbly.

"What about that new belt?"

"Oh, yeah, I reckon."

Estrellita smiled, snatched the belt off his shoulder, put it in the saddlebag.

"You'll need another scabbard for that new rifle. Maybe I ought to take the belt out and use it so you can hang the rifle from the saddlehorn."

191

"I carry it," he said.

"All right. Now, will you ride with me to a place where we can talk. Just you and me?"

"I don't know. I got to get on."

"Jeremiah! It's important." She looked at him earnestly. Her lips pulled together in a beseeching pout. "You have time. Please."

"I ain't never had no girl beg me before," he said.

"Well, I beg you. Let's go. We can ride over by the mounds or down by the levee. Or out by Planter's House."

Jeremiah really wanted to see Estrellita. More than ever, now that he was leaving St. Louis. Now that he'd seen her, he never wanted to leave her again. Her beauty radiated through him, infused him with powerful feelings, feelings he didn't sort out or understand.

"I reckon I can go—for a little while."

"Follow me," she said. "I know a quiet place by the river. It's not far." The two unhitched their horses and mounted up. Estrellita rode to Second Street, passed Convent, then followed the road south. A meadowlark trilled and the sounds of the city died away. Here, wildflowers grew, and prairie grasses waved graceful in the sun. Bees foraged among the blossoms of brown-eyed Susans and vagrant buttercups. A pair of prairie swifts darted overhead, slicing through the air in front of a brisk tailwind.

Estrellita turned her horse off the road, doubling back easterly, galloped the mare to the river. Jeremiah followed at a walk, not wishing to leave his goods strewn in the tall grasses or tire his mount. He looked back at the city. From this place it looked small and inconsequential, swallowed up and diminished by the wide expanse of sky and prairie. Still, he was nervous, although he knew he had time before he met with the Lalande brigade. It was just that he was anxious to be on his way west.

Estrellita was already dismounted by the time he rode up to her, the mare feeding on grass, snatching up clumps in her mouth, chewing silently. Jeremiah swung down, let the reins trail. His horse bent its neck to graze, and a flock of green-winged teal skidded to a landing in the river, a hundred yards downstream. On the other side of the river a lone redtail hawk whipped its wings, hovered over a field mouse or a rabbit, stationary in the sky. Seconds later, it folded its wings and plummeted to the earth in a fierce dive. Jeremiah waited for its scream but there was only silence, and moments later he saw the hawk skim low across the prairie, then flap its pinions to gain altitude.

"It's beautiful out here, isn't it?"

"Yeah, sure is," said Jeremiah.

"Away from people."

"That party still goin' on?"

"Yes. I told Lucia I wanted to go out riding."

"She didn't like it much," he said.

Estrellita laughed. That was the best thing about her, he thought. The way she laughed. The sound of her laughter. Like music, like dulcimer music, or his mother humming when she thought nobody was around, kind of low in her throat and yet high and pretty like a woman's voice should be, the way it came out of her throat, high and sweet. Pretty and bright as quicksilver. He could listen to her laughter forever. It made him feel bright inside, made him happy.

"It wouldn't surprise me if she came by on the next riverboat and stepped off on the shore right here."

Jeremiah laughed.

She took his hand in hers and the touch startled him. He looked around as if expecting to see Lucia, or someone. She moved close to him and there was that scent of her again, only earthier, more like earth and wildflowers, like the prairie flowers he kept seeing, different ones all the time, so many he had lost count of them.

"I wanted to talk to you," she said. "I didn't want you to go to the mountains with anger in you, being angry at me."

"Aw, I ain't angry no more."

"You're not angry *any* more."

"'At's what I said."

"You misunderstood what Augustino was . . . was doing to me. He . . . he was taking liberties."

"I don't like him much."

"Let's not talk about him. I just wanted you to know I didn't want him to kiss me."

"You didn't? Honest?"

"Honest," she laughed, and squeezed his hand. "I want you to come to Santa Fe when you come back from the mountains."

"How come?"

"I'll miss you. I won't be able to stand it being there without you."

"You make me feel warm all over, Estrellita." She squeezed his hand then, and she looked up at him, her eyes misting, and he felt something in him melt like soft wax, felt his stomach sink, float down.

"I . . . I can't tell you how you make me feel. I just know I want to see you again."

"I reckon you will," he said.

She put her arms around his waist, hugged him tightly, so tightly he could feel the soft cushions of her breasts. Then, as quickly, she released him.

"I must go," she said breathlessly.

He held her to him, not wanting her to go, not wanting her to take those feelings away from him. Feelings of want and need, a shivering of his heart that made him tingle all over.

"Estrellita . . ."

"Kiss me," she breathed. He felt his heart sink as his stomach had and he stood on strange, weak legs, stunned with the immensity of his feelings, the rapture that glowed in him like heat lightning.

He kissed her, and felt a tightness in his chest, a suffocation, like drowning in heat, just gasping on boiled summer air, breathing in heat and drowning. The kiss made him burn all over and made his heart jump and his head swim with dizziness.

"No . . . more," she sighed as she broke the kiss, stepped away from him. "I . . . I must go now."

"No. Don't go."

"I love you, Jeremiah," she said softly. "I want you always to remember that. Wherever you are, remember I love you. I love you."

"I . . . I love you, too, Estrellita. God, I really love you."

"I'll be your sweetheart, always."

Her words pierced him like thorns, made him feel good and sad at the same time. His sweetheart. He had never had one, never had someone to care for him. He opened his mouth to speak, but he was struck dumb by what she had said, the kiss still hot on his lips. She ran from him, to her horse, and rose easily in the stirrup, swung into the saddle. She waved at him through a shimmering haze and he waved back, fought down the tears that surged unbidden to his eyes. He kept waving as she rode off, to the south, to the Vial ranch, and she waved back just before she disappeared over the horizon and it was the most terrible moment in his life. He felt so empty. Lost in emptiness. Lost in self-pity, in exultation. She made him feel so grand, she made him feel grander than he had ever felt.

He wanted to go after her then. Go after her and take her with him.

He stood there for a long time, rooted to the spot, the wide river washing by him, swirling in mysterious eddies, muddy, powerful, changing constantly. He took a deep breath and kicked at a clod of dirt beneath his feet.

"I love her," he said aloud. "I love her and she loves me."

Then, he gave a warwhoop, and Fleetfoot looked up from grazing, shook his head. The reins rattled like hailstones on shingles.

He rode slowly back to St. Louis. He kept looking back, expecting to see Estrellita come riding his way. But she was gone and he was empty inside. Empty and full. Full of her and empty, too, because she was gone.

Chapter Thirteen

The winds blew off the Mississippi, carried the smells of St. Louis and the fine grains of grit from the sandy levee upon which it was built. Someone on shore fired a swivel gun and men shouted, cheered, as a cloud of smoke rose in the air. Seagulls wheeled over the anchored boats, screaming above the whitewashed stone buildings that seemed to follow no builder's pattern but were like a child's blocks tossed helter-skelter onto a giant sandpile. More than seven thousand people lived in the city now and their garbage added to the rank stench that floated southward on the warm April breeze.

Jeremiah rode down Second Street, turned on Market. Here, brick buildings had begun, some years earlier, to replace the homely stone structures built by the French when St. Louis was still the capital of Missouri Territory. Market was filled with men, horses and mules, Indians, trappers, merchants, hunters, streaming in both directions, talking, smoking, yelling to one another. It was not difficult to find the baked-brick warehouse where Lalande's brigade had gathered to outfit for the summer trip to the Rocky Mountains.

There were actually two large warehouses flanking a vacant lot. Wagons were lined up on both sides of the street, waiting to dump the loads of supplies onto the lot. Men shouted and cursed. Whips cracked like gunshots and there was a reek of whiskey in the morning air. Mules squealed and brayed, horses whinnied. The din surprised York from a block away. When Jeremiah rode up, he heard his name called.

"York, get your sweet ass off that horse and get to work!"

"Huh?"

Drew Ballentine stepped out into the street. He carried a twenty-foot bullwhip, coiled up like a snake, in his hand.

"There ain't no free trappers in this party, Son. Get down and get to sweatin' or I'll take yore goddamned hide and sell it to the Absaroky!"

Jeremiah leaped from his horse, led it to a hitchring, and tied it up. Drew had disappeared, gone into the cloud of dust that the mules and horses had roiled up on the empty lot. He choked on the flying dirt, fought his way through men and animals, dodging recalcitrant mules and skittish horses, to one of the warehouses, its doors opened like a gaping maw.

"York!" shouted someone, and Jeremiah squinted to see through the swirling dust. "Over here!"

Jim Karns stood on the sloping loading dock of the warehouse, shirtless, his chest sleek with sweat, his mouth crooked with a sly grin, his dark, kinky hair glistening in the sun, flecked with dust and dirt like everything else in the maelstrom of the yard. It took Jeremiah a moment to connect the face with the name.

"Yes," said York. "I'm comin'."

"York, you help me tally these trade goods and then we'll load them mules. Time's a-wastin'."

Karns had a slate in one hand, a chunk of chalk in the other. As soon as he filled one slate, a clerk seated at a small desk transferred the data to foolscap with a quill pen. Men wrestled barrels and crates to the loading dock, stacked them waist-high, then retreated into the dankness of the warehouse for more goods.

"Whatcha want me to do?"

"I'll sing 'em out, you tally 'em down like this," said Karns. "You kin write, cain't ye? Kin ye cipher?"

"Some."

"Take this slate and chalk then, an' jest foller my scratchin's, then when it's full up, hand it to the clerk feller there."

Jeremiah looked over the list the clerk was writing, scanned it quickly.

Coffee	30 bags
Hams	500 lbs.
Powder	100 sqt.
Lead	15 brls.
Horse Shoes	60
Beads, Large	10 brls.
Beads, Small	10 brls.
Sugar	55 pcks.
Knives	10 dz.
Tobacco	10 1/2 kegs
Cloth, Scarlet	250 yds.
Cloth, Blue	250 yds.
Vermillion	2 cases
Trinkets	40 packs
Lead bars	240 lbs.
Flint	2000 bags
Salt	50 lbs.
Cloth, plain	45 yds.
Ribbons	300 yds.
Axes	
Hoes	

The clerk had not yet written the figures down for the last two items. Jeremiah took the slate from Karns. Jim started pushing boxes toward the ramp where other men waited to carry the goods to those loading the items in panniers onto the mules. Others were breaking up the items into smaller bundles for packing, cracking barrels, smashing open crates.

York began tallying, and for the next hour, he marked down coffee, sugar, tobacco, powder, fish hooks, flints, scissors, knives, cloth, both blue and scarlet, lead, blankets, buttons, axes, rifles, pistols, castor, trinkets, tacks, until he was dizzy from it.

"Let's go load us some mules, Lucky," said Karns as Andersen and Asterwold relieved the two.

"Lucky?"

Karns grinned.

For the next two hours, Jeremiah worked at breaking open crates and barrels, wrapping knives and axes in cloth and weighing them by feel so that Karns could pack the panniers. The mountain man threw diamond hitches on the packs when they were loaded, cinched the ropes up tight. Soon the line of loaded mules began to extend out of the yard and down the block.

"What the hell we carryin' all this stuff for?" York asked Karns when they stopped to rest.

"Gettin' it to rondeevoo," said Karns. "Big doin's, you'll see. We had a poor winter or we'd still be up thar in the cool."

"I never saw so much stuff."

"Me, neither, York. We'll pick up food and sech when we gets to Independence. Maybe it means a good year, but I don't see it gettin' no better. More trappers mean less beaver for the rest of us, and I ain't never seed so many trappers as what was up thar last season. An' goods goin' outta here like I never seed. Sublette, now, he's a-tryin' to beat Wyeth and we're a-tryin' to beat 'em all to the Green."

Jeremiah didn't understand half of what Karns was talking about, but he knew who William Sublette was, and he'd heard the name of Nathaniel Wyeth more than once. They were mountain men, legends back in Illinois and even here in St. Louis. He was to hear more about these two men in the days to come, for there was, that summer of 1834, trouble brewing for the fur trade and dark clouds on the horizon for American Fur, indeed, for all of them setting out in April for the summer rendezvous.

Mike Finnegan loomed up on the lot, his wide shoulders

eclipsing a portion of the sun. His shadow fell on York like shade from a magnolia tree and Jeremiah looked up at Big Un's grinning visage.

"Har, Lucky," said the big Irisher, "and be ye all in one piece after such a night?"

Jeremiah rubbed his jaw, blinked in bewilderment.

"What'd Eyestone tell you?" he asked, flushing with embarrassment.

"Wal, now, he didn't tell me nothin' at all, at all, and now, why should he?"

"Why'd you ask after my health then?"

"'Cause I thought maybe you got in a scrape is all, and now enough of this talk, Lucky York, we've got a pack mule for ye and we'd best get him saddled and loaded."

"For me?"

"Sure, you got to pull a mule of your own same as the rest of us, and Baptiste picked this 'un out special for the likes of yourself."

Karns winked at him as he followed the waddling bulk of Finnegan over to the street. There, its halter rope wrapped around a crate, stood a swaybacked, moth-eaten mule, blunt-nosed, wild-eyed, slat-ribbed, mane bristled like a razorback hog's, ears jutted up like a pair of frog-stickers.

"Looks mean as cuss," said York.

"Why, that's ol' Beelzebub," said Finnegan, good-naturedly. "Harmless as gingerbread."

"I seen mules before. That one's got the wild eye."

"Well, he's your'n, Lucky, and, Baptiste, he's only takin' ten skins out'n yore pay. A bargain, sonny, and that critter knows the way to the shinin' mountains, knows where the beaver is, *begorra*."

"I'll bet he knows where my stones are, too," said Jeremiah warily. He circled the animal, and Beelzebub's eyes rolled back in their sockets, showing white and wild, and the ears lay back like a pair of nutting shears. The mule cocked one hind foot and he swung his head to follow the youth.

"Just talk sweet to him, York, and pat him some. Then you better throw a pack saddle on him and tie a longer rope to that halter. We got to make tracks for fair, we do, and time, the old bitch, she's a-wastin'."

Jeremiah kept his distance, completed his circle. Beelzebub tracked him every inch of the way, wall-eyed, its short-cropped mane bristly as a riled porcupine, ears laid back, nostrils rippling rubbery, lips pulled back from bared teeth.

A crowd gathered. Jeremiah recognized some of them. Lalande was there, Andersen, Ballentine, and Asterwold. Other faces swam before him, grinning faces that he did not recognize. Men stood in judgment over him, but they had come to scoff and to see him get mule-kicked into the dust. Jeremiah knew that. He could feel their scorn as he could feel the April sun on his face.

"Wal, get to it," said a voice from the throng.

Jeremiah looked around him, saw a stack of trade blankets atop a wooden crate. He snatched one up, dashed up to the mule, and whipped it open. Beelzebub squared away for battle, jerked backward until the lead rope tautened like a piano wire. York didn't give the animal time to think but quickly smothered its head with the blanket, blinding it. Then, as the animal kicked and brayed, Jeremiah grabbed up the wooden pack-saddle, slammed it onto the animal's back. Quickly, he cinched it up expertly. He removed the blanket with a flourish, refolded it and put it back on the pile as the mule blinked, snorted steam from its nostrils, and twitched its fight-scarred ears.

A cheer rose up from the assemblage of mountain men. Jeremiah grinned.

"You'll do, Son," said Andersen. "Never saw no mule skint that way. Last one tried to put a pack saddle on Beelzebub got a chunk bit out o' his laig."

"J.R., he got hisself kicked into the middle of next week," said Karns, "and that was on a Monday."

"What would you have done if they warn't no blanket?"

asked J.R. solemnly.

"Put some more bite marks on his ear," said York.

Asterwold suppressed a smile.

Men guffawed and one or two slapped Jeremiah's back before going back to work. York began to work with Big Un, filling panniers, attaching the canvas bags to Beelzebub's pack-saddle.

Lalande began going around to all the men and Jeremiah saw the train begin to form in the street as they lined up the loaded pack mules and brought their horses up. Karns yelled at him to get his horse and Jeremiah took off at a run. He tied a lead rope to Beelzebub's halter and hitched it around his saddle horn. Men began to mount their horses. Big Un rode a dray horse, but he made it look like a pony with his bulk and weight. He pulled a pair of mules as the pack train moved down the street. Jeremiah felt a thrill as Fleetfoot took his place in line, between Karns and Andersen. Some of the men fired pistols in the air. He looked back and saw Eyestone riding a horse unlike any he had ever seen before.

"What's Eyestone riding?" he asked Karns.

Karns stood up in the stirrups, looked back over his shoulder.

"He got him one of them Nez Perce ponies, I reckon," said Karns. He spat a stream of tobacco juice out of the side of his mouth. Some of it stuck to his dark beard. "Mighty fine pony."

"How come everybody's callin' me 'Lucky'?" asked York.

"Well, now, Eyestone figgers in that, I reckon."

"Huh?"

"Don't you know, boy? He got him a slice across his belly last night. After he left you, they was two men come up to do you in."

Jeremiah's stomach fell.

"What're you talkin' about? I never saw nobody."

"Howsomever. They was two a-follerin' you and Eyestone, he got into a tangle with 'em. He kilt one, maybe scraped hide offen the other."

York rubbed his face in bewilderment.

"How come he never said nothin' to me?"

"That's his way, Son. Lucky for you he was around. They was fixin' to gut you."

"Who were they?"

"Man he kilt was Sanchez. He trapped with Sublette one season, come to Lalande's brigade last spring. He kept to hisself, was a fair trapper till he joined the Army in Santa Fe."

"Who was he with last night?" asked York.

"Damned if I know. Eyestone don't know neither. Best lay it to rest, Son. You owe Eyestone a favor sometime, that's about it."

"I could have been killed?"

"I reckon the Mex was a-tryin' to put yore lamp out."

The pit in York's stomach deepened. He looked back at Eyestone, but they were pulling a corner and he didn't see him. He rode alone in silence, listened to the shouts of the mountain men and the farewells from the citizens in the street. He saw men and women waving, got choked up when a pretty girl waved to him. He kept looking for Estrellita, but he knew she would not be there. There was a sadness in him, and a fear, too. He was going to places where he had never been, with men he did not know. And, perhaps, one among them was with Sanchez the night before, had wanted to kill him.

"Don't you worry about it none," said Karns when they finally reached the prairie, the road to Independence. The line of men was broken up by then, stretched out, some riding together, some alone. He looked back, saw Big Un way in the rear. He looked closely at the other men around him, but did not see any that he knew, could not see murder on their expressionless faces.

"You reckon that other jasper is a-ridin' with us?"

"Oh, that's right likely, I'd say. No tellin' who it is, though."

"You make me feel real good, Karns."

"Wal, now, jest wait till you get to the mountains, York. There, now, maybe you'll find some shinin' times."

"What do you mean?" he asked Karns.

Karns cut off a chunk from a tobacco twist, jammed it into his mouth. His mouth appeared for a moment, lips small and sensuous as a baby's, then disappeared in the dark tangle of his beard.

"Did you ever see diamonds?"

"No," said York.

"Sometimes when I'm up there in the mountains, I see the streams running full with 'em. And I seed 'em in the snows, a-clingin' to the trees and dancing in the air like fireflies. And, blue, you ain't never seen blue like some skies when you're high up, close to God. I seen things in the mountains that chokes me up and makes me want to shout and jump like a crazy man, and I done that, too, more'n once't I can tell you. And when it's green and spring and the ice is breaking up on the rivers, you can feel it in your blood, it's like them waters is in your blood and you can feel it in your veins. It don't come quick nor all at once't, but someday you wake up and everything you see just makes your eyes pop out and it's like seeing everything new and fresh for the first time. But it's in you and around you and you get drunk on it. That's what shinin' times are, York, and if'n you spend any time in the mountains, you'll see what I mean, by God."

"How long do you have to stay up there before you see it like that?"

"Haw! Ain't no way to put it into a clock, boy. Season, neither. It comes when it comes and no sooner ner later. You'll see."

"How long you been goin' to the mountains, Possum Killer?"

"Haw, I come here in '23 or '24, when Saint Louie was full of gumbos, more Frenchies than they is now, and folks in Illinois said God didn't cross the river, but I crossed her anyways, and heard talk of beaver and money for pelfries. Heard talk that Ashley was putting together men to winter in the mountains. So, I spent all my money thinkin' of beaver pelfries sellin' fer five to eight dollars the pound, and this feller Clyman come got me out of the Green Tree and hired me on."

"And you went to the mountains?"

"I surely did and they was times I wanted to turn back 'fore we ever got there, what with the Rees killin' us and Injuns after our skelps at ever' turn and towin' the boats and goin' hungry. Wonder we ever made it. We had some mean niggers with us, I swear. The scum of St. Louis. Clyman, he was the clerk for Ashley, said Falstaff's battalion was genteel by comparison to our rough bunch."

"Is it any different now?" York asked.

"Ain't no different, Jeremiah. Men's the same anywheres you go. 'Cept most of these been after the beaver and has got some seasonin'. We was all mostly green as calf shit and twice't as rank. You keep an eye out for that other nigger what tried to gut ye last night. Likely he'll show his hand one of these days. When you least expect it."

"Maybe I better talk to Eyestone."

"You wait till he talks to you, you want my advice."

"Why?"

"Eyestone, he calls the turn pretty much."

Karns said no more and pulled his pony and mule ahead as if to signal that the conversation was finished. Jeremiah lagged back, hoping to talk to Eyestone about the night before, but the man kept his distance. There were stops as poorly packed mules dropped their loads and the train stretched out even more.

Jeremiah looked across the prairie and at the sky and wondered how the mountains could be so much different. He felt good to be alive and on his way to the Rockies. Yet he yearned for Estrellita to share it all with him. There was, also, a sinking sensation in the maw of his stomach, a swallowing that told him she was promised to another. Hers was a family of wealth and power. He was just a poor boy with no trade, no money, no friends. He had made brash promises to her, but now, lost in this vastness of sky and earth, he had never felt

206

smaller, more insignificant. Among these hardy, rough men, he was but a boy, untested, unproven. The road seemed to stretch forever, and he knew it would be many days before they reached the mountains. When he got there, would he be man enough to take his place beside these trappers?

There was fear in him as he thought of these things. A fear without name or substance, but a fear just the same. What was it? He wondered. Was he afraid of losing something? He had nothing. Estrellita? He did not have her, either. But he wanted her. He wanted her to love him, to marry him. Someday.

A warm April breeze blew against his face. A soft wind that might have come all the way from the Rocky Mountains. He swelled his chest with breath and breathed it in, and it steeled something in him. He was no longer afraid. He would match the mountains. There, he knew, lay wealth beyond any he had ever known. And there, too, lay his future, his manhood, his very destiny.

Chapter Fourteen

Lieutenant Merito Salcedo looked down at the dead face of Láncer Private Jesus Horcasitas. The body lay on a pine pallet inside a warehouse situated along the levee on Front Street. St. Louis Constable Guillaume Fourchet brushed away the flies that gathered at one of the dead man's eyes which refused to stay closed. Captain Augustino Armijo grimaced as the hairy insects took flight like a covey of miniature quail. The eye, as the flies fled and returned, seemed to be constantly winking at the three men.

"We found him early this morning," said Constable Fourchet, "in an alley behind a church on Vine Street. My men stripped the body so that you could see the wounds."

"He appears to have been in a fight," said Salcedo thickly. Flies swarmed over the winking eye.

"He had a knife in his hand," said the constable. "Do you know the man?"

"He was one of my men," said Armijo.

"Yes, he was in our company," said Salcedo, grimacing.

"Perhaps you will want to question your men?" beseeched the constable. "Perhaps one among them is wounded?"

"I will do so," said the lieutenant.

"Yes, we will conduct a thorough investigation," interjected Armijo. "But I doubt if a soldier did this."

"It is brutal enough," said the constable, "but I have retraced the man's steps of last evening. He was in rough company, to be sure."

"Eh?" Salcedo grunted.

The constable was a man in his forties, sallow-complexioned, with hooded eyes, a lean, hawkish nose, thin lips. His blue eyes were almost colorless as if he had lived underground all his life. His blue serge uniform was lightweight, threadbare at the sleeves. The seat of his pants were almost shiny enough to see one's face in, and the creases in his trousers had long since lost their memory. He looked, in the garish light of the warehouse, like a cadaver on the mortician's table, the pigments not yet added to his cheeks, formaldehyde gray as grease in his veins. In truth, he worked at night, patroling the raucous levee, the rough waterfront with its taverns and grogshops, where men fought over sluts or money or rum as often as they brawled for the sheer joy of it.

Like the vampire Dracula, Fourchet seldom saw the sun, and his vapid eyes squinted now as he looked at the two officers, resplendent in their uniforms. Shortly before dawn he had learned the identity of the dead man and where the New Mexican troops were quartered. It had taken him another three hours to track down Armijo and Salcedo. He did not expect them to turn over one of their men, but it was his responsibility to attend to the body and see that it was delivered to the proper authorities, after which, he would make out his report and forget about the dead Lancer. During his years of service to the constabulary, he had seen other dead men: wagoners, trappers, ex-soldiers, drifters, thieves, pimps, rivermen, stevedores, even some who lived in one of the limestone residences above the levee's foul stench, men who had wandered down from their mansions furnished with crystal, mahogany, cut German crystal, Parisian velvet, and Oriental lace. He had never seen a New Mexican soldier on the undertaker's slab before, but he knew the knife work well.

"Ah, what did you find out?" asked Salcedo, shooting a

worried glance in Augustino's direction.

Fourchet folded his hands behind his back, pooched his lips in a Gallic moue, drew himself up as if summoning a display of his mental notes from some deep part of his mind.

"The soldier was seen in the company of an unknown trapper last evening. He entered alone sometime around nine of the clock, perhaps as late as ten, and sat with this man in a corner of a grogshop called the Red Boar. Later in the evening a young man came in alone and joined a group of trappers who were drinking with Baptiste Lalande, who is known to us. The young man's name was York, I believe, and he is no longer in the city. When York left the tavern, the soldier and the trapper also left, a few moments later. A young tavern maid named Sally Brewer remembered that she had worried about the young man at that time."

"Do you know the name of this trapper?" asked Salcedo.

"I was hoping you might question some of your men about him. We do not know the name."

"What he looks like?"

"Sal—Miss Brewer recalls that he was a big man, with a heavy beard. She did not get a good look at him. He seemed not to want to be noticed."

"I see," said Salcedo, trying not to gloat. "Go on, Constable."

"Nothing more. I have since learned that York left with the Lalande Brigade and did not appear to have been wounded. We did find the place where the fight occurred, however, and we believe the unknown trapper might have been hurt. There were blood spots leading away from where the most blood was found. We are still looking for this trapper, but many have ridden out for Independence this day and we do not expect to find him in the city."

"I see," said Armijo calmly. "Sir, we thank you for your report. We regret this most unfortunate incident. We will send some men to remove the body of this Lancer."

"Will you inform the constabulary of any information you

may obtain regarding the death of this man?" asked Fourchet.

"We will do this," said Armijo officiously. "I will see to it that everything is done to bring the soldier's murderer to justice."

"Ah, then, there is nothing more to say about it," said the constable. "I will wait outside with my men until you arrange to have the body taken away. Gentlemen."

Fourchet saluted the two men and walked out into the sunlight, shading his pale eyes with a frail, bony hand. He crossed the street where two other police officers waited, leaning against the shady bricks of a building. Salcedo looked again at the wounds in the soldier's torso. The belly was ripped open. Intestines, severed like sausages, bulged from the gaping slit, gleamed a dull pewter. There was a deep cut over the heart, just to the right of the breastbone high up on the chest.

There was silence for a few moments. Somewhere, a church bell tolled the hour in twelve mournful gongs that lingered in the death-scented air of the warehouse like tendrils of incense, brassy, somber echoes in a dim-lit cave.

"It looks like someone drove the knife in with a hammer," said the lieutenant, speaking Spanish.

"Is this the man you hired to kill York?"

"He is the one I sent to get the job done, 'Tino. He knew one of the trappers."

"Well, you have made a fine tangle of worms out of this, Merito."

"Patience, my friend. This one got caught with his hand in the purse, but he is not the assassin."

"Not anymore," said Armijo dryly.

"No, he never was. It is the trapper who is to kill York, that burr in your hair."

"What is his name?"

"I do not know. He was a friend of Horcasitas."

Augustino's eyes clouded over like a thunderstorm sky. He and Merito had become strong friends, ever since the fighting in Tampico, under Generalissimo Antonio Lopez de Santa

212

Anna Perez de Lebron. In 1829, Santa Anna was jolted from his preoccupation with the American malcontents in Texas by a foolhardy invasion launched by resurgent imperalists in Spain. In August, three thousand Spanish troops landed at the port of Tampico. Merito and Augustino marched with Santa Anna, who easily routed the Spanish Army, whose members were nearly starving, broken down with fever and were ill-equipped to wage war on foreign soil. Santa Anna proclaimed the battle an epic victory and called himself the "Hero of Tampico." Later, he began calling himself the "Napoleon of the West." Now, he was president of Mexico, and he had rewarded Salcedo and Armijo with posts in Santa Fe. Merito had fought bravely at Tampico and Augustino trusted him. But now he was disappointed in his friend from the province of Coahuila, bright as he was, loyal as he was to his uncle, the ex-governor.

"I must know the terms you arranged, Merito."

Salcedo stiffened.

"I did this for you, 'Tino. I knew you did not want a rival, especially an American bantam cock like York. So I ordered Horcasitas to contact his friend, a trapper, and have this man put the blade to the gringo. He was paid half of the money to seal the bargain, with a promise of the other half when he brought proof of York's death to me."

"And where did the money come from?"

"Why, from my own purse, 'Tino."

"How will we know that this trapper will fulfill the agreement?"

"Since he did not kill York here, he will bring me his scalp in Santa Fe. If he does not, then I offer my own locks in fair exchange."

Augustino laughed. Merito grinned impishly as if to remind Armijo why he liked the man. He slapped Salcedo on the shoulder.

"Let us arrange to have this piece of meat carried off to company headquarters. Unless you have a better idea."

Merito grinned wider. He looked at the dead lancer.

"*Levantase Lazaro,*" he said soberly. "Arise, Lazarus."

"No, you fool," joked Augustino. "This man is named Jesus. He does not need your exhortations. He can rise of his own accord."

Merito laughed. The two men walked away from the corpse, friends once again. Jesus Horcasitas was forgotten in a few moments as the soldiers began to talk of other things.

"I believe we will return to Santa Fe soon," said Armijo.

"Why do you say this? We have just arived."

"I heard Don Miguel talking to Pedro Vial last night. He wishes to buy goods to sell in Santa Fe. He ordered thirty-five wagons."

Merito whistled. "He will be rich."

"And so shall we, someday. There is opportunity everywhere you look, is it not true?"

"It is true," said Salcedo, and his eyes shone like polished stones in the sunlight.

"Must we return to Santa Fe so soon, my husband?" asked Corazon that afternoon as the wagons pulled into the field outside the hacienda. The *fiesta de cumpleaños* would begin again in the afternoon, but now the dew was just burning off the grasses and the rancho was quiet except for the trill of meadowlarks and the catlike chirp of a mockingbird atop the trellis where the wisteria vines trembled in the soft April breeze. The flagstones quivered with leaf shadows all around the couple as they watched the drovers bring in the heavy wagons, line them up in orderly phalanxes.

"There is a profit to be made," said Don Miguel, "even with the heavy taxes. And we must demonstrate that the Santa Fe Trail is the *llave,* the key to progress in our valley, all along the Rio del Norte."

"But I am worried about Estrellita. Do you not think that we should stay away from Santa Fe for a few more weeks, or months, perhaps."

"We cannot hide forever," said Don Miguel.

"I am frightened of Tecolote. I keep thinking of Don Ignacio Baca and his daughter, Maria."

"That was a long time ago, my dove."

"Lucia, too, broods about it."

"Lucia broods about everything, *mi cariño*. In times of darkness, she draws the drapes tight and blows out all the candles."

Corazon laughed, but it was forced, strained like tautened leather, and Don Miguel put his arm around her waist, drew her to him. Like dancers in slow motion, they stood there, watching the wagons rumble up the road, each pulled by a pair of Missouri mules.

"I dread the trip, but I know it's important."

"More important than you know. General Armijo must learn that his arrogance and greed is costing all of us a fortune. Unless he protects the trail and welcomes trade, Santa Fe and Taos will dry up like gourds and we will all blow away like seeds in the wind."

"When will we leave, my husband?" she asked.

"Within a week."

"We must see to it that Estrellita is safe once we return."

"You have my promise," said Don Miguel.

Estrellita entered the Montez hacienda dressed as a servant girl, her long black hair tied up in symmetrical twin buns framing her veiled face. Her dusty peasant's dress, of gray muslin, hung loosely on her frame. She carried a carpetbag, wore moccasins and leggings to complete the illusion. Following her into the house, Lucia peered everywhere at once like a gawking turkey, her sharp eyes squinted to pick out the most infinitesimal speck of trouble, whether it be signal smoke in the mountains, a band of Comanches riding through the valley, or a sheep wandering off by itself. Other servants, these genuine, followed the *dueña* inside, single file, carrying

215

luggage and boxes from the coach and the freight wagons that lined the courtyard, their drovers gathered at the watering trough, wetting themselves down in the July heat.

"Put those in the parlor. That box goes upstairs to the don's bedroom. Put that crate over there," ordered Lucia in staccato Spanish. "Be careful. That box is filled with expensive vases."

The *mozos* scrambled at the whiplash of her tongue, some lugging boxes and trunks up the winding stairs, others streaming off into different parts of the house, their sandals clacking on tiled floors. Lucia took off her mantilla, shook the dust from the lacy shawl, and laid it atop a table. She inspected the room with a hawk-eyed glance, from the small statues called *bultos,* whittled from the soft root of the cottonwood tree, to the carvings on the walls, *santos* coated with a plaster made of animal glue and gypsum, painted with pigments made from plants and roots, iron ores and charcoal and laid on with hog's bristle brushes. There was the Virgin Mary, brightly painted, arms outstretched, a beatific smile on her faintly Moorish face, standing serenely atop an armoire; a *bulto* of San Isidore, the patron of farmers, tilling his soil behind miniature oxen on a small table in a corner of the spacious adobe-cool room, a set of religious cartouches carved on an amber-toned *retablo* portraying Nuestra Señora de Guadalupe that told of her revelations to a Mexican Indian, Juan Diego, in 1531, when she appeared before him in that Mexican city. Over the mantelpiece above the massive tone fireplace, a two-foot carving of Jesus dying on the cross looked down on smaller statues of his mother and John the Baptist. Lucia unfastened the cloth thongs of her cape and folded it neatly before placing it on the top of the divan.

"Well," she said, "we are home at last."

"I don't see why I have to wear these old servant's clothes," pouted Estrellita. "They make me feel poor and homely."

"Perhaps it is good for you to feel humble once in a while, my child."

"I feel wretched."

216

"It must not be known that you are the daughter of the don and his lady," said Lucia. "Those *peones Indios* have big eyes and ears. Did you not hear the story of Don Ignacio Baca and his daughter, Maria?"

"No," said Estrellita impatiently. "And I want to go upstairs and change into one of my new dresses."

"Inside the house, you may wear what you wish," said Lucia. "But if you venture from these walls, you must dress like a servant. That is the wish of your mother and father."

"How long must I do this?"

"Child, I do not know. Until Tecolote dies or no longer comes to this hacienda. Or until you marry Captain Armijo."

Estrellita sighed deeply. They had argued about Augustino all the way from St. Louis to this valley bordering the Rio del Norte. She was glad that Augustino and Merito Salcedo had accompanied her father's wagons in to Santa Fe, for the governor's nephew had been most persistent in his attentions toward her throughout the long and arduous journey. Although he had been most ardent, she had been cool to him, much to Lucia's annoyance and displeasure. Augustino, however, seemed not to mind, for he kept reminding her that once they were back in Santa Fe, he would resume the courtship right up until the day they married, at the January Fair, la Fiesta de Enero, in Chihuahua.

"I do not know why my father should fear an Indian," said Estrellita to change the subject.

"Tecolote is a Comanche, that is why. He thinks you are dead, and if he ever learns the truth, why, he might bring the whole nation of Comanches down on Don Miguel's rancho and kill us all. The Comanches have long memories. Tecolote would have you marry his son and bring shame to your family. Have I not told you about Don Ignacio Baca? What happened to him?"

"No. And I do not think I wish to hear this story."

"Well, you will hear it, young lady, and perhaps you will understand why you must comport yourself with wariness

217

until your marriage to Augustino Armijo."

"There you go again. Do not I have any choice in the matter?"

"None. None at all."

"Woe to me, then, Lucia. I feel as if I am just a pawn in a game of chess. Someone moves me here and then moves me there until I am finally captured—no, sacrificed for the sake of the king and queen. I don't care about the Comanches and I would not marry a man I did not love."

"Sit down, my mistress," said Lucia. "Listen to me, for you are not unlike Maria Baca, and everyone knows what a sad end she came to."

"I have never heard of her."

"Sit," said Lucia.

Estrellita shrugged. Her shoulders drooped as she sat down. She loosened the laces on her boots, loosened the garment she wore. The servants continued to carry in luggage, speechless but noisy with their clacking sandals and their grunts, made for Lucia's benefit so that she would be aware that they were working.

"Go on and tell your old story," said Estrellita. She affected a look of boredom on her face.

Lucia sat in a chair, ever prim and straight-backed, wooden as any of the carvings in the room. She drew herself up as an orator would and began speaking slowly, her voice hushed so that the servants would not overhear.

"There is a village south of Santa Fe, south of Albuquerque," said Lucia. "It is called Tomé. It is a small village, and these things I speak of happened many years ago, maybe sixty years ago. There was a wise man, a man *muy sabio,* who lived there. He was *rico,* but not so rich as the grand hidalgos who settled these lands. He had much respect because he owned more than a million sheep and the village looked to him for advice in important matters. On one occasion, he was asked to negotiate a truce between the village and a band of Comanches who were said to have come from the north, from the Sangre de Christo range of mountains.

"Don Ignacio made the truce and it lasted nearly ten years. It proved to be profitable for him, as well, because each year the Comanche chief would come to the village bringing fine horses or buffalo robes which he gave to the don as gifts. The chieftain had a son who often played with Don Ignacio's daughter Maria during the visits. Maria was very beautiful, and the chief thought that she would make a perfect bride for his son once the two children were of marriageable age. He asked Don Ignacio if a wedding might not be arranged." Lucia paused for breath.

"Surely the don did not agree to such a thing," ventured Estrellita.

"Ah, but he did, for he never thought such a marriage would come to pass. Maria had but ten years when the pact was made, the boy the same. They were two children who played in the plaza and made everyone laugh because they were so full of life and merriment."

"What happened?" asked Estrellita.

"Maria attained maturity. When she had sixteen years, her father began to worry about the agreement. He sent his daughter off to visit relatives in a nearby village. Sure enough, the Comanche chief and his son came riding up in full regalia to claim the right of matrimony. As your mother and father did, because they knew of this story, Don Ignacio led the chief and his son to a freshly dug grave that bore Maria's name. He told the Indians that she had died of the pox. The chief and his son went away grieving, for they believed the story the don had told them.

"But some other Indians told the chief about the deception. One day, when the people of Tomé were at Mass, they heard the thunder of hoofbeats. The door of the church burst open and Comanche warriors flooded inside. The Indians killed the priest, Don Ignacio, and several other men. Maria was kidnapped and carried off. She was given to the chief's son for his wife and lived her life, thereafter, with the Comanches. She

219

bore her husband many children, but she was never allowed to return to her people, to her heritage. The Indians call Tomé the 'village of the broken promise,' and I'm sure Tecolote knows the story as well as everyone else. One day he will think of it and come back to this rancho. If he sees you alive, he will bring his savages down on us and kill us all."

"That is a sad story, Lucia, but it happened a long time ago."

"History repeats itself," said Lucia.

Chapter Fifteen

Rifle shots barked from somewhere up at the head of the column. Jeremiah jerked upright in the saddle, reached for the butt of his Hawken. He fumbled in his possibles bag for a percussion cap as he swung the rifle across the pommel of his saddle. Nearby, a grinning Karns shifted a cud of tobacco in his mouth.

"Who you aimin' to shoot?" asked Karns.

More rifle fire crackled ahead of the two men. The sounds grew louder. Men shouted hoarse epithets that were drowned out by the explosions.

"We bein' attacked?" asked York.

"No, we ain't bein' attacked. That's Independence up ahead. You shoot off that fusil, mind where you p'int it."

Jeremiah's face flushed with the rosy flare of embarrassment. Still, Jim Karns slid his own rifle from its sheath, capped it, pointed the muzzle into the air. He cocked the set trigger, pulled the firing trigger. White smoke and orange flame belched from the muzzle. The explosion deafened Jeremiah. He put the cap he held between his fingers back into his pouch and hung the Hawken back on the saddlehorn.

"What? You ain't goin' to shoot?" asked Karns.

"I reckon not," said Jeremiah, hardjawed stubborn.

"Haw! Well, now, ain't that somethin'? Son, you got to git in the spirit. This is the last taste of civilization you're goin' to git, last place to spend your money, get wallowin' drunk and dip your wick."

"I don't need to clean no rifle again today," said York. He had been practicing with the Hawken every chance he got, sighting it in, trying various loads. He liked the rifle, liked it a lot. He kept it clean and had rigged a sling from a long leather thong, meaning to make himself a regular sling once he had some hide to cut and shape.

"You 'bout to wear that rifle plumb out, ain't you, York?"

"Likely it'll last me a while."

"Maybe as long as your h'ar," grinned Karns.

Rifles boomed all around them, and men began to ride from the rear, bunch up. Throaty shouts broke out all up and down the caravan and some of the men began singing bawdy songs. Jeremiah felt his veins race with excitement as the trappers began to gallop toward the town, their mules braying in protest, packs rattling on their panniers. Karns dug moccasined feet into his horse's flanks and galloped off, into the grit that rose in the air and sparkled like silver dust in the sunlight. York held back, sensing that he should wait and see where everyone went, not make a fool of himself. He watched the men ride by, feeling lost and alone, as he had on the trail. He remembered sleeping out under the stars, watching the fireflies paint golden spirals of light in the dark, the stars so close in the cloudless sky, he felt he could touch them, feel their cold glow on his skin. He smelled again the sweaty bodies of the men stacked around him on blankets, the fetid musk of their whiskey breaths as they snored or spoke mindlessly in their sleep. He had felt lost then, and alone, strangely detached from them, yet part of them, too, as if he were growing into them, slowly, like a vine around a tree trunk. They were strangers, still, but he was beginning to recognize their faces and attach habits to them. He had not seen Eyestone, but knew that he had left with them and kept to himself, somewhere up ahead or below the horizon alongside the column. When he asked Andersen about him, he said only that "Eyestone is hurtin'. He'll fair up and jine us bye and bye."

A few men lagged behind and York took up with them. Some, leading the mules that had not yet been fitted with packs and panniers, asked him to help and he took three mules by their ropes and saw Beelzebub nip at them, ears laid back along his skull. The mule's jealous, he thought, and grinned with the rapture of his pride.

The firing died away and the caravan streamed into town, gathered at Owens and Aull's store, milled around, greeting others of their kind, cracking jokes, poking fun at those already there, some drunk, all grimy, greasy, dirty, as if they'd rolled in pigsties for half the morning.

The streets were choked with wagons, immigrants heading west, and Jeremiah saw one wagon loaded down with buffalo robes that had the felloes and spokes wrapped with taut rawhide to keep it from falling apart. Men stood around, watching others unload the robes and carry them into a warehouse stacked high with peltry.

Some of the bigger wagons were drawn by oxen, and the men driving them different from the trappers, in dress and manner. As the trappers began to dismount and disperse, some of the big wagons passed through town, the bullwhackers cracking their whips across the backs of oxen and mules, bellowing over the creak of the wheels, the rumble and groan of wood under strain.

"Where ye bound?" called out Ballentine to one of the wagoners.

"Headin' fer the Cimarron Cutoff!" yelled back a grizzled drover.

"Haw! You'll waller in mud up to your bunghole," cracked Ballentine and a bunch of men laughed.

The wagoner roared and threw back his head, broke into song. Other men joined in.

"Ge up! Ge ho! Tho' the sun is burnin' o'er us,
Mula! Mulo! And the grass is short and dry.
Prick your ears, and go, for big timber is before us,

223

And we'll all fill our bellies where the grass grows high.

Oh, the world is turnin' round as our wagon wheels are turning

And to get through life we must sometimes meet a swamp,

But we're on the hills now, and our axle trees are burning.

And we'll grease our wheels and bellies when we stop to camp.

Ge up! Ge ho!

Of a Blind Buffalo you can make a 'blind bridle'

But we scorn Bull Buffaloes and Bridles now,

For while Jerry can crawl, and Valentine can sidle,

We shall never want a dinner from a young fat cow.

Ge up! Ge ho!

There's our wagoner Bell, and the gentle spoken Decker,

'You Pomp! You Nell! Get up! Get out of that!'

They would drive a team to hell, and never need a checker,

Provided they could grease their wheels with Buffalo fat.

Ge up! Ge ho!

And when a comrade goes to the world that lies before us,

And we make his last bed in the desert prairie,

His memory shall live in the numbers of our chorus,

And 'Ge up! Ge ho!' shall his requiem be!

Ge up! Ge ho!

Several cavalry dragoons rode by, caught up with the departing wagons. Jeremiah thought the soldiers looked fine in their uniforms, a sharp contrast to the scruffy men in his brigade. When the thunder of hooves died down, Big Un came waddling up to him, flashing a gap-toothed grin.

"Put them mules up, York, and come on out back, out of the crowd. We got whiskey in the horn and pledges to make before we cross the river."

"Where do I put 'em up?"

"Tie 'em to the sky, Son, don't make no whop where you put 'em. You find a stump or a knothole and get 'er done."

Jeremiah followed some of the other trappers who were leading mules away from the store. People jammed the streets and the reek of whiskey floated on the air. It seemed a madhouse to York as he rode through throngs of people coming and going. The other trappers rode to a pole corral, put up the mules, stripped them of packs, unloaded the panniers. Jeremiah did the same with Beelzebub. The panniers had not rubbed through the thick hair, but it was plastered down good. The mule shook itself gratefully. Jeremiah tied on a nose bag filled with a few handfuls of grain. He saw no water trough, but he could tend to that later. He wanted to see the town, look at the people, drink with the men. He could smell the river and the far-off hoot of a melancholy boat horn sent a ripple of electric current up his spine.

When he had finished, York started to walk back to Owens and Aull's. He looked at the skyline, saw the spires of stone buildings, the jumble of other buildings sprawling in two directions beyond where the main trail to the Missouri lay open and wide. Covered wagons moved along the road and smoke rose from the chimney of a long stone building that reminded him of St. Louis. Someone fell into step beside him and he looked up, saw Cooper Eyestone regarding him with solemn eyes.

"I wondered where you was at," said York.

"I been along all the while, Son."

Jeremiah saw the seam across the middle of Eyestone's buckskins, the rawhide stitches, the rusty patches of dried blood. Eyestone walked gingerly, not limping exactly, but leaning forward slightly, favoring his belly.

"I heard you got into a fight," said Jeremiah.

"Walk down to the river with me?"

"I'll do that."

Eyestone swept a buckskinned arm to the left, the fringes waving, making a soft leathery sound. York turned, walked

225

alongside the trail, his ears filled with the rumble and creak of canvas-covered wagons pulled by six oxen under heavy wooden yokes.

"You got you an enemy, Son," said Eyestone. "Mind you watch yore back."

"You killed a man." York's stomach fluttered.

"You know any soldiers, boy?"

"Soldiers? What do you mean?"

"That man I kilt was a soldier. Mexican Army."

Jeremiah felt the hot rush of sweat and then the cold drench as it cooled on his face. He thought of Augustino Armijo and Merito Salcedo. They were soldiers. They might mean him harm.

"It wasn't Armijo, was it? Or Salcedo?"

"Who be they?"

Jeremiah told him.

"This warn't no officer, Son." They walked down the gentle slope toward the river, watched as wagons crossed at the ford. Eyestone halted, stood there like a statue, his weight resting on one leg. His eyes narrowed. "This was just a regular lancer, I reckon, somebody hired."

"What about the other man?"

"He were a buckskinner for shore."

"Do you know him?"

"I know his smell. He's got my mark on him."

Jeremiah choked on it, gagged with the scent of violence that exuded from Eyestone like hard, sour cider.

"You know his name?"

"Nope, and didn't get no good look at his face. But I'll know him. He'll know me."

"And me."

Eyestone said nothing. The caravans moving across the river looked like disjointed parts of a fortress, with guns bristling from every seat. Every outrider carried a rifle at the ready as if they were all stepping off the edge of civilization into an abyss fraught with peril. The dragoons under the command of Captain Clifton Wharton streamed in formation in front of the wagon train in a column of twos.

"Town ain't been here long," Eyestone said, finally. "Warn't here in '26. We come back in '27, she was sprouting limestone buildings so bright and white they nigh to blinded a man. The steamboats come in and the outfitters moved down from Franklin. That town ain't there no more. Built her on a sandbar and it all washed away."

"You been trapping a spell," said Jeremiah.

"Went out with Ashley in '24. We had us fifty packhorses, a wagon, and a team. Had to leave the wagon 'cause of the deep snows, but we rode up the Platte to its south fork, then up to the Cache la Poudre. We come to the Platte again, headed west to Pacific Creek and down the Big Sandy. We got to the Green River in April, I recollect. Left Franklin in November. It was a trip. We went into the mountains, agreeing to meet at rondeevoo in July."

"What was it like, that first time up in the mountains?"

"Glorious. And hard. Me and my kid brother hadn't never seen no sights like them mountains, and grass on the Green so tall and bright it fair shocked your eyes. We split up and my brother went with Ashley, he warn't no more'n fifteen, and I thought he might do better helping cache the supplies for rondeevoo. Didn't see him no more until we come down at the tail end of June. Met up at Henry's Fork, then went on to the Green. We was about a hunnert and twenny men by then, some of the Hudson's Bay men deserted and jined up with us. We had two camps set up when Jim Beckwourth and some other trappers come down. Lord, it was a sight. More'n eight hunnert of us all jubileein' and dancin' with the wimmens. Beckwourth, now, he hadn't seen sugar nor coffee nor whiskey for many moons and Ashley, he got him some high prices for those goods."

"What did you do there?" asked Jeremiah, rapt at the image of that many trappers together all at the same time and place. "There were women there?"

"'Bout four hunnert wimmen and children, I reckon. We played Injun games and shot our fusils at targets, threw the 'hawks and drank whiskey like water. Jed Smith was there, Etienne Provost, Weber, Beckwourth. It was a time."

There was something in Eyestone's voice that made Jeremiah think of autumn and its sadness, the dying of leaves in a burst of color, the shift of light and the change in temperature, the quail going quiet in the thickets, the long lines of wildfowl flying south in erratic vees, the deer slinking furtive and quiet through the woods, restless as the skeletal oak leaves that rustled underfoot and blew like the ghosts of birds in the wind.

Eyestone seemed to stand there like a blustery tree clinging to a craggy slope, strangely detached from everything, yet oddly possessive of the small patch of soil on which he stood. He seemed to grow smaller, then larger, as if something inside him was pulling him up out of despair, out of some dark well of despondency.

"It . . . it sounds like a time, all right," said York. "Wish I could have been there then."

"We loaded the fur packs on the horses and headed for the Bighorn River by way of South Pass. Me and my brother went with Ashley. We dug up a cache of two dozen packs that Jedediah Smith had left up on the Sweetwater. Damned if the Blackfeet didn't jump us. He sent me to get help from the main bunch. I come back and we drove them Blackfeet off, but my brother took a arrer in his throat."

"Did he die?"

"It took about a week, but he died."

"I'm right sorry," said Jeremiah. "What was his name?"

"Same as yours, kid," said Eyestone, and he reached down and picked up a stone. He chunked it at the river. It struck the water and disappeared. Soon there was no trace of the ripples it made. "Come on, let's get to the drinking horn, wash some of this blamed dust out of our throats."

"You goin' to look for that other feller?" asked Jeremiah, a quiver in his voice, a tight feeling in his gut.

"You keep your eyes sharp," said Eyestone. "I'll do likewise."

"I will. I surely will."

"We don't talk about this no more, neither."

"No."

Jeremiah felt that he had been privy to some great secret. It was hard holding it in, keeping it to himself. He wondered how many of the others knew about Jeremiah Eyestone and how he died.

As they walked back up to Independence, they heard a man singing, far out on the trail.

> "I'm a bullwhacker far from home,
>   If you don't like me just leave me alone;
>   Eat my grub when hungry, drink when dry.
>   Whack, punch, swear, then lie down and die."

And, farther off, the lone boom of a rifle, as if someone just wanted to make sure there was no fouling in the barrel.

Chapter Sixteen

Baptiste Lalande introduced the new man to the brigade as they gathered in front of the corrals. "Mr. Cantwell Clayburn," said Lalande, "is our navigator." Clayburn was a lean, wiry man with a sardonic smile on his weathered face. His eyes seemed to be perpetually in shadow, but they were blue, and shiny as Indian beads. His hair was snowy, but he could not have been more than forty years of age. "He is a sea pilot from Missouri," continued Lalande, "who will chart our course by the stars. He will measure our path across the prairie and in the mountains, eh? And, by Gar, we are leaving in one hour. Mr. Wyeth will be eating our dust, no? Are you ready?"

Everyone was aware that Wyeth was camped about four miles from Independence, setting up an expedition that would set out for the mouth of the Columbia River. The outfit, calling itself the Columbia River Fish and Trading Company, had been formed in Boston. The firm had fitted out a brig of two hundred tons burden, which carried gear for the salmon and fur trade. It was under orders to sail for the mouth of the Columbia, while Wyeth would proceed overland, join up with the brig's company, and establish a post on the Columbia near the Pacific Ocean.

Nearly sixty men responded with lusty cheers. Some threw hats in the air and others, with tempers honed by terrible hangovers, grumbled and moaned. Jeremiah York stood next to Eyestone, looking at the navigator, who was dressed no different from the rest of them, in buckskins and leggings, unbeaded moccasins. He carried a knife, a 'hawk, a rifle, and a telescope, a square leather bag over his shoulder. He did not smile beyond that crinkle of thin lips that gave his lean face a cruel cast.

Clayburn stepped forward. He pointed to a large man standing next to Lalande.

"My assistant," he said. "Louis Vernon. He will take the notes and draw the maps. He is a draftsman, but like me, he can ride and shoot. He is good at his trade, as I am good at mine."

Vernon was tall, slope-shouldered, with close-set brown eyes, long simian arms. His eyes moved constantly in their sockets, and his buckskins appeared even more worn than Clayburn's. Unlike Clayburn, however, he didn't even try to smile. There was an arrogance about the two men that was almost palpable. Vernon's face appeared to have been carved out of stone. His hair was jet-black and he had a high forehead, bushy brows, a porcine cant to his nose. There was no honesty in his open face. Rather, he seemed to harbor deep and terrible secrets behind his dark eyes, and his flabby, slightly sensual lips seemed permanently sealed in a defiant sneer.

"What do you make of 'em?" asked Bloody Hand Andersen of Eyestone.

"Somethin' familiar 'bout that Clayburn feller."

"Used to captain a boat on the Mississip'," said Andersen.

"Why ain't he a-doin' it now?" asked Eyestone.

Bloody Hand shrugged and walked away. Eyestone stood there watching the two men as they spoke with Lalande. Lalande left them and went to fetch his horse and packmules. York stood there, too, and when the two surveyors strode away, he looked at their backs. Eyestone made a noise in his throat.

"What is it?" York asked.

"Maybe nothin'. But ain't that Clayburn limpin' a mite?"

"I can't tell."

Jeremiah looked intently, but he couldn't see the limp. The ground was uneven where the two men walked. They both appeared to walk perfectly normal.

"Well it don't make no nevermind right now. I'll keep an eye on 'em," said Cooper. "You best fotch your horse and mule. Be slow goin' at first, till the whiskey wears off. You'll see some country."

"I'm ready," grinned York. He had not drunk much at the gatherings. Mostly he had listened to the talk, listened to the tall tales the men spun when they were in their cups. They passed the horn around and he took some drinks, but he had not gotten sick. He had watched his back, wary of every man who came too close, looked at him too hard. He couldn't remember all their names, but there was talk of Bridger and Sublette, Jedediah Smith, who had been killed in '31 by a band of Comanche, his body never found, of Wyeth and his navigator, Captain Joseph Thing, like Clayburn, hired to accompany Ashley's party across the Rocky Mountains. Jeremiah had listened to the talk of grizzly bears and mountain lions and Indians just as he had back home and his veins sang with the delirium of his blood, his heart beat like the hooves of buffalo rumbling across the plains like a shaggy sea, and his mind flooded with the sights and sounds of his future, the allure of far-off mountains and shining beaver streams, the frozen fastness of high passes locked in by winter, the lush grasslands of meadows basking in golden sunlight where the air was so thin you had to breathe it twice.

Now, as Jeremiah walked to the corral, he realized that he was finally beginning his journey of adventure, going to the places he had dreamed of for so long. He was leaving civilization behind and going into the wilderness. He wanted to mark the day in his mind, remember always the tingle he now felt in his veins, hold forever this moment in time when he would join the brigade of men who made the mountains their home. He wanted to shout, to scream his joy, but he held it in, held down his excitement like some quivering bird struggling to break free and take flight.

Lalande led the party across the river and onto the plain, the men riding in double file, each leading two packmules or horses. At the rear of the column, Clayburn and Vernon rode with the men who drove an extra twenty head of horses and half as many cattle for emergency rations. Jeremiah understood that they would live off the land as much as possible, and he had been given an extra packhorse to lead, along with Beelzebub. The expedition traveled at a slow pace over the wide green prairie. York exulted at the pureness of the blue sky and the smell of the country, did not mind that they did not make a noon stop, but continued on until shortly after two P.M. when they pulled into a small grove of timber near a bubbling spring. Like the others, he unpacked his mule and horse, hobbled the animals. Men threw up a rope corral, lashed the ropes to the luggage at intervals. That night he drank spring water and ate beef and skillet bread, a ration of beans. He read by the firelight, fell asleep with one of Estrellita's books in his hands. He did not awaken until someone aroused him for the dog watch. He took up his rifle and walked a half circle around the camp, marveling at the closeness of the stars.

During the next few days, they crossed a number of small streams that sliced through the gently undulating prairie. The streams were easy to see since they were lined with timber and brush on an otherwise featureless landscape of tall, waving grasses on an unbroken sward. The prairie looked like a green sea in the soft wind that blew at their faces. When they reached the Kaw, some called it the Kansas River, Jeremiah saw the Kaw Indians for the first time.

"Filthy, ain't they?" said Eyestone, who had taken to riding with Jeremiah part of each day.

"They sure stink," said York. The Indians were not what he had expected. They lived in small oval huts about five feet high

234

hat were made with crisscrossed willow branches and covered with deer, elk, or buffalo hides. Lalande argued with the ndians, and later that day, they crossed the Kaw and made camp early. The next day, they rode over the endless rolling prairie, going deeper and deeper into the land, into a silence that York found awesome and serene. The vastness of the sky made him feel small and insignificant, so purely blue he thought it must have been painted by God's own hand. Hunters roved far and wide for game and brought back deer and antelope. One day, Eyestone shot a buffalo and he beckoned to Jeremiah, who had ridden with him on the hunt. It was the first such animal that York had ever seen and he was surprised at its large size, how easily Cooper had brought it down, with a single shot from his Hawken at four hundred yards. The animal was a stray and they saw no others.

Eyestone dismounted, drew his knife.

"Ever taste any mountain-man cider?" he asked.

"Nope," said Jeremiah.

"Get me that little pot out of my saddlebags."

Jeremiah fished around in the saddlebag, found a small boiling pot. "This what you want?" he asked.

"Be just fine."

Jeremiah stood over Eyestone as he checked to make sure the cow was dead. Then Cooper pushed it over on its side. Jeremiah saw the bluish tongue lolling from the animal's mouth, the frosty cast to its brown eyes. Eyestone ran the blade up the animal's gut, slit it open. A cloud of fetid, faint steam rose up and the reek of entrails assailed York's nostrils. They were curled in the cavity like glistening snakes. He fought for air as bile burned his throat, tossed up from his boiling stomach as it rippled with nauseated contractions.

"Hold it down," said Eyestone knowingly. "Take some deep breaths and think about sweetcakes."

The trapper rammed the blade of his knife into the distended buffalo paunch, held the tin pot against the opening. Green and gelatinous juices gushed from the stomach and into the pot.

Eyestone pushed one edge of the pot downward and drained off the water, leaving only the mush of the stomach contents. He stood up, drank from the pot, handed it to Jeremiah.

"Don't look at it, just swaller it," said the trapper. "We'll wash her down with blood when I take the heart out."

Jeremiah's knees turned to flannel and he thought he would go down. But he took the pot, poured some of the green mash into his mouth. He swallowed, fought the gagging. It tasted bitter, but it stayed down. Eyestone slapped him on the back, then took the pot, drank the rest of the bilious mixture.

As Jeremiah watched, Eyestone did some more cutting with his knife, carefully took the heart out of the dead beast. He punched a hole in the left ventricle, held the incision shut. He held the organ over his mouth, tilted his head back, and squeezed. A stream of blood jetted into his mouth. He smacked his lips, grinned at York.

"Open your mouth," he said.

Jeremiah tilted his head backward, opened his mouth. Eyestone held the bloody heart over the opening and squeezed. The warm blood trickled into York's mouth. He closed his eyes and swallowed.

"Boy, we're gonna have a feast tonight, beaudoins and fresh buff meat. You cut that tongue out, it's prime, and we'll cook its liver 'tween us. You watch while I skin this old girl out and you can help me do some quarterin'."

Some of the other hunters brought in buffalo that night, too, and the brigade feasted like barons. Men fought over the prime cuts, argued over meals past, and bigger buffalo killed until late in the night. Lalande laid over a day so that the *depoille* of the buffalo could be stripped out and smoked. This was the fat lying along the backbone, next to the hide, running away from the shoulder blade to the last rib. Men dipped the fatty substance into hot grease for half a minute, then hung them high over the fire to dry and smoke. It would keep indefinitely and was better than bread.

Jeremiah had never been so full. He could still taste the

granulated liver drenched in the juice of a burst gall bladder that Eyestone cooked for him. He ate half of the tongue and every morsel Eyestone handed him over the cooking fire. He could think of little else as they moved up the Kaw again to the forks, then forded the south fork and headed north.

Sometime early in May they reached the Laramie where it entered the Platte, and Jeremiah could see the Rocky Mountains looming like giants to the west. They followed the Platte until dark and camped. The next day they left the river and went into the Laramie mountain range. They came to the river again and crossed it at a place called Red Buttes. The next day they headed northwest, stopped that night on a small spring branch. There was no firewood and they left early the next morning, rode to the Sweetwater where it tumbled into the Platte. The going became more rugged and Jeremiah's eyes strained to see all the beauty around him. They saw elk and deer every night and morning, sometimes during the day, and once he saw a bear, smelled its scat for an hour as he fought his skittery horse. They crossed through South Pass, dwarfed by the grandeur, surrounded by magnificent snowcapped peaks that broke the skyline in all directions. They camped on Sandy Creek.

"The Sandy, she runs into the Green," Eyestone told York. "We'll move down her tomorry."

"I've never seen anything like this in my life," said Jeremiah.

"There's so much of it, you get glutted," Eyestone said, and his words proved true. They reached the Green and rode another twenty miles to Ham's Fork. It was two days of hard, slow riding.

Lalande laid out their camp. Men broke away to hunt and fish and Indians began stopping by. More traders began arriving in June. American Fur trappers streamed in under the leadership of Captain Drips and Fontanelle. Sublette and his men passed Wyeth, arrived about the middle of June. Wyeth's brigade pulled in noisily a couple of days later. Mountains rose up all around them and Jeremiah rode in every direction, discovering something new and exciting every day. He shot an antelope with his Hawken, brought it proudly into camp. He saw very few deer, and those only along the rivers, but there were elk and bear there aplenty. Lalande set up his trade blankets, laid out his goods. The heavy competition was between Sublette and Wyeth, but Lalande did well on the overflow, his camp being between those of the two rivals, some five miles from Wyeth, closer to Black's Fork.

Trappers, hunters, half-breeds, and Indians filled the valley that summer, bringing in furs and powerful thirsts. There were drunken brawls and dancing. Indian women smiled at Jeremiah, teased him with their eyes. Some of them wanted to touch his hair, feel its silkiness. He fought them off gently, but he was just as fascinated with them as they were with him.

York camped with some of the men he'd first met in St. Louis. Big Un, Bloody Hand, Possum Killer, Eyestone, J.R., White Buffalo. Over the days and nights of hunting and drinking he began to feel at home with them, but he never relaxed his vigilance. Vernon and Clayburn were often away from camp and most nights they were looking at stars through long brass telescopes and writing down figures in a book. Jeremiah read the books that Estrellita had given him and traded them back and forth for others that were dog-eared and the paper well-worn. He read Shakespeare without understanding all the words, but he heard the music in the language and he began to be conscious of his own speech and listen carefully to the patois of the mountain men. Each man seemed to have his own distinctive dialect and it seemed that each man's speech was as special as his medicine pouch or his clothing.

Each day he tallied the furs that Lalande took in from the Indians, other trappers. It was not difficult, for Baptiste used him to work the press every afternoon when the day's trading was concluded. He learned that all pelts were measured by the beaver. To the fur companies, only beaver existed in the Rockies, even though they bought other peltries.

A beaver, full grown and prime, was equal to one "made beaver." A cub was worth one half. A large, prime otter pelt was equivalent to two beaver skins, while a prime small was worth but one. Black fox in its prime was two "made beaver," and red prime was merely a half. The marten amounted to more than one third of a beaver on the books.

York kept his tallies a secret, writing them down at the end of a day on foolscap. He developed a unique method for keeping track of the various skins. He took a pouchful of beads with him each day. The pouch hung from his belt and he could dip into it, transfer beads to his pocket without anyone noticing. The beads were of different colors, red, green, blue, yellow, black, and brown. He assigned a color to each class of peltry, gave them values of ten. At the end of a day, in his lean-to, he would count the beads. Ten red beads amounted to a hundred prime-grown beaver. Green was beaver cub, blue was grown otter, black was small, yellow was black fox, brown was red fox. He used cuts of leather thong to keep track of the marten.

At many of the camps, when the trappers first arrived, he saw hundreds of beaver skins drying in the sun. These were stretched on willow hoops, varying from eighteen inches to three feet in diameter, according to the size of the skins. He noticed that the flesh side turned red since it was the side exposed to the sun. He learned to spot these red circles when he rode through the camps, and after they were dried, he'd see them marked, folded, and stacked, tied into packs.

He helped Big Un and Jim Karns make a fur press one day. They cut saplings to various lengths, finally making a boxlike rectangle from six poles about five feet long, lashing them at the top with shorter poles, at the bottom with thicker ones. A longer pole was attached to a chain that was nailed to the base. The furs were placed inside the skeleton of the box and two men rode the press pole until the furs were matched flat.

"Now we got us a chain, pole, and saplin' press," said Karns when they were finished.

"Makes 'em easier to carry," said Big Un, panting. "They'll press 'em again at the trading post."

Jeremiah saw that it took about sixty pelts, folded once, fur side in, to make a pack that weighed from ninety to a hundred pounds. The pack was encased in a wrapper of dry deerskin and lashed tight with leather thongs. It was hard work, but the men in the brigade took turns so that York didn't have to do this work every day.

He roamed the camps, sat and listened outside teepees, tents, lean-tos, went into lodges, drank, ate with men he did not know but who welcomed him to their campfires. He smelled the roasting meat, the smoked game, tasted rare viands, chewed on strange animal parts, ate greasy breads and dried fruits. Soon he was as dirty as any man there, and when he rode the high country it gave him pleasure to look down and see the camps, the pall of blue smoke hanging in the air, listen to the whoops of men who had become children for a time. He started learning sign language and found that it came very easily to him. He watched the Indians and the traders talk, asked questions, and tried the signs in secret, began to see a kind of poetry in the talking hands, a silent song with flowing lyrics.

York began to add beads and ornaments to his own buckskins and he made a pair of moccasins, sewed a capote from a four-point blanket after Eyestone cut him a pattern. He made some mistakes, but his personal possessions began to increase and he did some trading for beads, German silver, trinkets for his medicine pouch. He began to resemble the other buckskinners, and the wind burned his face and hands brown, the sun washed his hair, turned it a lighter hue.

He knew there was trouble between Wyeth and Sublette, knew that Fitzpatrick had deserted Wyeth and joined Sublette. There was talk of money and bribery and the liquor continued to flow. Jeremiah smoked many a pipe with the various men and listened to their stories without ever becoming bored.

Wyeth grumbled that he was in the company of scoundrels. He left the rendezvous on July 2 and York later heard that he had sold out to the Hudson Bay Company. He didn't understand all the intrigue and rancor, but he knew it involved sums of money and broken friendships. He began to think the only men worth knowing were the free trappers, who owed allegiance to no man. They lived wild in the mountains and they drank hardest and swore loudest at any gathering.

There were many shoots and throws of the tomahawk, competitions at which a man could bet or try to beat the best shots, the best throwers of knife and 'hawk. Jeremiah became proficient at all three events and began to make a name for himself.

On the Fourth of July, Jeremiah awakened to the rapid rattle of musketry. Big-bore guns boomed all around the camp. Groggy, he grabbed his Hawken, crawled out of his lean-to, ready to do battle. Men shouted that they were under attack and blossoms of white smoke hung over the dew-wet grasses like small clouds.

"Injuns!" yelled someone.

"Where?"

York saw J.R. crawling out of his bedroll. Jim Karns sat up, rubbed his paunch, blinked like a tousled owl, snorted at a wisp of smoke that fingered a tendril at his nose. Ballentine, across the way, clanged a pot with an iron spoon.

"Fourth of July!" he hollered. "Whooeeee! Independence Day!"

Then, everyone began shouting and hoorawing and firing off their rifles and trade muskets. Even the Indians got caught up in the spirit, yelling and whooping with the trappers, firing off their fusils, grinning like a pack of mangy wolves.

Ballentine broke out a keg of rum, and a circle of men soon crowded around his buffalo-hide lean-to. Someone put some fat to fry and skillets popped and sizzled with the sounds of venison and elk strips bobbling in hot grease.

The camps were strangely deserted as York rode through them that evening. Fitzpatrick and Sublette had already gone.

Drips's camp was still intact. York learned that one of the trappers had been called up to stand trial for murder, but had fled like a coward with a guilty conscience before anything could be done. Lalande had furs stacked in his storage tents, traded for from the Nez Perce, Bannock, and Shoshone. His pile of trade goods had diminished considerably. He was surrounded by other Frenchmen, all in their cups, all bleating vociferously in their native tongue.

In the dark, it was difficult to tell the Indians from the assemblage of French-Canadians, half-breeds, white trappers, so alike were they in dress and manner. York marveled at this strange encampment of peoples who whooped, howled, cursed, quarreled, and laughed with raucous abandonment, as if they had grown up together, were all one family.

Fascinated, he did not notice that two men followed him through the darkness, stopped when he stopped, urged their horses forward when he did. Jeremiah had ridden up to the bluffs that day, weary of the constant trading, glutted on the rum and tall tales that amounted to imaginative lies, and he had wanted to let the country seep into him, smell the firs and pine and spruce. He had watched a covey of grouse for over an hour, walked to within two yards of them, and sat in their midst. When the sun started to fall over the farthest range, he headed back to Ham's Fork, saw the flare of campfires brightening the dark.

The two men closed the distance as York left one camp, headed for his own. His first awareness of them came when he heard the faint pound of hoofbeats behind him. He turned, saw two dark shadows, the silhouettes of men on horseback coming toward him fast.

Except for the hoofbeats, their approach was soundless. They did not whoop or holler and he thought they were just re-creating their own horse race after the ones he had watched that morning. The two riders split apart and he thought they would ride on past him. He lifted his hand to wave at them.

That's when he saw the tomahawks in their hands, raised as if to strike him from his saddle, to strike him dead.

Chapter Seventeen

The deadly horsemen loomed closer, their voices silent, 'hawks poised for the kill. The moon had not yet risen and only the faint light of stars, the distant flickering of campfires, slashed the darkness, glinted off the blades of the tomahawks. The blackness of night hid the faces of the two men.

Jeremiah's upraised arm probably saved him from being killed. He felt a jarring shock in his arm as the rider on his right swung the tomahawk, aiming for his head. He screamed in pain, ducked. Seconds later the rider on his left swung at him. He heard the whish of the 'hawk as it sliced the air above his head.

He wheeled Fleetfoot, clawed for his knife. The two riders reined up, turned, came back for him. Jeremiah heard the screeching creak of leather under strain, the groan of saddles twisting the cinches. At that moment of fear all of his senses became honed to a fine, sharp edge. His stomach knotted, but he drew a breath and felt the tenseness drain away. He desperately wanted to live, to give a good account of himself if he must die. That was the thought that crystallized in his mind, made him dangerous. He would not wait for death to come, but meet it headlong, grin into its dark, empty face and make it pay for its audacity.

York knew what he must do as the pair of assassins closed

the yardage, came at him as one rider, galloping toward him with tomahawks upraised once again. Jeremiah touched heels to his horse's flanks, charged toward the nearest man, a plan already forming in the split second left before he must strike with his puny weapon. He held the knife close to his chest, blade toward his opponent.

Jeremiah opened his mouth, drew air into his lungs, and let out a blood-curdling war cry. At the same time, he drove Fleetfoot toward the nearest rider, lunged at him. He plunged the knife straight toward the man's chest. He stood up in the stirrups and drove the blade down until it struck flesh and bone. The knife sank like a hot poker through butter. The assailant gasped and dropped his 'hawk, reached out for York even as Jeremiah drove him backward.

Jeremiah pulled the blade from the rider's chest, pushed him with his free hand. He heard the man grunt and saw him slide out of the saddle, struggle to stay aboard his mount. The other rider galloped past, unable to stop, to see what was happening. York grabbed his reins, hauled his horse into a tight turn, and went after the other man. He screamed his warwhoops again, heard answering cries from the camps. The rider slapped the trailing ends of his reins against his horse's rump, clapped heels into the animal's flanks.

"You ain't gettin' away!" yelled Jeremiah.

Men shouted. Voices rose up out of the night.

"They's a fight!" someone yelled.

"Where?" called another.

Jeremiah raked Fleetfoot's flanks with his heels, pounded the soft webbing between the horse's flank and its hip. The man ahead of him turned his head. York whooped again, ate up ground in his wild, galloping chase. The man swung his horse in a slow circle, but Jeremiah cut him off. York's hand gripped the knife, his fingers slippery with blood.

"Now you'll die," growled the man with the tomahawk, and Jeremiah recognized the voice.

"Clayburn," muttered York.

"Shoulda kilt you in Saint Louie, sonny boy." There was a deadly menace to his tone.

"You?"

"Ain't no Eyestone to he'p you out now, youngster."

Jeremiah's anger flared, then seemed to calm him as it settled into a dark hatred. He hated a man who sneaked around like Clayburn. He hated a bushwhacker who came at a man from behind.

Clayburn drove his horse at York's, jabbed with the 'hawk. Jeremiah sidled away, using the reins with one hand, keeping the knife ready with the other. Then Clayburn rode in fast, leaped from the saddle. He caught Jeremiah off guard, smashed into him, knocking him from his horse. Jeremiah smelled his whiskey breath, the heavy scent of sweat and grease.

The younger man hit the ground with a thud, felt the weight of Clayburn knock the wind out of his lungs. He gasped for breath, wriggled to get free. He scooted out from under Clayburn, rolled just as the ex-sailor swung the 'hawk downward The navigator buried the blade in the earth and Jeremiah scrambled to his feet, dove sideways, jabbing with the knife. He felt the blade slash through buckskin. Clayburn cried out in pain, twisted away, jerking the 'hawk free.

Jeremiah lunged again, but Clayburn leaned to one side. He brought up a foot, kicked at York. Jeremiah took the blow in the knee, felt his leg collapse. He fell sickeningly, folded his legs up, and kicked outward as Clayburn leaped at him. His moccasins caught the man in the belly, propelled him backward.

Men raced into the clearing, some carrying pine torches. Some Flatheads were the first to reach the pair of combatants, and they laughed as the torches illuminated the struggle. Men shouted and jostled for position. Jeremiah rose to his feet, stalked Clayburn in a fighting crouch, holding the knife out to his side, his other arm distended like a bent wing.

"Now you won't get away from me, you whelp," grunted Clayburn.

"What you do?" asked Lalande, rushing into the circle of light. "You stop, Cantwell. York, put down your knife."

Jeremiah blinked, looked at Baptiste, then at Clayburn.

"Stay out of this, Lalande," said Clayburn. "Pup tried to carve me up. Think he killed Lew."

"Let 'em fight," said a drunken trapper. "I alluz liked to see two bucks go at it."

Lalande took a step toward York. Clayburn ran toward York from behind Lalande, using the Frenchman for cover. He shoved Lalande aside, stopped and hurled his tomahawk straight for York's chest.

A half dozen men in the path of the thrown 'hawk ducked instinctively. York fell backward a split second before the tumbling hatchet whistled past him. Clayburn fell on him, reached for his neck. He grabbed York with his hands, squeezed. Jeremiah felt the pressure on his windpipe. When he sucked for air, none was there. He jabbed with the knife, drove it into Clayburn's side. Once, twice, again. He felt the burning in his chest. Panic rose up in him as he struggled to breathe.

He felt a blanket of darkness creeping up on the edges of his mind. Clayburn's face wavered and shimmered, appeared distorted, flattened out of shape, elongated from his neck to his pate. His chest was bursting. He closed his eyes, looked inside himself for a strength that was no longer there.

With one last desperate effort, Jeremiah forgot about the strangling hands around his neck, rammed the knife into his attacker's side. He gouged and raked, pulling the knife through flesh.

Clayburn screamed and released his grip on York's neck. He fell to one side, clawing at the knife buried in his flesh.

Jeremiah felt the dead breath rush from his lungs. He gulped, gasped as he drew precious oxygen into his mouth. His mind cleared as his chest swelled with air. He crawled away from Clayburn, woozy from his ordeal. His breath rasped in his throat. He swallowed, trying to erase the soreness in his neck. He rubbed the bruises, stretched his neck. He still felt as if he was being strangled.

Eyestone appeared in front of him, reached down, grabbed him under the armpit.

"Can you stand up?"

"Arrgh!" All that came out was a rasp. Jeremiah struggled to his feet. He wobbled there, leaned against Eyestone. The blurring in his eyes was going away. He felt lightheaded, dizzy.

"They jump you?"

Jeremiah nodded.

"Be hell to pay until we set it straight," Eyestone said.

Jeremiah heard the tangle of voices, the murmurs and exclamations from the men. He couldn't make out what they were saying. Blood pounded in his temples. His ears filled with a sound like a blowing wind through autumn trees.

Clayburn lay on his back, moaning, rocking from side to side. A group of men stood over him. Lalande, who was one of them, broke away, approached Eyestone and York.

He swore in French.

"What you do, York? Eh?"

"Them two come after me. Tried to cut me in half with their 'hawks."

"Vernon's still alive," said Eyestone. "He's lost him some blood, but he's breathin'."

"How I know you tell the truth?" asked Lalande. "Those men, they pretty good men, do good work for me."

"You hold on there, Ba'tees'," said Eyestone. "York, can you stand on your own?"

"Yes."

Eyestone released his hold on Jeremiah, walked over to Clayburn. He drew his knife, cut him out of his buckskin shirt. Then he rolled the groaning man over with his toe.

"Looky here, Ba'tees'. He's got him a scar ain't too old. I reckon I put that there in Saint Looie when he tried to jump York."

"You sonofabitch," hissed Clayburn.

Lalande grabbed a pine torch and held it up as he looked at

247

the scar in Clayburn's side. It was still pink with the new flesh flaring an angry red around the edges.

"This true, Cantwell?" asked Baptiste.

"You go to hell," said Clayburn.

"I got to think about this, eh?" said Lalande. "Why they want to kill this boy?"

"Maybe somebody paid good money to do the job," said Eyestone.

"Eh? Who do this?"

"Coupla Mex soldiers maybe," said Cooper. He walked back to York.

Lalande scratched his head. He was hatless. He worried his beard, said something in French that was unintelligible.

"Best make litters for these men," said Andersen, taking charge. He was puffing from exertion. "That Vernon may not make it."

"He's cut purty bad," said Karns. To York, he said, "You stood off them two with a knife?"

York nodded. He was confused. He wondered if these were men sent by Armijo to kill him. Would a man stoop that low? Maybe. The Mexican wanted Estrellita, and maybe he didn't want any competition. He saw Augustino now, in his mind, and he burned with anger toward him. He wanted to see him face-to-face, challenge him. No, he wanted to kill him. There was just no other explanation. He didn't know Clayburn or Vernon. They had no reason to kill him. None that he knew of, anyway. But maybe Armijo did. That would explain why one of the assassins in St. Louis was a Mexican soldier. It would explain a lot of things.

"Let's get you back to camp, York," said Eyestone. Already, he knew the men were beginning to take sides. J.R. came up, then, grinning. He held two tomahawks in his hand.

"No blood on 'em," he said.

"Yeah," said Eyestone. "York, he's slippery all right."

The men around them laughed. Big Un waddled up, leading Fleetfoot.

"Can you ride, York?"

"Walk," said Jeremiah, his voice screeching through bruised vocal cords. "Better walk."

"I'll bring yore horse back," said Big Un. He spat a stream of tobacco juice through a gap in his teeth.

Jeremiah felt his strength returning. He walked past Lewis Vernon, who was lying on his back, staring upward at the sky. His eyes were glassy. He looked as if he was in shock. Blood drenched his buckskin tunic. Someone had cut away part of it to expose the wound. The knife had gone in below the heart, possibly through the ribs above his diaphragm.

"He don't look good, do he?" asked J.R., striding alongside the two men. He rattled the 'hawks, making the blades ring like iron bells. "He kicks the bucket, maybe . . ."

"Shut up, Asterwold," said Eyestone.

Jeremiah thought that Vernon might die. He didn't feel anything. He felt emptied out, maybe, cold inside, like old ashes. Dry and empty and numb. He didn't know why Lewis Vernon wanted to kill him. Money? Or was he just helping Clayburn? Birds of a feather.

His stomach turned. That could have been him lying back there, a tomahawk in his gut.

J.R. tramped on ahead, clanging the 'hawks together as if he were in a parade. The sound was unnerving to Jeremiah. It was dark without the pitchpine torches. Ahead, he could see the campfires, but they brought him no warmth, no welcome. He was glad of the darkness. It helped smudge out the image of Lewis Vernon lying there glassy-eyed, staring up at the sky as if he couldn't see anything. And Clayburn, the knife wound in him, maybe bleeding to death inside, he didn't want to think about him, either. It seemed he was in a living nightmare, that all these things couldn't have happened to him, but did. He was empty and numb and he wanted to crawl into a dark hole and just hide from it all. Make it all go away, as if none of it had ever happened.

Jeremiah started to shake after he crawled into his lean-to.

He couldn't control the shivers. His teeth rattled together like dice in a leather cup.

Eyestone knew that York was in shock. He sat there, just outside the lean-to, his rifle across his lap, puffing on a clay pipe. His eyelids were clamped almost shut, but he saw everything he needed to see.

"Kid, I think you better make tracks come mornin'."

"Huh?" Jeremiah was grateful for the sound of a human voice. He had been living inside his mind for several moments, thinking about those two men chasing him in the dark, silent as wraiths, trying to cut him to pieces with tomahawks. The images were too much for him. Now the fear grew in him, writhed inside his belly like a pack of poisonous snakes.

"Maybe go up in the mountains for a spell. Let things cool down. Or go back to Saint Looie."

"No. I won't go back there."

"Santa Fe, maybe."

Something clutched at Jeremiah's heart.

"Santa Fe? Why do you say that?"

"Fine times there. Taos, too. They got a fair there. July. August. Bad whiskey, purty wimmen. I be goin' there pretty quick."

"You?"

"Yep. Best tradin' place this time o' year. Taos just a spit from Santa Fe."

Jeremiah felt better already. He scooched out to the edge of his skin roof on his elbows. His face took on the shadows and light from the small fire that Eyestone had kept feeding. The cooking irons were bare, the pots cleaned and put away.

"Close, huh?"

"Yep, mighty close. Be some boards a-dancin' in Taos, come next month, the month after. Lots o' traders. Injuns, Mexes, whites from Saint Looie. Firewater they call lightnin'. Ooooh, I swear."

"Long ride there?"

"Long ride. Good country. Be trails and such. A man can

ke his way."

"We'd come back and trap?"

"You can cut notches on it."

"I'd be proud to go with you, Eyestone."

"You call me Coop, Son."

Jeremiah beamed. He said the nickname over and over in his oughts. He looked at the man squatted there by the fire oking his pipe and he felt a kinship with him. Yet there was mething about Eyestone's manner that tugged at him, made m wonder why the trapper had taken him under his wing. It emed to him that Cooper, Coop, had something heavy on his nd.

"I . . . I feel bad about what happened. What if those men ?"

"Likely one or t'other will. That ain't your big worry now, rk."

"Huh?"

"Lalande. That Frenchie been watchin' you like a hard-eyed wk at a pullet. An' today, he come to your lean-to and did me scoutin' on the sneak."

Jeremiah felt his heart drop through his rib cage.

There was only one thing that Lalande could have been oking for, reasoned York. His tally sheets. He crawled back der the lean-to, searched under the stack of clothes where he pt the papers. He had kept them carefully flat in his copy of ashington Irving's *The Conquest of Grenada*.

"They ain't here," exclaimed Jeremiah.

"What ain't there?"

"I been keepin' a tally on the furs Lalande took in."

"You, what?"

"I . . . it's somethin' I been doin'." Jeremiah searched inly through his clothes and in between the pages of the her books, but the tally sheets were not there. Chagrined, he thered back to his former position on his elbows. He looked Eyestone, swallowed. "I had to do it, Coop."

"Had to?"

251

"I got reasons. One of 'em is a debt Lalande owes [M]
Morrison back in Kaskaskia. I mean to see Mr. Morrison g[et]
his money. He's pretty old now. I want him to have the mo[ney]
before he dies."

"I heard tell some about that. Warn't Baptiste what owe[d]
but his pa."

"It's still owed. Debt passes from father to son, don't i[t]"

"I don't rightly know," said Cooper. "Baptiste's pa, now,
was a rogue for sure. Been talk about him for years, and y[ou]
ain't the first one Morrison sent to collect that debt."

"Huh? What'd you say?"

"Pike, he got throwed in jail for tryin' to collect. Back [in]
ought four it were. Hell, Baptiste, he must be laughin' at y[ou]
plumb hard right about now. Thirty year ago, his pa sold M[or]
rison's goods, kept the money, and they's still talk of i[t. I]
heard the story when I first come to the mountains. Morri[son]
don't really know the half of it, or he'd a sent a army for t[hat]
money."

"I don't know what you mean," said Jeremiah.

"Lalande, Baptiste's pa, he was a French Creole, met up w[ith]
your friend, William Morrison, back about a year after [we]
bought the Louisiana Territory from the French. Lalande to[ok]
Morrison's goods clear to Santa Fe, sold 'em for a fair pri[ce.]
Hell, he was treated like a hero when he rode in. The gover[nor]
sent him a army escort and they paraded him up and down [the]
streets like he was a king."

"Mr. Morrison never told me any of this."

"Haw! Mr. Morrison never set eyes on Baptiste Lala[nde]
again. Likely he don't even know the half of it. Pike went af[ter]
him, got throwed in jail. Lalande, he got top dollar [for]
Morrison's goods, was given land and a free hand with [the]
ladies. Some say he was the first American to trade in Santa [Fe,]
that he was the one what give 'em the idea of a Santa Fe Trai[l in]
the first place."

"Lalande?"

"Yep. Baptiste's pa. Now some say he meant to send so[me]

money back to Morrison. Others say he had wickedness in his heart like some men got blood. He died a rich man and his son appears to be mighty enterprizin' hisself."

"I wonder why Mr. Morrison didn't tell me all this?"

"Maybe he took you for a fool. No matter. Lalande, he'll be primed with eighty grains of mad-powder now. I think you best lay low for a while."

"That why you say I oughta go to Santa Fe, Taos?"

"Mebbe so, but you cut a couple of men Baptiste put stock in and he ain't goin' to take it kindly. Don't help none that you been keepin' a tally on him. Why, Baptiste, he might get the idee you don't trust him none."

"I don't."

"And now he don't trust you, Son."

Jeremiah heaved a sigh. Eyestone was right. He had made an enemy there. Lalande hadn't liked him from the first moment when he'd asked for Morrison's money. Now he had reason to dislike him even more. He should have kept the tally sheets in a safer place. Maybe kept them with him all the time. Now it was too late. He had failed Chouteau and he had failed William Morrison.

Big Un heaved into view, loomed up behind the lapping flames of the fire. He cracked a snaggle-toothed grin, panted for breath. His buckskin shirt seemed about to pop like a sausage skin as his chest filled out, strained against the hide.

"That Clayburn feller's callin' fer ye, York," said Finnegan. "Wants to get somethin' off his chest."

"Where is he?" asked Jeremiah.

"Lalande's got him and Vernon laid out in his wickiup. Ain't much time."

"He dyin'?" asked Eyestone.

"I dunno. That Vernon don't look none too pert now, and that's the truth of it. Cain't say about Clayburn. He's jest real set on havin' a smoke with ye, York. Maybe he hears old Gabe a-blowin' his horn."

"Want to go?" Eyestone asked York.

253

"I don't know, Coop."

"Maybe you'll find out somethin'."

"Yeah." York stood up. His legs didn't shake anymore. The queasy feeling in his stomach had gone away. "Let's go," he said.

"Take your rifle, was I you," said Eyestone softly. "Prime that pistol, too."

"You think the—there'll be trouble?"

"There already is," said Eyestone. Big Un grinned wide. His chest seemed to swell like a barrel about to burst.

Jeremiah tucked his pistol in his belt, grabbed up his Hawken. Big Un waddled off into the night beyond the campfire. Eyestone fell into step with York. Jeremiah noticed that he no longer walked with a limp.

Chapter Eighteen

The two wounded men lay on buffalo robes just outside Lalande's trading tent. Lalande, Andersen, Asterwold, Karns and a couple of other white men, a Flathead brave, and a young Blackfoot woman, sat on kegs or on a squared-off log around the fire. Jeremiah saw that someone had bandaged up Clayburn. A pot of water hung from the irons over the fire, steam surging up from its surface in wispy swirls.

A buckskinned man knelt beside Clayburn, bent over the wounded man. Jeremiah saw Clayburn twitch and then smelled the aroma of burning flesh, heard the hiss of hot iron searing the wound. Clayburn grunted in pain, shoved the man with the poker away.

Lalande saw York and turned away from him, scowling.

"Go on, kid," said Eyestone, "hear what the man has to say." He jabbed a thumb in Jeremiah's back, urging him toward Clayburn.

"I don't want to," said York, but he stumbled forward.

Clayburn grimaced, propped himself up on one elbow. As York drew closer, he heard the Indians chanting low, singing a song in their language. The fire raked the night with flaming fingers, lashed at the darkness with lapping tongues. Bright sparks fluttered skyward, tiny coals that winked out like distant fireflies disappearing in tall grasses. Beyond the flames, the gaunt face of Clayburn shimmered with shadow and light, his eyes invisible in their hollows like sockets in a skull.

For a brief moment, Jeremiah saw Clayburn's face distorted into something less than human, something evil and grotesque. As he drew closer, the flames dropped lower and no longer seemed to lick at the face beyond, a face floating in the darkness like a hideous mask.

"You . . . you wanted to see me?" York stammered.

"Aaaah! York, you sumbitch. Come close. Look what you done to me."

"No. I—I . . ."

"You come here!" The wounded man's voice rasped with authority and hatred. It seemed to boom in Jeremiah's ears like a voice from hell. "You will look at me and see what you've done."

Eyestone stood silently a few yards away. Lalande looked on from the shadows, his eyes hooded, noncommittal. The Indians chanted the death songs softly, keening words that Jeremiah did not understand, words that chilled him, nonetheless, clear to the bone.

"I . . . I'm sorry you got hurt," said Jeremiah. "You oughtn't to have come at me like that."

"Hurt? You little snot-nosed bastard, you've killed me and Vern there. He won't last the hour and I'll be dead afore mornin'."

Clayburn pointed to his wound. The cauterization had not helped much. His flesh was sodden with blood. Jeremiah had never seen so much blood on a man before.

"You know why I come after you, York? Money, that's why. They's a Mex soldier who wants you dead. Name of Armijo. Payin' good money to see you dead. Should be you a-lyin' here, York. Not me. You . . ." Something bubbled and rasped in Clayburn's throat and his face contorted in pain. He sagged back on the buffalo robe. Beads of sweat oozed out of the pores in his forehead and his face blanched in the firelight as if all the blood had drained out of his skull. He recovered, propped himself up again. "You," he continued, "are gonna die just like me. I mean it. Armijo will get to you one day. He might even do it himself."

"Armijo paid you to kill me? Why?"

"He don't like you. He aims to marry that gal and he don't want you around. Hell, you won't get within five paces of her again."

"You know about Estrellita?"

"She's promised to the ex-governor's nephew," croaked Clayburn. "He told me that much. Your life ain't worth a tinker's hammered thumb."

"Why are you telling me this?" Jeremiah believed him, but he could scarcely believe he was hearing it from Clayburn's own mouth.

"Because, you little sumbitch, I want to see you sweat your last remaining days on God's green earth. I want you to jump at every shadow. I want you to sleep a-sweatin' and look over your shoulder wherever you go. He's gonna get you, York. Armijo wants you dead and he's gonna hire somebody else to crack your brain wide open like a walnut. Someday, somewhere, somebody's gonna come up behind you and slip some steel in your gullet. I hope to sweet baby Jesus you die real slow and real hard, like me."

Clayburn fell back then, exhausted, and his eyes closed, the lids quivering like the wings of infant birds. His breath was a bellows wheeze in his chest, sawing horribly at his vocal cords, producing a sound that was more animal than human.

The Indians began to chant more loudly and they swayed from side to side in unison. Jeremiah started to back away. He did not want to watch Clayburn die. He turned, stumbled, and almost fell atop Louis Vernon. Vernon lay there, his mouth open, his eyes staring up into nothingness.

"He's already dead," said Eyestone, suddenly coming up behind York. "Let's go."

"York!" called Lalande. "You and me, we talk, eh? You see me after sunup. I think you bad luck in this brigade."

"Lay back, Ba'tees'," warned Eyestone. "There's been enough blood spilled tonight."

"Go on," said Lalande, dismissing the men with a wave.

Eyestone took York's elbow, led him past the corpse of Vernon, beyond the ring of firelight. York staggered along, like a man tipsy from drink, stumbling because he could not seem to lift his moccasined feet high enough to clear the stony ground.

"God," said Jeremiah, blowing the word out of his lungs as if expelling foul air.

"Don't let it get under your blanket, York," said Eyestone. "Man wanted you in his own damned sweat lodge. You can keep it in your craw or spit it out."

"He acted like to lay the blame on me."

"Man's wrong, he's wrong, right enough. You done what you had to do. Other way 'round, why you'd be lyin' there on that robe a-bleedin' to death and him laughin' and pourin' whiskey down his throat in pure jubilation. Drinkin' a toast to your trip to hell."

"I can't get him out of my mind."

Eyestone stopped. They were out of earshot of Lalande's campsite, stood in the middle of the sward between other tents and lean-to's. Some of the campfires had died down. York could hear men snoring in their lodges, talking softly somewhere in the distance. The looming mountains now seemed hostile, dark and threatening. He felt trapped, a prisoner held for some nameless reason, locked away from friends, his feelings choked in bewilderment by unseen hands.

"Look, kid, that's what he wanted to do. He put some p'izen in your head. Forget about Clayburn and that Vernon bastard. Ain't two more worthless human bein's than that pair. Why, you done us all a favor. Likely, when the truth gets knowed, some will think you're a pretty fine feller. You stood up for yourself against two growed men and you beat 'em fair. Be glad it ain't you ridin' up to the stars this night or down some rocky canyon to hell. You got your life and they lost what they tried

258

to take away from you. It's that way anywheres you go. Some live and some die and they ain't no explainin' it. Just be grateful it warn't you this time."

"Maybe Armijo will get me kilt," said Jeremiah.

Eyestone started walking toward Jeremiah's camp again. Jeremiah followed.

"And maybe you'll kill him," said Eyestone.

Lalande sat on a crate draped with several deerskins. Another crate served as his desk. Atop it were Jeremiah's tally sheets, a mug of steaming coffee, a clay ashtray that cupped his smoking pipe, a ledger, some slates and chalk, and a quill pen in a hide well that had been lacquered stiff to hold the ink. His eyebrows arched when he saw Eyestone stoop to come in under the flap, but he said nothing. Jeremiah stepped inside the large tent right behind Eyestone.

"Eh, *bonjour*, Coop. You want some whiskey? Coffee, no?"

"I'll just set," said Eyestone.

"York, you sit, eh? We make some talk."

Jeremiah saw his tally sheets on the crate, heaved an inaudible sigh. He did not sit down, but stood there, shoulders slumped.

"Did Clayburn . . . Is he . . . ?"

"He cursed you with his dying breath. Did you not hear the shot?"

"No! What happened?"

"Clayburn, he kill himself, *non?* He take the pistol and he put it to his head and poof! He blow his brains out, eh? He dying anyway, but he don't want to suffer no more."

Lalande's face bore no expression. His eyes appeared dull as agates. He spoke in flat, even tones, without a trace of emotion in his voice.

York looked at Eyestone. Cooper shrugged, looked away.

"He come at me," said York feebly.

"No matter," said Lalande, sweeping the subject away with

259

his hand, as if he was clearing off a desk of unwanted papers. "We got other fish to fry, *non?* You make the fool of me." Lalande picked up the tally sheets, shook them until they rattled like dry corn husks. "What you do? You watch Baptiste. You mark down his trade. You check up on him, eh? I think you plenty stupid kid."

"I was keeping a tally. Yes." York's jaw hardened. His eyes flashed like struck flint. "Ain't no law agin' it."

"Eh, you talk law to me? Baptiste, he the law in the mountains. You work for me, you don't make marks on paper if I don't tell you to make marks on paper." The Frenchman stepped close to York, crumpled the papers up in his fist. Eyestone stiffened, but did not move.

York did not back down. He straightened his shoulders, squinched his eyes to narrow slits.

"What's yore point, Lalande?" asked Eyestone.

Lalande wheeled, glared at Eyestone. The papers continued to twist in his hand.

"I do not want this boy in my brigade. He is bad luck, *non?* He bring plenty trouble, I think. Plenty trouble."

Eyestone stood up.

"That's for you and York to work out. I'll be outside if you need me, Jeremiah."

York watched Eyestone walk out. He felt betrayed, but he realized that Coop was right. This business was between him and Lalande.

"I want the money you owe Mr. Morrison," said Jeremiah. "Soon as you get it."

"Eh? My father, he make the debt. Maybe he pay. You don't say Baptiste he pay. You don't tell Baptiste nothing."

"I aim to collect that debt."

"Why you tally my hides, eh? Mr. Morrison he say do that?"

"No," said Jeremiah.

"Who tell you do this thing?"

"I . . . I can't tell you."

260

Lalande swelled up with rage. His face billowed as air filled his cheeks. He seemed about to explode, his eyes threatening to pop from their sockets.

"Get out. Get away from me. You don't trap for Baptiste. You go, quick."

Jeremiah blinked in confusion. He did not know if he worked for Lalande or for Chouteau. None of this seemed real to him. His mind swirled with scraps of vagrant thoughts. He could pin down none of them. He had no defense, no plan of attack. He backed away from the angry Frenchman. Lalande began to shred up the tally sheets. He ripped them up into tiny pieces. As York backed out under the tent flap, Lalande hurled the confetti at him. The papers fluttered like snowflakes.

York turned, stalked away, his senses scrambled. He wanted to run. He wanted to hit, to cry out, to rage and scream. He wanted to hide and to cry. He wanted to fight something, someone, but he didn't know who the enemy was. He didn't know where to start. He had been sent away like a child, stripped of his job with the Company, exiled before he had trapped a single beaver, skinned a marten or a mink. The injustice of it surged up in him like a terrible swirling storm. Tears stung his eyes, but he clenched them back, shook off the suffocating feeling of self-pity. He stumbled blindly toward his camp, hardly aware that men were looking at him strangely, watching him as they would a dog gone rabid.

The world had turned on him, the land jerked from underneath his feet. Worse, he had killed two men. He had not meant to kill, only to defend himself, but they were dead. And he was responsible. He wanted to run, but his feet seemed rooted to the earth. His heart flew against his ribs like a bird trapped in a cage. He felt the pumping in his temples, heard the sound of beating wings in his ears. He plodded toward his lean-to as if walking through a quagmire, as if walking against the wind.

The tears he had fought back gushed forth, filling the wells of his eyes. His throat burned as he tried to quell his anguish, keep from sobbing. Something turned bitter inside him, something he could not name, something sour and twisted that seemed to penetrate his flesh, shrink him back to boyhood, away from the man he wanted to be. He felt unwanted, alone, exiled from the company of men.

It was a terrible moment for Jeremiah York. He looked out into blackness and shadows, even though the sun was shining, burning green across the mountains, shimmering silver in the creek. He looked up and the light blinded him, the trees wavered in magnification through his tears, and he could not look at them without feeling the emptiness inside him. All of the beauty around him had been distorted, dulled, smashed into a wreckage that he could not untangle. He lurched onward, sobbing deeply now, his heart hurting as if he had been stabbed.

He fell upon his blankets and buried his head in the smoke-scented capote he had sewn himself. His sobs shook him mercilessly, would not stop, would not be silent. He cursed and raged wordlessly, unable to articulate his pain, unable to find coherence in the terrible jumble of self-pitying thoughts.

When the tears no longer came, still he sobbed, until his throat raged with fire, until his heaving lungs burned with a scorching heat. Then, as suddenly as it had started, the hysteria died in him, and he lay there, breathing like a man washed up on shore from a drowning sea, his heart slowly calming, his hurt subsiding on a wave of calmness.

It was as if he had been through a storm and now the wind had died and he was alone but alive, battered but unbeaten. He felt the calmness wash through him, sensed the rational thoughts returning shyly, on tiptoe, like creatures sent to shelter by the klaxons of thunder and lightning. He turned over, his ribs cracking into his traps, making them jangle like broken shackles fallen away from his limbs. He heaved a deep sigh, threw an arm across his tear-stung eyes, lay there, gathering his strength.

He had taken a life. Maybe two lives. Yes, Clayburn had

killed himself, but he was dying anyway. Jeremiah had to accept the truth that he himself had killed two men. Their blood was on his hands. He had dispatched their souls, whether to heaven or hell, he had no idea. He felt hollow now, unable to grasp the awesome concept of death in such cosmic proportions. He did not know whether to feel guilty or relieved. The men had tried to kill him. He had killed them. Was this not justice?

But what of the other? Death itself. Depriving another human being of life. What did that mean? Would he always see the faces of Vernon and Clayburn as they lay mortally wounded? What had happened to them? Where had they gone? Would he be punished? By whom? By God? By man? Had he broken some unknown law, a commandment? Thou shalt not kill. Was that it? Period? Could one kill to save one's own life? The questions shot through his mind now, like accusing arrows, too fast to dodge, too fast to grasp and answer. The questions thudded into his brain and lodged there, vibrating with resonances he did not understand.

He wanted to feel something. He wanted to feel sorry for the two men who had died. But he felt nothing. Nothing he could touch or magnify in his mind. It had happened and it seemed as if it had not really happened. As if he had dreamed it or just thought it and then they had just died without his having done anything to bring about their deaths. As if someone or something else had actually done the killing. As if Vernon and Clayburn had just been taken away from life, without anyone being able to stop it.

"Awwwrrgh!" Jeremiah groaned.

He felt a presence, jerked his arm away from his eyes. He squinted at the light, saw the silhouette of a man at the opening of his lean-to. He recognized the beadwork on the buckskins, the leggings tied with bright cloth sashes.

"Jerry," said Eyestone. "Come out. We'll make some smoke, talk."

"Coop."

263

"You got to get it out."

"I know." Eyestone had called him Jerry. That was something. First time that. Nobody had called him Jerry before. He liked it.

"I'm empty," said York.

"Maybe I got some news for you." Eyestone hunkered down, grinned. Jeremiah had seldom seen the man smile. So many changes now. So much happening. He couldn't sort it all out. He sat up, crawled outside, into the sun.

Eyestone sat on a log by the dead fire, stirred the ashes with a stick he picked up. Jeremiah squatted on the bare ground, drew his knees up toward him.

"What news?"

"Lalande's sending his furs on down to Santa Fe. He's not going to ship 'em back to St. Louis by boat."

"What's that mean?"

"Means he's cuttin' out Chouteau."

"Can he do that?"

"He's a-doin' it. You want that money for your friend, maybe you ought to go to Santa Fe, too."

"I ain't welcome here, no more, you mean." Jeremiah tugged a blade of grass loose from the earth, stuck the stem in his mouth. He sucked the sweet juices into his mouth.

"Maybe you're better off goin', then comin' back."

"Huh? Come back here? Lalande don't want me to trap for him. He don't want me."

"I had me a talk with Ba'tees'. He's goin' his own way. Over the mountain. Thinks the beaver is done trapped out. Goin' to Oregon, maybe. He'll stick Chouteau, just like his pappy stuck ever'body. Haw! Ain't that somethin'? That Frenchie's just no damn good."

"What about you?"

"Same as you, Jerry."

"Huh? What do you mean?"

"I mean we're both free trappers now. We ain't got no company, we don't have to sign on no brigade. I told Lalande

264

so. We're going to Santa Fe, Son, and we'll come back in the fall and trap these mountains, have us a high old time."

"Free trapper? Me?"

"'At's right. You, me, a passel of free trappers. Bunch of us made up our minds. We're all quittin' Lalande. Karns, Ballentine, Andersen, Asterwold, Finnegan, a Frenchie name of Jacques Lescaux I knowed a long time, some others."

"You just up and made up your minds all of a sudden?"

"Been a time at it. Didn't want to say nothin' till we saw whichaway Lalande was a-goin' to jump." Eyestone looked off to one side, raised a hand. "Here comes Lescaux now. He wants to talk to you."

Jeremiah followed Eyestone's line of sight, saw a man coming toward them. The man was short and stocky, with bowed legs. He looked more Indian than white, with dark skin, a full bushy beard, a wolfskin hat, buckskins dripping with horsehair and ermine, bright with beadwork and dyed porcupine quills. He carried a rifle and a clay jug. His possibles pouch, beaded with Crow designs, flapped against a brawny leg, and his powder horn clattered on the bone breastplate that hung from thongs around his neck.

"That's your friend?"

"Ain't seen him in two years. Thought he was dead."

"What's he want to talk to me for?"

"He wants to thank you."

"Me? How come?"

"You killed two men he dearly wanted to send to the devil hisself. You got to 'em first and he's mighty grateful."

Jeremiah looked at Jacques Lescaux closely as the man approached. Lescaux halted, drew his tomahawk from behind his back. He looked at Jeremiah, took careful aim. Then he took two long strides and hurled the 'hawk straight at Jeremiah. *Whoof, whoof, whoof,* the 'hawk whistled through the air.

Jeremiah hurled himself flat on the ground, his heart pumping like a triphammer.

He heard a war whoop as he skidded on his belly through the grass.

Then Eyestone's laughter broke from his throat like a roaring river as the 'hawk soared by, thunked into a stump.

Jeremiah sat up, angry, ready to do battle. Before he could get to his feet, Jacques Lescaux was all over him, wrestling him to the ground. He was strong, his breath was laced with whiskey. It seemed to Jeremiah that the man was trying to kill him.

In fact, he was sure of it.

Chapter Nineteen

Lescaux's braids hung down like black ropes as he straddled Jeremiah, pinned the youth's arms to the ground. Jeremiah looked up into the mahogany face with its deep wrinkles, the dark eyes sunk like olives behind appled cheekbones, the nose hooked over the wiry mustache that blended seamlessly into the thick beard. The Frenchman's mouth opened a small hole in the underbrush of his face.

"Waugh! Eh, you big tough guy, *non?* Jacques Lescaux, he tink you leetle runt kill zee giant. Maybeso, you make pretty good trapper someday."

"Let me up!" Jeremiah grunted. Lescaux sat on his diaphragm, making it hard to breathe.

"Sure. I let you up, we talk zee bevair, *non?* I tell you many things, eh?"

Lescaux slid away, stood up. He bent down to pick up his rifle and jug, squatted on the log next to Eyestone. Cooper still wore a wide grin on his face. His eyes twinkled with merriment.

"What'd you have to go and do that for?" asked Jeremiah, rising up and brushing himself off.

"Eh, we see what you made of, Giant Killer." He said "Killair."

"I didn't like it none."

"Maybeso, you get leetle more smarter, eh? Maybeso next

267

time nobody jump you like zat."

"Damned right," snorted Jeremiah.

The Frenchman and Cooper laughed in unison.

"Set down, Jerry," said Eyestone. "Jacques, I'll have a pull of that jug."

Lescaux handed the jug of whiskey to Eyestone. Cooper took a swig, offered some to York. Jeremiah shook his head.

"You kill doze two rascals, Jeree," said Lescaux. "You do me big favor. Zey took my squaw, skulled her, and make her veree sick. They took her favors lak she zair woman. Goddamn sonzabeech, no damn good man take squaw like zat. I keel zem myself if zey live long enough, eh?"

"I wasn't tryin' to kill them," said Jeremiah, pouting. He squatted some distance away from the volatile Frenchman, still not able to bring himself to trust him. "They was a-tryin' to kill me."

"No mattair. You keel zem. I mighty glad."

"Jacques here showed me how to trap beaver and such," said Eyestone. "Long time back. Saw him this mornin' and told him I was breakin' with Lalande. He was a-lookin' for you, Jerry. He can tell you why he's a free trapper, eh, Jacques?"

Lescaux grabbed the jug from Eyestone, tipped it up. Jeremiah could hear the whiskey gurgle down the French trapper's throat. When he brought the jug down, he didn't even blink. His eyes were clear and dry.

Jacques set the jug down between his feet, smacked his lips. They disappeared back into the thicket of his beard.

"Lalande he do you big favair, I tink, Jeree. The brigade, she own you. She own your soul. No good, eh? You go with zee brigade to trap zee bevair and you tink zees is *bon*, no? *Mais*, I do zee same ting and I am enlist for t'ree year in de fur company *pour* zee bounty, *n'est-ce pas?* Ha! Eighty dollair zey geeve me. And, if not for zee damn 'Rickaree, zee Crow, and ze damn Pieds Noir, zee Blackfoot Injun, I make *beaucoup* monee, *non?* But I am rob-rob-rob too damn focking much. Lak' five time I am rob. I am being zee free trappair *pour* seven year, eh, I am rob five time. Zey take all zee horse. Take my gun. Take all my clothes. Zey take all zee bevair, eh, I come back St. Louis on foot like beggair, *non?* I tell you, Jerree, zis trapping she make a man vairy rich, but you got to watch out for zee robair, zee t'ieving redskins."

Jeremiah listened raptly to Lescaux, making out the words despite the thick accent. The voice was high-pitched, but went up and down the scale chromatically, making the narrative sound almost like a song.

"Lalande, he no good. He steal like the redskin. He steal from you, me, anybody he can. You be free trapper. You make much money."

"That's what I want to do," said Jeremiah.

"*Bon!* You hunt with Coop, he show you everything."

"What about you? Are we gong to trap with you?"

"Maybeso. I live in the mountains. I sell my pelts to Ashley, go back pretty quick. I see you one day, uh?"

Jeremiah looked at Eyestone. Coop nodded. Jacques picked up his jug and rifle, stood up. As suddenly as he had come, he was gone, around the bend of the stream. It was quiet after he left, seemed as if he had never even been there.

"Funny man," said Jeremiah finally.

"He knows you're hurtin'. Trying to take your mind off it some."

"What?"

"Same as me, I reckon. It's got to be talked out. Else you got it stuck like a arrer in your craw. Ever kill a man before?"

"You know I ain't." Jeremiah's tone reeked with sullen undertones.

"Mighty bad feelin'. Don't get no better, neither. Man feels like he's tamperin' with somethin' mighty big. With life, maybe. Death. Somethin' bigger even. He gets a deep hole in his innards for a spell afterward, like somethin' wrenched your gizzard out and is gnawin' on it.

"Don't make no difference if it's a redskin or a whiteman. It's different than killin' a deer or elk, buffalo. Different kind of feelin'. You shoot a man dead, or cut his life out with a knife or 'hawk, it's like the ground drops out from under you."

"That's the way I felt. Kind of." Jeremiah drew a deep breath, lost some of his trepidation. "Made me feel real bad. All over. Inside. Like God was watchin'."

"First man I kilt," said Eyestone, "made me want to crawl in a hole and pull the hole in after me. I reckoned lightning would strike me dead for what I done. I kept waitin' for hell to open up and drag me down into the fire. Took me a long time to get over it. I run a long ways and never looked back.

"Who'd you kill?"

"My pa," said Eyestone. His voice was so soft, Jeremiah almost didn't hear him say it.

"You kilt your own pa?"

"He was killin' my ma. Crazy drunk, like always, and she was turnin' blue. I asked him to stop, and my ma not breathin', and I taken a Pennsylvania squirrel rifle what was loaded and primed, aimed it at his head. I never thought I'd have to use it. I didn't want to shoot my own pa. But he wouldn't quit chokin' her. My ma went limp and I squeezed the trigger. I never knew what a .41-caliber ball could do to a man's head at close range. Took me a half hour to get my ma breathin' right again. She helped me clean Pa up and bury him, but she never looked at me the same no more. I left, but that man's death is still with me. I just didn't see no way out of it. Don't make it right, though."

"No." Jeremiah let out a breath, seemed to take forever to draw some air back in his lungs again.

"You had to kill those men," said Eyestone. "Same as I had to kill my own pa. I made some smoke with a feller or two what knowed Clayburn and Vernon. Clayburn, he had him some enemies. He liked to do anything for a buckskin or a greenback dollar. Vernon, he was a man who'd stick you in the back and never blink over it. Used to work together down on the wharves in St. Louis. Clayburn, he was runnin' passengers up the Mississipp', and he'd tip Vernon which ones had the cash.

Them travelers'd get their skulls bashed in or get run through with a dirk, and them two water rats split the money."

"How could they get away with something like that? I mean, if people knew about it."

Eyestone shook his head.

"I don't know. They was slick as pig shit on a peeled log. Nobody could prove nothin', but they suspicioned that they was a-doin' it, put Clayburn off his boat. Him and Vernon took some pilgrims out from Independence a few times and they'd come back with their pockets full. I reckon that Armijo feller promised to pay 'em good money to take your gizzard out's why they come with Cap'n Lalande."

"I . . . it's all hard to believe. Why people do such things."

"They's rotten in ever' apple barrel, Jerry. Them two was at the bottom, putrid as a three-day skunk carcass. World's better off 'thout 'em."

"I don't know what to say. I guess I wish your friend Lescaux had kilt 'em first."

"They wouldn't be no deader."

The mountains made their own weather. They made their own storms. One minute the skies would be a flawless blue, the sun naked and brilliant, not a trace of wind, the land serene as a basking lizard. Then, great snowy clouds would boil up from some far-off canyon and spill over the jagged peaks like gigantic bolls of cotton.

Towering over the land, the clouds blocked out the sun, threw monstrous shadows across every tree, every blade of grass, darkened the creeks and rivers, brought the strong winds sniffing, gathered force behind the massive stone faces of treeless peaks. In moments, the weather changed. The clouds blackened and rumbled. Jagged streaks of lightning split the heavens. Hailstones as big as musket balls rattled on granite outcroppings. Snow fell on the white peaks, rain danced at the lower elevations like curtains of isinglass, lancing down in silvery needles.

The storm grew over the place where they buried the two men, belched a torrent of wind-thrashed rain over those who dug the holes, and shoveled the dirt over Louis Vernon and Cantwell Clayburn, wrapped in moth-riddled blankets. In seconds, the graves turned to mud. There were not many at the gravesite and most of them ran to their lodges when the rains struck. The Indians broke off their keening and the trappers scurried away like startled prairie chickens. Only the two shovelers remained, hurling mud into soupy graves.

Jeremiah watched from a distance, fairly dry under the graceful boughs of a blue spruce. He felt numb and empty, could not think of the two men as they were when alive. He saw them only as misshapen grotesque forms in sodden blankets, lifeless lumps that would soon enough be eaten by worms, corroded to bone by the earth itself.

The images were ugly and he wondered if the mountains were thundering their disapproval of him. He had slept fitfully the night before. Some of the other trappers had come by, tried to give him solace, offered him drinks, but he wanted to be alone. It seemed to him that his life was a jumble, that all of his past was in disorder. The events of the day before did not blend in with his experience in the mountains or along the trail. His boyhood in Kaskaskia did not fit in with his life now. He no longer knew for sure who he was, nor where he belonged. He was no longer in the brigade and Lalande had turned out to be a thief. Who was there among those he knew who was honest, who was trustworthy? Was this not what his father and mother had drummed into him most every day of his life? Where was the goodness in life if men killed and stole and cheated? How was a stranger to life, as he now felt he was, to make his way? Something strained inside him, something bolted in harness that wanted to be free, wanted to be aligned with those lessons he had learned back home. Yet he had looked inside himself last night and thought of the things Lescaux and Eyestone had told him and wondered how they could be so casual about life and death. Especially death.

Now, in the slashing rain, he saw men making mud in holes where dead bodies wallowed like drowned hogs wrapped in moldy blankets and he tried to make sense of it. What had happened to him? Why was he not punished? What did the rain mean? Was it a cleaning force that renewed the land, filled up the streams and rivers, made fresh mantles on the high peaks, and thrashed the underbrush with hailstones? Or was it God weeping, bellowing at him in thunderous tones, cursing him for a murderer?

The men finished piling the mound of dirt into the grave and ran for shelter, their shovels slung over their shoulders. They disappeared behind the phalanx of rains and Jeremiah could see only the barest outlines of teepees, tents, lean-tos, hide huts, bereft of life and movement, shadows that cringed under the downpour. He sat there, with the needles dripping softly on his buckskins, tasted the brine of wood-kissed rain on his tongue, and looked at the grave puddles bouncing with miniature waves like miniature seas.

"I'm sorry," he said to no one, and he drew his knees up, made a platform of his arms. He bowed his head and listened to the tink of rain on the spruce boughs, twitched when the thunder boomed, cringed when the lightning crackled. The air smelled like burnt metal as a ragged bolt touched the ground not far away. His spine tingled and he felt the hackles on the back of his neck bristle with an electric charge.

He had seen lightning hit a calf back home one day. The calf bawled and bucked, bleated for hours afterward. The lightning had peeled a streak of hide off its back like a potato peeling. The calf had survived, but it wore that jagged pink stripe on its back the rest of its life. No hair ever grew back over it. It was like a brand, hideous as anything he had ever seen, but fascinating as well. He would never forget that calf, though it had long since been butchered and eaten.

He tried to shake off the backward thoughts, the childhood memories. He was here now, and could never go back to that

273

time and place. He wondered what Estrellita would think if she knew he had killed two men. Would she think less of him? Hate him, maybe? He wouldn't tell her right away. Maybe never. But maybe somebody would and then she would look at him differently. What if she knew that the men had been hired by Armijo? Would that make a difference? Would she believe him? Armijo would never admit it.

He wished he was with her now. Wished he had never heard of Augustino Armijo. Wished they could just be together, alone, without troubles. Was that possible? No, he would have to face Armijo, have to show him up for what he was. Punish him, perhaps.

The thoughts were more complicated now. He could not see himself with Estrellita. Maybe she had forgotten all about him. Armijo would be around her, strutting and preening like a gamecock. He felt the burn in his senses when he thought of the Mexican holding Estrellita in his arms, kissing her. He made a fist and saw Armijo's face, wanted to pound it to pulp, make him ugly, smash his lips, pummel his black eyes until they swelled shut.

The feeling of anger passed, but the image of Estrellita remained. He saw her riding across the plain, free as the wind, her dark hair blowing like a proud mane behind her, her breasts pushing against her blouse, a flash of leg above her boottop. He saw her in bright sunshine, all dappled and mysterious as a face behind a lace veil, and in shadow, comely and vibrant, waiting for him with a smile on her lips. He could almost feel her as he unclenched his water-slick wrist, could smell the scent of flowers in her hair, the heady musk of her womanhood, so oddly thrilling he felt he could fly to her over the mountains, wingless, and drop into her bedroom. As if time and distance were no more than imaginations of the mind, flimsy obstacles that could be brushed aside with the brute force of thought. He was not homesick, he realized. He was lovesick. Estrellita, for all her distance, was the person most dear to him. He wanted her, more than he wanted anything else, and yet he had nothing to give her.

Nothing but trouble.

And dreams. He had those. Plenty of them. Dreams like gossamer spiderwebs, bristling with jeweled dewdrops, stretched across a lush green meadow between two sturdy trees. Dreams like gold coins in his pocket, heavy and shining, burnished to a high sheen. He had dreams as rich as any king's treasure, resplendent dreams, dreams of wealth and power and Estrellita standing by his side, his arm around her waist, hers around his. Dreams, yes, but so fragile he dared not breathe them aloud.

He realized now that Eyestone was right. He must go to Santa Fe. He must leave these mountains for a time, let the rains wash away the mounds of the graves, let the sun grow grasses over them. He must see Estrellita and make a stand against Armijo. Then he would come to the mountains again and be a free trapper. He would become wealthy. He would begin to give the dreams form and substance. He would have gold in his pockets and wear fine clothes. He would make Estrellita proud of him. He would drive Armijo away, put him to shame.

These were the hard dreams he could realize. These were not shadows or spiderwebs, but solid, true actions he could take. Suddenly he realized how very much he wanted to go to Santa Fe. He wanted to talk to Estrellita about the Irving books, about his journey, about the game and the wild crags of the Rocky Mountains, the shining streams. He wanted to talk and dream with her. He wanted to hold her in his arms. He wanted to taste her sweet kisses, wanted to feel her soft breasts pressing against his cheek.

He crawled out from under the spruce boughs and stood up. He strode down the slope, past the sopping graves. The rain splattered against his face, soaked his buckskins. He felt the cleansing rain on his face, did not jump when the thunder pealed and the lightning washed out all the shadows, made the camp stand out in brilliant relief.

275

"Coop! Coop!" he called, as the rumble of thunder fell away in a fading descrescendo of drums.

But the wind blew his words away and the rain swallowed them up in a spattering tattoo.

Jeremiah didn't care. He grinned and tasted the rain on his lips. His buckskins weighed a thousand pounds and he slipped in the mud, skidded on his belly across the path that had been worn to earth by moccasins and horses and mules. He came up laughing and staggered drunkenly through the healing cleansing rain, toward the warmth of his lean-to, toward the dry harbor of his dreams.

Chapter Twenty

San Fernandez de Taos gleamed in the late-morning sun. The adobe houses seemed to spiral outward from the small, shadowy plaza, but there were *jacals* on the outskirts, little primitive thatched huts, and *cholas,* dugouts, or caves, where the people lived. The adobe houses had few windows, but women and children appeared at the openings and began to yell in Spanish.

Los americanos! Los americanos! Ya vienen!"

Jeremiah heard the cries picked up and carried throughout the village, and soon the trail was packed with waving men, women and children, yapping dogs. He rode in the back of the caravan, leading Beelzebub, whose panniers were filled with furs, knives, blankets, beads, things he had traded for before leaving rendezvous. He and Eyestone had cached their traps and winter gear, caught up with Lalande's pack train along Bitter Creek, journeyed with them down the North Platte, crossed the Cache la Poudre, heading ever southward. They had met others along Fountain Creek and still more trappers when they crossed the Arkansas. Their numbers had grown, and York had talked to men from Bents' Fort and the Pueblo. Other trappers and traders streamed in from the mountains and from dwellings along the Huerfano and the Purgatoire rivers until they were more than a hundred strong as they rode down from Cumbre Pass to Taos.

And, Taos, Jeremiah knew, was very close to Santa Fe, where Estrellita made her home.

He felt lightheaded, giddy. What would he say to her? Would she even remember him? Would her folks let him see her? Hell, he didn't even know where she lived. But he could find out. He could ask. Her family was prominent, he knew that. Folks would know where she lived. Maybe, he thought, she would come to Taos for the fair.

"They call it a ransom," said Eyestone, jarring York out of his thoughts.

"Huh?"

"This here fair. Mexes call it a ransom. Big trading times. Lots of strong liquor, plenty of women."

"Town looks asleep," said Jeremiah.

"Looky over yonder." Eyestone pointed and Jeremiah followed the line, shifting his gaze to take in the surroundings. His eyes caught the rows of pines streaming down from the Sangre de Cristos, the clearing on a high plateau. He saw them then, the tents, the teepees, the smoke from cookfires. The haze hung thick over the camp, almost hiding it, but he saw it all right.

"God A'mighty," he breathed.

"Purty sight, ain't it? Not much stirrin' this mornin', but you wait till afternoon. Be some foofarawin' and fandangoin', some fists flyin' and heads bustin'."

Finnegan, Big Un, shot off his rifle first. Others in the caravan followed suit. Jeremiah sent off a volley of his own, the weariness of the trail draining away with the pull of the trigger. The acrid aroma of burnt black powder stung his nostrils, made him feel good and tingly all over. He yelled with the rest of them, and Beelzebub got froggy and tried to pull off the trail. He fought the mule into submission, rejoined the pack train. Jim Karns rode by, grinning and waving. Jeremiah grinned back. He looked again at Taos, saw its green meadows, its shorn fields of wheat, the icy streams lacing the hills below the majestic peaks of the Sangre de Cristo range, regal ermine-clad peaks that rose like women's breasts to the blue sky, glistened blindingly white in the sun.

Jeremiah's face and arms were burnished to a tawny gold and there was iron in his backbone. He had grown some, he knew, and he had put the deaths of two men behind him. Eyestone had told him he had to live with it. He could live well or he could live bad. Jeremiah decided to live well. Worry was baggage. Excess baggage. Guilt was more of the same. He could not bring the men back to life, but they could bring him to death if he kept fretting over it. The miles helped rub away a lot of it. The distance helped. Time and the worms would take care of the dead in their graves. They were no longer his worry.

And then they were riding into Taos and the New Mexicans were shouting *Fandango! Fandango!* and there was the cool smell of adobe and tortillas, fresh bread baking in the ovens. He saw the beautiful women and the children. The children wore no clothes, and most of the women wore full blouses and colorful gathered skirts. Some of them wore *topolas* or *rebozas* covering their heads or flung over their faces and shoulders so that only their bright brown eyes showed.

The men, too, cut fine figures as they strutted along the street, smiling and throwing greetings to the trappers. Some wore simple white trousers and shirts, but others wore the calf-length trousers, also white, and brightly colored sashes at the waist. Some of these men wore loose-fitting shirts and some wore the loose *bolero*, a jacket somewhat like a vest. All of the dandies wore the broad-brimmed, high-crowned *sombrero*, usually tilted at a rakish angle. Jeremiah thought the men, with their bronzed faces and chests, were handsome and they seemed proud as they smiled and waved.

Some of the trappers had already turned their grimy shirts clean side out, exchanged their fur hats for rumpled beavers, their buckskin shirts for linsey-woolsey. Men dropped off at the cantinas and disappeared inside, leaving their goods to be pawed over by giggling urchins who ran beneath the legs of the horses and mules with fearless abandon.

Eyestone and York made their way to the encampment on the banks of the Rio Grande. The air was cool, even at midday, and they pitched their lean-tos among the pines. There were traders there from Chihuahua, Mexico, trappers down from the nearby mountains. Some had already begun to load their wares, take them to the marketplace at the edge of town.

"Like rondeevoo," drawled Jeremiah, when he'd had a chance to walk around the camp.

"Some, 'ceptin' ain't so wild in camp. Tonight they'll have parades and candles, some dancin'. More guitars than ever I seen in one place. You'll be stone deaf by mornin'."

"Should I do some tradin' today?"

"If you want. I generally look first day in, see what the others brung. Tomorry be soon enough."

"What'll I do with my goods until then?"

"Be all right in your lean-to. Ain't much thievin' 'mongst these folks."

"I'll wait, too, then."

"You want to shuck out of them buckskins?"

"Sure."

"Maybe we'll take a swim and put on some cloth."

They swam in the Rio Grande, which the New Mexicans called el Rio Grande del Norte, and Jeremiah put on the finery Estrellita had given him, found that the clothes had shrunk some. When he next saw Eyestone, the older man was dressed almost like a dandy New Mexican. He wore the sombrero, and the white pants, the sash. Jeremiah laughed.

"Well, I been here before," said Eyestone sheepishly.

Trading tables and tents rimmed the eastern outskirts of Taos. Banners flew from some of the tent poles. There were teepees, with buffalo robes and blankets laid out before them. Eyestone pointed out various Indians to York—Comanches, Pawnees, Utes, Arapahoes, some Shoshones and Delawares.

"They ain't fightin' now, but they get back home and it's horse-thievin' as usual," said Cooper. "Be more here tomorry and you'll likely find offers for your knives, blankets, trinkets,

They'll want to buy a pot or two. Be more tradin' in town on the plaza, kind of like a town square, but all crowded and such."

Some of the Indians wore white-men hats and York thought they looked ridiculous. He wondered why white men wearing Indian clothing didn't seem at all out of place.

The Indians were selling pieces of chamois, buffalo hides, horses, stolen and worn-out muskets, meat.

"What about Lalande's furs?" asked York.

"He'll sell 'em in Santa Fe. Bring a better price there."

"When will he go there?"

"In a few days. He ain't in no hurry. Money'll be there, the buyers won't."

"What do you mean?"

"Most of 'em'll come up here. Today, maybe. Word gets around pretty fast. The *ricos* will ride up on fancy horses, maybe even the governor, and they'll try to get the trappers drunk and buy the pelfries cheap. Lalande knows better."

"You think the rich Mexicans will come to Taos?"

"Looky yonder," said Eyestone, pointing southward.

Dust in the sky. A long way off, but a lot of it. Jeremiah's heart pounded hard in his chest.

"Comin' from Santa Fe?" he asked.

"Noplace else," said Eyestone. "Be nightfall 'fore they get here. You lookin' for someone?"

"My girl, maybe. Estrellita. She might come, with her father, Don Miguel." Jeremiah had written a letter to Estrellita, sending it on south with a group of men going straight to Santa Fe. She should have received it two weeks ago. If so, she would know he would soon be stopping in Taos, then go on to Santa Fe. His heart went weak every time he thought of her.

"Well, let's have us some of that fiery poteen they serve in Taos. Pass whiskey. Clear the dust outen our throats. Come on. My pockets are plumb burnin' up to spend a skin or two."

Don Miguel Santos de Rojas y Montez, his wife, Corazon, his

daughter, Estrellita and the *dueña*, Lucia, rode in the caravan with the governor, Manuel Armijo, and his two nephews, Augustino Armijo and Manuel Chavez. Chavez was but a youth and his uncle detested him. It was their privilege to ride slowly at the head of the column, away from the dust, while the column of servants and lesser luminaries followed at some distance behind this body. Lieutenant Merito Salcedo rode alongside the don's carriage in charge of two columns of cavalry lancers flanking the caravan, more for ceremony than for protection.

"I resent that man riding so close to our carriage," fumed Estrellita.

"Who, Merito?" asked her mother.

"You know very well who I mean," snapped her daughter.

"You needn't be so cross," said Corazon. "The man is only doing his duty. Why do you resent his presence?"

"Because he spies for Augustino," said Estrellita, her eyes blazing.

"Hush, child," said Lucia. Estrellita gored her with a fierce, barbed look.

"He is always around," said Estrellita. "When Augustino is not pestering me, then Merito is looking at me."

"They are only trying to protect you," said her father. "They know the dangerous times we live in. It was your mother's wish that they not let you out of their sight."

"I feel like a prisoner." Estrellita sulked. For the past month, Augustino had been a guest at their home at every week's end, and sometimes in the middle of the week. When he was not there, Salcedo and some of his men lounged about the yard. She could feel the cloying grip of their penetrating gazes on her, as if they were undressing her in their minds.

But these were not the only reasons for her protest. This past week she had received a letter from Jeremiah. She did not know that Lucia had steamed the letter open and resealed it after showing it to Captain Armijo. She was unaware that Augustino was paying the *dueña* to tell him everything. Yet, she knew she must be free in Taos to look for Jeremiah. She had no wish that Merito should be her shadow, Augustino her guard, and Lucia her girdle. Somehow, she must avoid their spying eyes so that she could see Jeremiah alone. Her heart yearned for him, even more strongly now that she had gotten a letter from him in his own handwriting. She had read it a hundred times and every word was burned into her memory.

"Dear Señorita Estrellita,

I have been missing you a lot. But I am coming to Taos for the Faire. I hunted Buffalow and I Killed 1 Elk and 1 Deer in the Rockie Mountans. I am going to come to Santa Fee pretty soon. I hope you can See me. I am going to trade some Stuff. I saw some Indians. Maybee you have forgotton Me But I have not forgotton You. How is your Horse??? I Hope you are Fine.

Your Friend
Jeremiah York"

She had slept with the letter pressed against her bosom every night. She dreamed of him when she went to sleep and she thought of him every morning. Now, as they drew closer to Taos, she could hardly contain her excitement.

Estrellita toyed with the hand-strap that dripped from the fine leather interior of the coach. She looked out the window at the steep dropoff they called the "Fire Jump." It made her dizzy to look down. She looked back at her father, who sat opposite her. She saw the worry lines in his forehead, the slight frown that sculptured his lips. She knew what bothered him. He wondered if any of Tecolote's band would be at Taos. No one had heard a word about him and each day seemed to make the don more nervous. She still felt like a prisoner, having to wear peasant's clothing when she rode around the ranch, her mother jumping at every strange sound. And she knew that men rode the ranch carrying rifles and others watched from the hills for any sign of the Comanche chief.

"One day he will come," Lucia said almost every day, and Estrellita had finally told her to keep her fears to herself.

But she knew the same thought was on both her mother's and father's mind. It was wonderful to get away from the ranch and from bustling Santa Fe for a few days. A change of scenery, with the promise of meeting Jeremiah again. If only he knew that she had thought of him every night since he had gone to the mountains! If only he knew how much her heart ached for him. Augustino's persistence as a suitor had not dimmed her ardor. Rather, she was more determined than ever to avoid the arranged marriage and seek her own path. There was something about Augustino that made her wary of him. He seemed so sure of himself, so sure of her hand in marriage, that he was almost arrogant whenever they were together.

"We are coming into the pueblo," said Corazon, breaking Estrellita from her thoughts. "I want you to stay close to us, Daughter. Do not go wandering about."

"Your mother is right," said Don Miguel. "There are rough men in Taos this season and they will be drinking the local spirits."

"Oh, Father, don't treat me like a child," said Estrellita. "I want to see everything."

"You mean you want to look for that American ragamuffin," said her mother.

"If he is there, I will see him," said Estrellita defiantly.

Lucia's eyes rolled in their sockets, but she made no sound beyond a soft clacking of her teeth that could scarcely be heard above the creak and rumble of the coach. Her lips moved silently as she prayed her rosary. The beads and the large crucifix lay in her lap like a coiled serpent. Patience was not a virtuous quality with Lucia; it was an iron creed, a sword made of Toledo steel that she used like a needle. She could prick a person to death over a long period of time and they'd never even know they were dying until the very last moment. Her patience made Job seem impetuous. If Lucia wanted a thing, wanted to make something occur, she would wait forever. She was like the continuous drops of water that can wear down stone, or, falling on a bald man's pate, drive him literally insane.

Estrellita, Lucia thought, was headstrong, impulsive, inconsiderate, impetuous, coltish. In other words, she was typical of most other young women at that age. The girl didn't know her own mind. She was responding to urges of the blood and the loins. This young man York had managed to snare her heart—for the time being. Infatuation, that's all it was, deep down. But the attraction was making Estrellita disobedient. Lucia could not tolerate disobedience. And Augustino, she mused, could not tolerate Estrellita's fascination with *el americano*.

Just yesterday morning, when the soldiers had come to escort Don Miguel's family to Taos, she had told Captain Armijo about the letter.

"Your rival will be in the pueblo of Taos, *Capitán*."

"How do you know this thing?"

"Estrellita has received a letter from York."

"Ah. The worm can write, can he? And what did this letter say, exactly?"

"You ask a great deal, Captain. A breaking of confidence. The telling of a secret."

"You have seen the letter then?"

"I have seen it."

"You know what it says."

"I have told you some of it."

"What is it you want? Money? Some little present for yourself?"

Lucia laughed harshly. Captain Armijo went right to the heart of a matter. It was more than money. It was a high moral obligation to see that Estrellita married this nephew of the ex-governor and became part of the ruling class of New Mexico. It would help Don Miguel and his lady, it would help them all. She saw herself as an intermediary, working behind the scenes, in secret, to bring about a marriage that was right in heaven, right in the world. Money was a consideration, of course, but only as a measure of her true worth in this matter, a meter stick that would remind her of her value as an ally to both the Rojas and the Armijo families.

"A woman can always use some extra silver," she had said to Augustino.

So she told him what was in the note and more, besides. She told him how Estrellita reread the letter each day and went to sleep with it under her pillow. She saw the rage build in Armijo and she gloated that she had effected this change in him. A jealous man, she knew, was soft, wet clay in her hands.

"You must tell me everything that happens between Estrellita and this York. I want to know what she says about him and if there are to be meetings. Everything, do you understand?"

Lucia waited for the rest of it. Her patience was like a tree growing for centuries.

"You will be well paid."

"It shall be done," said Lucia.

So they had made this pact between them, Lucia and Augustino. She looked out the window of the coach now, saw the blue of the sky and the snowcapped peaks of the mountains in the distance. She recalled another thing Armijo had said that morning, something that both chilled and thrilled her heart. She was still listening to the assuring clink of the silver coins in her purse when Augustino spoke to her.

"I do not understand why this York is still alive."

"Eh?" Lucia grunted.

"I mean," he said, "that it is very dangerous where the American has been. I did not expect him to come out of the mountains."

"Sometimes such things must be guaranteed, Captain Armijo. Arranged."

"Yes. That is what I was thinking."

"Maybe," said Lucia, probing further, "York will not live long, even so. Maybe he will not even come to Taos."

"That is possible."

"Do not give up hope. Never. There is many a rock in a man's path, many the turns in the road."

Augustino laughed.

"You know something, old woman? I think I like you. I think we two think very much the same."

"We both want what is good for our young lady, the daughter of the don," said Lucia, smiling.

"Yes, yes, we do."

"Even if it means . . ."

"Yes, even if it means a, shall we say, sacrifice?"

"I would hold no pity for a thief of the heart. A bandit is a bandit."

"You would make a good soldier, Lucia."

That had made her proud, to hear Captain Armijo compliment her so. She felt commissioned now to join Augustino in his suit for Estrellita's hand in marriage. She already had the moral approval of her conscience, but the captain's seal on her deeds made her role even more important and vital than it was before she had entered into this conspiracy.

A prodding elbow in her ribs broke into her thoughts, jerked her back to the present.

"Lucia," said Estrellita, "move over. You are wrinkling my mantilla." They had traveled nearly sixty kilometers yesterday, wearing different clothing. They had spent the night at a rancho, and this morning they had dressed as if for a fiesta. It was probably a mistake, but her mother had insisted they arrive in style. She was glad she had worn a dark-red dress. It did not show the dust so much as the white one she had brought for evening wear. Nor the wrinkles, perhaps.

"Oh, I am sorry, my mistress." Lucia scooted away, and the coach lurched over a stone in the road, jolting all of them from side to side.

"I will be grateful when we get off this wretched road," said Corazon. "My clothes must have gained ten kilograms from the dust."

"We will be there soon," said her husband. "One more hill."

"Always," said Lucia to herself, "it is one more hill." But she saw the smoke from the pueblo through the window and she knew it would not be long before she would use her wiles and her wits to prevent a meeting between Estrellita and York.

She looked at Estrellita, smiled, and patted the back of her hand.

"Is it not very fine that Captain Armijo is with us?" she said. "I look forward to seeing you dance with him again."

Estrellita gritted her teeth.

Why was it that Lucia had to spoil everything all the time, even her thoughts, which were certainly not on Augustino at that moment. Quickly, she moved her hand away from Lucia's. It was a rude and thoughtless thing to do, but it gave Estrellita a brief moment of wicked satisfaction.

Lucia finished the last bead on her rosary, lifted the crucifix to her lips. She kissed the tormented face of Jesus, unaware of the faint smile she wore so briefly that it was like a small summer cloud, blown vagrant by a high wind, passing over the sun for only a second yet blotting out the light and casting an ephemeral shadow over mountain and plain for as far as the eye could see.

Estrellita felt the sudden chill in the coach as it lurched up a grade, pinning her shoulders to the seat. She grasped the strap and held on grimly to keep from being tossed from side to side.

In the distance she heard the peal of a bugle, and her heart quickened.

The cornets drowned out the lone bugle call and the sound was like a chorus of Gabriels announcing Judgment Day.

"Taos," she breathed.

Chapter Twenty-One

Jeremiah heard the brassy bleat of cornets gracefully flaring into a rolling fanfare as the caravan topped the rise and surged over the hill and onto the valley plateau. Lancers, stiff-backed in their pale-blue uniforms, held their prancing horses to a graceful single-foot gait as they fanned out, driving back the crowd so that the carriages could pass.

"Here comes the Santy Fee bunch," said Eyestone.

York stood there, openmouthed as the cavalry troops dazzled the crowd with a precision exhibition of horsemanship. Banners streamed from guidons like oversize ribbons and the cornets wove a fluting martial melody in close harmony.

"*Ay! Ay! Los coches! Miran, miran. La entrada del gobernador!*" shouted the New Mexicans.

"Wal, iffen it ain't the governor hisself," said Karns. "An' looky them horses. He's some nigger in them fancy braids and gold buttons."

A pack of Arapahoes scattered as the soldiers widened their circle. Sabers flashed in the sun, and the crowd cheered. People began streaming from the village, running through the filthy, hard-packed streets that ran with urine and feces, both animal and human, shouting their greetings as they flowed onto the plain like a procession of scarecrows wrapped in white bedsheets.

The lancers re-formed in a column of twos and pranced their horses into the village, heading for the main square. Behind them, one man stood out from the other horsemen. He wore a plumed hat and a uniform adorned with gold epaulets, a gold belt and sash. He doffed his hat and grinned idiotically at the crowd.

"Who's that?" asked Jeremiah.

"Why, that's Manuel Armijo hisself," said Eyestone. "He's the governor, or used to be. I heard tell he's the customs officer now. Collects all the money from the St. Louis wagons. Most of it sticks to his palm like honey to a grizzly's paw."

"Armijo," Jeremiah breathed. Then he saw Augustino riding a few horse lengths behind the ex-governor. York's blood raced hot and he felt the familiar churn in his stomach, the boil-up of fluttering insects deep in his gut.

Augustino saw Jeremiah at the same time. A look of dark hatred flashed in his eyes. He scowled and turned his head. Eyestone saw the look pass between the two men.

"You know that soljer," he said.

"That's the man that paid to have me killed," said Jeremiah.

"He don't look none too happy to see your face."

Jeremiah snorted. He saw Merito Salcedo riding alongside a carriage. The lieutenant did not see him. He was too busy preening for the ladies, doffing his hat, and grinning like a coon eating fermented persimmons. York was not interested in him, however, but only in the face he saw in the window. At first his brain did not catch up with his senses. He thought he must be imagining that face, but the harder he looked, the more he knew it was right. He yelled hoarsely, began to wave.

Estrellita turned at the sound, looked at him through the window. Then she leaned out, smiling, and waved her fan at him. The lace on her mantilla flowed across the side of the carriage. Jeremiah flushed a bright pink from his forehead to his toetips.

"Estrellita!" he shouted. "Hoooo!"

Then Estrellita's face disappeared and the shutter came

down hard as if someone had pulled on it violently. The carriage rolled away toward the village, followed by others, and the dust blew toward York and Eyestone, settled on them like ashes.

"That's my girl," said Jeremiah softly. "That's the girl I aim to marry up with soon as I get rich."

Eyestone said nothing. He didn't want to piss on the boy's plate. But he knew how those *ricos* felt about Americans. They might smile and act friendly, but they put a mighty high price on their women marrying gringos. Religion was part of it, but they were jealous of their territory, too. Ever since Mexico broke away from Spain back in '21, the New Mexicans ruled with a high hand.

He and his brother Jeremiah had been just kids then, taking up with Bill Becknell. They rode out of Franklin in Missouri Territory, headed out to trade with the Indians. Word of the revolt in Mexico City took some time to get out to the plains, but Becknell ran into some New Mexican hunters who said the gates of Santa Fe were open.

They headed across the Sangre de Cristo range by way of Raton Pass, dropped down to Santa Fe. Cooper had spent about fifty dollars on goods and he sold them for almost eight hundred. His brother made five hundred dollars. They felt rich. When they got back to Franklin, they showed their gold and silver coins, watched the people go crazy. He and his brother left the next spring with Becknell, who took a different path to reach Santa Fe.

Back then, Cooper thought Becknell might be a couple of bricks shy of a load. Instead of turning toward the Rockies when they reached the Great Bend of the Arkansas, Bill headed south into hell, following the Cimarron. The sun baked their brains and fried their throats. The desert sand was hard on the horses and mules. They ran out of water and started killing their dogs, first off, and drinking the blood. When they ran out of dogs, they killed their mules. Coop had never had such thirst. They were all slowly going mad when they spotted a lone

291

buffalo, its belly swollen with water. Cooper shot the animal, slashed open its stomach, and twenty-nine men drank warm water until there wasn't a drop left. Eyestone had never had a drink that gave him so much pleasure as that first quenching swallow from the buffalo's belly.

Jerry Eyestone found the stream where the buffalo had drunk and they drank until they were all sick. The party made a hundred thousand dollars profit on that trip and Cooper took his brother to the mountains. Becknell had guessed right. Going down the Cimarron was a shorter route to Santa Fe and it gave Eyestone some small satisfaction to know that the shortcut was now the favored trail to New Mexico. They called it the Cimarron Cutoff, and though it was hellish at times, especially when the rains turned the trail to mud, you could get wagons to Santa Fe a hell of a lot quicker than by going over the mountains.

Eyestone watched the coaches and empty *carretas* rumble into the pueblo. York stood there, then started running. Cooper let him go. This was Jeremiah's party. He would either get the gal or get killed.

Ex-governor Manuel Armijo had arranged for his entourage to be put up in some of the larger, finer adobes near the plaza. Estrellita thought the quarters quaint, but her father deplored the Spartan accommodations. Lucia was given a small room of her own. Estrellita's was next door. The house smelled of goat and mule, of onions and fried cornmeal. The walls were whitewashed, decorated with animal skins and woven blankets. There were few windows, little light. The first thing Estrellita did was to search her purse for the quill pen, a sheaf of foolscap. Hastily, she wrote a note to Jeremiah, hoping she would see him before the day was over. She pursed her lips and blew the ink dry, carefully folded the note, put it inside her bodice. After unpacking, Estrellita joined her mother and

Lucia for a stroll to the plaza. Don Miguel had business with Manuel Armijo, inspecting some prime New Mexican mules, looking over the packs of prime pelts brought in by the trappers, and they would not see him again until evening when they were to dine at the ex-governor's quarters a few doors away.

The plaza was ringed with makeshift benches piled high with foodstuffs, cheeses, meats, sausages, soap, blankets, trinkets. Handmade jewelry glittered in the sun. Brown-faced women peered from behind the stacks of goods, smiled wanly, flashed decayed teeth. Men and women strolled from bench to bench, examining the various wares, picking them up, putting them down, sometimes making a purchase. Estrellita and Corazon were the two most beautiful women in the plaza and the men stopped to look at them with admiring glances. Lucia scowled at every one of them and they looked away, only to steal a glance at Estrellita again once the *dueña* had passed.

The smells were overwhelming. Dogs roamed the plaza, and naked children scurried across the open court on mysterious missions, disappearing between adobes and into dark doorways. Someone plunked on a guitar and the noises from a cantina drifted on the afternoon air, a jumble of talk and laughter sprinkled with the clank of pewter tankards and the soft thunk of clay mugs on wood.

Corazon looked at a lace shawl, but it was crude and heavy. Estrellita's attention was fixed on the young men, looking for Jeremiah's face in the throng. Lucia hovered at her elbow, but was soon distracted by some handmade crucifixes at a bench watched over by a pretty young maiden with high cheekbones, the natural vermilion of her strong Indian blood softening the sharp ridges. Estrellita drifted away from the two women, scanned the various entrances to the plaza.

She heard a soft whistle, turned, saw Jeremiah standing in the shadows of an adobe. Her heart turned to hot wax, seemed to melt with a sudden intense heat.

He beckoned to her. She looked around, saw that Lucia was

engrossed in looking at the crucifixes, and her mother was still riffling through piles of lace shawls as if searching for something delicate enough to suit her fancy. Estrellita slipped away through the crowd, threaded her way to Jeremiah. Her red gown stood out, even amid the colorful attire of the natives, and her mantilla bobbed above the sea of raven-haired men and women, proud and flowing as a showhorse's mane.

Jeremiah stepped out of the shadows, rushed to meet Estrellita. He stopped just short of taking her into his arms, looked into her dark eyes. She looked into his, smiled.

"Howdy, Estrellita."

"Hello, Jeremiah."

"I'm right glad to see you."

"It is a pleasure for me."

He shuffled his feet, looked down at them. The pants she had bought for him were too short, the sleeves of the shirt seemed to have shrunk as well. His nostrils filled with the scent of her perfume. The scent reminded him of gardenias and honeysuckle, of morning glories and every prairie flower he had ever picked along the trail to the Rockies. Estrellita seemed suffused with beauty from every imaginable source. The direct sunlight shone through Gypsy strands of hair, the light bouncing off the adobe softened her features, smoothed them to perfection. The mantilla gave her a regal air and the dress seemed to flow from her shoulders to the ground like fire.

"You've grown," said Estrellita.

"I reckon," he said, and then, as if realizing what he had said, he straightened. "I read those books you give . . . *gave* me. Liked 'em."

"I'm pleased."

"Can . . . can we walk somewheres? Can we talk, private-like?"

"You want to kiss me, don't you?" she whispered.

The question caught him by surprise. He stuttered, stammered something. They both laughed.

She touched his hand, then reached inside her bodice, withdrew the note she had written him.

"I can't talk to you now, but this note will explain where I'm staying, where to meet me tonight. If you want to."

"Want to? I can hardly wait."

He took the note, started to unfold it.

"No, don't read it now," she said. "No one must know about it."

She looked around, failed to see Merito Salcedo inside one of the adobes, looking on. She folded Jeremiah's fingers over the note, pushed his hand away. He put the note in his pocket.

"Yes, I want to kiss you," he said.

"Not now," she protested as he leaned toward her. She looked frantically over her shoulder, spotted Lucia. "Uh oh. I've got to go. Lucia must not see us together."

"Why?"

"I can't explain it to you now. Will I see you tonight?"

"Nothing could keep me away, Estrellita. It's mighty good to see you."

He saw Lucia then, over Estrellita's shoulder, striding through the crowd like some ungainly buzzard after carrion. Impetuously, Jeremiah grabbed Estrellita's hand, brought it to his lips. He bowed slightly, kissed the back of it. He whispered good-bye and melted back into the shadows. It took the strongest effort of will to turn his back on her and walk away from the plaza. His heart was pounding in his chest and his stomach swirled with what Big Un called "the-bad-whiskey-scairt-of-dyin'-mornin'-jitters."

He had the almost insane desire to go back and wave to Lucia, flash her an idiotic grin. It was a passing thought, one that he took to be a sure sign that Estrellita made him feel like an addled schoolboy. Still, the idea that he could irritate Lucia for just a moment was appealing. He didn't hate the woman, he reasoned, but she was a pebble in his boot, right enough.

When he escaped the shadowy clutch of the pueblo,

Jeremiah stopped near a water trough, fished the note from his pocket. He opened it, felt a thrill as he looked at the words written in a flourishing hand.

"Most Esteemed Jeremiah,

I am so happy to know that you are in Taos. I am staying in a house on Calle Hernandez. I would like to see you this evening. We are dining at the Cantina Obregon. It you will stop by, perhaps we can see each other for a few moments.

With love,
Estrellita"

He read the note again and again. He would have to find out where this Cantina Obregon was and Calle Hernandez, too. He didn't know how he could wait for the sun to go down. Knowing she was here, so close, was almost too heavy a burden for him to bear. He wished now that he had snatched her away from that old chaperone and taken her to his camp or up into the mountains. He needed to talk to her. He had been thinking of her for months, and the things he wanted to say were all stored up in him, ready to burst out in a flood. He put the note away, walked back toward camp. He wanted to think about her, think about what he would say to her tonight.

York did not feel comfortable in the clothes Estrellita had bought him. After being in the mountains, living in buckskins for so long since leaving the East, he felt out of place, too noticeable among men he admired and respected to wear such finery. He realized that he had wanted to impress people he did not know, did not care about. It wasn't that the people of Taos were not elegant; they were, it was just that he felt awkward in St. Louis clothing. He wondered if he looked like the fool he felt he was. It didn't matter. He did not feel like Jeremiah York. He felt like something patched together, some creature on display. As he approached the camp, he heard the talk and it was not the dandified speech of St. Louis, but the booshway

296

talk of trappers and hunters, the barking guttural rasps of Indians, the soft patois of the French, the burr of the Scots, the lilt of the Irish singing voices and the broad accents of the Kentuckians, the Tennesseans, and Missourians that made him feel at home, part of the grand heart of peoples from everywhere on the face of the earth who came to the wilderness and asked for nothing but a chance to hunt and trap the wild places, make their own paths in places where few white men had ventured, where even the Indians had to struggle to survive, year after year.

"York!" someone called as he strode into the camp by the Rio del Norte.

Jeremiah saw the men gathered around a stone-circled firepit with cooking irons dangling pots and utensils. He squinted into the dazzling afternoon light, saw the men of Lalande's brigade sitting on logs and buffalo robes, smoking and drinking.

"Ho!" Jeremiah replied.

"Come, have a smoke," hollered J.R. Asterwold. "Have a taste of lightnin'."

There it was, Jeremiah thought. The friendship. That something among men that made him full inside, made his heart swell.

"Let me get into my 'skins," he told J.R.

Jeremiah stripped naked, put on his buckskins. Now he did not feel out of place or awkward. He looked at the cast-off garments lying in a puddle at his feet. The only time he had worn those clothes, he had gotten into trouble, first with the bull, then with Estrellita. They did not fit well now, if they ever had. He kicked them away from his feet. Somehow the small act of violence did not seem enough. Although the clothes had been a gift from Estrellita, he no longer wanted them. He did not want to be reminded of that disastrous night when he had run away. He should have stayed and fought for Estrellita. He should have taken her away from Augustino Armijo then and there.

He strapped on his knife, laced up his moccasin boots. He snugged down the rabbit felt hat with the seed-bead band he had bought from a Blackfoot up on Ham's Fork. Satisfied, York left his lean-to, walked to where the men had gathered.

"Set, York," said Andersen. "We been havin' an argument amongst ourselves. Maybe you can settle it."

"Whiskey?" asked Karns, lifting an earthen jug over his head.

"Don't drink none of that," said Big Un. "It'll burn your throat clear through to your asshole."

"After it hits bottom, you don't give a damn," said Andersen. "You have a swaller or you'll still be a pilgrim."

Jeremiah sat down, wiped his lips with a buckskinned sleeve. The men passed the jug down. He upended it and his mouth filled with fire. He swallowed quickly and a molten ball struck his stomach. His breath shut off as fumes filled his lungs and nostrils. His eyes blurred with tears and he gasped.

The men laughed. Jeremiah wondered if the fiery liquid would stay down. He gulped desperately, drawing great draughts of air into his tortured lungs.

"Ah, ah, ah," he hawked and grasped his queasy stomach as if to stay the liquor from belching back up and burning his throat all over again.

"Now, thet'll put some pepper in yore pecker," said Karns, the liquor slurring his speech to a lazy drawl.

"Lucky," said Drew, looking cock-eyed at Jeremiah, "we beeen talkin' 'mongst ourselfs. Seed you prancin' aroun' like some Mexican booshway in them fancy clothes. Now you got yourself back into buckskins and it got us to wonderin' if'n you wasn't Meriwether's Sambo after all."

"What?" asked Jeremiah.

The men laughed, slapping their knees. Too much laughter, thought the youth, for what had been said. Andersen's eyes filled with tears; Karns bent over, his body shaking and quivering as if he had the ague. Then Drew slapped Big Un on

298

the back and rocked backward on the log serving as a bench for the men. They laughed a long time, as Jeremiah's puzzlement deepened.

"What's so goddamned funny?"

No one answered. The laughter rose to a crescendo again. All of the men gasped for breath. Andersen clamped hands to his sides, bobbed his head.

Jeremiah stood up, anger boiling just beneath the confusion in his mind.

"Ah, York," wailed J.R., a chuckle still gurgling in his throat. "Fetch me my boots, York. Fetch my coat."

"My fowling piece, York," bellered Andersen. "Fetch it, boy."

"York, bring me my pipe," cracked Drew, and the laughter broke out again, contagious as the whooping cough.

Jeremiah's fingers contracted into fists. He wanted to lash out, strike the nearest man. He took a step toward Karns, drew back his right fist. He felt a hand grip his arm at the elbow.

Jeremiah turned, saw Eyestone.

"It ain't worth no fightin'," said Cooper. "Them niggers is just havin' some fun. Some joke they had stuck in their craws. Likker loosened it up is all."

"Huh? They was laughin' at me."

"No harm meant. It's your name, Son."

"My name?"

The laughter died away in a series of coughs and heavy sighs.

"York," said Eyestone. "The name's like a feather ticklin' their toes."

"I don't see nothin' funny about it," said Jeremiah as Eyestone released him. "No more'n any other name."

"Before your time," said Eyestone. "Before mine, too."

"So, why are they funnin' me?"

"York was with the Lewis and Clark expedition," explained Eyestone. "Did everything for them two."

"Fetched stuff?"

The mountain men stifled contagious titters.

"Yeah," said Cooper. "York was a servant, kind of. A slave."

"A black slave?" asked Jeremiah.

"Black as the inside of a stovepipe," said Karns. "York was some nigger, I'd say."

Jeremiah glared at the men.

"Any of you ever laugh at me again," he said, "I'll break my 'hawk over your goddamned heads."

He stalked away, back to his lean-to. He grabbed up the bundle of St. Louis clothes and carried them over to the fire where the men sat. He threw them into the flames without a word. The men all looked at him soberly. Eyestone smiled, walked away, toward a circle of young Arapaho playing the bone game under a pine tree.

The clothes caught fire and sent sparks shooting upward. The men around the fire had to move to keep from being stung by the tiny coals. Jeremiah gave them all one last scathing look and then turned on his heel, started toward the pueblo.

"I believe that boy's got him some backbone," said Andersen softly.

Chapter Twenty-Two

Shadows filled the streets and alleyways of Taos, relieved only by the flicker of lanterns and lamps spilling smoke and light through windows and doorways. The Cantina Obregon, just off the Plaza Mayor, on Calle Dos, had been taken over entirely by Manuel Armijo and his guests, including the Rojas family. Estrellita had listened to the boring speeches from Manuel Armijo and others, had sat through the endless toasts, the raucous laughter, glancing at the door, expecting Jeremiah to come walking in at any moment.

Finally, as the governor was expounding on the riches coming into New Mexico from the United States, warning his listeners about the greed of the Americans, Estrellita excused herself from the table and, without waiting for Lucia to accompany her, slipped out the door and onto the shadowy street. Her pulse throbbed in her temples like dozens of little triphammers, faster and faster, louder and louder.

She stood there, silhouetted by the light for several moments, catching her breath.

Where was Jeremiah?

A small boy padded out of the shadows, ran up to her. He thrust a scrap of paper in her hands, then raced off in the opposite direction. Estrellita held the paper up under the glow of one of the lanterns, squinted as she tried to make out the handwriting. Her heart seemed to stop for a second then begin beating again. The note was from Jeremiah.

"Meet me in the plaza. I will wait for you at the cantina called La Copa de Plata. Hurry my love."

The scrawled signature was barely legible.

She looked both ways, saw the dim light from the lanterns in the plaza, and headed in that direction. She shuddered involuntarily when she looked down the dark street. Her glance was so swift, she did not see the bulky shadows a few yards away. She did not hear the furtive breaths of the men watching her from the security of deep shadows.

Jeremiah saw Estrellita leave the cantina, but he was powerless to follow her. He could not even call out her name. Seconds before, as he walked toward the cantina, two men emerged from the shadows, pinned him to an adobe wall. One man clapped a hand over York's mouth, the other held his arms. There was a small boy there, too, and this was the one who ran up to Estrellita the moment she emerged from the Obregon. He couldn't make any sense of it. He just knew that things were going all wrong and his heart sank to think that Estrellita was right in the middle of it.

Jeremiah struggled, but the two men were too much for him. One of them was Merito Salcedo. He held a sword to York's throat.

"Do not yell, gringo," Salcedo whispered into York's ear, "or I will take off your head."

Jeremiah watched as Estrellita turned the corner into the plaza. He felt the cold steel blade nudge against his throat, knew that if he moved he was a dead man.

York could not see the face of the other soldier, but he was small, muscular, obviously cavalry. He was not an officer. Where was Armijo? He looked into the dark hollows of

Salcedo's face. He knew this one, all right, and his anger overrode his fear.

"Let me loose," he said.

"You wait. Shut the mouth."

Salcedo increased the pressure of the blade. Jeremiah winced as he felt the razor-sharp edge push against his Adam's apple. The cavalryman's fingers dug into Jeremiah's arms. York's shoulder blades sank into the cool dank adobe wall behind him.

A moment later, the door to the cantina opened again and Lucia stepped into the street. She closed the door and looked toward the three men, her face obscured by shadow.

"Sssst," Salcedo hissed.

Lucia hurried toward them, hiking her skirts above her ankles. Her bootheels thunked on the hard-packed dirt of the street.

"Merito?" she called.

"Yes. I am here," Salcedo replied in Spanish.

"*Dónde está Estrellita?*"

"*En la plaza. Se fué, despues de leer aquel mensaje.*"

"*Bueno,*" the woman replied.

Lucia stopped when she came to the three men. She peered closely at Jeremiah.

"So I was right. The American came to meet her."

Jeremiah did not understand all the words, but he knew Salcedo and Lucia were talking about him.

"She did not see the American," said Merito.

"Good. All is going according to plan."

"Shall I kill him? That would be better, I think. I could slice his throat very quick."

Lucia sucked in a breath. She did not speak for several seconds.

"No, Merito. This is not the way. Not yet. I think my plan is better. She will soon see what a *pendejo* this gringo is. Augustino will take care of the rest. You just do what I told you."

"With pleasure, *señorita,*" said Merito.

"Wait until I am gone and make sure that no one sees you do this thing."

"It will be done as you instructed. The girl will never look at this man again without thinking of filth."

"I do not want any mistakes, Merito."

Merito drew himself up, jutted out his chest.

"I know how to do this thing. Trust me."

"I trust only in God," she hissed in Spanish.

Jeremiah watched the woman whirl and storm down the street. She turned the corner, headed for the plaza. At that moment, Merito rammed a knee into York's groin and clamped a hand over Jeremiah's mouth.

The pain bludgeoned him, spread from his testicles to his brain in a fiery instant. His stomach roiled with bile, turned queasy.

Dame la botella, Pedro," snapped Merito.

The other man, a private, handed Merito a bottle of Taos lightning. Merito pulled the cork with his teeth, gagged at the strong smell.

"Now, gringo," said Merito. "You are going to drink this or I will cut off your balls."

Salcedo rammed the bottle into Jeremiah's mouth before he could protest. The fumes made his stomach turn over, and his throat burned as the foul-tasting whiskey boiled downward. He gasped for air and Merito jerked the bottle from Jeremiah's mouth for a moment. Then the lieutenant jammed it in again. Jeremiah went to his knees, fighting off the sickness. Merito grabbed York's hair at the neck, jerked his head back. He poured more alcohol down the young man's throat. Jeremiah's brain filled with a swirling fog.

"He's getting drunk, eh?" Salcedo said to Pedro Arminta, the private.

"I think he will be much drunk, Lieutenant."

Jeremiah tried to rise. Merito slammed the sword guard down on the side of his head. The flesh cracked open and blood

304

spurted down the side of York's face. Salcedo kept pouring whiskey down Jeremiah's throat. He splashed some of it over York's buckskins until the young man reeked of alcohol.

Merito sheathed his sword.

"Help me to lift him," he told Pedro.

The two men brought Jeremiah to his feet. He swayed between them like a boxer on the ring ropes. The Mexicans laughed and started walking toward the plaza.

Jeremiah's vision wavered in and out of focus. The adobe buildings seemed to be made of rubber. They swam before his eyes, rippled like desert mirages. His head throbbed and his testicles sang with an excruciating pain as if someone had driven nails into those tenderest of organs.

"Where you taking me?" Jeremiah asked, his voice slurred.

"You are going to drink some more, have a lot of fun," said Merito. "Isn't he, Pedro?"

Pedro didn't understand a word he'd said, beyond his own given name.

Jeremiah lost all feeling in his legs. His tongue thickened and thoughts floated around loose in his brain like corks bobbing in a rain barrel. He could retrieve none of them, could not connect them up or make any sense of them. Finally, the thoughts faded away and the darkness of inebriation swarmed over his consciousness, blew out the last light of reason like a candle snuffed by a sudden wind.

Estrellita reached the plaza, almost deserted now, with the trade goods put away, some of the shops battened down for the night. She heard muffled laughter, strained to find the source. Lamplight buttered the shadows and she walked toward the loudest sound. This seemed not a place for a lover's tryst and she wondered why Jeremiah would want to meet here in this deserted, ghostly place. Perhaps, she reasoned, it was because he did not want to risk being discovered by her family or Lucia.

She looked for a cantina, saw two doorways spilling

yellowish light where one might be. She started toward the nearest one, saw a shadow detach itself from one of the adobe buildings. For a moment, she was startled.

"Ah, *buenas*, Estrellita." The man strode directly toward her. She stopped, knowing that it was not Jeremiah, but momentarily bewildered because he was the one she expected to see.

"Augustino?"

"For certain. Whom did you expect?"

Flustered, she batted her eyelashes, struggled to open her fan.

"Why, no one. I was just . . . just out for some air."

"You did not enjoy the supper?"

"Oh, yes. What are you doing here?"

"Taking a stroll. I did not expect to see you wandering the streets alone. It is very dangerous at night. This pueblo is full of thieves."

"I have seen no thieves," she said, regaining her composure.

Augustino laughed politely. He recognized the line as a rephrasing of an old Spanish joke.

"If you are looking for someone, perhaps I could help you find that person."

"What do you mean, Augustino?"

"It appears to me that you came here to meet someone. I wish it were me."

"What gave you that notion?"

"Ah, well, a beautiful woman out alone in a deserted plaza. Perhaps a tryst. Perhaps a clandestine meeting with someone she is forbidden to meet with."

Estrellita's temper flared.

"You are most impertinent, Augustino. You assume a great deal for one in whom I place little or no confidence. Certainly I do not think you should concern yourself with my private affairs."

Augustino grasped her shoulders much as a kindly old uncle might. Estrellita shook herself free.

"My, but you are very much on the edge this evening," he

said. "I merely wished to calm you down, since it may be that you are in for some unpleasantness."

She looked at him sternly.

"What is it that you are saying?" she asked. "It sounds to me as if you might be threatening something."

The shadows etched a cruel cast to his face. His eyes were dark sockets and she could discern no meaning from them; they were invisible in the darkness. A pair of soldiers strolled past, two women on their arms. She saw a man go into one of the lighted doorways and she heard laughter for a moment as the door opened and closed.

"I would not threaten one so lovely as you, my cherished one," he said.

"Well, you are entirely too familiar. My chaperone is not here and you let such words fall from your tongue as if to take liberties with me."

"That is not my intention," he said stiffly. "I don't think the *dueña* Lucia would approve of your being out alone. Neither of you should be here without escort. If you are finished taking your air, I will be happy to take you back to the Cantina Obregon."

"I am not finished," she said, and she knew her voice was too sharp, too loud.

"Then, if I may escort the señorita someplace that she wishes, I am at her service."

"Damn you, Augustino!" she snapped. "You just leave me alone."

"Ah, but I cannot, don't you see? If your father, or your mother, knew that I had seen you all alone and left you to the mercy of savages and thieves, why, they would tell my uncle and I would be in very deep trouble."

Estrellita snorted at his wry speech, delivered, she thought, with malicious undertones. But, what he had said was true. Now that he had seen her, as a gentleman he had no choice but to protect her. Panic welled up in her, stroked her slender neck with constricting fingers. For a long moment, she was indecisive. What should she do? She could not just go off

307

without seeing Jeremiah. He would think she was snubbing him. She could not bear that. No, she had no choice but to get rid of Augustino or take him into her confidence. Perhaps it was time he was taught a lesson. He did not own her. He was not her husband, and if she had her way about it, he never would be.

"Very well, then," she said. "If you must know, I came here to meet a friend of mine. I assure you that he is perfectly capable of escorting me back to the Obregon. He would certainly protect me from these savages and thieves you speak about as if they were personal friends."

The bitterness tinged her words, but she could not help herself. Augustino was an annoyance in her life. Especially now. He seemed always to be around when she wanted to be alone with Jeremiah. He was worse than a chastity belt.

"He? Then it is a man you came to see?"

"Yes," she said. To herself, she added, "Damn you."

"Not a boy?"

"What are you saying, Augustino? What do you mean saying that to me?"

"I had thought you meant that gringo stableboy you met in St. Louis. I am so happy to hear that you are meeting a man, may his lips fall off with leprosy, instead of a mere boy who has infatuated you."

"Jeremiah is not a boy!"

"Ah, then that is the one."

"You know very well he's here, that we are good friends."

"I think you have a poor choice of friends, Estrellita. But, if that is the case, then I may still be of some help to you. I was in the cantina a while ago, and I did see the boy. Alas, he was in his cups. Quite inebriated."

"I don't believe you," she said coldly.

"I do not lie," he said, lowering his voice. "But, do not take my word for it. I believe he is still there. Drunk, no doubt. *Borracho.*"

"Where?" she said, the panic besetting her once again. She looked around, a wild look in her eyes.

308

Augustino chuckled, jerked a thumb over his shoulder.

"That place there," he said. "La Copa de Plata. It is a pretty sordid cantina, most truly. Full of drunkards and braggarts, peons and Indians. I do not think you would want to enter such a place alone."

A bullbat streaked by overhead, silently scooping up insects in its maw. Its wings flashed a pair of hazy silver pesos, natural markings on the undersides. Somewhere, the notes of a sad guitar leaked through a doorway and a voice intoned a *son huasteco,* a Mexican folk song about infidelity, murder, and a mother's love for her wayward son standing at the gallows tree. Estrellita envisioned a dire scene inside the bawdy cantina, with drunken men cursing like *carreta* drovers, half-dressed native women slinking between tables as men fondled their breasts. She could not picture Jeremiah in such a setting, however, no matter how hard she tried.

"Take me there, then. I will see for myself if what you say is true."

"Do not say I did not warn you. I will protect you from bodily harm, but I cannot control the tongues of the *borracheros.* They may say crude things, insulting things."

"I will deafen my ears to vulgarities," she said crisply, holding out her arm. She never did get the fan to open, and the note from Jeremiah was burning a hole through her palm. She had no place to put it, unless she swallowed it.

Augustino led her to the first doorway limned in yellow light. She heard now the muttered tones of men, the clunk of tankards, the faint thunk of clay cups striking together. The sounds of the *son huasteco* faded away and she knew the guitar player must be in another cantina.

Augustino opened the door, stepped inside, turned to let her in. The moment she stepped into the room, the talking stopped. It was as if someone had sucked all the sound out of the men's throats. She saw dozens of pairs of eyes looking at her. She dipped her own, then lifted her head boldly. She scanned the room, looking for Jeremiah.

"I do not see him," she whispered sotto voce.

"I believe he is at one of those tables back there. Where it is so dark."

"I don't believe you," she hissed.

"Come along and let us see."

The talking resumed again, although the men spoke low. She heard a number of exclamations. The floor was dirt and she knew she was scuffing the shine on her shoes. She didn't care. She just wanted to see for herself if Jeremiah was in such a place. She could not imagine him wanting her to meet him here. It was full of bleary-eyed Mexicans and a few women wearing plain dresses of cheap linen. There were no soldiers that she could see. There was a back door, probably leading to an alley. A man staggered through it, trying to button his trousers. She turned away in disgust.

Augustino reached the back table. He bent over it as Estrellita came up behind him. Then, he stepped away, and she saw Jeremiah. Her hand rose to her mouth as she stifled a scream.

Jeremiah sat slumped in his chair, his legs sprawled out, lifeless. He reeked of alcohol. His face appeared to be dirty until Estrellita saw that it was streaked with dried blood. She gasped as he tried to still his wobbling head. His eyes seemed unable to focus on her.

She wanted to run, to scream. She could not bear the sight of Jeremiah York sitting there in a drunken stupor.

"Why?" she asked. "Jeremiah, why did you do this?"

Jeremiah squinted one eye, cocked his head back. He opened his mouth, moved his lips. At first he made no sound, then he rasped her name.

"Essalita," he said, his voice slurred with the effects of the liquor. "Sorry, Essalita."

"I'm ashamed of you," she said. "How could you do this to me?"

"Don' unnerstan'," he mumbled.

"Of course not. You're drunk."

"Not 'runk."

"Jeremiah, I never want to see you again," she said.

"You've proven yourself as a man with no character."

Then Estrellita burst into tears. Augustino put his arm around her shoulders, drew her to him. He looked at York and smirked with satisfaction.

Jeremiah tried to rise, but his legs would not respond. He fell back against the chair, swayed there.

"Essalita," he muttered.

"Good-bye, Jeremiah," she said. "Augustino, take me from this place."

Armijo turned her toward him, was about to make his way back through the tables when the front door burst open. Lucia strode into the tavern, followed by Don Miguel and Corazon. Lucia forged ahead, lunging past the gawking patrons.

"Estrellita!" shrieked Corazon. "Dear God, what are you doing in a place like this?"

"Be quiet," said Don Miguel. Corazon followed Lucia to the back of the room. Don Miguel shrugged and stalked in her wake past the startled drinkers who watched the gentleman and the ladies sweep by them.

Lucia grabbed Estrellita's arm, pulled her away from Armijo.

"Look," she said, "this is the American she came to see."

Don Miguel and Corazon looked at Jeremiah. Corazon gasped. Her breasts heaved in anger. Estrellita broke into a tearful spasm.

"Oh, Mother!" she exclaimed.

"Why, he's drunk," said Corazon, looking at Jeremiah.

"That is clear," said Don Miguel. "Augustino, what do you know about this?"

"Sir, your daughter is blameless. This drunkard lured her here and I escorted her inside merely to show her York's true colors. I beg your forgiveness."

"We'll speak of this later," said Don Miguel. "Corazon, you and Lucia bring Estrellita. This American should be thrown in the *calabozo* for his drunkenness."

"Come, child," said Lucia, her voice dripping sweetness like syrup.

"Yes," said Corazon, "we must leave this place at once."

"Oh, Mother, I'm so sorry," wailed Estrellita. "I didn't know. I just didn't know."

"Come, my daughter. Do not give this man another thought."

Corazon and Lucia braced Estrellita between them and marched her toward the door. Don Miguel and Augustino followed.

"Shall I inform the authorities, Your Grace?" asked Augustino.

"What would be the point? Let the drunkard drown in his own juices. We will return to the rancho in the morning."

"Yes, Your Grace."

"In November, we will not go to the fair at Chihuahua, as planned. Instead, we will arrange for your marriage to my daughter sometime after the new year. Perhaps in January or February. Would you agree to such an arrangement?"

"I am most pleased, Don Miguel."

"Soon, she will forget all about the American."

"*Claro que sí*," said Augustino, with relief. The party swept through the doorway and out into the plaza. The voices of the patrons rose up behind them.

Jeremiah tried to align the room, hold it steady in his wavering gaze. He knew something terrible had happened. Estrellita had been there, and Augustino. Who were the other people? He had seen them before, but now he could not put names to their blurred faces.

"*Ay, gringo*," someone called to him, "you have the fancy friends. Buy us some drinks."

The room boiled with laughter.

Jeremiah sank into a slump. He could not fight his way out of his stupor. He leaned over the table, felt his head blessedly drop onto the wooden surface. He closed his eyes and the voices began to fade. The laughter died out, smothered by the dark cloak of sleep.

Chapter Twenty-Three

The shock stunned him at first. Then, as the cold struck through to the bone, consciousness returned in a rush, jerking him out of sleep. He gasped as he sucked in water through his mouth. He gagged, flailed his arms to keep from sinking. He pushed upward, drew clean air into his lungs. The shore swept by as panic seized him. Where in God's name was he? The sky was just turning pale, the stars fading away like the lights of a distant town winking off one by one.

He heard footsteps, saw the dark silhouettes of men running along the riverbank. He flapped at the water, realizing then that he was stark naked. The coldness bit deep into him as he fought to stay afloat, swim to shore.

"Haw, lookit him. Like a goddamned frog."

"Swim, York, swim!"

"Hey, Yorkie, you sober yet?"

The voices bombarded him from the bank, strangely disembodied. The men were still shrouded in shadow, faceless, moving shapes that had no names.

Jeremiah felt the current pull at him and he began swimming more strongly, fighting against it, fighting against the chill that speared his bones, numbed his feet and fingers. Pain throbbed in his head, in a head robbed of all recollection, all memory. Fuzzy thoughts emerged, only to be swept away by others, like

313

cobwebs blown to shreds by the wind. He could make no sense of his situation, could not fathom why he was naked and swimming for his life against a current that threatened to drag him under.

Clouds changed from dark puffs of smoke to vermilion-smeared cotton wads. Some pinkened to a salmon color and then turned to gold as the sun rose. Jeremiah swam, angling now with the current instead of fighting against it.

"Atta nigger," shouted Karns, and Jeremiah saw his bearded face, then the wide grin.

"Come on, let's catch him," said J.R., racing ahead.

There was Big Un lumbering along behind the pack of laughing men, his fringes flapping from his sleeves and shoulders, jiggling like limp, crooked sticks. Jeremiah kicked hard and spaded his hands through the water, scooping downward. He felt his body warm with the exertion, felt his skin tingle as his blood pumped a faint heat through cold tissue.

He rammed into the shore, grabbed at a stone. Eyestone was waiting for him. He reached out, grabbed York by the hair, pulled him onto the bank. Jeremiah realized that he had been waiting downstream all the time, that he was not one of the men who had followed his course down the river.

Cooper clawed under Jeremiah's armpits, hauled him onto dry land, dropped to a squat beside him.

"You ain't a fair swimmer," said Eyestone.

Jeremiah crawled until he brought his knees up under him. He rolled over and sat there, sopping onto the rocks and dirt, shivering in the chill of morning.

"You was hopin' I'd drown," replied Jeremiah, puffing short bursts of air from his lungs, huffing air back in to soothe the burning.

"I reckon not. I knowed you could swim some was you awake. Thought when they throwed you in you might sink like a stone."

"Who did it?"

"Couldn't rightly tell."

"How . . . how did I get—I mean, what happened? How come they threw me in?"

The others ran up, sprawled facedown on the ground, sucking air into overworked lungs. None of them could speak. J.R. was the only one not winded. He came walking up from farther downriver. He squatted, Indian-style, on the other side of York.

"You was plumb drunk when some Mexes dragged you back to camp," said J.R. "Woke us all up."

"Mexicans? What was they doin' that for?" asked Jeremiah.

Eyestone shrugged.

"They didn't say. Not in English anyways," said Andersen, the first to catch his breath. "But you looked like something drug in by a she-griz all right. Waugh! Stinkin' of Taos lightnin', plumb under like somebody cracked a stone over your skull."

Jeremiah winced, shivered as a light breeze blew up off the river. He looked back at it. The big river. His mind cleared. He remembered it all now. Waiting for Estrellita, then Salcedo jumping him, smashing that sword into his head. Pouring whiskey down him.

The rest of it was a jumble. Merito and that other soldier had dragged him to a tavern, taken him in through the back door. Poured more whiskey down his throat until the room spun like a top. Estrellita. Had she been there? Or was that only his imagination? Someone had spoken to him, but he couldn't remember any of it.

Something sank in him, sank in his belly like a lead ball through mush. Estrellita was part of it, but she was all tangled up in his mind like a cat in twine and he couldn't unravel any of it.

"Jesus, York, you gonna stay nekkid all goddamned day," said Karns. "You look like a drownded muskrat."

The others sat up, laughed easily as the sun rose, painted the mountains and the land, brought out the green and the gold of

315

morning like daubs on a painter's pallette.

"Anybody bring my moccasins?" he asked.

They all laughed.

"Son, you got to walk like a Injun," said Andersen.

"Well, thanks for the bath, boys," said Jeremiah, rising to his feet. "I won't hold it against you that you didn't bring me a blanket at least. Less'n dumbness is a crime, you fellers are free to go your own ways."

Eyestone stood up and slapped him on the back.

"You'll do, Son," he said, and the others chorused their assent.

Jeremiah was woozy as he started walking back to camp, the men poking fun at him, joking with him as he stepped painfully over rocky ground.

"Watch out for cactus," said Big Un.

"And rattlesnakes," said J.R. "'Specially them little pigmy rattlers."

"Scorpions," said Andersen, with glee.

"Shut up," said York good-naturedly. His head throbbed, not so much from the blow Salcedo had dealt him, but from the ravages of the bad whiskey. His stomach was sour, the taste in his mouth like copper soaked in piss. He wanted, at that moment, to die painlessly and be resurrected without a head that was as sore as a hammered thumb.

Later that morning, after he'd scrubbed the blood and whiskey out of his buckskins with lye soap, he told Eyestone what had happened the night before.

"I got to see her, Coop," he said. "Explain what happened."

"Hell, you don't even know what happened."

"I got chunks of it. I know that damned Augustino was behind it."

"They could have killed you."

"Would have. That Mex shadow of Estrellita's wanted to show me up. Make me look the fool."

"Well, you got a ways to travel if you're gonna do any 'splainin'," said Eyestone.

"What do you mean?"

"Them Mexes pulled out early this mornin', troops and all. Saw 'em go before the sun cleared the junipers."

"Estrellita, too?"

"She was among 'em, lookin' a mite pasty-faced, but I seen her."

"Damn, I got to go there. To her father's ranch."

"You might get a ball in the gullet for your trouble."

"I can't just let her think I got drunk on her. Wonder what that bastard Armijo told her, huh?"

"Well, Jerry, we're goin' to Santa Fee in a couple of days ourselfs. You ride along and maybe I'll see that you don't get bushwhacked again."

"No. I got to go there now."

"You want that money Lalande owes your friend, don't you?"

"It was a promise made."

"Then you be sure you're there when they sell the pelfries. Bloody Hand or Possum Killer will be handlin' the silver. You got to get it from them."

"Will Andersen or Karns fight me over it?"

"I reckon those old coons are prepared to spin a tall yarn for Baptiste. They'll cook somethin' else. You just ask 'em."

Jeremiah grinned.

"I may not be able to go back up to the mountains with you, Coop."

"We got our goods cached up at Cumbre Pass, not far to go. We can trap the Sangre de Cristos. Plenty of beaver up in them hills. They's some creeks no more'n a couple of days' ride from Santa Fee. 'Course we got to look out for Utes and such."

"Estrellita's more important."

"You do what squares up for you, Son. I'll help you load your packs. You want to sell your goods here, I'll do it, save the money for you."

"Thanks, Coop. I'm mighty obliged."

"Just watch your topknot, Jerry. Santa Fee is Mexican

owned and they don't like 'Green grow the lilacs.'"

"I'll be careful, Coop."

Jeremiah saddled Fleetfoot. He left his packs and Gideon with Eyestone, promising to meet him in Santa Fe within the week at La Fonda. He was on the road to Santa Fe when the sun was straight up noon.

Estrellita sulked in the carriage, talked little all the way home. They arrived at the ranch late that same night, tired, famished. The servants scrambled to set the table for a late supper.

"I have no hunger," said Estrellita. "I am just going to bed." She was starved. She just didn't want to listen to any more lectures from her parents. Lucia had scolded her enough the night before.

"We will talk in the morning," said her mother, removing her mantilla.

Lucia looked scornfully at Estrellita but said nothing. They all bade her good night and Estrellita went upstairs, so weary she didn't think she could walk another step. Her traveling valise seemed to weigh a hundred pounds. She kept seeing Jeremiah sitting in the tavern, so drunk he was witless. Somehow, she felt sorry for him, even though she had suffered the worst humiliation of her life because of him.

She lighted the lamp in her room, undressed in a weary daze. She donned a nightgown, removed the ribbon from her hair, shook her head to fluff it out. She wanted a hot tub drawn but was too tired even for that. She must manage to comb her hair, however. While searching through her small valise for her comb, she found the crumpled-up note that she had saved, the one from Jeremiah asking her to meet him at La Copa de Plata.

She unfolded the paper, was about to read the note again when she heard the knock on her door. Hastily, she stuffed the note under her pillow, grabbed up her tortoiseshell comb, and raked it downward.

"Enter," she said.

The door opened. Her mother stood there for a moment, then came in. She closed the door behind her. Estrellita sighed, forced a smile.

"I want to talk to you before you go to sleep," said Corazon.

"If you must, my mother."

"Your father asked me to speak to you." Corazon sat on the edge of the bed. Estrellita began to comb her hair in earnest. "Don't do that," said Corazon.

"Mother, I am very tired."

"So are we all. This will not wait. Your father has spoken to Augustino, your betrothed. He wants a wedding sometime early in the new year. Augustino will come here, make a formal demand for your hand in marriage. Possibly before the week is out."

Estrellita's heart seemed to skip several beats.

"So soon?"

"You're of age, my daughter. I agree with your father. It would not be good to wait too long. If we have your wedding in February, that will give us time to plan, order your gown, announce the banns. There are relations to write to in Mexico and in Spain."

"Must I marry Augustino?"

"Surely there is no other worthy of you."

Estrellita sighed.

"I do not love him."

"Perhaps not now, but in time . . ."

"He is so arrogant. He takes me with his eyes. Even when he does not touch me I feel his hands on me."

"Young men do that. He is no different than any other. He loves you, I'm sure."

"Love or lust, Mother?"

"Do not joke. Now, as for the wedding. We will have the ceremony in the Chapel of Our Lady of Guadalupe. I will speak to Father Horcasitas when next I am in town. You must choose your ladies-in-waiting and we will look at fine fabrics, secure a seamstress. Oh, it will be a grand wedding. Augustino's uncle, they say, will someday be governor again. At present, he is very rich from collecting the taxes on the caravans. It is important that you be closely associated with one so destined."

"I have heard stories about Manuel Armijo, Mother. I have heard that he was lowborn, that his parents were both disreputable persons of Albuquerque. They say he was born a thief. He pilfered when he was a child and then engaged in serious larcenies. They say he boasts of his past, of stealing sheep and selling them to his neighbors, sometimes over and over again. I wonder if Augustino has not inherited his bad blood."

"For shame!" exclaimed Corazon. "It matters not what people say about Manuel Armijo. He is very rich and will soon be even richer. Augustino is his favorite and we know that Manuel looks with favor on your union with his nephew."

"Mother, if I must marry Augustino, I will, but I will not be happy with him."

"Surely you have forgotten all about the American who shamed you so."

"Yes, Mother. I have forgotten him," she sighed.

"Very well then." Corazon stood up, brushed out the wrinkles in her dress. "I will tell your father. You will make a most beautiful bride. I am very proud of you."

"Good night, Mother."

"Good night, Estrellita. Lucia will be pleased, as well. She cares for you very much."

Estrellita said nothing, and her mother frowned just before she turned on her heel and left the room. The lamp flickered and Estrellita turned up the wick. She started to pick up her comb, then remembered the note. She slid it out from under her pillow and held it close to the lamp. She read it again, looked carefully at the handwriting. She went to the small desk and pulled out Jeremiah's letter. She compared the two. The handwriting was similar, but it was obvious that the phrasing, the script of the note, was not the same as that which she read in the letter.

She knew then, knew for certain, that the note the little boy had given her was a forgery.

But who had written the note? Why?

Augustino? Lucia? Someone had wanted her to see Jeremiah at the cantina. Perhaps someone had made him drunk. But who had known that she was to meet him?

Estrellita's thoughts floundered in confusion. It was difficult to fathom such a conspiracy, but as she thought back to that day in the plaza when she had talked to Jeremiah, she knew that there was only one person who might have seen her and Jeremiah together.

Lucia!

She put the letter and the note back in the desk drawer and flung herself onto the bed. She began to pummel the pillow with her fists.

"It's not fair! It's not fair!" she squawled. "Oh, Jeremiah, what have I done?"

Then the tears came, and she buried her face in the pillow, muffling the sound of her sobs in soft eiderdown.

Jeremiah saw the city from the shadows of the Sangre de Cristos, rode toward it, across the edge of the great plateau that stretched westward toward the valley of the Rio Grande and the far-off Sandias and Jemez mountain ranges. As he drew closer, the city took on shape, its scattered white buildings shining in the sun. At the center of a broad plain, the buildings were larger, built more closely together. Beyond stretched a line of foothills and a vast, rolling plateau that seemed endless. In the clear, thin air, he could see the country as if it was etched to a crystal clarity with the hard sharp edge of a diamond. He was glad now that he had camped out the night before so that he could arrive in Santa Fe by early morning. He had rubbed up some, combed his hair only minutes before. Now he wondered how he would find Don Miguel's ranch and if he would be allowed to see Estrellita, speak to her.

He followed the hard-packed trail into the pueblo, past the little adobe houses much like those he had seen in Taos, all painted with gypsum to a dazzling whiteness. The streets leading to the *plaza pública* were unpaved and filthy. He rode along a continuous and forbidding wall, arcaded to keep out the sun and rain, with barred windows and large doors every several feet. He rode through an arched opening in the wall and followed the street to the main plaza, gawked at the palacio, the principal building on the north side of the square. The plaza itself was virtually treeless. Unlike the houses he had seen when he rode in, there were no flowers growing on the hard-packed adobe and no shade to shield one from the blinding sun.

He dismounted, hitched Fleetfoot to a rail near the edge of the plaza on the south side. Here, he gazed up at a large military chapel with two lower towers. He saw a cluster of bells. There were two other churches ringing the plaza, the Chapel of Our Lady of Guadalupe and a parochial church. A few women talked outside the latter building. La Fonda stood there, too, a large inn where he was to meet Eyestone and the other members of Lalande's brigade later in the week.

His attention was drawn to a group of men talking in front of the presidio, which was part of the palacio. This building stretched four hundred feet east and west and twice as far north and south. It was enclosed by an adobe wall. The main building was roofed with pine and spruce logs that had withstood two centuries of weather. As he drew closer, Jeremiah saw soldiers inside the adobe wall, drilling on the *plaza de armas*.

The men he approached stood with their horses at the hitching rails, resplendent in their braided *chaquetas*, their laced *calzoneras*, trousers, colorful sashes that were like cummerbunds, and boots of embossed leather shined to a high sheen. Most of them wore silver spurs, and the bridles of the horses were also decorated with silver trappings. The New Mexican men were dressed more finely than the women he had seen in front of the little church. The women wore blouses and flannel skirts or linen dresses, some of which were dyed red or green or blue. A couple of the men wore serapes and straw hats and they dressed in white garments. These Jeremiah took to be of the poorer class of New Mexicans. He wondered if any of them spoke English.

"Good morning," said Jeremiah. "Do any of you speak English?"

"I have the English," said one man, stepping away from his fellows. "Which is it you desire?"

Jeremiah grinned.

"I am looking for the ranch of Don Miguel Montez."

"I know him," said the gentleman. "Do you have the business with him?"

"Yes," said Jeremiah. "I want to talk to him, sure."

"His rancho lies that way." The New Mexican pointed to his left, to the east. "You have a horse?"

"Yes."

"Ride along the mountains. There is a road. You will see his rancho and the sheep. Maybe seven *kilometros,* maybe not so many."

"Thank you, sir. There is one other thing I need to ask."

"I am at your service."

"I want to buy a locket of gold. And some flowers."

"For Don Miguel?"

"The locket is for his daughter. The flowers for her mother."

"I see. You can buy flowers over there by the little church. See the cart?"

Jeremiah nodded.

"There is a little shop around the corner. They sell jewelry there. It is called La Joya."

"Once again, thank you sir."

"Buenos días," said the New Mexican. Jeremiah tipped his hat and strolled back to his horse. He did not know how far it was to the ranch, but he knew that it lay to the east. He bought

a bouquet of flowers, placed them gently in a saddlebag. They were wrapped in cheesecloth. He hoped they wouldn't wilt. He walked around the corner, found the jewelry store. He picked out a gold locket with a small silver eagle on it. It was beautifully shaped. He paid ten dollars for it, wondered if he could not have done better if he could have spoken Spanish. He returned to the plaza, mounted Fleetfoot, and rode under the arch, heading south for a time. At the main road, he turned east, and the country stretched out before him, radiant in the morning sun.

At the officers' barracks in the presidio, Augustino finished brushing his pomaded hair.

"What do you think, Merito?" he asked, turning away from the mirror. He tugged the bottom edge of his tunic, squared his shoulders.

Merito, sitting at a table in Augustino's quarters, looked up from the deck of cards laid out in a game of solitaire.

"You are a handsome rogue, 'Tino."

"Is my horse saddled?"

"It waits outside for your majesty." Merito grinned. "Just wait until you ask a girl to marry you."

"I would not ask."

"Just take her."

"Yes."

Augustino donned his hat, checked himself in the mirror one last time.

"I am nervous, Merito."

"Why? You will ask her, she will accept. Her father has already agreed to the marriage."

"She is wild yet."

"Tame her, then."

Augustino smiled. His confidence returned.

"I will do that, my friend. I will break her like a colt. She will

324

be eating out of my hand like a bird."

Merito laughed and stood up. He raked the cards together, left them in a stack on the table.

"I will miss having you in barracks, 'Tino."

"You must dine with us often."

"What shall I tell Señorita Dolores?"

"You stay away from her."

"But she is so sweet, so delicate. She will be heartbroken."

"She is a peasant."

"Peasants have hearts, too."

Augustino laughed. Dolores was a girl he had met in a Santa Fe cantina. He supposed the girl loved him. It did not matter. She was just one of many.

"When I am finished with her, you may have her, broken heart and all."

"Thanks, 'Tino. *Por nada.*"

The two men walked out of the barracks into the sunlight. Augustino's horse stood hipshot at the hitchrail, its saddle gleaming in the sun.

"Good luck, 'Tino."

Augustino mounted his horse, looked down at his friend.

"I am glad you took care of the American. I wish you could have seen Estrellita's face when she saw him."

"I wish I had cut his throat."

"You would take away all of my pleasures, Merito."

"*Vaya.*"

Augustino saluted his friend, took command of the reins. He rode slowly across the *plaza de armas*.

His confidence returned once he was on the familiar trail to Don Miguel's ranch. He could not wait to see Estrellita again, take her into his arms.

Perhaps, he thought, she would let him into her bed before the marriage. He would like to sample the wine before buying the vineyard.

Three quarters of an hour ahead of him, Jeremiah was riding

up to the huge adobe hacienda through a sea of bleating sheep. There was the fragrant scent of pines in the air, wafting down from the foothills onto the plain. The sheep parted to allow him to pass. Fleetfoot eyed them warily, ears cocked, and began prancing in a graceful sidestep.

Jeremiah waved to the shepherds.

They did not wave back.

Chapter Twenty-Four

Jeremiah tied his horse to the hitchrail. He tapped his pocket to reassure himself that the locket was still there. He took the flowers, red and yellow carnations, out of his saddlebag, exposed the blooms by peeling back the cheesecloth. He sniffed them, filled his nostrils with their fragrance. They were still fresh.

He opened the gate, walked under the arch into the exterior patio. He saw a massive oak door with intricate carvings and a brass knocker. He fidgeted nervously for a moment, took off his hat, smoothed his hair. He lifted the heavy knocker, rapped smartly three times.

He heard footsteps, saw the curtains rustle at a nearby window. The door opened and Lucia stood there like a rock barring his passage. A look passed between them. Jeremiah saw her stiffen. Her eyes flashed with a light that might have been fear, might have been hatred.

"You go away," she said in her thickly accented English. "Go now."

"I came to see Madam Montez, er . . . Mrs. Montez, and her daughter, Estrellita." He did not know what to call Estrellita's mother. And, despite his dislike of Lucia, the memory of what she had done to him, he knew that she was a powerful figure in the Montez household. She was Estrellita's guardian, her watchdog. He didn't hate her; he just wished she were somewhere else.

"*Quien es?*" called a voice. Jeremiah recognized it as belonging to Estrellita's mother.

"*No es nadie, señora,*" replied Lucia. She gestured with her hands as if to shoo Jeremiah away. The door started to close.

"Please, ma'am," said Jeremiah loudly. "I don't want no trouble. But I rode a long ways and I aim to see Mrs. Montez, give her these flowers."

Corazon appeared behind Lucia's back. She saw Jeremiah and frowned. Lucia stepped aside.

"What is it you want?" Corazon asked in English."

"Ma'am, I brought you these flowers and I want to see Estrellita. I want to explain what happened the other night in Taos."

Jeremiah felt the pressure of Corazon's scrutiny. He did not look at Lucia but could feel the intensity of her gaze. Corazon looked him over, and he wondered if his hair was mussed or too plastered down from sweat. He held out the flowers to her.

Corazon smiled wanly.

"Come, young man," she said, "for I cannot turn away a guest who brings me flowers. If you will be seated, I will have Lucia bring my daughter to talk to you. Will you take something to drink?"

"No, ma'am," said Jeremiah. He stepped inside, handed the bouquet to Corazon. "I'm too nervous. I'd spill anything you'd bring me."

Corazon laughed. Lucia, her expression knotted into a dark ferocity, did not even crack a smile, although Jeremiah believed that she understood every word.

"*Traiga* Estrellita *aquí,*" said Corazon to Lucia.

"*Pero . . .*"

Corazon stifled the woman with a look, strode past her to the living room. Jeremiah looked smugly at Lucia, followed Corazon.

Lucia stalked up the stairs, her bootheels thumping on the

hardwood steps. Corazon sat in a chair, waved Jeremiah to a settee. He barely glanced at the room, saw that it was beautiful. The walls were covered with white gypsum, but there was calico draped over them to shoulder height because the mineral rubbed off at the least touch. He looked at the rugs on the polished floor. The ceiling was beamed, the fireplace constructed so that the wood had to be placed upright against the back wall. The furniture looked to be of oak and the wood finely turned. He sat down, his hat between his knees, looked at Estrellita's mother closely for the first time.

She held the flowers cradled across her lap, seemed to be enjoying the fragrance.

"How's Mr. Montez? Is he here?"

"He is taking his siesta. He is well."

"Good." Jeremiah fell silent, wondered when Estrellita would be down.

"I hope you realize, Mr. York, that Estrellita is engaged to be married," said Corazon as if reading his thoughts.

"No ma'am, I didn't know that."

"Her engagement will be formalized this afternoon."

"You mean . . . ?"

"Augustino Armijo will ask my husband for her hand in marriage."

"Well, maybe I'd like to ask him the same thing."

Corazon's smile was patronizing.

"I do not think my husband will consent to such a marriage. You are not Catholic?"

"No ma'am. I'm a Protestant."

"Then it would be out of the question."

"What if I was to become a Catholic?"

"Even so. The marriage has been arranged."

"Doesn't Estrellita have anything to say about it?"

"No, truly she does not."

"I still want to talk to her."

"Only for a few moments. Then you must leave. My husband would not like for you to be here."

"Where I come from, every man is given a chance to prove himself."

"Our ways are different. Now if you will please excuse me, I will put these flowers in water. I give you thanks for bringing them. They are very beautiful."

Jeremiah stood up as Corazon arose from her chair. He watched her walk through a doorway. He stared at the religious icons in the room, admiring the furnishings.

"What's taking Estrellita so damned long?" he muttered to himself.

He heard a commotion at the top of the stairs, looked up to see Lucia flying down them, three at a time.

"Where is the señora?" she hissed.

"She went through that door," said Jeremiah, pointing.

Lucia, hiking her skirts, raced past him, disappeared through the doorway.

"Se fue, señora, se fue!" he heard Lucia say.

He rose from the chair, listened to the rapid exchange of Spanish between Lucia and Corazon. A moment later, Corazon and Lucia entered the room.

"Mr. York," Corazon said tightly, "Estrellita is not in her room. Lucia says that she climbed out her window. I'm afraid you'll have to leave."

"But . . ."

"Please. Go now. I do not want to wake my husband until we find her. I am very . . . how do you say it? Disturbed."

"Maybe I should help you find her."

"No. We will do this. Please go."

"Yes'm. I'll go, but I'll be back."

Lucia and Corazon ushered him back out onto the patio. He walked to his horse. The door closed quietly behind him. He mounted Fleetfoot, rode slowly down the lane. Then he saw her. Estrellita waved to him from beyond the road. She was riding the Arabian mare, the one he had sold to her father in St. Louis. In fact, he recognized the horse before he did Estrellita. She was dressed in white and she wore a sombrero that shaded her face. He put the spurs to his horse, galloped toward her, his heart thumping hard in his chest.

Estrellita turned her horse, rode off toward the foothills. Puzzled, Jeremiah slapped the trailing ends of the reins against his horse's flanks. Fleetfoot broke into a run. Estrellita disappeared into the pines.

Jeremiah saw the trail, followed it up through the thick pines. In the distance, he heard sheep bleating. When he looked back, he no longer saw the hacienda. The scent of pines filled his nostrils.

"Over here, Jeremiah," called Estrellita.

He tugged the reins lightly, slowed his horse to a walk. A moment later, he rode into a small glade.

"Hello," he said.

She stood in the shade of a pine, holding on to the Arabian's reins as it grazed at a patch of grass. He was surprised to see that she was wearing the white trousers and blouse of a peon. Her hair was coiled up under her flat-crowned sombrero.

"I saw you ride up to the house. I was afraid they would not let you in."

"So, you climbed out the window."

"Yes." Their glances met and she giggled. Her eyes danced with a mischievous light, then the light faded away as she sobered. "My father will be very angry."

"I reckon so."

They looked at each other for a long time. Then Jeremiah swung down off his horse. Estrellita rushed up to him, embraced him in a moment of desperate abandon. He wrapped his arms around her. In his eagerness to kiss her, he knocked her hat off. He chucked her under the chin and she closed her eyes. They held the kiss for several seconds. When they broke, they both began talking at once.

"You didn't send me that note . . ."

"I want you to know what happened . . ."

"You first," she said.

"No, you. What note?"

331

"See? No, you tell me about that night in the cantina."

They laughed, but he told her all of it, leaving nothing out. They sat on pine needles, in the shade. She told him about the note and her discovery that it was forged.

"I want to ask your father to let us be married," he said finally. "Would you marry up with me?"

"Oh, Jeremiah, I would, but you know my father will just say no."

"I think I ought to have the same chance as Armijo."

"I don't want to marry him."

"Your mother asked me if I was a Catholic."

"Uh oh. What did you say?"

"I said I'd become one."

"You could, you know." She became very excited. "Listen, you could see the priest in Santa Fe, Frey Bonifacio Algodon. He instructs Protestants who want to marry Catholics. Oh, Jeremiah, would you?"

"I'll see him today. After I talk to your father."

"What if my father says no?"

"Then I might just carry you away. Would you marry me if I was a Catholic?"

"It would not be easy," she admitted. "How would we live? Where would we live? Oh, Jeremiah, you do not know how different our worlds are. I have been to St. Louis and it is very strange to me, as Santa Fe must be strange to you. Our customs are so different, and so very strong that if we broke them, our lives would change. We would be outcasts. My family would probably never speak to me again."

Jeremiah sighed deeply. "I would hate that," he said.

She took his hand in hers.

"You are very sweet," she said. "I wish we could be together like this always."

"Me, too."

Then he remembered the locket. He reached into his pocket, pulled it out.

"I brought something for you, Estrellita. I want you to wear it and think about me."

The locket was in a little cloth bag. He placed it in her palm. She took the locket out of the bag, held it up by its golden chain.

"It's beautiful," she said. "Oh, look, it has an eagle on it."

"That eagle, now, it's just one bird, common all over the West. Mexico, it's got itself a golden one, and, well, the States has the snow-headed one. But they're both eagles and they ought not to fight one another."

"Oh, Jeremiah, you make me very happy. I will wear it always."

She placed the locket around her neck, stared down at it. She leaned over, kissed Jeremiah lightly on the cheek. It was a very special moment and they both felt it. The locket seemed to forge a bond between them. Its tiny gold chain linked them together for the first time, a man and a woman, where once there was only a boy and a girl, strangers in a strange land.

The silence rose up between them, blossomed into a serenity that grew out of their secret thoughts. Jeremiah studied Estrellita's face, knew that he wanted her more strongly than he ever had before. This was what he wanted: to sit on a hillside, among the trees, with the blue sky above them, the earth beneath. He wanted her then, and he wanted her forever. He wanted her for his wife, with or without her father's consent.

"Jeremiah? What are you thinking?"

"About you and me."

"I am thinking the same thing. It just seems impossible to me that we can marry."

"Ain't nothin' impossible, Estrellita."

"Maybe. Augustino is to come today and formally ask for my hand in marriage. My father will approve."

"I'll do some askin' myself."

"The wedding is to be in February, I think. The bishop. Oh, Jeremiah, I'm so scared just thinking of this. It is not what I want."

"Let's go. I want to talk to your father. Your mother is probably worried."

"Yes. Please don't say anything to anger my father. Be polite."

"I'll just ask him like a man," said Jeremiah.

They rode up to the grand house together, saw the horse at the hitchrail.

"Augustino is already here," she said.

"Maybe I'll ask him about the two men he sent to kill me." It had just slipped out. Jeremiah hadn't meant to mention this to Estrellita. He did not want her to know that he had killed two men.

"What do you say?"

"Oh, nothing. There was some trouble up in the mountains."

"How do you know Augustino did this?"

"It wasn't the first time. He sent two men to kill me in St. Louis. One of them was a soldier."

"Ah! What happened?"

"Someday, Estrellita, I'll tell you all about it. Right now I got a heap of things on my mind."

"Yes, yes," she said. They dismounted and tied their horses next to Augustino's. Estrellita took his hand, dragged him through the patio to the door. They entered the hacienda like a pair of lost children, shy and full of fear.

Don Miguel sat sternly in his big chair in the living room. Augustino sat stiffly on a smaller one. Lucia and Corazon were on the settee. Estrellita curtsied, forced a smile. Jeremiah stood awkwardly next to her. She was still holding his hand. Every eye in the room fixed on those two hands. Jeremiah felt the burning in his own hand.

"Good morning, Papa," said Estrellita in Spanish.

"Sit down," said Don Miguel in English. "What is that American doing here?"

Jeremiah nodded to Estrellita. She sat, alone, on a hassock

near the fireplace.

"Sir, I am here to ask for your daughter's hand in marriage. I love her. I want to marry her."

The words sounded strange to Jeremiah. But no one laughed. He wondered if anyone could see that his knees were shaking. He wondered if Don Miguel knew how scared he was. It seemed as if it were someone else, just then, a different person, one with a strong loud voice, and timbre to it.

"Young man, you do me a dishonor by coming uninvited to my home. My daughter is already promised to Captain Augustino Armijo. He has formally asked for my permission and I have granted that permission. You must now leave my house and never come here again."

Don Miguel spoke coldly, dispassionately, without emotion. He was the master of this house, Jeremiah knew, and he had every right to order him out. But there was more at stake here than hospitality or custom. His future, and Estrellita's, hung at the center of a fulcrum which could tip either way. Either in his favor, or Augustino's.

"Please hear me out, sir," said Jeremiah. "I mean no disrespect, but I've come a long way to talk to you and I won't ride off like a cur with my tail between my legs until it's done, done right and proper."

He saw Estrellita looking at him wide-eyed, a rapt expression on her face. The others in the room stared at him, too, but he looked only into the storm-depths of Don Miguel's eyes. He could feel Augustino skewering him with a glance shot full of hatred.

"You have no money, York," said Don Miguel. "You have no position in life. You are an American in a foreign country. You are not of our faith. There are many reasons why you have no right to even think of marrying my daughter, but above them all there is only one thing that matters. Custom. Our custom. My custom. Now that is something that you cannot question nor overcome. I again ask you to leave my house and say no more about this matter."

Jeremiah looked at them all now. He looked at Estrellita, then at Lucia and Corazon. He looked at Augustino and then he looked at Don Miguel once again.

"Custom," he said, choosing his words carefully, remembering that Estrellita had chided him about his improper speech. "That is no matter to me. Custom doesn't tell what's in a man's heart. Custom doesn't mark a man's worth. Custom doesn't point Cupid's arrow. I love Estrellita and she loves me. She doesn't want to marry Captain Armijo. She wants to marry me. Ask her, if you don't believe me.

"All I want is the same chance as that soldier over there. I am young and strong. I would not marry your daughter if I did not think I could make her a good home, buy her the things she wants. You are rich, sir, but I will be even richer, for I will have a good woman by my side when I go after my fortune. I am a trapper and I aim to make a good living at it, for a time. I have seen the money there is in furs and in trading, between Mexico and the States. I am in good physical health and I am not inexperienced in commerce. If I did not have confidence in myself I would not ask your daughter to marry me. I ask you the chance to prove myself, both to you and to Estrellita. And, sir, I am going to see the priest in Santa Fe and become a Catholic. If it is necessary for me to become a Mexican citizen, I will do that, too. There is no one going to marry Estrellita but me, with or without your permission, begging your pardon."

Estrellita gasped.

Lucia let out an exasperated sigh. Augustino burned with a cold fury. He looked about to explode inside his uniform. Corazon looked at Jeremiah, stricken with amazement.

Don Miguel rose halfway out of his chair, sat back down slowly. His eyes strained at their sockets, bulged like a pair of swollen olives bobbing up in a cream pitcher.

"You would give up your country, your religion?" Don Miguel demanded.

"I would give up my life," said Jeremiah, bowing his head.

"*Por Dios!*" exclaimed Augustino, breaking his silence. "I

will gladly oblige this stupid gringo!"

"Captain Armijo, please restrain yourself," said Don Miguel, spearing the captain with a lancing look. He turned to Jeremiah, cleared his throat. "Mr. York, you have impressed me with your sincerity, with your uncommon boldness. I am a man of honor and I have made an agreement with Captain Armijo and his uncle, Manuel. This was not a formal contract, to be sure, but it was always understood that someday I would offer my daughter's hand in marriage to Augustino. He has formally asked me to honor that gentleman's agreement and I have accepted."

"Does that mean . . ."

Don Miguel held up his hand for silence.

"Let me finish," said the don. "There is another kind of honor at stake here. A gentleman's honor. While I do not think much of your chances in your appeal for my daughter's hand in marriage, I do respect your ambition. I will not grant you permission to court her at this time. But I will not deny it, either. However, I think you must prove yourself before we speak again. You are going to trap the mountains this season?"

"I am, sir."

"Very well. After the snows lock the passes and you come down from the mountains with your pelts, I will receive you in my home. If you can show me two thousand dollars that you have earned by your own hand and wits, then I shall grant you permission to ask for my daughter's hand in marriage."

"What about Armijo there?"

"While you are away, he will be courting Estrellita, just as I promised him."

"And the wedding?"

"We will set no date for a wedding at this time."

Corazon looked at her husband, smiled wanly. Her admiration for him was plain to see. Estrellita's eyes glittered like diamonds. Lucia glowered like a fuming volcano. One could almost see dragon's smoke spume from her nostrils.

Jeremiah strode across the room, stuck out his hand to

337

Don Miguel.

"Done," he said, "and thank you, sir."

"Done," said Don Miguel, rising to shake Jeremiah's hand.

Augustino bristled and stood up.

"Don Miguel," he said, "I beg your permission to leave. I must talk to my uncle at once."

"Go, then," said Don Miguel. "I hope you will behave like a gentleman in this matter."

"It is only with the greatest restraint that I do so in your home," said Augustino. "Else I would challenge this gringo to a duel this very instant."

Estrellita gasped.

Augustino saluted, wheeled, and stalked from the room. A moment later, the door slammed.

Estrellita ran to her father, embraced him. She peppered his face with kisses, murmured thank-yous into his ear.

Don Miguel smiled.

"I will be going, too," said Jeremiah. "If I might speak to Estrellita for a moment."

"Corazon, let us leave these two to talk for a moment. Lucia, do not stay so close to them that they cannot enjoy each other's company for a brief moment."

Lucia glared at Jeremiah, nodded.

Estrellita watched her parents leave the room, then ran to Jeremiah, grabbed his hand.

"You spoke well," she said.

"I love you," he whispered. "I will earn the money."

"That is such a great amount, and so little time."

"Don't you think I can do it?"

"Yes," she breathed. "I think you can do anything."

He would remember that light in her eyes for a long time. He kissed her, despite Lucia's protests, held her for a long moment, savoring the softness of her for the long months ahead when they would be apart.

"Good-bye, my love," he said.

"Until we meet again," she said. "*Hasta luego.*"

338

Chapter Twenty-Five

Frey Bonifacio Algodon genuflected, dipped chubby fingers into the font of holy water, crossed himself. Jeremiah wondered if he should do the same, but since the priest walked toward the altar without looking back, he saw no reason to mimic his actions. Algodon genuflected again at the altar, climbed the step beyond the wooden railing, turned into a door to his right. Jeremiah followed him, gaping at the huge figure of Christ on the Cross that peered down at him from above the altar. The statue's face was thin and gaunt, the fleshtones dark olive. Red paint dotted the Christ's forehead just below the crown of thorns that ringed his skull. The altar, draped in white linen with gold borders, seemed serene compared to the depiction of Jesus on the wall, with the gory wound in his side, the painful expression, touched with a look of pity, on his visage.

Frey Algodon entered the sacristy, stopped, and beckoned to Jeremiah. The priest sat at a desk, pushed a primitive wood-and-hide chair toward York.

"Sit," he said, puffing for breath. The priest was corpulent, his face cherubic. His black robes stretched to the breaking point around his ample belly. His chasuble hung from a wooden peg on the wall. The room smelled of wine and incense. Jeremiah sat down. "Ah, it feels good just to sit. I

339

have been walking the plaza, saying my office." He put down a small book bound in black leather.

"I come here to be a Catholic," said Jeremiah.

"You are a Protestant, then?"

Jeremiah nodded. The priest spoke perfect English, as York had learned when he encountered the cleric on the steps of the small parochial church a few moments before. He had stayed at La Fonda the night before, slept late.

"Why do you want to change your religion, my son?"

"I want to marry a Catholic girl. A woman, I mean."

"Ah, one of the lowborn women of our squalid little settlement, I suppose."

"No, sir. The daughter of Don Miguel Montez. Her name is Estrellita."

"I know the family. Don Miguel is a *rico*. But I thought his daughter was marrying the nephew of Manuel Armijo—an arrogant pair, one a scoundrel, the other a martinet in uniform."

Jeremiah didn't understand half of what the priest was saying, but he got the gist of it.

"Well, I spoke to Don Miguel yesterday and he will allow me to court Estrellita. I aim to do that if you will make me a Catholic. The quicker the better."

Frey Algodon fixed a myopic blue eye on the young man, suppressed a fleshy smile.

"Do you think it's just a matter of my waving hands over you, sprinkling you with holy water, perhaps saying a few pertinent incantations over your American Protestant soul?"

"I don't know. Is that what you do?"

"My boy, no. You must study. You must learn to have faith. You must comprehend the divine mystery of the Holy Trinity. You must learn your catechism. It is very difficult to make a Catholic out of a Protestant, easier, however than to transform a Buddhist into a Christian."

"I don't know anything about this. I just want to be a Catholic."

Frey Algodon smiled.

"And so you shall be, my son. After all, the bishop has sent me to this godforsaken post in the Indian wilderness to save souls, to convert heathens into God-loving creatures. If I can make a poor *Indio* into a kneeling, pious, praying, Sunday church-going Catholic, I can most certainly take a strapping young man like yourself and teach him the tenets and dogma of the Roman Catholic Church."

"I reckon," said Jeremiah.

"You will have to come for instruction every day for a month. After that, we will see how you progress."

"I am going to the mountains in a day or two. I am a trapper."

"And when will you return, my son?"

"When the snows get too deep. November. December, maybe."

"Then you will have to study the catechism. The books I give you. Do you read Spanish?"

"No, sir."

The priest crossed himself, looked skyward for divine guidance.

"It may be that I have some instructions in English. We have had some Americans come here and convert. Give me a moment to think."

Frey Algodon left the room. He returned moments later with three books. One was a catechism, written in English. Another was a worn, ragged book of Catholic dogma. The third was a book specifically written for those Protestants planning a conversion to Catholicism."

"Take these with you. Read them over and over again. If you have any questions when you return, ask them. I will then ask you a number of questions. If I think you are ready, I will baptize you. You will be a Catholic. If you ever get to the point where you want to read Thomas Aquinas, I have a copy of his writings in English."

"Who is this Thomas Aquinas?"

"Never mind. You will find a lot of mystery in our religion. You may want to learn Latin. Do you know Latin?"

Jeremiah shook his head.

"No, I thought not. Go with God. Call on me when you return. What is your name?"

Jeremiah told him.

"Go then, and avoid the Jesuits at all costs."

"Who are they?"

"Rival priests. They carry fusils and swords instead of Bibles. Good luck with the beaver, Jeremiah York." Algodon reached under his desk, pulled out a bottle of sacramental wine. He pulled the cork with his teeth.

"Thank you, sir." Jeremiah took the books, left the sacristy. He heard the gurgle from the wine bottle as he crossed in front of the altar. He did not look up at the crucifix again. He was already intimidated enough by the priest and the trappings of this strange church.

Two days later, Eyestone and the rest of the brigade took over La Fonda. The trappers traded and drank for three bewildering days. Jeremiah filled his pockets with silver coins from the sale of his trade goods, but he knew he was facing a formidable obstacle. He didn't see how he could possibly earn the huge sum of two thousand dollars by the onset of winter.

He told Eyestone all about his visit to the Montez ranch, his plans for the future. He didn't tell him that he had been reading the Catholic books every night until his eyes burned. He hadn't made much sense of it yet, and he had a thousand questions to ask the priest whenever he saw him again.

He left the *bailes* early every night and yearned for Estrellita. So near and yet so far.

"Coop, I got to make that money. Can we trap enough by then?"

"Trap and trade for it. Free trappers make the most, if they don't get gutted out of it. I figure to make close to a thousand this season. Maybe."

They sat under the meager shade of an acacia tree outside the walled city of Santa Fe.

"Maybe I need more traps."

"You'll be hard put to service the ones you got."

"I sent that money off to Mr. Morrison."

"Knew Possum Killer would give it to you."

"Lalande ain't gonna like it."

"Baptiste don't like nothin' much. Money, maybe. He likes that some. He'll probably wind up a booshway trader out in Oregon. Doubt you'll run into him anytime soon."

"Are we going to trap those mountains over there?" Jeremiah pointed to the Sangre de Cristos.

"Can't. Mexes would be all over us like maggots on wolf meat. You and me'll pick up our cache, go on up the Arkansas, maybe. Way back in, some of those streams got prime beaver. I been there once't."

"Far?"

"Not too far. We better get to gettin', even so."

"I'm ready."

"Been here too long as it is. Karns and the rest pulled out this morning."

"They did?"

"Just you and me left, but we're not goin' so far."

"I need to know if I can make that much money up there."

"First season, likely not. Be good to skin out half that in plews."

Jeremiah moaned, dropped his head. Eyestone cut off a chunk of tobacco from a twist, stuck the wad in his mouth. They were running out of shade. He got up.

"We can cache the furs, go on over to the Cimarron and hunt some buffalo. We'll have to get some wagons. Might make up the difference. Take us a month or more. Hard work, I'm thinkin'."

Jeremiah saw his dreams crashing before he even trapped his first beaver. Time was his enemy. Time and distance. He looked at the Sangre de Cristos, so close and yet so far. The mountains made a man feel small. But they made him feel big, too. The more he stayed in them, the stronger a man would get, the bigger. He thought of the men he'd met at rendezvous that summer. They seemed bigger than life now, bigger than the biggest person in this small town of mud and limewashed walls.

"Well, it's not going to beat me," he said suddenly.

"Chile, what in the name of Jehosaphat's ass are you jabberin' about?" asked Eyestone.

"Time," said Jeremiah, rising from the ground.

"Time?"

Jeremiah grinned. "Time we got to movin'," he said. "There's beaver up there, and marten and mink, and I've got traps and skinnin' knives and strong arms. What say, Cooper? You want to stay in Santa Fe and do them fandangos and watch cockfights all winter?"

Eyestone jumped up, clapped Jeremiah on the back.

"Hell, no! Let's be about men's work. Let's see what beaver there be up on the other end of those Sangre de Cristos. Let's trap the Culebras and the Wets, if need be. Skin 'em clean, Jerry, skin ever' goddamned one of 'em clean. You'll get your money, by God. We'll trap until the beaver skate on the creeks and snowshoe over the passes if we have to. By Jesus, we'll show American Fur what free trappers can do with the stink of castoria and a steel trap."

"Whoooeeeee!" screeched Jeremiah.

The two men whooped all the way back to La Fonda, staggered like drunken men. Within an hour, they were mounted and riding for Taos, jubilant as boys let out of school for the summer. The mules brayed and the horses whickered. Jeremiah laughed.

"They know it, Son," said Eyestone. "These animals know we're headin' for the high country."

Jeremiah looked back at Santa Fe, shining in the sun like a town made out of chalk. He saw the mountains and the plain, the great vastness of the land and sky and felt the enormous

344

gravitational allure of the country. He had come here an alien. Now, a door had opened. Where once there had been only despair, now there was hope. The land seemed new to him, big enough for all who roamed its limitless expanse.

He turned, looked off in the distance to the hazy mountains rising from the plain. In their majestic heights, in the secrets of their rivers and plains, he would realize his boyhood dreams. There he would find his manhood and his fortune. The air he breathed was as fresh and bracing as mint, aromatic of pines, cool as the snowtips of the distant peaks.

Estrellita would wait for him, he knew. He would return to her as a man. He would lay out the fruits of his labors before her. In the mountains he would find the seeds for his fortune, for his future in a grand new land with the woman he loved.

"Wait for me," he said to himself.

It seemed, in the fresh breeze that riffled his hair, blew soft against his face, that he could hear her answer. In the tugging zephyrs he could feel her caress. In the golden sunlight that burnished the land, he could feel her warm radiance. In the solitude of his mind, he could see her smile just as if she was there with him, riding the trail that seemed to stretch clear to the faraway mountains, clear to the sky itself.

Epilogue

The rider gave his report to the commandant and changed horses at the presidio in Santa Fe. But the fresh horse, an army mount like the other, was lathered by the time the rider reached Rancho Montez. The man who rode up to the hacienda was a scout for the Mexican Army. His name was Juan Fortuna. Juan was half Yaqui, but he spoke the Comanche tongue as well as Spanish. His mother had once been a Comanche prisoner and he had grown up among them. He wore army trousers, moccasins, a fringed buckskin shirt, and a battered felt hat that was stained with sweat and dust. He knew Don Miguel well, knew that his information was of vital importance.

Juan rode up to the gate, dismounted. He loosened the cinch strap of the light Santa Fe saddle, hitched the heaving horse to the rail. His side ached; his lungs burned.

Don Miguel opened the door before Juan was halfway across the patio. Corazon stood behind her husband, trembling. They had both seen the rider through the window, recognized him as their friend.

"What news, Juan?" Don Miguel asked in Spanish.

Panting, Juan removed his hat, nodded to Corazon. He was a small, wiry man with a leathered face, dark-brown eyes. He carried both pistol and knife on his brass-studded belt. His rifle remained in its boot on the saddle.

"The Comanches are coming," said Juan.

"Come into my house, friend," said Don Miguel.

Corazon closed the door.

"Tecolote?" she whispered.

Juan nodded.

"Come, let us sit and talk about this," said the hidalgo. "You have ridden far, Juan?"

"Yes," said the scout, doffing his hat. His lungs did not hurt so much now. The ache in his side was going away.

They took chairs in the living room. It was cool in the room. A strong wind had come down from the north during the night. It was only the second day of September and some said there would be an early winter. Juan seemed out of place in a chair. He sat stiffly, his moccasins flat on the woven rug beneath the chair.

"Do you want something to drink, Juan?" asked Don Miguel. "Some *tepache*, perhaps? Milk or wine?"

"No, nothing," said the half-breed.

"Do the Comanches come to trade?" asked Corazon. Her husband gave her a sharp look, then softened. This was her concern, too, but he was annoyed that she would join in the conversation of men.

"They come to trade," said Fortuna, "but then they go to hunt the buffalo and the antelope for their winter meat."

"Yes," said Don Miguel, a faraway look in his eyes.

"I have been with my mother in the Jemez mountains. Tecolote and his band summered there. Now the scouts have come back from the East and have told of many buffalo on the plains."

Juan looked away from Don Miguel and the hidalgo knew there was more. He must have patience. Juan would tell it in his own way.

"These scouts of Tecolote," said Don Miguel, "they passed by here?"

Corazon stiffened visibly. The corners of her mouth quivered. She held her tongue, as well as her breath. She folded her hands together to keep them from trembling.

A sound on the stairs interrupted the trio, drew their

attention. Don Miguel looked up. Lucia and Estrellita descended the stairs. The hidalgo frowned.

"Papa, what passes?" asked Estrellita.

"Come and sit, my daughter. Lucia, you might as well hear this, too."

Juan stood up, bowed to the two women.

"Juan," said Lucia. She and Estrellita sat on the settee.

"Continue," Don Miguel told Juan.

"It is bad, Don Miguel. Very bad. The scouts watched the hacienda for a long time, many times. They stayed in the hills and watched. These Comanches were two warriors of the tribe of Tecolote. They call themselves Many Lances and Red Lizard. They are like shadows on the hillsides. You do not see them, but they are there."

Juan paused, looked at Corazon, then looked away.

"You tell us, Juan," said Corazon. "You tell us what they saw, what Tecolote said."

"*Sí, señora.* I will tell you. The scouts came to the grave of your daughter." He looked at Estrellita. "They say that no one comes to the grave. They say that no one puts flowers on the grave. No one weeps there. No one mourns."

Don Miguel swore. He and Corazon exchanged knowing glances. Lucia clenched her teeth. They made a loud clack in the brief silence.

"I did not think of it," said Don Miguel.

"No, it was my fault," said his wife.

"Do not blame yourselves," said Lucia diplomatically. "I could have picked the flowers."

"The Comanche know these things. They have seen Estrellita and they say your daughter is not dead. Tecolote was very angry to know these things. He said bad things."

"What did he say?" asked Don Miguel.

Juan hesitated for a moment, drew a breath. His side no longer ached and his lungs had stopped burning.

"He said that he does not like to be fooled. He does not like men to lie to him. He said that you cheated him and his son, Yellow Wind. He said that you deceived him."

"That is true," said Don Miguel.

"He knows this and he is very angry. He says he will come for your daughter. And he says he will come for your wife, too."

The woman gasped.

Don Miguel scowled.

"When?" he asked.

"In this moon, he will come. He speaks of war, and I have reported what I heard to the commandant at the presidio."

"And does he take this seriously?"

"He has issued orders for the lancers to take the field. Even now, they are making ready their horses and their arms. Captain Armijo is riding to the south for reinforcements. He asked me to tell you this. He thinks that you ought to leave the hacienda and go far away until the Comanche are defeated."

"Juan, you have done well. I am surprised that Tecolote did not stop you when you wanted to leave."

"I think Tecolote does not care if you know that he is coming. I think he wants you to know."

"But he did not speak to you directly," said Don Miguel.

"No, but he spoke loudly and to many braves for many days. He knows that my ears are big."

"Thank you, Juan. What will you do now?"

"I will guide the lancers."

"Be careful."

"You take care as well."

"There is a fresh horse for you in the stable. Ask my stableman, Lazaro Quintano, to give you the horse called Cazador. Lazaro will care for your army mount, return it to the army post."

"A million of thanks, Don Miguel."

"For nothing. Go with God, my friend."

Juan stood up, bowed to the women. He put his hat on. Don Miguel walked him to the door, returned in a few moments. The women's whispers sounded like a pack of ghosts gone mad. They fell silent when he entered the room, took his chair.

"Well," he said, "we must go. We must leave at once

for Chihuahua."

"Must we always run like this?" asked Estrellita. "I do not want to go to Mexico. It is too far."

"Silence, child," said Lucia.

Estrellita turned on the *dueña*. Anger flared her nostrils, sparked lightning in her eyes.

"This is like the story you told me," said Estrellita. "Does this Tecolote think I am promised to him? What is happening here?"

"Lucia," said Corazon, "you did not tell my daughter . . ."

"No, my mistress," said Lucia. "I promised I would not. I told her of another, of Don Ignacio Baca of Tomé."

"You make me angry, Lucia," said Corazon. "You should not have spoken of these things."

"I was only trying to make Estrellita see the reason for hiding when we returned from St. Louis. I did not mention that you were the daughter of a Comanche chieftain."

"What?" exclaimed Estrellita. "What does she mean, my mother?"

Corazon looked at her husband, a pleading in her eyes.

"Perhaps," said Don Miguel, "it is time that our daughter hear the story of your mother, of her capture by the Comanches."

"If it is your wish, my husband," said Corazon meekly.

Slowly, Don Miguel told the story of Corazon's origin, the chilling tale of revenge against the Comanche, the terrible secret they had carried for years. Estrellita sat there, stunned, a growing fear in her heart.

"So that is the story of your mother and me," said Don Miguel, finishing up his story. "Now you know why we must leave. If Tecolote finds us here, he would slaughter us all and never even blink an eye."

"Yes," said Estrellita. She touched the locket on her neck and thought of Jeremiah. She wished he were here. By now, he would be up in the mountains. He would not even know that she was gone. "When will we return?"

Don Miguel shrugged.

"When it is safe. When Tecolote is killed or captured."

"We must make preparations to leave immediately," said Corazon. "Lucia, you help Estrellita pack."

"I will see to the coach and horses," said Don Miguel, rising from his chair. "We will leave before the sun sets."

Estrellita began to tremble then. She felt herself engulfed in sadness. She was sad for her mother, sad for her father, sad for herself. They no longer had any control over their lives. A savage held them all in the grip of fear.

Corazon noticed her daughter's trembling, put her arm around her shoulder.

"Do you have fear?" she asked.

Estrellita nodded.

"Do not worry. Your father will keep us safe. He would never let Yellow Wind take you."

"Mama, what about you?"

"I would kill myself before I would let a Comanche touch me. I think of what they did to my mother."

"You and I have Comanche blood, is this not so?"

"Yes, through no fault of our own."

"Papa did not mind?"

"No. Your father is different from most men."

"That's the way I feel about Jeremiah," Estrellita said softly. And she no longer trembled. She felt Jeremiah's strength within her, felt his love swell her heart, brace her from harm as though his arms were around her. Now that she knew about her mother, and her father's love for a half-Comanche woman, she had the gift of hope. Her father would know, eventually, that she and Jeremiah were destined for each other, no matter the obstacles, just as he and Corazon had been destined for each other.

She touched the silver eagle on her locket and drew comfort from Jeremiah's words. She and Jeremiah were like two eagles. Eagles of destiny. Together they would scale the heights, soar freely above the earth and its turmoil, safe from harm.

TO BE CONTINUED

352